ONE BITE *Per* NIGHT

BROOKLYN ANN

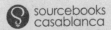
sourcebooks
casablanca

Published by Sourcebooks Casablanca, an imprint of Sourcebooks,
Inc.
P.O. Box 4410, Naperville, Illinois 60567-4410
(630) 961-3900
Fax: (630) 961-2168
www.sourcebooks.com

Printed and bound in Canada.
WC 10 9 8 7 6 5 4 3 2 1

Dedicated to my mother, Karen Ann.
The finest painter and teacher I've ever known.
And to my grandmothers, Ruth and Sharon.
Your love and hugs are priceless.
And to my best friend, Rachel.
We have the best adventures.

One

1822

"I WILL BE BRAVE," LYDIA PRICE WHISPERED TO THE portrait of her dead father.

Her voice held a faint tremor, though perhaps that was from the constant bobbing of the ship, carrying her away from her home and across the Atlantic to a grandmother she'd never met.

Lydia shifted on her bunk. Papa would be disappointed in her lack of confidence; an earl's daughter must be resolute. Now more than ever, she must live up to his faith in her.

Lydia sighed and sat up, gazing through the porthole at the endless span of whitecapped ocean. "I wish you were here with me, Papa. You and Mama."

Taking a deep breath, she tried to soothe the worry gnawing at her belly. Her father had barely followed her mother to the grave when his solicitor arrived to read the will. Lydia was coldly informed that all of her father's assets were to go to her uncle, now the Earl of Morley, and she was to be packed off to England

and delivered into her grandmother's care. Her grandmother, the dowager countess who'd disowned her son for marrying below his station. Would she welcome her granddaughter? Lydia had no idea. She hadn't received so much as a note from her.

The ship lurched again, and Lydia gripped the portrait's frame tighter. These maudlin thoughts would not do. Perhaps her grandmother wouldn't bear her any ill will for her father's defiance in marrying a merchant's daughter. If the dowager had misgivings over Lydia's common blood, they would be laid aside when Lydia proved she'd been raised as a proper lady. Her father had groomed her for the possibility of returning to England. She could dance, curtsy, make polite conversation, and handle a fan with grace.

She'd received several marriage offers when she made her debut in New Orleans, so there was no reason to believe she wouldn't have similar success when she made her London debut.

Perhaps I'll become a countess as well. If Lydia made a prestigious match, surely she and her father would be redeemed in Lady Morley's eyes.

Of course, there was just as good a chance she'd disgrace them all over again by falling in love with a commoner. Lydia had vowed to marry only for love, just as her parents had.

If that happens, I'll simply make a living from my work. Her paintings had always fetched good sums at the annual charity auctions. Her landscape of the bayou alone had fetched five hundred dollars.

"*You have a gift, sweetling,*" Papa had told her when she'd first picked up a brush and palette. "*Never abandon it.*"

He'd hired the best tutors and turned a room in their town house into an airy studio for her. She had mastered landscapes and was beginning to learn portraiture. One day, she hoped to paint like Sir Thomas Lawrence, president of the Royal Academy of Arts and the artist who first inspired her love of painting. Her father had sat for him before he left England. Lydia held that very portrait in her hands.

Looking into tawny eyes identical to hers, Lydia could almost imagine they were real. The wavy black hair, Roman nose, and strong, square jaw held the same vitality. She longed to be able to capture such detail, such life, to immortalize a person so their loved ones could look at their portraits and see life long after death. Every time her memory tormented her with her parents' faces, ravaged by yellow fever, Lydia had only to look upon Sir Lawrence's painting to banish the nightmarish images.

"Sir Thomas Lawrence is in London," she whispered, carefully setting the painting aside. Apprehension gave way to excitement. "I *must* meet him."

Three years ago, when the paper announced Lawrence's return to London and his subsequent knighthood and induction as president of the Royal Academy, Lydia had begged to go to England. She wanted to take lessons at the Academy. To train under such a master was a dream she'd nurtured since Papa had taken her to her first art gallery. She was determined to make that wish come true.

"Maybe next year," her father would say with a smile.

That year had never come, until now. If only the circumstances weren't so tragic.

Lydia swallowed the lump in her throat. Once she

was settled in London, she would implore her grandmother to enroll her in the Academy.

Fingers itching to create once more, Lydia rose from her bunk and picked up her sketchbook and charcoals.

"I will be brave," she repeated, sketching the ocean view through her cabin's porthole. "And I will become the finest painter in the world."

∞

Cornwall, 1822

Vincent Tremayne, Earl of Deveril and Lord Vampire of Cornwall, ran his tongue over long curved fangs as the blood thirst roared through his body.

Impatient to quell his hunger, he charged up the stone steps and out the secret passage from his chamber. Unlocking the door, he raced out into the corridor and nearly crashed headfirst into his butler.

"Good evening, my lord." Aubert bowed. His pinched face was the only indicator of nervousness. "The Dowager Countess of Morley is here to speak with you regarding what she claims is an urgent matter. Since she has had to wait for quite some time, I took the liberty of placing her in the library and providing her with refreshments."

Vincent suppressed a growl at the delay to his hunt. Who the hell did this woman think she was? He'd spent centuries cultivating the reputation of every incarnation of the Earl of Deveril as that of a reclusive madman. Yet this dowager had the gall to ignore the implied warning. As he stalked down the stone steps to the library, his stomach roiled in unholy hunger.

Morley…the name niggled at his memory. Had he met this woman before?

He opened the heavy oak door with more force than was polite. His uninvited guest lifted prominent gray eyebrows beneath a jeweled lorgnette.

"Lord Deveril, it *is* a pleasure."

Vincent favored her with a mocking bow as he concealed a bitter smile. A pale-faced maid lurked nervously behind the settee, apparently trying to make herself invisible. Damned if this dowager wasn't the ultimate virago. Her blood likely tasted of bile.

"My lady, to what do I owe the pleasure of this visit? It is a rare occasion when I receive callers."

The hag sniffed with such violent derision that her yellow turban was nearly knocked askew. "I have come to speak of the ancient alliance between our families."

"Alliance?" His brow rose as the woman's identity became clear. *Morley…How could I have forgotten?*

Her thin lips pursed before she gave a brisk nod and held out an ancient scrap of parchment that Vincent hadn't seen since his mortal days. "Yes, the earldoms of Deveril and Morley have a documented alliance dating back to 1651."

Vincent closed his eyes, remembering the blood, stench, and screams of the battlefield. He remembered Joseph Price, his comrade in arms. He remembered tearing his uniform to staunch the blood flowing from the man's shoulder. He remembered Joseph later returning the favor. Yes, he remembered the former Earl of Morley.

"*Let there always be friendship between our families,*" Joseph had said when the war was over.

As his heavy eyelids lifted, Vincent beheld the sour countenance before him. Friendship did not seem to be a likely prospect with this descendant of his old friend.

Lady Morley continued, oblivious to his reverie. "The terms of the alliance include providing aid to the other's strongholds in the event of attack, vouching for one another's good character"—she paused and fixed him with an icy gaze—"and becoming guardian to the other's children in the event of death or incapacitation."

At the latter, the dowager's steely gaze flickered momentarily, giving way to worry.

"I see." He was afraid he did.

"My son, the former earl, and his wife perished of yellow fever in the Americas over a month ago. They left behind a daughter, who is being sent to me." Her mouth twisted as if tasting something sour. "I request that you honor the alliance of your forebears and become her guardian."

A vampire as guardian to a young girl? Vincent frowned. "Are you unable to care for her?"

The woman's eyes narrowed to slits. "Allow me to speak plainly, my lord. My son caused a horrid scandal when he ran off with…this girl's mother. It was all I could do to hold up my head. I will *not* have the offspring of such a mésalliance in my house." She lifted her chin. "My true granddaughter will make her debut in Society this Season, and the presence of that… other one would bring back old gossip and harm my Georgiana's chances of making a successful match."

Pity for this unknown orphaned descendant of his old friend pierced his conscience. Vincent forced his voice to remain level. "Look about, madam. I hardly think my home is suitable for a child." He gestured at the gray stone walls and austere furnishings.

Lady Morley sniffed. "She is twenty…or somewhere thereabouts, hardly a child."

"Ah, so she is ready to debut as well," Vincent's voice was low and silky as the implications of the woman's panic became clear. *And ripe for the marriage market… Perhaps this won't be such a problem.*

The dowager flinched at his words before straightening her spine back to its customary ramrod posture. "She is in mourning."

"By the time the Season begins, she'll be nearly finished mourning," he countered, enjoying her discomfort.

Though her laughter was scornful, the look in her eyes was uncertain. *The Mad Deveril bringing out an uncouth American?* "You would launch her this year?"

"I did not say I would take her in," Vincent countered, though his competitive nature relished the prospect of a challenge. "This residence is unsuitable for a young lady, and I daresay I am ill equipped to present a debutante."

Lady Morley favored him with a petulant frown. "Then I shall have to find some other way to dispose of her…perhaps I may have her committed to an asylum."

Vincent recoiled in disgust, but he kept his expression bland and noncommittal. Damn his sense of honor. He would have to take the girl. He'd made a vow to a friend. However, he would do everything in his power to see that Lady Morley would regret approaching him.

"Does she have a dowry?"

"Indeed she does." Desperation tinged her voice.

She knew the game was not yet won. "I will also supply a bank draft to cover a portion of her expenses."

His eyes narrowed. "Double the dowry."

Lady Morley quivered with indignation. She opened her mouth to deliver a scathing retort, but Vincent held up a hand, his patience at an end.

"I am willing to take this girl off your hands, but you must endeavor to give me the opportunity to see her off mine." The words ended in a growl, bringing a terrified squeak from the maid in the corner.

After a few moments of apparently taxing mental debate, the dowager relented with a frigid nod and stood. "Very well. I shall send my solicitor with the proper documents straightaway."

Suddenly the maid leaped forward. "No, my lady! You cannot do this! You cannot send a maiden into the clutches of the 'Devil Earl'!"

The vampire grinned at her Cornish accent. As a local, no doubt her parents had frightened her into obedience with threats of the "Devil Earl."

The dowager, however, was not amused. "I have had enough of your nonsense on this matter, Emma. You are dismissed from my employ."

Emma's face paled further. "B-but, my lady—"

Lady Morley swept past her as if she did not exist. "I thank you for your assistance in this matter, my lord. The girl's ship is due to arrive in Plymouth on the sixteenth of February. Now, if you will excuse me, I am quite exhausted and must seek a decent inn at once."

Jaw clenched, Vincent pulled the bell cord to summon the butler. "What is the girl's name?" he asked.

She clipped out, "Her name is Lydia Price. My solicitor will contact you with further information as to her arrival."

Turning away from the dowager, he addressed the trembling Emma. "Miss Price will require a maid. If you would care to fulfill that situation, I'll double what Lady Morley paid you." In a gentler tone, he added, "I am aware of the stories circulated about me, and I swear on my honor that no harm will come to you under my employ." He was already taking one of the dowager's castaways, what was one more?

Dazedly, Emma curtsied. "Thank you, my lord."

Lady Morley gaped and sputtered like a landed trout, and Vincent grinned at the small triumph of unsettling her so efficiently.

The butler arrived and gave the dowager a quizzical look before bowing. "Yes, my lord?"

"Aubert, please see Lady Morley out and ask Mrs. Hodgkin to prepare a room for Miss…?" He turned to the maid expectantly.

"Fiddock, my lord," she murmured, staring at the hem of her homespun gown.

Aside from a slight twitch of his eyelid, Aubert appeared indifferent to this unusual request, although Vincent hadn't had a long-term guest during the butler's entire employ. "Yes, my lord."

"Lady Morley, it was a *pleasure*." His saccharine smile nearly revealed his fangs.

"If you think you can make a decent match for this American, then I'm afraid you will be sorely disappointed."

"We shall see."

She laughed a low, ugly cackle and retreated with

such long strides, Aubert nearly stumbled in an effort to keep up.

Returning to the maid, Vincent fought back his raging blood thirst, exuding the most nonthreatening aura possible under the circumstances. "Your employment begins now. Fetch me a quill and parchment from the desk. I want you to make a list of everything a young lady requires to make a successful debut."

Emma gasped. "Do you mean...?"

He favored her with a conspiratorial grin, concealing his fangs. "Yes, I shall bring Miss Price out into Society. *And* I fully intend for her to make a better match than Lady Morley's precious favorite granddaughter." He frowned. "We had best start with seeing a chaperone settled here before the young lady arrives. Would you have any knowledge of how I may go about that?"

Finally, a ghost of a smile touched the maid's lips, and she curtsied once more. "Lady Morley is seeking to hire Miss Hobson. Her ladyship says she is the best."

Vincent returned the smile. "Perhaps I can give this Miss Hobson a more attractive offer. Now, what else is required?"

Once he and Emma finished making the list, Vincent departed the castle to seek his meal. He glanced at the moon and climbed the ragged cliffs of the coastline, soon finding the group of smugglers he knew would be there. Their sort always made an easy meal. Blocking the supernatural aspects of the encounter from their memories, he was thus obliged to take a cask of French brandy in exchange for his silence on their illegal activity.

With his head cleared of blood thirst, Vincent wondered if he was pursuing a wise course of action. One mistake, and his secret would be out. The Elders would execute him...if the inevitable vampire hunter or crazed mob didn't reach him first.

On the other hand, if his plans were successful, he would have the pleasure of watching Lady Morley's stricken face as his charge defeated hers in the game of wedlock. Vincent smiled. It had been too long since he'd indulged in a good competition.

Two

LYDIA AWOKE TO A LOUD RAPPING ON HER CABIN door. The wooden floor bobbed under her feet as she stumbled like a drunkard to answer the knock.

The first mate greeted her with a gimlet gaze. "There's been a change in plans, miss. Ye're ta depart here at Plymouth."

Confusion warred with relief that her long voyage had come to an early end. "Ah…do you know why, sir?"

He shook his head and chewed on his pipe. "Ye'll have to take that up w' the cap'n. All I know is he received a note. Put on yer warmest frock, an' I'll get yer trunks loaded up."

Lydia sighed and donned her black traveling dress and woolen cloak. Her mind raced as she struggled to pin up her thick black hair. *Why Plymouth rather than London? Did Grandmother take ill? Or did she retire to the country to take the opportunity to meet me sooner?* Praying it was the latter, she hurried out of her cabin to the captain's quarters.

The captain grumbled impatiently. "All I know is a carriage is waiting for you here, so you'd best

run along and pack your things. I have work to do."
Before Lydia could respond, he walked away, barking
orders to his crew.

Lydia deftly avoided the rushing people on deck
and returned to her cabin. The crew had already
begun hauling her trunks, grumbling at their weight
and number. She shoved her charcoals and sketchbook
into her valise as her mind raced with excitement to
at last meet her English grandmother. Perhaps Lady
Morley would be interested in hearing about her
adventurous voyage…and all about her papa and their
life in America. Perhaps she had even forgiven him.

As she returned on deck, moisture filled her eyes,
blurring the spectacular vista of the bustling port city
before her. Limestone cliffs gave way to a turbulent
blue-green sea. Never before had she seen such a
beautiful place. And the people, so lively and animated,
their lilting voices echoing like a new song. Stevedores
shouted and hauled crates up and down winches. Ships
of all sizes crowded the harbor. Carriages and carts of
all kinds lined the road beyond.

Oh Mama, Papa, I wish you could see this. With a
deep breath, Lydia swallowed a lump in her throat and
joined the line of passengers on the gangplank.

All was chaos as couples and families shouted joyous
greetings and exchanged tearful embraces.

Lydia looked left and right for someone who
appeared to recognize her. But the melee of reunion
continued around her, indifferent as the waves lapping
against the pier.

She hugged her valise tight and fought to stay
calm. The cold, salty sea breeze assaulted her body,

competing with the creeping chill in her heart. *It will be my turn soon. A kind face will smile my way and beckon me—*

There she was. A tall, regal matron accompanied by a maid and footman beckoned near the end of the docks.

Forgetting the weight of her valise, Lydia rushed forward. "Grandmother?" she cried, breathless with joy for the first time since her parents died.

The woman shook her head and Lydia's face burned in humiliation. She had approached the wrong person. Now that she was closer, she saw that the woman was too young to be her grandmother. There was more blonde in her hair than gray, and she couldn't be older than fifty.

Before Lydia could apologize and make a hasty retreat, the woman spoke. "Are you Miss Lydia Price?"

She nodded, dread sinking into the pit of her stomach. Something was wrong.

"Welcome to England. I am Miss Hobson." Her narrow face was stark under her gray bonnet. "Your guardian, the Earl of Deveril, has hired me to be your chaperone and educate you in social graces."

"Deveril?" Lydia repeated dumbly. Had there been another Miss Price aboard the ship? "I-I was under the impression that the family name was Morley."

Miss Hobson bowed her head, but not before Lydia caught a glimmer of pity in the woman's eyes. "Let us have you settled into the carriage, and I will explain what has transpired."

Oh God, my grandmother has died. A lump formed in her throat. *Am I cursed? Is all my family dead?*

Oblivious to her grief, the footman gathered her

trunks and loaded them onto the carriage. The maid adjusted her starched cap and approached her with a tremulous smile on her mousy face.

"My name is Emma, Miss Price. The earl has hired me to be your maid." Her lilting accent was so different than the chaperone's clipped cadence.

Lydia smiled. "I am pleased to meet you, Emma."

Emma curtsied. "What beautiful hair you have, miss. It's like spun onyx. I will be pleased to dress it."

Miss Hobson silenced her with a stern glare. "It is time we were off."

Once settled in the carriage, the chaperone cleared her throat. "I do not know how to say this easily, Miss Price, so I apologize for my forthright manner. Due to the scandal your father caused with his marriage to your mother, Lady Morley refuses to have you in her home, so the Earl of Deveril will be acting as your guardian. There was an old alliance between the families."

Lydia discovered that it was indeed possible to feel worse. Her grandmother didn't want her. She'd heard that English folk were snobbish, but she hadn't expected this. Her heart felt as if it were cleaved in two. *Now I understand why Papa never returned home.*

Lifting her chin and blinking back tears, Lydia faced her chaperone. "Well, I daresay, she does not sound like a person I would like to know." Forcing a smile, she spoke past the lump in her throat. "Please, tell me about the Earl of Deveril. Was he a friend of my father?" *Please tell me he is kind.* He'd have to be, to take in a complete stranger.

Miss Hobson's eyes widened a moment at Lydia's cheery tone. "I know little about the earl as I have only recently come under his employ. It is doubtful he knew your father. His lordship resides at Castle Deveril in Cornwall and is known to be a recluse."

"A *castle*?" A measure of her dismay fled at the prospect. It would be just like a gothic novel. What sorts of secrets resided within its stone walls? Were there hidden passageways? Ghosts?

Before her imagination could take flight, Miss Hobson began questioning Lydia on her accomplishments. The woman did not smile. The only indication of approval Lydia received was a placid nod at the mention of her painting.

Displeasure, on the other hand, seemed to be the chaperone's forte. Her brows rose to her hairline in outrage when Lydia spoke of shooting with her father.

"In England, an unmarried lady does *not* handle firearms," the chaperone said sternly.

Lydia sighed. "I suppose that means fishing is out of the question as well."

Miss Hobson's lips twitched slightly before she sniffed. "Quite."

As the carriage rolled down the rutted road, Lydia gazed out the window in rapt fascination at the Cornish landscape. Stone houses perched among the rolling green hills on one side and cliffs fell away to the sea on the other. Ruins of castles dotted the horizon like aging sentinels. Something within her awakened at the sight. There was something magical about this land and its wild beauty. She stared for hours, absorbing the colors and textures, her fingers itching to capture it all on canvas.

Night had fallen by the time they reached the castle.

The carriage rattled and shook violently as it rolled down the rutted, rocky path. Lydia clung to the leather straps, terrified that the conveyance would topple over. When the wheels ground to a shuddering stop, she let out the breath she'd been holding. Thunder sounded in the distance as the footmen helped the ladies from the carriage.

"You had best hurry inside," the driver grunted as the trunks were unloaded. "A storm approaches."

Lydia only half heard him as she stared up at Castle Deveril. Iron-gray stone gleamed in the waxing moonlight. Wind howled through ancient arrow slits, and shadows engulfed the turrets. A thrill rushed through her body at the realization that she would live in a real castle, just like a princess in the stories Mama used to tell.

Mama… Lydia's eyes stung with unshed tears. She blinked and focused once more on the castle. Could this place become her home? Much of that would depend on her guardian. She peered toward the towering entrance.

"Come now, Lydia," Miss Hobson urged as the wind picked up and clouds raced across the face of the moon.

Lightning flashed, and a figure seemed to materialize before them on the stony path. Emma let out a cry that was immediately drowned out by a crash of thunder.

Miss Hobson remained composed, though her voice cracked. "My lord, you startled us." Straightening her spine, she continued. "As you can see, Miss Price has arrived safely."

The Earl of Deveril stepped forward with a bow. Long, wild hair fell forward to shadow his face. "Miss Price, welcome to my home. I hope you will be happy here." His accent held the same musical cadence as Emma's.

With shaky legs, Lydia managed a curtsy. "Thank you, my lord."

Entranced, she looked up at her new guardian. Tall and lean, he loomed over her like a specter, his greatcoat flapping in the wind. Lightning illuminated his silvery-blond locks sweeping across sharp, angular features.

Her spine tingled. Never had she seen a more striking person. Though his hair was the color of moonlight, his face and form were those of a young man. Lydia choked back a gasp. She longed to render him in charcoal…no, *oils*.

Lord Deveril interrupted her thoughts, his lyrical voice holding her captive. "Please, go inside before the storm strikes. A warm bath and a hot supper await you." Genuine kindness filled his tone, a soothing balm from the coldness and pity she'd faced from others. "We may further our acquaintance tomorrow evening. Tonight you must rest from your long journey."

"I am well, my lord. Where are you going?" The thought of this mysterious stranger who held her entire fate in his hands leaving her so suddenly was alarming.

Her grandmother's rejection taunted her. Perhaps she *was* cursed. As if to concur, a lock of her hair slid from its pin to slap her cheek in the biting wind.

Paying the weather no mind, Lord Deveril regarded her calmly. "I am going for a walk."

The absurdity of his statement made her chuckle. "But it is dark out, and a storm is coming. Surely you should not risk your health in such inclement conditions."

Miss Hobson made a small sound, no doubt to scold her for such pertness. Lydia didn't care. She didn't want him to leave. He was to be her only link to her new life, her only sense of stability. What if he didn't want her either? Was that why he was so eager to remove himself?

Lightning flashed again, illuminating his eyes. A captivating shade of blue tinged with gray, they glittered like the turbulent sea. Her breath halted. It was as if his eyes *were* the storm.

Lord Deveril smiled, displaying gleaming white teeth. "Your concern is most touching, though unnecessary. I have taken my nightly walk every evening for many years. The weather never stops me."

He stepped closer, gently lifted the loose lock of her hair with long, graceful fingers, and tucked the strands behind her ear. Lydia's heart pounded at his whisper-light touch. The earl bowed once more and departed with smooth, powerful strides. Lydia's stomach quivered as if she were back aboard the ship.

Three

AN OLD MAN STUMBLED OUT OF THE PUB, SINGING AN ancient Cornish love song, oblivious to the torrential rain. Vincent was upon him in a heartbeat. As soon as Vincent's thirst was slaked, the drunkard shambled on, still singing. A catchy tune—Vincent found himself humming as he entered the smoky establishment. Silence fell for a breath as the patrons gripped their mugs and stared, followed by the usual whispers of the *"Devil Earl."*

Ignoring them all, he made his way to a shoddy table in the rear corner where his second in command waited.

Emrys Adair raised a brow at the puddles of rainwater trailing behind him. "You forgot your umbrella again."

Vincent sat and shook out his sodden hair. A reluctant smile tugged his lips as he recalled Lydia's concern for his well-being in the storm. No one had cared for him in centuries.

His second in command sipped his ale and related his weekly report on Cornwall's small populace of vampires. Aside from a rogue being chased off to Devon, all remained placid and dull. Vincent only half listened, pondering his ward.

"Has the girl arrived?" Emrys asked suddenly.

Vincent cocked his head to the side. "Are you invading my thoughts?" he jested, knowing full well that the vampire lacked that degree of power.

"Of course not!" his second huffed. "I only remembered that the chit was due this week."

He smiled. "Yes, she is here."

"And?"

"She is comely enough that I have every confidence in seeing her settled with no trouble."

Truly, Lydia Price was far more than comely. With that silken onyx hair and eyes so pale brown they appeared gold, his ward was a breathtaking creature. And her voice…he'd expected Americans to have brash accents, but hers was liquid music. The suitors would line up in droves just to hear her speak.

Emrys shook his head, interrupting his thoughts. "I cannot believe you are doing this."

"Why? You've known for over a month. I distinctly remember you being awake when I announced it at the gathering." Vincent leaned back in his chair, stretching his long legs under the table. "All that aside, I have been in charge of looking after the misfits of our kind for seventy years. An unwanted mortal is not too much of a stretch."

He frowned. Truly, *unwanted* should not be a word used to describe Lydia Price.

"And you've done an admirable job," Emrys replied levelly. "You've saved countless vampires from giving themselves up to the fatal dawn, and you've never had to execute any, no one denies that. Yet what exactly are you saving this human from?"

"An insane asylum, if her horrid grandmother is to be believed."

The vampire gasped. "*Is* the girl cracked?"

"Not as far as I've discerned." Vincent rubbed his temples, weary of the discussion. "Speaking of which, we need to look in on the Siddons sisters. I have found something for them to do. How were they the last time you saw them?"

"Much better. Maria says that Sally's bouts of depression have grown shorter, and reports that her own blue devils are much more tempered."

Vincent nodded. "That is good news. Whom do you have supervising their hunts?"

"Bronn for now. I think he's become smitten."

"Poor lad. Those two will probably refuse to entertain any romantic entanglements for at least a century...if they survive that long." He adjusted his damp greatcoat. "Shall we be off?"

Emrys rose reluctantly from his seat and grabbed his umbrella.

The rain had abated somewhat as they left the pub, coming down in a cold drizzle. The second huddled beneath his umbrella, cursing under his breath. The moment they were out of view, Emrys folded his umbrella, and both vampires took off in a burst of preternatural speed.

The sisters lived in a secluded cottage some ten miles outside the village of Portloe. Before Vincent could knock, the door opened to reveal a frail vampire resembling a girl of sixteen. She'd been nineteen when she'd been illegally Changed. "Good evening, Maria."

Maria Siddons, daughter of the infamous actress, Sarah Siddons, curtsied deeply. "M'lord. Mr. Adair." Her voice was almost a whisper. "Please, do come inside."

The cottage was warm and cozy with a blazing fire in the hearth and myriad embroidered cushions and lacy doilies. The sisters had taken the hobby of sewing to an astonishing level. It seemed to ease their minds.

Sally Siddons rose from the plump sofa, setting her sewing aside. "My lord!" She gazed at him with wide gray eyes, wringing her hands. "Is everything all right?" The tips of her fangs were revealed through parted lips.

"Everything is fine. I only wanted to look in on you both and beg a favor."

She sat back down and resumed stitching the hem of a dress. "Oh, we are quite well, aren't we, Maria?"

"I understand you are going to London soon, to present that human girl." Maria eyed him with sudden intensity.

Vincent held up a hand. "Do not trouble yourself by asking. You cannot accompany me."

"But—"

"You're supposed to be dead, don't you remember? It's been only twenty years. You cannot run the risk of being recognized." He met her angry gaze with all the authority of a Lord Vampire.

Dying from consumption and devastated by the heart-wrenching end of a scandalous three-way love affair with the portrait artist Thomas Lawrence, Maria

Siddons had charmed a rogue vampire into Changing her without sanction from the Elders.

Five years later, she'd found another rogue and convinced him to Change her elder sister.

One of the rogues had been caught and executed by Ian Ashton, the Lord Vampire of London. However, that didn't stop the sisters from scheming to kill the painter who'd broken their hearts. Ian had caught the vengeful sisters before they succeeded. Not knowing what else to do with the frail, half-mad pair, he'd delivered them to Vincent.

Vincent himself had been suddenly Changed, with no vampire to mentor him through even basic methods of survival and no one to help him keep the madness and grief at bay. He'd had the deepest sympathy for the Siddons sisters, who'd endured their first years without guidance.

When the Siddons sisters came under his care, they'd seemed to be a lost cause, alternating between bouts of suicidal depression and murderous rage. With Vincent's patience and sheer unwillingness to see such sad creatures put to death, they'd made progress over the years and were at last able to live and hunt independently. Slowly he'd been easing them into interacting with mortals, and now he would attempt the next step.

"What is it you require of us?" Sally asked, wringing her hands once more.

He eyed the stacks of *La Belle Assemblée* on the table, the mannequin in the far corner, and the gowns the sisters wore. Both rivaled garb made by the most coveted seamstresses.

"My ward requires a wardrobe for her debut this Season," Vincent ventured cautiously. "I wonder if you ladies would be up to the task."

Sally's eyes lit with immediate interest, and she reached for a magazine of fashion plates. "My lord! We would be honored. When may we come to the castle and—"

"We *require* a price," Maria interjected, folding her arms across her chest.

Vincent sighed. "I will *not* bring you to London."

"For a wardrobe of that size, along with the inevitable repairs needed, you have little choice in such a short time frame. Besides, we can paint up our faces and disguise ourselves beyond recognition. We grew up in the theater, don't you recall?"

Sally rallied behind her sister. "And I feel we have the right to look in on our mother. She is in her dotage, and it would break our hearts not to see her before she dies. Please, my lord, show us some mercy."

In the face of Maria's logical argument and Sally's emotional appeal, Vincent's resolve crumbled despite his better judgment. "Very well. I will ask the Lord of London for permission for you to accompany me, which he may very well refuse. If he consents, you must remain out of sight as much as possible. And, by all that is holy, you will stay away from that infernal painter."

Maria's green eyes hardened. "Will *you* look in on him for us, and tell us how he fares?"

He sighed, willing patience. "No good can come from bothering Lawrence. It won't help you forget him."

"We don't want to forget, not until we see him dead."

"Killing humans is illegal," he replied for the thousandth time. "However, he will die eventually. Like all mortals, he grows older every day. I've seen many people perish from age. It is a more torturous death than you could imagine. Can't you take comfort from that?"

Sally gave her sister a hard look. "If you will see him and tell us of his suffering."

"I hope he's bald and his teeth have rotted black and pain him daily," Maria grumbled.

Vincent chuckled. "All *right*. I'll take a peek at the sod. Perhaps he has gout. Now will you help me outfit my ward?"

"She will shine like a diamond of the first water, and all other debutantes will chew their livers in envy." Sally smiled sweetly. "That is, if you supply us with the fabric, thread, and all other accoutrements we request."

He returned the smile, pleased to see genuine enthusiasm light her usually bleak countenance. "You will have everything you ask for, along with my eternal gratitude."

After he and Emrys took their leave, his second shook his head. "Are you certain it is wise to bring *that* pair to Castle Deveril and expose them to your pet mortal and servants, much less bring them to London?"

"They've done well by the woman who comes to clean, and have not caused trouble with the mortals in town when they venture out." Mention of *his* pet mortal brought an inexplicable urge to see her once more. "The night grows late. We'll discuss it later." Vincent took off toward his castle…and his ward.

Miss Hobson accosted him the moment he returned. "We must discuss Miss Price."

"Allow me to divest myself of my wet coat, and I shall meet you in the solar," he replied over his shoulder, already shrugging out of the sodden garment.

Pausing in the doorway to the solar, he observed the stern woman. On the surface, she appeared to be as snobbish and cold as Lady Morley. He had been assured that Miss Hobson was the best, and though she might be strict, females under her charge constantly defied the worst of odds to emerge as winners in the marriage game. Lydia Price needed a chaperone of that caliber.

"Would you care for some brandy, Miss Hobson?" He removed a decanter and two snifters from the sideboard.

"A lady does not drink strong spirits, my lord." Contrary to the prim decline, her eyes gleamed at the smoky liquid.

Vincent smirked and filled both glasses. "Come now, who is here to judge you? I believe after your arduous journey, you have earned a robust drink."

Finally, a genuine smile crossed her thin lips. "Very well, my lord, if you insist."

Vincent handed her a glass and added another log to the fireplace before settling in a burgundy velvet wing-backed chair across from the chaperone. They shared a brief companionable silence, sipping their smuggled brandy.

He set down his snifter with regret. Too much would upset his digestion. "You wished to discuss Miss Price. What is your impression of her?"

Miss Hobson sighed before taking another fortifying

drink. "As I told you before, securing a match for the young lady will not be easy. Aside from the scandal surrounding her birth, the fact that Lady Morley refuses to receive her will discourage Society from acknowledging her." She lowered her voice. "And I have a feeling that Lady Morley will endeavor to make things worse when Miss Price is presented. *That* woman will stop at nothing."

Although the news was bleak, Vincent felt a measure of encouragement at Miss Hobson's animosity toward Lady Morley. He would need a strong ally in this game. "Very well, may we now discuss the young lady's assets?"

The chaperone nodded. "Her appearance is satisfactory, though her accent is unfortunate."

She is beautiful, Vincent thought, calling to mind Lydia's tawny eyes and luxurious hair. And her southern American drawl was like warm honey.

"She has many accomplishments, though not all are ladylike," Miss Hobson continued. "I will encourage her to hide the latter while I work on nurturing the former."

As the chaperone droned on, Vincent took another drink, letting the brandy roll across his tongue, and speculated on the taste of Lydia's smooth flesh. Perhaps she would taste as sweet as she sounded... He shook off the thought, alarmed at the intensity of his desire. *Good Lord, what is happening to me? Has my solitude driven me mad in truth?*

Miss Hobson remained oblivious to his sinful musings as she finished her inventory. "Finally, Miss Price seems to be quick-witted and very brave. These things will ensure her survival and possibly garner respect among the *ton*."

He nodded. "Yes, she does seem to possess ample courage."

Pride filled him. Lydia's gaze had been bold as she faced him, without a glimpse of terror at the prospect of being placed at the mercy of a stranger.

"Given that she's an American and has been rejected by her family, this will be the biggest challenge of my career." Miss Hobson sighed, pulling him back to the matter at hand. "Though I believe I may carry it off."

"That is why I hired you," Vincent replied blandly. "I was informed you are the best."

"Yes," she replied without arrogance. "Also, her substantial dowry will help matters considerably. However did you wrangle such a sum from the Morley purse?"

"I required Lady Morley to double the existing dowry in exchange for my taking on the responsibility. *Then* I doubled the amount yet again from my own coffers."

A strange snort that may have been a laugh came from Miss Hobson at the last. "The dowager countess will not be pleased to hear that." Taking a sip of her drink, she leaned forward. "It is rumored that the Deverils have always been a miserly lot."

He smiled over his glass of brandy. "Well, their frugality has been enough that it shall be no trouble for me to break the tradition." It was astounding the fortune one could amass in two centuries. The bitter rub was that he'd had nothing or no one to spend it on…until now.

"That is excellent news. You will need it for this endeavor to succeed."

Miss Hobson then filled his ears with talk of tutors, dresses, fans, and other such frippery. Vincent only half listened as he mulled over other more serious challenges: the first being that a Lord Vampire needed permission before entering another's territory. Typically, that would not be of great concern, as he was on good terms with the Lord Vampire of London. However, Ian was due to depart soon on an extended wedding trip, and his second in command would rule London for the next half century.

Vincent was not well acquainted with Rafael Villar, though if the dour expression on Villar's scarred face was any indication, relations between London and Cornwall would become less amicable. Likely Rafael would refuse Vincent's request to bring Lydia to London for the Season, as he had vocally disapproved of Ian's marriage to a mortal.

Hell, Ian might refuse if he was still in charge. He'd involved himself with a human out of necessity, and solved the conflict eventually by Changing his bride. Vincent's involvement was voluntary…and hell would freeze over before he destroyed such a vivid life as Lydia's.

As soon as Miss Hobson retired, Vincent headed up to the chamber he'd prepared for Lydia. He wondered momentarily at his sense of urgency. *I am only doing my duty in seeing that she's settled in properly.*

He paused at her door long enough to reach out with his senses and verify that she was asleep before stealing silently into the room. It wouldn't do to frighten her.

She was so full of life. Vincent watched Lydia's

sleeping form with awe. Her hair spread across the pillow like a midnight waterfall. He longed to touch it as he had earlier. No, *more*.

He remembered how her large eyes had sparkled despite the dark circles of fatigue beneath them. Yet she had seemed concerned for *him*. An odd ache pierced his chest at the memory.

Her hair whispered beneath his fingers like satin. Vincent snatched back his hand and left the room, guilt roiling through him for touching something so pure.

Four

LYDIA AWOKE TO THE AROMA OF BACON AND FRESHLY baked bread. She smiled at Emma, who was carrying a heaping breakfast tray. "That smells heavenly."

Emma nodded and placed the tray on the table near the bed. "Cook was pleased to prepare a nice meal. His lordship rarely dines at home."

"Why not?" Lydia reached for the food, stomach rumbling. A pang of disappointment struck her at the maid's words. She'd looked forward to dining with her fascinating guardian.

The maid shook her head. "It seems to be a custom among bachelors."

"Well, it's a terrible custom." She bit into a piece of crisp bacon. "The man is much too thin." That hadn't stopped him from haunting her dreams last night. He'd been caressing her hair as though she was something cherished. Her cheeks heated, and her pulse quickened.

Oh no. Her fork fell from nerveless fingers. She knew this feeling. It was the same sensation she'd experienced when she'd first seen the dashing Monsieur

Delacroix at the opera last year. She'd yearned for the better part of a month until her maid had informed her that the man was engaged to a planter's daughter, and he also had a quadroon mistress tucked away in the French Quarter.

Now I'm attracted to my own guardian. Her lips curled in a self-deprecating frown. Was she destined to always pine over the wrong man? A guardian was supposed to be a figure of familial authority, like an exalted uncle. Unfortunately, Lord Deveril was too damned handsome to be anyone's uncle.

Unaware of Lydia's plight, Emma opened the curtains and tended the fire. Lydia buttered her bread and looked around the chamber. Far from a gothic horror scene, the room epitomized luxury, with its plush rugs covering the stone floor, elegant tapestries, and cheery fireplace. Lydia didn't know whether to be relieved or disappointed. At least there were no cobwebs. She abhorred spiders.

After she finished eating and completing her morning ablutions, Emma helped her into a gown of black muslin trimmed in lace.

"Is the earl about this morning?" Lydia ventured curiously.

"No, he remains abed during the day. The sunlight gives him a terrible sick headache."

"The poor man!" Lydia's heart clenched with sympathy. "How is he to enjoy himself? Much less look after his estate?" *Or me?* "What is he like?"

Emma paled and glanced around as if expecting to see Deveril over her shoulder. "I cannot say, miss. I have not been long in his employ."

It seemed her maid was afraid of the earl. Was the man a tyrant? She wouldn't be able to abide that for a moment. *Though if he's strict, my silly infatuation should abate.*

Miss Hobson awaited her in the solar with a pair of fans in hand. The chaperone looked pale. "Good morning, Miss Price. We must begin cultivating your manners so you are ready for the London Season."

"London?" Lydia's heart raced. "I only now came here."

"We won't be leaving for another month."

Lydia nodded. At least she had time to become acquainted with this wild, sea-kissed land. Although admittedly, the prospect of seeing England's capital was exciting. Her dream of meeting Sir Thomas Lawrence might yet be possible. "Do you suppose Lord Deveril may take me to see the Royal Academy of Arts?"

Unaffected by her excitement, Miss Hobson handed her a fan. "He may, though we must make you presentable in time. Now show me how you learned to open a fan."

Just like that, her lessons began. Lydia's instructors in America seemed not to have been good enough, for Miss Hobson drilled her in things she'd thought she'd mastered years ago. After an hour with the fan, they spent even more time on walking, and yet a longer period on sitting. By the time they finished luncheon, Lydia was twitching with boredom…and Miss Hobson had paled further.

Miss Hobson absently rubbed her temple. "Do ladies nap in America?"

"We do when the heat is terrible. As it is much cooler here, I do not feel in the least tired. Perhaps Emma could give me a tour of the castle while *you* rest?" Lydia suggested gently. "I know I have been a trying pupil."

"No, no, not at all," Miss Hobson assured. "However, your suggestion has merit. It is time you become acquainted with your new home. We shall continue your lessons at supper."

Finishing her tea, the chaperone departed, still rubbing her temples as though her headache was worsening. Perhaps the malady was a common reaction to the climate, since the earl suffered from them as well. Lydia prayed it was not so. Frequent headaches had plagued her when she'd had yellow fever.

She forced the ugly memory away and stood, brightening at the new prospect before her. "Let us explore the castle."

Emma shivered as she secured the needle in her sampler. "I've not been here long enough to know this place well, miss. I fear we shall become lost."

Lydia chuckled. "What fun that would be."

"*Fun?*" The maid quavered in fear.

Taking pity on the woman, Lydia sighed. "I'll ask the butler to come along. I do not suppose this castle has many callers to tend."

At last, the maid giggled. "I suppose not."

Aubert proved to be an informative guide, navigating the corridors with ease as he explained the purpose of each room. Worn tapestries depicting pastoral landscapes covered nearly every inch of the walls in an attempt to block out the musty dampness. Lydia listened to Aubert's descriptions, rapt with fascination as she pictured rushes adorning the stone floors and knights rushing off to battle, wearing their ladies' favors for luck.

Several renowned paintings also adorned the castle walls. Lydia gasped in delight as she spotted a Goya, a Lorraine, and even one by Thomas Lawrence. The earl appeared to be fond of landscapes. Lydia's fingers itched to render her own images on canvas. Perhaps Miss Hobson would nap long enough for her to venture outside with her paints.

"Miss Price." Aubert's voice turned sharp when she turned the corner to the south wing. "We cannot continue that way."

"Why not?" She peered down the corridor. The lack of lit wall sconces engulfed the area in shadows. Was there a dark secret? She'd read that castles contained secret passageways.

"Those are his lordship's quarters." Aubert's voice was hushed and wary. "He *must not* be disturbed."

Lydia sighed at the depressingly commonplace explanation. "Very well. Are there dungeons?"

The butler nodded. "Most of that area has been refurbished into a wine cellar." As if sensing her need for further entertainment, he added, "A few old prisoner cells remain. Would you like to see them?"

"Oh yes, I would be most obliged!" Lydia vowed she would search for secret passageways the moment she was alone.

⤜⤝

Vincent bit back a curse as he returned from his first hunt of the evening. Lydia had been under his care for less than twenty-four hours, and she'd already gone missing.

"Where is she?" he demanded once more to no avail.

The maid trembled and babbled incoherently.

"What is amiss, my lord?" Miss Hobson's voice was groggy as she entered the room.

"My ward is missing." He vowed to use a less heady vintage the next time he plotted with the chaperone.

Aubert shuffled between them. "Miss Price is painting on the west hill, my lord. Miss Hobson was indisposed…" He squared his thin shoulders and continued. "Miss Price wanted to walk the grounds and paint. I saw no harm in her doing so, as we can see her from the window…"

Vincent glared at the dark window.

"Well," the butler stammered. "We *could* see her before we began preparing for supper."

Miss Hobson flushed. "I shall fetch her straightaway!"

"No," Vincent countered. "Why don't you… check on the supper?" He turned to the maid. "And you will…do whatever a maid does to prepare for a meal. *I* will collect Miss Price."

Utterly out of his element, he left the castle and hurried through the moonlit evening. Devouring the distance in long strides, he wished he could use his powerful speed and flash to the west hill in seconds. It wouldn't do to frighten Lydia. He had to behave as a mortal man.

Clenching his teeth, Vincent realized he wasn't the only one upset by his ward's arrival. Although he had hired Miss Fiddock, she would not have lost her position in the first place if it were not for Lydia. Miss

Hobson would not have come here if not for the sum he offered…and she would have done a better job of keeping track of her charge if he hadn't doused her in brandy the night before. His servants were in a state of bewilderment, since they were unaccustomed to long-term guests.

By the time Vincent crested the west hill, he was infuriated. It would be all well and good to blame Lydia, but she was innocent. Lady Morley was a far likelier target…yet even then she was only the catalyst. He had only himself to blame, and though if he could go back and refuse the dowager's plea to honor the alliance, he knew he wouldn't. He should have planned better, enacted further preparations.

The chaos in his household was solely his fault. The fact only increased his temper.

"What do you think you're about?" he demanded.

Lydia turned from packing away her paints, tawny eyes wide as a doe's. "My lord!" She managed an awkward curtsy despite her heavy canvas apron.

Vincent frowned. The cumbersome apron made her resemble a drudge. Were things more lax in America? "A lady is not safe alone outside, especially after dark."

"I was perfectly safe." With a jaunty grin, Lydia removed her hand from beneath the apron. A flint-lock pistol was in her grip. "I am not a fool. My father told me I shouldn't be alone without some means of protection. I've had it pointed at you since you startled me."

Shock and admiration warred within, until all he could manage was a burst of laughter. His ward had spirit. Lydia glared at him like the wrath of hellfire even as the moonlight glistened on her hair like an angel's nimbus.

Catching his breath, he managed to gasp, "I am not laughing at you, Lydia. I am laughing because you had the upper hand all along." He regained his composure. "I am unused to being surprised."

She released the hammer on the gun with delicate precision before tucking it back into the massive pocket in the apron. "I shall endeavor to do so more often, for your reaction was quite diverting."

Not knowing what to say to that, Vincent approached the canvas propped up on an easel. His eyes widened at her skill. "You've rendered the castle well."

"That is only the preliminary outline," she said demurely as she finished packing her supplies into a worn leather case. "Besides, how can you tell? I had to stop because I couldn't see the end of my brush."

"I can see well at night, due to my nocturnal schedule." With his heightened vision, even the tips of her eyelashes stood out in vivid detail. "Allow me to escort you back to the castle. It is time for supper." He reached for the painting.

"Be careful, the paint is still wet." She gingerly snatched the canvas before he could take it. "You may carry my easel."

Vincent folded the contraption and picked up her case. Lydia strode down the hill in brisk strides. As he matched her pace, the scent of gardenias rose over the acrid odor of turpentine.

The moment they entered the castle, Lydia was swept away by Emma and Miss Hobson, for one to primp and the other to scold. However, in a surprisingly short time she arrived in the dining room no worse for wear and radiant in a black taffeta evening dress.

"You look fetching this evening, Miss Price," he said, pulling out her chair.

Her cheeks flushed an entrancing pink. "Thank you, my lord. I know it is a bit much for a country supper. Unfortunately, I do not have many gowns."

"Oh?" He raised a brow as the soup was served. "You brought many trunks."

She tasted her chowder and dabbed her lush mouth with the napkin. "One contains my paints, charcoals, canvases, and sculpting clay. Two hold my paintings. Another, my books."

"And the rest?" He stirred his soup, wishing he could eat more than a miniscule amount.

"Well, one contains my fishing rods and tackle, and the last holds my gun collection." An impish smile teased the corners of her lips.

"Gun *collection*?" Vincent was thankful he did not have a mouthful of soup, or else he would have sprayed the table. "So, one is not enough?"

Miss Hobson's face turned an alarming crimson as she choked on her dinner roll. Lydia gave her a hearty thump on the back. "Most were my father's, but three are mine. He enjoyed taking me shooting."

Vincent grinned. "It appears you are a lady of many talents."

Miss Hobson interrupted with a brisk cough. "I have discussed Miss Price's, ah, unconventional pro-clivities with her, and I assure you they will not be revealed to others."

Lydia nodded, expressionless, but Vincent could feel her sudden sadness. He suppressed the urge to glare at the chaperone, despite the fact that she was likely correct.

He forced a bright tone as the next course was served. "All the same, that should not prohibit her from enjoying herself here until we go to London. With my forests and lake, I'm certain you will be able to indulge your passion for the fresh air."

"You have a lake?" she nearly squealed in delight.

"Well, it is more like a very large pond," he joked, happy to bring back her spirit. "But the fish are plentiful, I assure you."

To his surprise, Miss Hobson smiled in what appeared to be relief. He realized she must have feared his disapproval of Lydia's hobbies.

As the next course was served, Lydia's cheer dissipated as Miss Hobson attempted to engage her in the practice of polite conversation.

"You must strive to do better in hiding your boredom," Vincent said after the topic of the weather had been exhausted.

Lydia hid her pained frown behind her napkin. "Yes, my lord."

Sympathy for her welled within. "I know these things can be tedious, but you must master them before the Season begins. However, I think you've endured enough for the evening. Let us speak more freely. Tell me about New Orleans. Did your father own a plantation?"

Lydia brightened at the change in subject. "No, we lived in the city, although we enjoyed frequent visits to the bayous. My father made his income from lucrative investments. He did *not* believe in slavery."

Vincent chuckled at her vehement tone. Slavery was a practice he disapproved of as well. "So all of your servants were white?"

"No, but all were free and were paid wages. *Gens de couleur libre*, they are called. 'Free people of color.'" She sighed. "I hope someday all Americans will be free."

"I wouldn't count on it." Vincent eyed her as he sampled his custard. A gentle heart and a revolutionary spirit could be a tragic combination.

They embarked on a spirited debate of the complex issues involved, with Lydia stubbornly maintaining that slavery could be abolished without an outbreak of civil war.

Vincent smiled at her naive passion. "All the same, the labor costs money, while slaves do not. American landowners save much coin that way." Pressing his point, he continued. "Never underestimate the power and depth of human greed, Miss Price."

She considered his words as the dishes were carried away. "I believe you are correct, my lord, though it saddens me." She managed a wan smile. "I must say, this was a much more stimulating conversation than the last."

Miss Hobson sniffed. "It was a distasteful subject, not at all suitable for Polite Society."

Vincent and Lydia exchanged glances, both fighting back laughter at the chaperone's pious disapproval.

As dinner concluded, Lydia glanced at him with concern. "Are you well, my lord? You have scarcely eaten."

Before he could fabricate an excuse, Miss Hobson

changed the subject. "Will you be adjourning to have a cigar and port? I have a matter to discuss with Miss Price."

No doubt to scold her for being so forward. "I do not smoke, so I feel no need to excuse myself." Pleased at thwarting her, he added, "However, we may all depart to the game room, and I would be delighted if you joined me once more for a glass of brandy."

The chaperone's lip curled at the jab, but her eyes glittered with amusement...and respect. "I do not suppose you have anything less potent?"

"Certainly," he said. "I have the finest champagne, imported from France."

"No doubt smuggled," Miss Hobson muttered.

"Quite so," Vincent said agreeably. "This is Cornwall, after all."

Five

"CHECK," LYDIA DECLARED WITH A TRIUMPHANT GRIN.

Lord Deveril merely blinked at her before slowly moving his rook. "Mate."

"Damn! I walked right into that, didn't I?" She ignored Miss Hobson's disapproving cough at her language and looked at the remaining chess pieces with awe as his strategy became clear. "That was brilliant, my lord! May we play again?"

The earl gave her a quizzical look that made her feel as if he was peering into her soul. "You are not bothered that I trounced you so?"

She shook her head and smiled. "I enjoyed myself thoroughly. I hope to learn more and win the next round."

As he set up the board with graceful, long fingers, she asked, "Tell me about smugglers. Are they like pirates?"

Deveril chuckled. "I have never encountered a pirate, so I couldn't say. Though I assume they'd taste—" His brow furrowed, and he shook his head. "Er, I assume their tastes are coarser than the usual smuggler, who is a combination of unscrupulous businessman and skilled sailor."

Lydia concealed a giggle behind her hand and took another sip of her delicious champagne, relishing the tickle of the bubbles on her tongue. As they played, she asked more questions about Cornwall's smugglers, in hope of distracting him.

"Most of what is smuggled here are luxury items from France, such as Brussels lace, brandy, champagne, tea, and spices," he explained, taking her queen. "And smuggling likely accounts for a larger portion of Cornwall's income than fishing and mining combined."

Lydia attempted to take his knight with her bishop. "But isn't there a death sentence if one is caught?"

"Yes, but one must feed one's family." He seized her knight with a pawn. "Besides, why should the Crown reap all of the profits?"

Lydia mulled this over as she brought her pawn to the end of the board, winning back her queen. Alas, it was too late, for Deveril had her king trapped. She again lost the game, but at least she earned an education. Her guardian was extremely intelligent, a quality she'd always admired in a man. She could never tire of conversing with him.

The earl's admiring smile made her loss worthwhile. "You nearly had me a few times, you know. When I'm finished with you, you will be quite a formidable player."

Lydia flushed at the compliment. "May we play billiards next?" Her father played, but Lydia had never tried her hand at it.

Miss Hobson cleared her throat, doubtless to decry the request as unladylike. "It is getting late, Miss Price. Perhaps you should retire."

Deveril held up a hand. "Actually, I believe we should adapt ourselves to city hours, in preparation for the Season. It would not do to have Miss Price wilting from exhaustion shortly after her first ball begins."

Lydia's heart surged. It appeared the earl was an ally.

Miss Hobson's eyes widened a moment as myriad expressions played across her stern face. At last, she dipped her head with a hint of a smile. "A capital idea, my lord."

The earl arranged the balls near one end of the antique, yet newly clothed, table. Lydia selected a cue from the oak rack, admiring the carved lions' heads adorning the rack's edges.

"Would you care to break, Miss Price?" Deveril invited.

She frowned. "Break?"

His brow arched. "Is it called something else in America?" He pointed his stick at the ivory cue ball and the triangle of colored balls.

Lydia gathered she was supposed to knock them apart. "I apologize. It has been some time."

Gritting her teeth, she approached the table and leaned over, positioning the cue in what she hoped was the correct manner. She took aim, drew it back, thrust it forward…and the dratted thing merely skimmed the cue ball. The white sphere rolled toward the triangle with agonizing slowness. It struck the first ball with a barely audible click, and the mass remained still.

"You've never played before, have you?" Deveril chuckled. Though his voice was amused, she could detect no trace of mockery.

Lydia returned his laughter. "No, for some reason Papa never taught me. He said darts were sufficient." A memory had her frowning in confusion. "He played with mother, though."

"Darts?" That quizzical glint returned to his gaze, making his eyes shift to a light blue, like the sea on a clear day. "How proficient are you at that game?"

She beamed. "Very."

He gestured to a mahogany cabinet at the far end of the room. "I have a board. Shall we play that instead?"

"Not tonight," Lydia replied. "I've always wanted to learn billiards…and piquet, tennis, and cricket."

Deveril sighed and started to say something but stopped and shook his head, opting instead for another draught of brandy. "Very well. We shall begin with the break."

With fluid grace, he bent and poised his cue, striking the white ball with the tip in a solid clink. The colored balls scattered across the table, faster than her eye could track. But she could hear them. Three flew into the corner pockets with resounding thumps.

Beautiful. The word echoed in her mind, and Lydia longed to match such skill, but knew if she failed, she'd be content merely to watch him…and the strong shape of his backside beneath his buff trousers.

She took the cue and made her shot. This time, the white ball bounced off the table.

"You need to put more effort in your balance to better make the proper angle," Deveril said before handily knocking in another ball.

He gave her the same advice after she sent the ball careening across the green, ricocheting off the corners, only to sink into the left pocket.

Deveril moved to make his shot and missed as a loud snore erupted behind him.

"I see I have further reason for us to grow accustomed to London hours," he said as the cue ball meandered lazily into the right pocket.

Miss Hobson rested her head on her shoulder, embroidery askew on her lap. She appeared to be sound asleep.

"May we please continue the game?" Lydia whispered, grateful to be away from the chaperone's scrutiny. "We can wake her afterward."

"Enjoying respite from the dragon, are you?" Deveril teased in his musical voice. "Surely it cannot be because you hope to win, although you have earned a penalty shot."

"You surmise correctly, my lord," she replied, fetching the white ball.

"Wait," Deveril said before she took her shot. "Would you like me to show you how it's done?"

Lydia grinned, eager to master the skill. "Please do."

For some reason, his features darkened. He took a breath, and his countenance settled, though his eyes remained stormy. She froze as he stepped toward her. "To do this, I will have to stand behind you and guide your hands."

"Yes," she whispered in answer to his unspoken question.

Tension charged the air as Deveril approached. A few locks of hair had escaped its binding and framed his face, making him appear rakish and predatory.

Her breath caught as he moved behind her. Though only his hands touched her, one on her shoulder and the other on her wrist, Lydia felt him against her, as if his presence transcended his body.

"Though you must lean over the table, you need to straighten your spine and bring up your shoulder." His breath tickled her neck and ear.

"Then you need to hold your arm level, like this." Those long fingers pressed against her flesh with suppressed strength as he gently moved her arm to the correct position.

Lydia's knees felt like custard, and her hips quivered in instinct to melt against him. It took all of her will to process his words. "All right."

"Now focus on that ball at a point just to the right of the center. Are you ready?" His hair brushed her cheek like a silken feather.

"Yes," she gasped, struggling to focus on the game.

With his hands guiding her, the cue moved back. Lydia felt his firm, warm chest against her back…then the cue struck. For an instant, her hips bucked against him, and something hot and primal rose up in her lower body.

Deveril moved away quickly as if burned. They watched the white ball strike its target.

The blue sphere fell into the pocket, along with another, and Lydia whooped in triumph. "I am catching up now, yes?"

Deveril shook his head. "I'm afraid not. You pocketed the black, which means the game is forfeit to me."

Her eyes narrowed in irritation. "You did that on purpose!"

"I did no such thing," he countered in such a stern

manner that it could only be the truth. He sighed and smoothed his hair from his face. "It was a mistake. A great mistake for which I humbly apologize."

Lydia suspected he wasn't talking only about the game, and shivered at the memory of his touch. "All right. May we play again?"

"No. It is time for my walk." His eyes were luminous, hypnotic.

"May I accompany you?" she asked, not yet ready to relinquish his company. To walk with him in the moonlight...

"*No!*" he said hoarsely.

Lydia jumped at his sudden harshness. Had she angered him?

Deveril gave her an apologetic look and returned to his earlier formal tone. "It would not be appropriate, Miss Price. Thank you for an enjoyable evening."

Without a backward glance, he left the room, crossing the plush rug with long strides.

Lydia's breath remained trapped in her throat as she put away her cue. She could still feel the brief, intense contact his body had made. And the fire in his gaze seared her soul.

"Well." Miss Hobson yawned and fetched a candelabrum. "It is past time we retire."

Lydia followed the chaperone like a puppet, her mind continuing her fixation on the earl and his quicksilver change in mood. "Whatever came over him?" she murmured.

"His lordship merely appreciates his solitude," Miss Hobson said as she held the candelabrum aloft, illuminating the dark stairway. Her voice gentled. "I'm certain he didn't mean to frighten you. It is likely the effect of being awake at this ungodly hour."

"What do you presume he does on those walks? Does he have a mistress?" Envy curdled her insides at the thought.

"No, his clothing is always in order when he returns, and he does not smell like perfume," Miss Hobson replied distractedly. She spun to face Lydia, eyes wide with outrage. "A lady does not speak of such things…and a maiden should not even know of them."

Lydia chuckled. Were English girls so cosseted? "Perhaps he gambles?"

The chaperone shook her head. "His demeanor remains unchanged. No sign of joy from winnings or dismay at losses. Really, this conversation is unseemly."

"Perhaps he's smuggling? Visiting an illegitimate family? Practicing witchcraft?" Lydia rushed on, undaunted. "Come now, you cannot tell me you are not curious."

Miss Hobson sighed as they reached Lydia's chamber. She glanced left and right for eavesdropping servants before ushering her inside and closing the door. "Very well, I admit one cannot refrain from a bit of curiosity at such odd behavior."

"What do you suppose he does?"

"I can see from your impish expression that you think he's involved in something scandalous," Miss Hobson scolded. "I regret I must disabuse you of such a notion. From all I've observed, his lordship shows no sign of tawdry behavior. Therefore, it is my belief that he goes on his nighttime walks merely because his headaches prevent him from doing so during the day." She lit the lantern and rang for Emma. "Or, it is a mental compulsion of some sort."

"Mental compulsion?" Lydia asked, intrigued.

Miss Hobson nodded. "I've seen such an occurrence. There was a duke who felt the need to wash his hands every hour. It was odd, though harmless. Otherwise, he was sound of mind."

"Ah, so Deveril is cracked?" Lydia whispered. That could explain his odd shifts in mood.

Before Miss Hobson could respond, Emma entered the chamber. "All Deverils are mad," she whispered loudly. "Every single one! My mother says—"

"That it is rude to eavesdrop?" Miss Hobson cut in with an arched brow.

Emma flinched. "No, miss. I was only answering your summons and overheard."

The chaperone nodded. "Prepare Miss Price for bed…and do not wake her until noon. His lordship wants us all to adopt London hours in preparation for the Season."

Emma curtsied, visibly relieved to have avoided a scolding. Miss Hobson bade them both a good night and retired to her chamber.

As the maid helped her out of her gown, Lydia whispered, "What *did* your mother say about the Deverils?"

She felt Emma stiffen. "It's really nothing, miss. J-just silly gossip. Miss Hobson will have me out of the house if I repeat it."

"She doesn't have to know," Lydia wheedled, curious about her enigmatic guardian.

Emma opened her mouth then shut it with a shake

of her head as she hung up Lydia's dress. "I must not say anything, other than his lordship has been kind to me." Lifting her chin, she added, "And he has been kind to *you* as well."

Lydia flushed with guilt at her speculation. Deveril *had* been kind to her. "All right, Emma, I'll not pester you." She climbed into bed. "Unless Deveril does something truly mad."

Emma nodded. "If he does, I will happily leave my position."

Despite the late hour and warm fire, sleep failed to entice Lydia into its embrace. Her flesh continued to tingle at the memory of Deveril's hands on her arms and the heat of his breath on her ear.

∾

An hour before dawn, Vincent strode back to his castle in a foul mood. Bronn, his third in command, had reported another rogue, or perhaps the same one who'd been sighted the previous week. Rogue vampires, those who had been Changed without sanction, or who'd been exiled or left their lord's territory without leave, were always a problem. His vampires were usually able to defend themselves from such cretins, but Lydia was not...and she'd been out alone after dark.

As he headed up to his chamber, he cursed himself for a fool. How could he have failed to consider the danger she could have been in? He needed to Mark her. He should have done so the first night she came here. He needed to be able to know where she was at all times, and Marking made that possible. If the

Siddons sisters had enticed rogues, Lydia would be even more tempting. After all, she had tempted him.

Memories of her husky laugh and warm smile assaulted him with a savage desire that grew more crippling when he entered her chamber and caught her sweet scent. Oh yes, she had tempted him. His fingers curled at his sides as he stood over her bed, resisting the urge to touch her once more. *Not for me.*

The thought sobered him, bringing his duty back to mind. He had set himself on this course of action, and he would carry it out to the best of his ability. Lydia would remain safe under his care, even from his own kind. His eyes narrowed as he bit his index finger, drawing blood. *Especially* from his own kind.

A shudder wracked his body as his finger touched Lydia's silken lips. *So warm...so soft.* Her unique aroma of gardenias and woman's musk taunted him even more than the sweet scent of her blood. Gritting his teeth, he forced his mind back to his task and began the ritual.

As his blood dripped into her mouth, he whispered, "I, Vincent Tremayne, Earl of Deveril and Lord of Cornwall, Mark this mortal, Lydia Price, as mine and mine alone. With this Mark I give Lydia my undying protection. Let all others, immortal and mortal alike, who cross her path sense my Mark and know that to act against her is to act against myself and thus set forth my wrath, as I will avenge what is mine."

A hot tremor engulfed his flesh as the preternatural magic took effect. Lydia moaned in her slumber. Reflexively, he caressed her black tresses in reassurance as he willed her to remain asleep. "It is all right, my dear."

Her pink tongue licked her lush lips. Vincent bent down to kiss her and froze. *No, she is* not *mine.* Rigid with arousal and self-loathing, he hurried out of her room, vowing never again to cross this threshold until she left his castle. The sooner that happened, the better.

∽

Sleep came with difficulty to Sarah Hobson. Scorning her bed, she sat in the rocking chair before the fire. As she rocked, her mind raced. The *ton* hailed her as the best chaperone in all of England. So skilled was she at ensuring successful matches for her charges, Society matrons actually bid for her services as if it were an auction. The highest bidder had been the Dowager Countess of Morley for Lady Georgiana—until the Earl of Deveril doubled the offer.

At first she was willing to chalk it up to the famed Deveril madness, but when she arrived at the castle and saw the furnishings—from Aubusson carpets and Chippendale chairs to beeswax candles, rather than tallow, she suspected the earl possessed deeper pockets than she'd anticipated. Her suspicions were confirmed when he did not blink at the cost of Lydia's debut, and most importantly, doubled her dowry.

It was Deveril's goal to arrange a more successful marriage for Lydia than Lady Morley would for Georgiana. It was Sarah's duty to ensure Miss Price made the best match of the Season. A titled gentleman with ample wealth was imperative…and the Earl of Deveril met these requirements. When they arrived in London, *he* would be the biggest catch of the Season.

However, Sarah was reluctant to encourage such a match on those factors alone. It did no good to push a girl into the arms of a man for greed. She preferred for there to be at least a measure of amiability between both parties, lest scandal erupt mere months after the wedding.

In the case of Miss Price, Sarah had further incentive to encourage a harmonious match. Orphaned and scorned by her remaining family, the poor child had no one. A good husband could help heal that hurt... and include a dower house and funds for her in his will. Normally Sarah did not think much on these matters. However, she *liked* Lydia. The girl had wit and spirit.

Lydia possessed many eccentricities, and Deveril was eccentric in his own right. It was apparent from the start that he admired Lydia for her unique qualities, that he would nurture her, rather than attempt to snuff the flame of her spirit. Sarah remembered how Deveril had smiled at Lydia, and how he could not refrain from touching her...and she hadn't missed the stars in Lydia's eyes when she looked at his lordship.

Deveril could be the perfect match for Lydia if he were not so fixated on his competition with Lady Morley that he missed the possibility that was right before him. Typical male. She yawned. It would be a tricky plan to carry out. These things must be done delicately. She must ensure that Miss Price and Lord Deveril had opportunities alone for their romance to bloom without the earl catching on to her meddling. And she must take care that things between them didn't venture into impropriety, for if that happened, then Miss Price would not be the only one with a ruined reputation.

Six

I AM A FOOL. VINCENT SIGHED AS HE HEALED THE doxy's wound and cleared her memory of his feeding. Though his blood thirst was slaked, the desires of his body remained as rampant and unquenched as they had been since his ward arrived. He could have made use of the whore's body along with her throat, but Lydia's large eyes sprang up in his mind, killing his inclination to make do with a substitute. Only Lydia would suffice. Yet he could not have her.

His teeth clenched so hard his fangs pricked the inside of his lower lip. Vincent growled, tasting blood, and loathing himself for wishing it was hers.

He cursed under his breath as he strode back to the castle, head bent against the rain. What was it about her that captured his fancy? She was beautiful, yet he'd seen hundreds of beauties in his near two centuries of life. She was not demure or ladylike. Hell, she'd pointed a gun at him on their second encounter.

Yawning, he returned home. Evenings in the company of Lydia Price were exhausting. He should pity her future husband, rather than possess an unreasonable urge to strangle the nonexistent sod.

Aubert took his soaked coat with a frown. "I see another storm has arrived, my lord."

For years, the butler had tried to dissuade him from his nightly walks, especially during inclement weather. He wondered how Aubert would react if he knew those walks kept Vincent from feeding on the servants. Doubtless it would be quite a scene. "I'll wear my cloak the next time I venture out."

Aubert's brows creased in disapproval, and Vincent changed the subject. "Miss Price must be upset that she was unable to work on her painting."

"Not at all, my lord. She's been tucked away in the library all day with a book and hot chocolate." Aubert hung the coat near the fire. "Reading seems to be another of her favorite pastimes. I daresay she is quite content."

It was obvious to Vincent that the servants genuinely liked Lydia. At first he presumed their solicitous behavior toward her was borne from pity for her circumstances, and perhaps relief to have someone relatively normal to look after. The butler's warm smile revealed that she had charmed them as well. Likely they would miss her when she was married off and gone.

For some reason the thought irritated him. "Well, I hope all that chocolate has not spoiled her supper," he muttered and headed for the library.

She wasn't there. Sighing, Vincent headed up the stairs to look. As her guardian, he should know where she was.

Emma gave a startled squeak as his shadow passed over the bed she and the housekeeper were turning down.

"I beg your pardon. I was looking for Miss Price."

The maid composed herself. "She's in the library."

Could no one keep track of his recalcitrant ward? Vincent sighed and closed his eyes, opening the Mark between them. Immediately, the connection he had forged with his blood sang in his marrow. Just as potent as her gardenia scent, he felt her presence, sweet and delectable. She was in the south wing...in *his* bedchamber. He shook his head and headed in that direction. Hadn't Aubert told her to stay away from that part of the castle?

Once he reached his room, he stood in the doorway, watching her, curious as to what she was doing in his room. Candlelight gleamed on her hair. Her hands were folded demurely behind her back as she walked slowly through the chamber, peering at the furnishing and tapestries with avid interest. When Lydia approached the large bed built to accommodate his height, she paused and reached out a tentative hand to touch the coverlet.

The innocent gesture made his blood boil with lust. *Curious about my bed, are you? I don't sleep in that one, though I could show you——* He broke off the dangerous thought, holding his breath as she passed the bed, still looking around.

He smiled at the sight of her futile tiptoeing. What *was* she so curious about? There was nothing in here except——

Lydia paused at a wall sconce, reached up toward it...

"Damn it," he growled, crossing the distance between them and snatching back her hand.

Lydia gasped and looked up at him, eyes wide with abashment and alarm. "My lord! I was ah…"

Before she could stammer an excuse, Vincent grasped both her wrists and captured her gaze. She seemed to forget what she was saying. Repugnance tormented him at the act; with her it felt like a violation. Alas, it was necessary. She had almost found the entrance to his lair. She couldn't discover what he was. As she stood mute and mesmerized, Vincent was suddenly aware of the pulsing vein in her throat that sang to him.

*Just a taste…*his inner demon whispered. Slowly, he slid his hands up her arms, grazing his fingertips across her collarbone before bending down to inhale the sweet bouquet of her blood and humanity. His lips lightly caressed her neck, as lust and hunger warred within.

He wanted more.

His mouth slowly trailed along the column of her throat as his hands reached up to cradle her face. He moved to kiss her lips and froze at the lack of spark in her glazed eyes. *No, not like this.* Repulsed with himself, he drew back.

"Your hair…" she murmured drowsily. "It's so beautiful." Slowly, she reached up and caressed his locks.

Remorse washed over him at her gentle touch. Vincent released her mind.

Lydia blinked at him and shook her head. "I was ah…"

"You were *what*?" he prodded huskily. Would she lie?

Her face turned rose red. "I was looking for secret passageways." She gave him a sheepish smile. "I've read that every castle has at least one. I-I have a fondness for gothic novels."

Vincent sighed, almost undone by her innocent curiosity. *Oh, if you knew, Lydia.* "Well, there *is* one, but you must promise to keep your silence." If he showed her another passage, perhaps she would stay away from his...and she deserved some sort of recompense for what he had done.

"I vow to keep the secret, even under the pain of torture," she declared with melodramatic flair.

"Your loyalty is commendable." Vincent laughed, taking the candelabrum from the table. He offered his arm. "Shall we?"

Her scent engulfed him at once as her small hand curled around his bicep. He could feel her quivering with excitement.

He led her out of the south wing and down a long corridor to a vacant room. Pressing a finger to his lips, he crossed the room and lifted a faded tapestry to reveal a wooden panel. When he pressed the panel's well-worn corner, it opened with a bone-wincing creak. The hinges needed oiling again.

Her enthusiasm was contagious. Feeling young for the first time in ages, he grinned at her. "Shall we explore it?"

Lydia's eyes danced with unabashed glee. "Oh, yes!"

Fighting to maintain dignified composure in the face of her eagerness, he forced a stern tone. "This passage has not been used in a very long time, so you must stay near me in case it has fallen into disrepair."

She nodded solemnly and grasped his hand as he guided her inside. The darkness was musty, yet strangely intimate in her company. Their steps were muffled on the packed dirt floor. Vincent grimaced and lowered his head as cobwebs brushed his face. He drew Lydia closer, grateful the light was too meager to reveal them.

"Where does it lead?" Her voice was suddenly shaky, whether from his proximity or fear of the dark, he could not tell. Little did she realize that he was the most dangerous thing here.

Vincent brushed aside another cobweb. "It merges into a tunnel leading outside the castle grounds. The purpose was to enable the castle's inhabitants to escape during a siege."

"How very fascinating—" She broke off suddenly. "What is that?" A dim light gleamed from a hole in the wall a few feet away.

Vincent squeezed her hand as they drew closer. "Look and see."

Lydia peered through the hole and gasped. "I see a bedchamber...my view is so obscured, as if...the opening is hidden by a tapestry. These holes are for spying on people!" She turned to him, eyes burning in accusation. "Whose room is it?"

"Emma's, I believe." Again, he concealed a chuckle, well aware of her indignant suspicions. "Though I cannot be certain. It has been a long time since I ventured here."

"Since you were a boy?" she asked.

He avoided the question. "I do know your chamber is blocked by the wardrobe."

Her body relaxed next to his, and she looked up at him. "What about *your* chamber?"

Vincent tamped down a fresh wave of guilt for mesmerizing her. "It is blocked as well."

Why did he feel such remorse? He'd been hypno-
tizing humans every night for centuries. It did them no
harm. *Because I did it to one I vowed to protect.*

They continued down the narrow passage, peering through the holes when opportunity arose.
Suddenly, Lydia let out a skull-piercing shriek.
She threw her arms around him and pressed herself
against his body with enough force to topple a
mortal man.

A low growl trickled from his throat as he pulled
her closer with one arm and disengaged the other to
destroy whatever frightened her. He frowned. He
neither saw, smelled, nor sensed anything that would
pose a threat.

"What is it, Lydia?"

Her face pressed so tightly against his chest that
he couldn't make out her response. The feel of her
mouth against him made his arousal flare painfully.
This is wrong.

"I…cannot…hear you," he bit out in agony.

A semblance of the sweet torture ended as she lifted
her head. "It was a spider." Her grip loosened, and he
fought the urge to pull her back.

She uttered a derisive laugh. "I apologize. It is a silly
fear, I know. I cannot help my revulsion for the horrid
creatures." Lydia shuddered against him, making him
suck in a breath. "May we go back now?"

"Yes." Vincent prayed his response to her embrace
would fade before they emerged.

Lydia chattered amiably as they made their way
back to the entrance, her terror forgotten. As they
exited the empty bedchamber, she looked up at him

with a mischievous grin. "Perhaps I can use the passage to escape my lessons—"

"There you are!" Miss Hobson rounded the corner. "Miss Price, I have been looking all over for you." Her hawklike gaze darted to Vincent, and she raised a brow. "My lord."

Vincent's jaw clenched as he gave her a polite nod. Her scrutiny made him feel like a recalcitrant school lad. "I was giving Miss Price a tour of the rest of the castle."

Miss Hobson eyed him suspiciously, then she smiled as if his answer pleased her. "I see. Come, Lydia. We must change your frock for supper. Good heavens, it is covered in dust. *Someone* should have a word with the housekeeper."

Lydia gave him a conspiratorial smile before she was whisked away. Vincent sighed and leaned against the wall. He was proving to be a terrible guardian.

Seven

THE NEXT AFTERNOON, LYDIA'S STEPS CARRIED HER TO the chamber containing the entrance to the secret passage. She shivered, remembering Deveril's smile when he took her there…and the firm, secure feel of his body in her arms when she'd seen the spider.

I want him, her inner voice declared with an ache.

For what? Her rational side asked. Lydia knew that when he was with her she felt safe and happy. She knew she wanted to run her fingers through his hair. She wanted to feel his arms around her. She wanted his lips upon hers…and more. *If only he weren't my guardian.*

Sighing, she pressed the corner, and the hidden door slid open with its usual protest. The passage seemed to be dimmer than on the previous evening.

She turned back to fetch a candelabrum, then stopped when she heard muffled voices. Someone was in one of the chambers. It had to be Emma. Shoving aside a momentary flicker of guilt, she continued down the passage, following the sounds.

The third viewing hole revealed the pair.

"They say he roams the countryside at night, steals

the milk from cows, and stops the chickens from laying their eggs!" a waifish blonde girl exclaimed.

Lydia's eyes widened. Now *this* was interesting.

"Hush, Beth," Emma admonished. Lydia had never before heard such authority in her maid's voice. "Do you want to get sacked on your first day? Mother cannot afford for you to lose this position."

"But we are under the roof of the Devil Earl!" Beth wailed.

The Devil Earl? Lydia fought back a gasp. They were talking about her guardian! The man *was* mysterious, but a devil? *Surely not.* Devils were not kind. A devil would not give her a home and company and laughter.

Emma sighed with all the exasperation of an elder sibling. "Stop behaving like a ninny. If the stories were true, I would have been dead weeks ago. I also wouldn't have recommended you when he sought a scullery maid." She nodded at Beth's wide gaze. "Yes, I am the one who had you sent here, *not* mother. And I do not see why you are carrying on so. *You* won't ever see him, as you'll be in the kitchens."

Beth continued to quaver. "Oh, Emma, I didn't think. You have to see him every day. Does he—" Her voice dropped to a whisper. Lydia couldn't hear the rest.

"Of course not!" Emma bristled. "He has been very kind, and I can assure you, he is no monster, much less a lecher." She chuckled and tweaked Beth's nose. "I think he may be somewhat cracked, yet I doubt he sucks the breath from babes or changes into a sea dragon during the full moon."

"What about the lady who is his ward?" Beth

prodded. "No one in the village has seen her. Is she mad as well?"

Lydia clapped a hand over her mouth to muffle her laughter. Beth was not the first to speculate on her mental faculties.

"She is in mourning. Ladies in mourning are not permitted—" Emma broke off and cocked her head toward the door. "Someone is coming. I think it may be Hobson."

Damn, teatime already. Lydia needed no further warning. She darted through the passage and out of the empty bedchamber just in time to greet her chaperone in the corridor.

She was tempted to question Miss Hobson during tea, though she did not dare, lest she endure a long lecture on eavesdropping. *Why are there such silly rumors about the earl? Is that why he isn't married?* Lydia frowned as she sipped her tea, wishing for café au lait.

Right after tea she bundled up in a thick woolen cloak, gathered her supplies, and had Aubert carry her easel outside to the west hill, where the light was best. The late afternoon sun shone brightly in the clear blue sky, though the air held a nipping chill. Lydia hardly noticed, so wrapped up was she in the beauty of Cornwall. Castle Deveril stood like an ancient sentinel poised before the jutting cliffs. The muted roar of the sea danced in her ears like forgotten music, calling her home. Craggy hills adorned with the greenest grass stretched down the coast; she had seen a wild, unkempt garden on the east side of the castle. To the north, a dark, dense forest beckoned her imagination and paintbrush with its haunting shadows streamed with mist.

Now the castle captured her attention. Already she was in love with the ancient fortress. As the sun dropped lower in the sky, the rosy light highlighted the wind-worn curves of ancient slate-gray stone. Sighing at its romantic beauty, she set up the canvas under the spreading limbs of a great oak tree at the summit of the hill, and mixed her paints.

As she painted, Lydia pondered her guardian. Perhaps the villagers' fear of him was understandable, for he did indeed resemble a character in a gothic novel. Tall, enigmatic, and captivating, the Earl of Deveril was the stuff of dark dreams.

Her fingers itched to render his striking features on canvas. She frowned, mixing colors on her palette. Those stormy eyes and moonstruck hair were meant to be immortalized. A small sigh escaped her at the thought of tracing the shape of his lips.

"Good evening, Lydia," Deveril called as he crested the hill. "How is the painting?"

A shiver ran down her body. He said her name only when they were alone…as if they shared an intimate secret. Lydia set down her palette and brush and pulled the folds of her cloak tighter. "It is going as well as it could be, with so few hours to capture the dusk. What is your Christian name?" she blurted as she removed the canvas from the easel. "I've known you for a week, and I feel I am at a disadvantage."

"It is Vincent," he replied in an odd tone. "I didn't realize you were unaware."

"Vincent." She tasted the word. Now she knew what name to invoke in her dreams. "That is quite a name for a devil. Do you truly steal milk from cows at night and change into a sea monster during the full moon, devouring hapless fishermen along the way?"

Deveril stiffened, and his eyes turned glacial. "Emma has been carrying tales, I see." Rage deepened his voice to a feral growl. "How dare she try to frighten you after I gave her shelter and employment when your grandmother sacked her? By God, I shall—"

"It was not Emma, my lord. It was her sister who said these things." Her face burned with guilt as she confessed her indiscretion. "I was in the passage, eavesdropping... Emma then assured her sister that you are not a monster." *Although she believes you are* somewhat *cracked.*

Then, his words struck her. He'd employed Emma after Lady Morley dismissed her. Lydia's heart warmed at his kind gesture.

Vincent continued to glower. "Perhaps I shall have to find a new scullery maid."

Lydia shook her head. "I do not think so, for you would only encounter the same problem with the next one. I understand the rumors are widespread." She attempted to make light of it as she packed away her painting supplies. "You should be flattered to be such a part of local lore. Perhaps one day 'The Devil Earl' will be as popular as 'Jack and the Beanstalk.'"

"I do not believe I've heard that one before." The hostility left his countenance, and he leaned against the great oak tree. "Would you tell it to me?"

"Of course." Relief washed over her. She had not caused Emma or Beth to lose their employment.

Taking a deep breath, she recited the tale. Lydia took extra care to insert appropriate drama when the giant arrived. "'Fee, Fie, Foe, Fum, I smell the blood of an Englishman.'" She stomped toward Vincent. "'Be he live or be he dead, I'll grind his bones to make my bread!'"

When she finished, Vincent applauded. "Now I must add storytelling to your list of accomplishments. We should return to the castle and meet the dressmakers."

"Not yet, my lord." Lydia stopped him, unwilling to relinquish the evening's beauty and his company. "Now you must tell me a story."

He sighed and nodded. "Very well." Vincent stepped away from the tree and began. "A young girl was told to bring a basket of food and herbs to her grandmother, who was ill."

Lydia had heard this tale, yet the way Vincent told it with his melodious voice and sinister narrative had her listening with anticipation. She watched entranced as he adopted the persona of the wolf, stalking around the tree like a sleek predator.

As Vincent neared the end of the story, he stepped closer to her. "'What big eyes you have,' said the girl. 'The better to see you with,' the wolf replied."

Lydia sucked in a breath as he circled her, eyes glittering with savage hunger. She could almost believe he *was* the wolf. Her knees trembled as he continued.

"'What big teeth you have,' the girl said next. To which the wolf answered, 'the better to *eat* you with.'" Vincent snarled and seized her shoulders.

Heat flared low in her body at his touch. Lydia shivered as she looked up at him. A trick of the moonlight made his teeth appear sharp and deadly. A gasp tore from her throat as he lunged forward. For a moment it seemed he was going to bite her.

She *wanted* him to.

Instead, his lips caressed her neck as he whispered, "Then the wolf swallowed her whole."

Liquid tremors wracked her form. She reached up to cling to his shoulders, to beg for more. Vincent stepped back, leaving her to grasp at the air.

Shielding her embarrassment at her reaction, she managed a small giggle. He'd only been telling a story, after all. "In the version my mother told me, the girl got away."

"Yes, that would be best." His voice sounded rough. "She *should* get away." He fetched her case and easel, avoiding her gaze. "We ought to head back now."

Lydia took her canvas and followed his long strides down the hill. A strange ache pulsed between her thighs with every step. What was it about Lord Deveril that made her feel this way? In New Orleans, she'd danced with countless beaux, yet none had elicited such a hypnotic response. None made her want to scream in longing for something she only half understood.

Vincent remained silent on the walk back to the castle. Once her painting materials were deposited in Aubert's arms, he stalked off without looking at her.

Miss Hobson marched into the foyer. "Thank goodness you've returned. The dressmakers are waiting in the solar."

Lydia blinked, watching Vincent's retreating form. "I'm sorry I had forgotten. I should change."

"Don't bother. You'll only need to undress for the measurement, so just wash your hands and don your gloves. Let's not keep them waiting." Despite the stern look in her eyes, the excitement in her voice was distinct. "They have fabrics and fashion plates that are absolutely divine."

Lydia frowned. Had she done something to upset her guardian? Stomach churning with worry, she rushed up to her chamber and cleaned her hands in the basin. With less haste, she made her way down to the solar. She didn't want to look at fabric. She wanted to play chess and converse with Vincent. She wanted to hear him laugh and see him smile.

He was speaking with the dressmakers when she entered the solar. They gazed up at Vincent as if he were a god descended from Olympus. Lydia completely understood.

"Have you been offered refreshment?" he asked them politely.

The elder, a young woman with large gray eyes, replied in a far too intimate tone, "We declined, for we had sustenance before we arrived."

He smiled at the seamstress and her equally lovely companion. Lydia had an unreasonable urge to claw their eyes out. Ethereal and delicate, they epitomized perfect English femininity.

Vincent's compelling gaze turned to Lydia, banishing her hostility. "Miss Price, I'm pleased to introduce Miss Sally and Miss Maria…Sidwell. Their skills with a needle are unparalleled."

Lydia managed a polite smile and a demure, murmured platitude as her senses reeled with the realization that he apparently was well acquainted with these women.

"Miss Price." The Sidwell sisters curtsied in flawless unison, speaking with one voice.

Vincent surveyed them with a strange smile. "You have my eternal gratitude for your assistance in outfitting my ward for the Season."

She studied them more closely as they looked at him. There was respect in their eyes...and no sign of heat or longing. The tightness in her chest eased.

"And you have ours," the younger, Maria, replied, glancing at Lydia with such intense curiosity that she shivered. "It will be an honor to adorn such a rare and brilliant flower."

"That she is, and I am certain you will do her justice. I shall leave you to it." There was a strange edge of command to his voice.

Her heart fluttered at his agreement that she was "rare and brilliant." Most important, Vincent didn't look at them the way he'd looked at her earlier, as if he wanted to devour her. Whatever his relationship with the seamstresses was, it was not the sort of intimacy that would give Lydia unreasonable ire. She warmed to the pair.

As soon as her guardian left, the room seemed to dim. Maria pointed to a stool by the fire. "If you would stand on that, miss, we can remove your gown and take your measurements."

Frowning, she obeyed. The younger sister appeared to wield more authority, yet the girl looked to be Lydia's age or even younger. Sally unbuttoned her black wool gown with astoundingly gentle rapidity. As she wrapped the measuring tape around Lydia's waist, Maria opened a case laden with rolls of fabric.

The bright colors were overwhelming to Lydia after months of wearing only black. Sally exclaimed

about Lydia's figure and coloring, selecting and rejecting bolts of cloth with a practiced eye as Maria showed
her illustrations of the latest fashions. Their choices
were bold, brilliant, and divine. She hadn't realized
how weary of mourning she'd grown.

"You will be *the* Original of this Season," Maria
declared, holding up a panel of violet silk embroidered
with silver leaves. Lydia wondered if Vincent would
like her in that color.

The novelty soon wore off as she was poked and
prodded within an inch of her life. Fittings in England
were much more aggressive and tedious than they had
been in America. The draftiness of the castle added to
Lydia's discomfort. By the time the session was over,
she was covered in goose bumps, despite the blazing
fire in the hearth.

Sally cooed sympathetically as she helped her back
into her gown with deft speed. Maria packed away the
fabric samples and fashion plates with equal dexterity.
Lydia marveled at the how quickly their hands moved.

Vincent returned to escort the dressmakers to the carriage. "I have a prior engagement, so I will not be joining you for supper," he said tersely before he departed.

"They seem competent and skilled enough," Miss
Hobson said to Lydia once they were alone. "The
seams of their gowns were invisible. I swear I've seen
those girls before. Perhaps they worked in Madame
Dumont's dress shop."

Supper was a dull, bleak affair without Vincent's
presence. Miss Hobson spoke in a steady stream about
the preparations for the Season. Lydia could respond
only with halfhearted smiles and comments.

An ache grew in her heart when he didn't return later. Lydia tried to absorb herself in sketching, yet it did little to improve her mood. Eventually, she gave up and went to bed.

What did I do wrong? She sighed, watching the shadows dance on the stone ceiling of her chamber. *Did I wound him when I spoke of the Devil Earl rumors?* She recalled his anger when he'd thought Emma had been gossiping. *That must be it. With all of the villagers afraid of him, he must be very lonely. I will make amends tomorrow.*

To her dismay, the next evening Vincent didn't join her on the west hill, though she stayed and painted until it was too dark to see. Miss Hobson sent a footman to collect her, and Lydia's heart sank when the earl yet again did not attend supper.

Her despair deepened as he avoided her for the remainder of the week. She attempted to raise her spirits by making a game of evading Miss Hobson and sneaking out through the secret passage to wander the castle grounds and practice target shooting, but it gave her little cheer, because Vincent wasn't with her.

Eight

"I BEG YOUR PARDON IF I AM TOO FORWARD, MISS Price. You look to be plagued by blue devils," Maria said as she adjusted the hem of Lydia's new gown.

Lydia glanced at the doorway for any sign of Miss Hobson before the words came pouring forth. "I think I've displeased Lord Deveril." Immediately she clamped her mouth shut, humiliated to share her personal pain with a virtual stranger. However, Vincent's absence had turned her into a veritable cauldron of worry.

Maria paused at her work and gave Sally a long look. Lydia's embarrassment deepened.

After a moment, Sally rolled her thimble between her elegant fingers and shook her head. "I doubt very much that you displeased him. Lord Deveril is a very, ah, complicated man who shoulders much more responsibility than most."

"Have you known him long?" Lydia burned with curiosity.

Maria smiled, gray-green eyes brimming with tender nostalgia. "We've been acquainted for a time. Lord Deveril rescued us both from dreadful circumstances."

Lydia was about to inquire further, then Sally spoke up abruptly. "Is this your sketchbook? May I look?"

"Yes." She realized that the dressmakers did not want to elaborate.

Sally opened the leather-bound book and gazed at Lydia's drawings. "These are very good. Maria, come see."

Despite her pleasure at the compliment, Lydia's cheeks burned. In between drawings of Castle Deveril and the Cornish landscape were many sketches of Vincent. Just as she expected, when they flipped through the pages, Maria gave her a knowing look.

"You are a very talented artist, Miss Price. You've captured Lord Deveril perfectly. Do you paint as well?"

Blushing, Lydia nodded. Surely they knew she was hopelessly infatuated with her guardian.

"Oh, you must show us your work!" Sally exclaimed.

In the face of such genuine enthusiasm, Lydia could hardly refuse. It might not be proper to invite hired help into her bedchamber; however, Miss Hobson was napping and thus was not present to object.

Both Sidwell sisters gasped the moment they beheld the paintings Aubert had hung in her chamber. Maria seemed most fascinated with the ones depicting the Louisiana Bayou, while Sally studied Lydia's paintings of sprawling plantation houses and the French Quarter. Lydia was beginning to tell them about New Orleans when both sisters spotted the portrait of her father.

"You have a *Thomas Lawrence*!" Maria breathed. Myriad strange expressions flitted across her angelic face.

Lydia nodded. "My father sat for him before he left

England with my mother. I wish more than anything to be able to paint with such skill. I hope to meet Sir Lawrence when I go to London."

Maria glanced at her sister before nodding. "Oh, you certainly *must* endeavor to make his acquaintance. Have you asked Lord Deveril if he will take you to the Royal Academy?"

If he will speak to me again. "I intend to ask him soon. Perhaps Sir Lawrence would be willing to provide advice on perfecting my own portraits." Then she could do Vincent's striking masculine beauty justice.

"He may be willing to tutor such a talented artist. But if he does, you must be on guard," Sally replied with sudden severity. "He is a notorious flatterer and despoiler of innocents."

Such candid and scandalous gossip tickled Lydia's fancy. She hadn't heard anything like it since she was in America…aside from the time she'd eavesdropped on Emma and her sister.

Unfortunately, Miss Hobson bustled into the room, eyeing all three of them with patent disapproval for gossiping instead of working. With hastily mumbled excuses, all returned to the solar with the chaperone marching in the vanguard.

The final adjustments to Lydia's two new gowns were made with a modicum of reserved propriety, though once in a while either Sally or Maria would meet Lydia's gaze, and they'd have to muffle their giggles in their handkerchiefs. Too soon, Vincent's coachman arrived to take the sisters home.

"That is as queer a pair as I've ever seen," Miss Hobson commented after they departed. "Though one cannot deny their extraordinary skill." She lifted the newest gown, a pale blue morning dress with embroidered forget-me-nots on the hem and bodice. "I can't believe they created such a dress in mere days. I know many in the *ton* who would pay a small fortune for such haste. However, it is such an inconvenience for them to come here in the evening and delay our supper."

"I don't mind." Lydia quickly defended them. "I cannot wait to wear these dresses."

The chaperone favored her with a rare smile. "You'll be permitted to wear the mauve dinner gown soon, when you enter half mourning."

"Thank God. Although I rather like black, it *has* become monotonous. Why does mourning have to be so much longer in England?"

"Because we are more civilized," Miss Hobson replied sternly, though there was a gleam of humor in her eyes. "Come now, it is time to change for supper."

Lydia nibbled her lip and asked tentatively, "Will Lord Deveril be joining us?"

"I do not think so." There was a glimmer of pity, or possibly anger in her tone. Perhaps she thought Vincent was being rude.

As she took her seat at the massive dining-room table, Lydia eyed Vincent's empty place. He *was* being rude. He was the lord of the castle and her guardian. He *should* be here. His absence was like a sore, relentlessly gnawing at her senses. The discomfort quelled her appetite, and as soon as was polite, Lydia excused herself, pleading a headache.

Miss Hobson gave her a sharp look, then her

countenance softened and she rang for Emma to help Lydia prepare for bed.

Once her gown and stays were removed and Emma departed, Lydia collapsed into her bed, utterly exhausted and aching with loneliness.

Though Deveril had been absent in her waking hours, he joined Lydia in her dreams every night—vivid, intoxicating, and disturbing dreams in which he danced with her in the moonlight. Slowly, he would bend to kiss her. Lydia would gasp in desire and reach to pull him close. Then he would change into a wolf and chase her through the forest. Her heart would pound in exhilaration, for she wanted him to catch her. Just as his arms closed around her, she would awaken, shudders wracking her body.

"This will not do, my lord." Miss Hobson fixed Vincent with a formidable stare. "As Miss Price's guardian, you need to see to her well-being. She was so lonely last night that she took to bed right after supper."

Vincent sighed. He should have locked the door to his study. "As I have told you time and again, Miss Hobson, I am very busy."

"If you are to see Lydia wed, she needs to learn the ways of courtship," she persisted.

He raised a brow. "Is that not why I hired you?"

"She needs to practice with a true gentleman." She favored him with a stern frown. "As she is in mourning, she cannot attend country parties to learn these things along with other debutantes."

Vincent bit back a curse. The woman's logic was

sound. Yet he could not be around Lydia any longer. For God's sake, he'd once more nearly bitten her! Self-revulsion knotted his gut. It was his responsibility to protect Lydia. How could he protect her from himself? Avoidance was the only solution.

And it wasn't as if he were not truly busy. He'd been meeting with his small population of subordinate vampires, explaining the situation to them as best as he could, and appointing his second in command to stand guard over Cornwall while he was in London.

"Surely there must be some other way. Perhaps I can hire someone." Pointedly, he flipped through the pages of his account ledger, all of which were up-to-date. "I have some columns that have yet to add up, so—"

"Lady Morley will be anticipating this," Miss Hobson interrupted in a deceptively casual tone. "She likely believes Miss Price will be presented to the King with a lack of polish. She wouldn't expect one of the 'Mad Deverils' to be capable of preparing a young lady for Society." Her gaze narrowed. "If you want to be successful in this endeavor, you must help Lydia. You are the only one who is able. Or do you want her to be the laughingstock of the *ton*?"

Vincent slammed the ledger shut. "Damn it!" Yet again, she was right. He supposed he should be grateful for the chaperone's advice. The Cornish sea would turn to swamp before he'd allow Lady Morley to triumph. A bitter smile curled his lips. "Check and mate, Miss Hobson."

The woman acknowledged her victory with a regal nod. "I rather thought so."

When Vincent arrived in the drawing room, Lydia's eyes lit with such joy he flushed with shame. Miss Hobson's words taunted him. *She was so lonely last night that she took to bed right after supper.*

"Good evening, Miss Price." He bowed.

Lydia said nothing to this and merely curtsied before sitting back down on the chintz sofa. The dark circles under her eyes compounded his guilt.

"That is a lovely gown," he ventured, feeling like a cad.

"Thank you, my lord," she murmured, looking down at her feet.

Was she upset by his avoiding her this past week? Or had he frightened her during that night on the west hill?

Sitting next to her on the sofa, he lowered his voice. "What is the matter, Lydia?"

She took a deep breath and met his gaze. "My lord, did I do anything to displease you? Is that why you have not spoken to me for so long?"

The hurt in her voice nearly undid him, along with the look in her eyes. Vincent was struck by such yearning it was like a blow to the chest. If only he could take what she offered.

"You have done nothing wrong." *I have*, he added silently. *Every time I touch you, it is wrong.* When she did not appear convinced, he gentled his tone. "I have been up to my ears in estate matters."

Her cheeks pinkened. "Oh, I am sorry. I hadn't realized…" She shrugged. "Of course you have work to do and cannot spend every evening with me, conversing and playing games."

"Perhaps we may play a game or two after supper tonight." He had missed her company as well. The nights without her laughter and inquisitive discourse had been cold and empty.

"My lord," Aubert announced from the doorway in a rattled tone. "The Duke of Burnrath is here."

Vincent stiffened. The Lord Vampire of London was here to discuss the situation with Lydia…and he saw fit to see to it in person. This could not bode well.

With monumental effort, he maintained his composure. "Miss Hobson, see that Miss Price is dressed for supper."

Ignoring everyone's wide gazes, he strode out of the room, fighting back a growl as he heard Miss Hobson whisper to Lydia, "It is a shame His Grace is married. He would have been a prime catch."

The duke awaited him in the entrance hall, tapping his gloves on his thigh.

"Ian." Vincent pointedly greeted the duke by his given name. Instinct commanded him to avoid humility, though he bowed low in respect for the other vampire's rank.

"Vincent." Ian returned the bow, silver eyes glinting without hostility. His long black hair had escaped its tie to fall in his face.

The duke must have flown here. Vincent felt a twinge of envy for that particular power of Ian's. He tamped it down and concentrated on the matter at hand. "I see you have not yet turned over the reins to your second and departed for Paris."

Ian nodded. "For your sake it's a bloody good thing I have not. Rafe would not have taken kindly to your

news"—his brows drew together in annoyance—
"which is precisely the cause for my delay."

"It appears I owe you my eternal gratitude."
Vincent couldn't hold back his relief. Perhaps His
Grace would be willing to help. "Would you care to
join me for a glass of brandy in my study?"

Ian inclined his head. "Quite so."

"Shall I set another place at the table, my lord?"
Aubert asked as he fetched the candelabrum.

Vincent looked to the duke, who nodded in assent.
"Yes." If Ian was staying that long, it was likely they
would hunt together as well.

"Very good, my lord." Aubert escorted them to the
study and lit the fireplace.

"Have you gone mad?" Ian demanded the moment
they were alone.

Vincent ignored the question and poured them
each a glass of brandy. "Are you refusing my request?"

Ian took a sip of his drink and ran his fingers
through his hair. "No, though I am hoping I can help
find a solution to this problem so you might avoid
coming to London completely. I have mingled with
Society for centuries now. Have you any idea how
difficult it has been?"

Vincent nodded. "I can imagine. Believe me, I
would not do this if I didn't believe it was completely
necessary." He explained matters in greater detail,
emphasizing the utter hatefulness of Lydia's grandmother. "Lady Morley intended to have Miss Price
forcibly committed to an asylum had I refused to
honor the alliance."

Ian's brows rose. "By God, I see now why you agreed."

He shook his head. "A London Season appears to be the best option after all. It would be far worse for her to remain too long under your roof, lest she discover what you are." His expression hardened. "I am, however, reluctant to allow the Siddons sisters to return to London."

"I need them to outfit Lydia. No mortal seamstress could carry off such a task in this short a time," Vincent argued. "Besides, their mental faculties have much improved, and they promised to stay out of sight and not make trouble."

Ian nodded. "Fine, if you believe they are necessary in getting your charge married off quickly. Though be sure to keep a close watch on them."

Vincent tried to ignore the ache in his heart at the thought of losing Lydia. It was for the best. She'd already come dangerously close to learning his secret. "Will the duchess agree to sponsor her?"

The Lord Vampire sighed and drank more brandy. "That, old friend, is another reason why I am here. My wife is…well, she's reluctant to take on such an endeavor."

"Why?" Vincent frowned. "Is it due to the scandal of Miss Price's parentage?"

"No, nothing of the sort." Ian raised his gaze to the heavens. "Angelica frowns upon Society's way of arranging marriages. She says she wants 'no part in auctioning innocent flesh to the highest bidder.'"

Vincent gaped. "This, from a duchess who secured that very title by wedding you?"

Ian laughed, silver eyes twinkling with mirth. "Ah, if you knew how hard she fought to avoid such a terrible fate."

The duke's courtship had not been completely amicable? He frowned in confusion. "She seemed cheerfully resigned the night of your wedding."

"Yes, by then I'd persuaded her I wasn't a fate worse than death," Ian replied, not offended. "And, I am certain Angelica will soften on the matter once she is assured Miss Price is receptive to the task of husband hunting."

Was Lydia receptive? Vincent wondered. He had not broached the subject of suitors with her. Surely Miss Hobson had. "I believe she is…why wouldn't she be?" he finally replied.

"Who can fathom the workings of the female mind?" Ian shook his head. "All that aside, please let me know if I can help you in any way."

Nine

"YOUR GRACE." LYDIA SANK INTO A DEEP CURTSY, grateful for Miss Hobson's instructions.

This was the first duke she'd ever met, and from what she knew of English nobility, they were a matter of great consequence.

"Miss Price, it is a pleasure to make your acquaintance." Burnrath raised her hand to his lips. Without his lofty title, he would still be an imposing man, with his well-muscled frame, gleaming raven hair, and intense silver eyes.

"The pleasure is mine," she responded, taking her seat.

Throughout the meal, the duke kept a steady flow of that same dull, polite conversation in which she had been trained. Yet somehow he possessed enough charisma to make the weather and local goings-on seem interesting.

Despite Burnrath's charm, Lydia could not help but feel a twinge of hostility at his presence. Just when Vincent ceased neglecting her, the duke had to intrude on her opportunity to renew her coziness with her guardian.

With His Grace here, there would be no games of chess, and certainly no chances to speak freely. She suppressed a defeated sigh. What was the purpose of the duke's arrival anyway? Vincent had greeted him as an old friend, and yet he appeared to be wary of the man. Perhaps they were partners in an illegal venture?

"...do you think, Miss Price?" Vincent was saying.

Lydia inclined her head in apology. "I beg your pardon, my lord. I was woolgathering."

Vincent gave her a forgiving smile. "I said, His Grace has offered to allow us to use his private box at the opera when we go to London."

"Oh, that would be lovely." It had been years since she'd been to the opera.

As the next course was served, Lydia could not help noticing that the duke ate as little as Vincent. Perhaps a meager appetite was an affectation of the upper classes. Lydia prayed such was not the case, for she would starve to death.

"What brings you to Cornwall, Your Grace?" Miss Hobson asked.

Burnrath gave Vincent an enigmatic look before answering. "Lord Deveril has requested that my wife sponsor Miss Price's debut in Society."

The chaperone's eyes widened, and she turned to Lydia with a smile. "This is momentous news! With such connections, the offers should pile in."

"Offers?" Lydia asked, though she was afraid she knew what Miss Hobson meant.

"Of marriage," Vincent said curtly, as if angry with her confusion.

"Marriage," she repeated through numb lips. The

purpose of the trip to London and all the training in preparation became clear. Of course it was to be more than a diverting vacation. Her stomach pitched.

The duke nodded, giving her a quizzical look, as if she were an interesting species of insect. It was no wonder, for she was behaving in an incredibly foolish manner. She'd known she'd eventually be encouraged to find a husband, but the suddenness struck her like a hammer on an anvil. She didn't want to marry a stranger in London. She wanted to stay with Vincent.

The room was suddenly too hot, and the walls seemed to be closing in around her. She had to get away, to get fresh air, before she screamed.

"Please, excuse me," Lydia said before fleeing.

⤔

"Well," Ian drawled, leaning back in his chair. "That went well."

Vincent ignored him and turned to Miss Hobson with an icy glare. "You did inform Lydia that she is to wed, did you not?"

The woman's chin lifted in a vain attempt to hide her anxiety. "I'd assumed she understood her responsibility as a young lady of noble birth." Her voice quavered defensively. "She'd spoken of having a Season in New Orleans. How was I to know things may have been different there?"

Vincent cursed as the matter became clear. "Because her father failed to perform his responsibility to Society when he married for love... Bloody hell, *I* should have known!"

"Vincent." The duke's voice was implacable.

"My wife will not sponsor the young woman if she is not willing."

Miss Hobson sighed. "Surely she could not expect something so fanciful as love."

Vincent ignored the chaperone and faced Ian. "I am certain we can persuade Miss Price to see reason. She has been receptive to all other aspects of taking her place in Society."

Ian swirled the brandy in the glass before giving a slight nod. "No doubt her grief remains for the loss of her parents."

Miss Hobson nodded. "A reasonable assumption, Your Grace. I'm certain she'll collect herself after a while and be down soon."

Ten minutes later, a gunshot exploded in the castle bowels.

Miss Hobson froze, putting a hand to her throat. The duke's eyes echoed the terror in Vincent's soul. "Dear God, do you think she—"

Vincent didn't hear the rest of the dreaded question, refused to hear it. In a burst of preternatural speed, he dashed from the room and up the stairs to the entrance to the secret passage, tracing the sound and the Mark between them.

"Lydia!" he roared as his heart threatened to pound itself out of his chest.

The moment he entered the tunnel, the scent of sulfur, gardenias, and salt consumed his senses...but there was no blood.

"Lydia?" His voice cracked with unadulterated hope.

"I'm all right, my lord." Her voice echoed from far away, near the end of the passage.

Vincent released the enormous breath he'd been holding and nearly flew to her side. She sat on the steps, halfway down to the rear door. The smell of black powder and sulfur permeated the confines to the point of near suffocation.

Her large eyes blinked at him, swimming in unshed tears. The gun lay in her lap, quivering in her trembling hands. He took it from her, hissing as the hot barrel burned his palm.

"I could have told you it was still hot," she muttered.

Vincent set the pistol out of reach, keeping an eye on her eerie calm. "What happened?"

Even in the darkness, he could see her cheeks color in embarrassment. "I saw a spider. I know it was foolish to take a shot at the damned thing, but it frightened me. I *hate* being afraid."

"A spider," he echoed like a half-wit. "You tried to shoot a spider." Relief replaced his terror. "I thought you—"

Mirthless laughter broke off his tirade. "You thought I tried to do myself in?" She wiped a tear from her cheek. "Do you truly think I would take such a drastic measure after hearing a bit of unpleasant news? And if I did, that I would utilize such a messy, crude method? In such a case I would likely use poison…or leap from one of those high cliffs into the sea…"

"Enough!" Vincent cut her off.

"I am sorry I caused you undue alarm, my lord." Her voice remained unnaturally brittle. "I merely wanted a few minutes of solitude, a peaceful nighttime walk. Y-you may return to your guest."

The smell of salt grew stronger as a tear spilled

down her cheek. Vincent's heart ached as the Mark between them pulsed in agony.

"I will not leave until you tell me what has upset you so." He sat beside her on the dusty stone steps.

"I have been such a fool," she choked out. "Papa would have allowed me to marry for love, and now he's gone." Her body shook with pent-up despair. "I know the rules are different now, yet I was so upset by the loss of my parents…"

Vincent placed a hand on her shoulder. Lydia took a deep, resigned breath and pressed on. "Then I came to this cold new land to reside in the care of strangers. My only remaining family didn't want me." Her chin tilted up, and she favored him with a watery smile that quickly shattered with her next words. "And now I realize I will go from one stranger t-to another."

The declaration undid her, and she broke off with a muffled cry. Vincent pulled Lydia into his arms as she cried. Each gasp pierced his heart, while her tears burned through the front of his shirt.

"Hush now. Do not cry." When the empty words had no effect, instinct took over. Vincent stroked her hair and her back in slow, soothing motions. He bent to kiss her forehead, but once his lips touched her delicate flesh, he could not stop there. His lips brushed her temples, her eyelids, her cheeks. Salt and sweetness drowned his senses, stirring his blood thirst. Recoiling at the predatory response, Vincent lifted his head, though he could not relinquish her embrace.

"Surely we are strangers no longer." The words fell dry and as useless as ashes.

Despite the inane statement, Lydia clung to him

tighter. "That is the very thing that makes this predicament more difficult. I've only just come to know you, you see. And I…" She shook her head. "I am such a fool."

His chest tightened as the impact of her words struck him. *No, Lydia. It is I who am the fool.* The bitter truth lodged in his throat. He'd thought it would be so easy to take her into his home, polish her up, and foist her off into another's hands. He'd thought of her only as a burden, a debt to a long-dead friend, and a means to spite her loathsome grandmother. Now, as he'd come to know Lydia, he'd only regretted his attachment to her, never considering that she'd form one to him. He'd thought only of himself.

"I will not be going anywhere." Vincent regretted the words the second he uttered them. Eventually he would have to depart from her life. The sooner he did so, the better it would be for them both. He lightened his tone and continued to stroke her silken hair. "I am certain you will meet a fine man, one who will shower you with jewels and adoration."

She snorted. "I don't care about jewels *or* adoration. I only want a friend."

Possessing a will of its own, his fool mouth responded, "I'll always remain your friend."

She met his gaze, her lashes spiky with moisture. "Do you promise?"

Unable to bear her tears, Vincent lied. "I promise." Eager to remove himself from his deceit, he brought the subject back to her impending marriage. "And I will not see you married to just anyone. It must be a good man, who will treat you with kindness and respect."

Lydia rested her head on his chest. "Will he love me?"

"Who could not love you?" Before they could venture further into dangerous territory, Vincent reluctantly disengaged from Lydia's embrace. Forcing a light tone, he said, "Come, we must assure the others you are all right. Miss Hobson was quite undone when she heard the gunshot."

❧

Lydia cursed herself as she met her chaperone's panicked gaze. *I've been such a ninny.* "I apologize for causing you undue concern, Miss Hobson. I merely wanted some air, and when I went to fetch my cloak, I…tripped over my gun."

"Are you feeling feverish?" Miss Hobson asked, worried.

"Not at all." Lydia willed herself not to tremble at the duke's intent stare. It was as if he knew what had transpired in the passageway, knew that Vincent had held her and kissed away her tears.

Her cheeks flushed at the memory. She turned away to pick up her glass of wine, draining the rest of it in one swallow. To hell with them if they thought her uncouth. She'd already discharged a firearm indoors, displayed hysterics before her guardian, balked at her womanly duties, and engaged in an improper embrace with a man…that man being none other than her guardian. A little wine could only improve the evening.

As she met Vincent's stormy gaze with her own, her mind raged with unsatisfied longing. *I must not let this man affect me so. I must save these feelings for my future husband.*

Yet, when the men departed for an evening walk, Lydia could not stop the cold ache of loneliness from piercing her heart any more than she could stop reliving the feel of Vincent's embrace...and his lips caressing her flesh.

❧

Vincent took a deep breath of the night air and regarded Ian as they walked toward the village. "Thank you for your keeping Miss Hobson occupied while I saw to Lydia."

"She gave us all a fright. I am relieved no harm came of it. By the by, I could not help noticing that you are covered in her scent," Ian noted drily. His eyes glittered molten silver in the moonlight.

"She needed comfort." Vincent resisted the urge to look away.

The duke raised a skeptical brow. "You must have been very thorough. You're not feeding from her, are you?"

Vincent stiffened and nearly tripped over a rock. "Good God, no!" *Though I almost stole a taste.*

Ian's eyes narrowed. "You want to."

Oh, yes. The beast within concurred. Self-disgust rose up at his desire. "My control is stronger than that." Forcing a level tone, he tried to change the subject. "As the moon is all wrong for smuggling, we shall have to seek our meal at an inn. The Carp's Head is usually full of sodden prey at this hour."

Ian ignored the bait. "You cannot become too attached to Miss Price...unless you intend to make her one of us."

"No!" Vincent roared, halting his rapid steps. "She is too full of life. It would be a crime to turn her into a monster."

"I had thought the same about my wife," Ian countered lightly. "I was wrong. Angelica has taken to this existence as if she were born for it."

"*No.*" Vincent remained adamant.

"Then we must see her wed as soon as possible." Ian's brow creased in thought. "There is the matter of my wife to contend with. However, I am encouraged to believe Angelica will like Miss Price, as she tends to admire unconventional sorts. Will Miss Price take well to Her Grace? I daresay that would help the situation."

"How am I to know?" Vincent said as the meager lamplights from the village came into view. "I've met your wife only twice."

Ian shrugged. "Well, tell me more about the young lady and her interests. Perhaps I may find something the two have in common."

Vincent sighed. "I've never encountered a mortal with so many interests as Lydia. It would take hours to catalog her pursuits. She paints, shoots, fishes, plays chess, and has a penchant for horrid gothic novels, to name a few."

Ian chuckled. "Gothic novels, you say? Well, that certainly helps. I believe Miss Price will be eager to meet my duchess."

"Why do you say so?" Vincent eyed two drunkards stumbling from the Carp's Head.

The duke smiled. "Have you heard of the author Allan Winthrop?"

Ten

LYDIA BREATHED A SILENT PRAYER OF THANKS THAT, after her lessons, Miss Hobson permitted her to retire to the library. Vincent and the duke had not yet come down for supper.

"It appears his lordship has left you a gift," Miss Hobson commented as she settled near the fire with her embroidery.

A delighted gasp escaped Lydia's throat. On her favorite settee lay a novel. "*The Haunting of Rathton Manor* by Allan Winthrop" was embossed on the cover in silver script.

Vincent had given her a novel to cheer her and perhaps apologize for neglecting her. Lydia hugged the book to her breast in delight before settling down to read.

The story was so chilling and engrossing it seemed she was halfway through in minutes. Dusk had fallen in the blink of an eye.

Lydia looked up from the novel as she heard footsteps approaching. "My lord, thank you for the book. It is so delightfully ghastly, it is giving me the shivers!

Do you—" The words died as the duke's imposing form filled the doorway.

"Miss Price." He bowed courteously.

"Your Grace!" She leaped to her feet and sank into a deep curtsy, darting a nervous glance at Miss Hobson. "I apologize. I had thought you were Lord Deveril. He left me a book, you see."

The duke chuckled. "No, it was I who left it for you. Vincent told me you enjoy such tales. Do you like it?"

Her cheeks flushed at his kind gesture. "Oh, yes, very much, thank you."

"Very good." Burnrath smiled strangely. "I am well acquainted with the author."

"You know Allan Winthrop?" She tried to suppress her excitement.

"Yes, I know her very well."

Lydia frowned. "*Her?*"

The duke winked. "Mr. Winthrop is my wife, Angelica Ashton, Duchess of Burnrath."

Her jaw dropped. "Truly? I look forward to meeting her!"

"I am certain she will be delighted." He smiled and left them with another bow.

"Well," Miss Hobson said the moment the duke was out of earshot, "His Grace seems to approve of you. That is a very good sign for your future prospects." The clock chimed the seventh hour, and the chaperone smiled. "It is time to change for supper. You may wear the mauve silk tonight."

Lydia brightened. At last she was in half mourning, and the gowns the Sidwell sisters had delivered were divine. She couldn't wait for them to finish the rest of her wardrobe. Right now they were working on her court dress.

As if to celebrate the reintroduction of color to Lydia's life, the dining room was adorned with flowers. When Vincent rose from the table, she observed he wore new clothes as well. From his snowy neckcloth, down to his gleaming black boots, he radiated gentlemanly elegance.

Lydia smiled in appreciation. "My lord, you look very dashing." His eyes were such a stormy blue she felt she could drown in them.

The duke cleared his throat, and her cheeks heated. "And you do as well, Your Grace."

Burnrath looked down at his equally fine garb and sighed. "Perhaps I am due for a new wardrobe." His silver eyes gleamed with teasing laughter.

The meal was another dull affair with all proprieties observed. Miss Hobson's extreme scrutiny of Lydia's use of her utensils and how she held her napkin was vexing. Lydia knew it was because they were going to leave for London in a month. Her appetite fled as excitement for the unexplored warred with apprehension at the unknown.

Miss Hobson's instructions continued after supper. Lydia ground her teeth behind her fan, on the verge of pleading a headache. Then she heard Vincent utter a muffled curse when the duke corrected his manner of sitting.

My God, he has to endure nearly as much preparation as I! Her eyes widened at the realization. The earl had been a recluse before she'd arrived on his doorstep.

Of course he would be unaccustomed to Society. A twinge of guilt gnawed in her belly. If it were not for her, Vincent wouldn't have to suffer this discomfort.

When the duke suggested they practice their dancing, Lydia and Vincent shared a pained smile.

∽

By the time Vincent and Lydia perfected the quadrille, his ward was nearly panting in exhaustion. Her breasts heaved within the confines of her gown, and Vincent almost groaned in desire. With her flushed cheeks and parted lips, she resembled a woman finished with a more pleasurable activity.

"I find it overwarm in here. Would you care to walk in the gardens?" Vincent asked before Ian or Miss Hobson could subject them to further exertion.

"I would like that very much." Palpable relief filled Lydia's eyes.

"You must fetch your cloak and wear your walking boots," the chaperone admonished. "It is likely damp out."

Lydia met Vincent at the door, and he offered her his arm. The cool breeze was indeed a relief after hours of dancing. Appreciatively, he breathed in the scent of rain and newly bloomed roses. A lantern glowed from the parapet above. Vincent waved at Ian, concealing his annoyance. Lydia glanced at Miss Hobson's reserved figure and sighed. As if by mutual agreement, they walked to the edge of the garden, out of earshot.

"How are you getting on with the dressmakers?" he inquired carefully. He'd lurked in the shadows outside the castle during those sessions, senses tuned for the slightest tremor of danger.

Lydia gave him the first genuine smile he'd seen all evening. "Very well, my lord. Not only have they produced the most exquisite garments I've ever seen, they also told me about Thomas Lawrence, my favorite painter. I've been wanting to ask—may we visit the Royal Academy and meet him?"

Those clever minxes. Vincent bit back a chuckle. *They wish to make certain the painter and I cross paths. At least there is little harm in it.* "Perhaps."

"The flowers are lovely in the moonlight." Lydia's voice was oddly tremulous.

Vincent studied her face a moment. "I know that look. You are curious about something, and reluctant to ask me. Speak up, Lydia. You should know by now you have freedom with me."

She bit her lip, then said, "I realize you have been greatly inconvenienced by my presence here."

His eyes widened. Was she aware of his desire for her? "Whatever do you mean?"

She sighed. "I mean…everything. I've observed you enjoy your privacy, yet since I've arrived, your home has been inundated with people. Now you must prepare for the London Season alongside me, though I know you wouldn't go if I hadn't been placed in your care."

The sweetness of her words warmed his soul. He forced a teasing tone. "Are you apologizing for being a burden to me?"

Plucking a wild rose blossom from a nearby bush, she avoided his gaze. "Yes, and I also want to know why you did this thing. What made you agree to become my guardian, to open your home to me when my own family would not have me? Why did you sacrifice your peace for a stranger?" She yanked the petals from the flower, allowing them to drift to the ground. "Miss Hobson told me there is an alliance between our families, though she didn't speak further on it."

Vincent met her gaze. He hadn't spoken of his friendship with Joseph or its tragic ending to anyone. But Lydia was his old friend's kin, and as such, she deserved to hear the tale—at least some of it. "In 1651, I...er, my ancestor was stationed alongside yours, Joseph Price, third Earl of Morley, in the army of Charles II. During the battle of Worcester, Joseph saved my...ancestor's life. A vow of eternal friendship was made. While the King was in exile, the two earls aided each other in avoiding Cromwell's spies and concealing their royalist leanings."

Vincent shook his head. Those had been dangerous times, with imprisonment and possible execution only a hairbreadth away. "The alliance was to be cemented further with the betrothal of the Earl of Deveril to Joseph's sister. Alas, there was an accident."

Vincent closed his eyes, remembering being drunk in celebration of his betrothal and the return of King Charles. He'd foolishly indulged in his favorite hobby of climbing, and tumbled from the cliffs near his castle, his body shattered on the rocks below. A dark figure had appeared over him. He'd thought it was the angel of death. The being knelt down and whispered to him in Gaelic: "*I have killed many Englishmen. I atone for it by leaving you with eternal life.*" Twin daggers pierced his throat. Then all was blackness punctuated by moments of extreme pain and a savage, alien thirst.

Lydia interrupted his thoughts. "What sort of accident?"

"I do not know," Vincent lied. "Only that it left the earl horribly disfigured."

He'd awakened as the tide came in. His body was perfectly healed, and with obscene strength, he climbed up the cliff, aware of nothing except a burning thirst. The gamekeeper found him, shouting in alarm at his tattered clothes. Vincent tore the man's throat open and satisfied the hellish hunger. As the corpse dropped at his feet, he realized he'd become a monster.

"The betrothal was broken," Vincent said flatly. Seeing Mary again had been out of the question. "Though Joseph visited his friend's bedside every month the first year after the accident, and twice a year thereafter."

His throat tightened at Joseph's loyalty as guilt crippled him at the times he'd covered himself in bandages and pretended to be an invalid so Joseph wouldn't see what he'd become.

"How very sad," Lydia whispered achingly. "The alliance lasted all these years?"

Vincent nodded. "So it has, though I did not know until Lady Morley arrived, brandishing those ancient papers."

Her eyes widened in the realization that it had been a forgotten alliance. She managed a shaky smile. "So there is friendship between our families once more."

"Well, between you and me, at least." He chucked

her under the chin. "As for your grandmother, I do not believe I can ever abide that harpy."

"Thank you for that," Lydia said quietly. "When I learned she did not want me, I'd thought there was something wrong with me...perhaps I was cursed."

He kissed her brow, savoring the taste and feel of her silken skin. "You are blessed, Lydia, and I intend to see you remain so."

For the first time since he'd been Changed, Vincent did not regret lacking the courage to end his existence as a new purpose made itself clear. As they walked back to the castle, he made a silent vow to Joseph's spirit, wherever it was. "I *will* see her safe and happy, old friend."

Eleven

"THIS IS THE WORST TORTURE I'VE BEEN SUBJECTED TO in my life," Lydia groaned as Emma helped her regain her feet. "What diabolical person devised such a horrid custom?"

She scowled at her new court dress, displayed in the solar as incentive for learning how to walk in it. The Sidwell sisters had created a masterpiece of gleaming white satin overlaid with petticoats adorned with hundreds of seed pearls, and embroidered with gold rosettes and wreaths. Miss Hobson remained in awe over the sisters' perfection and their speed in sewing it.

Not daring to risk ruining the elaborate creation, Emma had fastened a tablecloth to the back of Lydia's gown. With that, Miss Hobson bade her to practice walking…backwards. One was not allowed to turn her back on the monarch, yet one's court dress was required to have a long train—which made obedience to such a rule damn near impossible.

Miss Hobson was completely unsympathetic. "In my day, I had to wear a gown with enormous hoops and stiff panniers, as well as a train that was twice as wide."

Lydia frowned at the mitigation of her plight. "Was your headdress this cumbersome?"

"No, those seem to have grown over the years."

In truth, Lydia liked the elaborate confection of pearls and white ostrich plumes. It reminded her of a voodoo priestess's crown, or perhaps the headdress of an Indian chief. Unfortunately, the damned thing persisted in falling off whenever she bowed.

"May we be finished for the afternoon?" she pleaded. "I will be mortified if Lord Deveril sees me wearing a tablecloth."

Miss Hobson looked as if she was about to argue, then she glanced out the window at the sun sinking behind the west hill. "The hour *is* late. Emma, bring the court gown upstairs so we may put it on Miss Price before the earl arrives. I assume he would like to see the picture she presents."

The gown was like a complex piece of machinery. Even with the aid of Emma and Miss Hobson, the ordeal of dressing Lydia took nearly an hour. Emma had barely arranged Lydia's hair when Aubert informed them that the earl was downstairs.

Assuming what she hoped was a stately air, Lydia carefully made her way down the stairs as Emma carried her train, and they both prayed she wouldn't fall. When she made it to the solar, Vincent's eyes widened. Her heart lodged in her throat. Did he find her beautiful? Then his features settled into what looked like boredom.

"No hoops?" he asked with a raised brow.

Lydia's heart sank. He was concerned with the dress, not her.

"The custom has been abandoned since the Regent was crowned," Miss Hobson told him.

"Ah." He nodded. "It will do, then."

As Emma and Miss Hobson helped her back upstairs to her chamber, Lydia bit the insides of her cheeks to keep from shrieking. After all the hard work it had taken to dress, all he could say was, "*No hoops?*" and "*It will do*"?

While Emma removed the elaborate gown, Miss Hobson attempted to soothe her. "Men are ignorant of the complexity of ladies' fashions. You cannot expect them to appreciate such delicate nuances."

When they joined him for supper, it seemed Vincent had an inkling of her trial.

"Have you mastered the art of walking backwards yet?" he asked as the soup was served.

Lydia opened her mouth to deliver a crushing set down. Then her pride stopped her from showing her hurt. She forced a light tone. "Not quite yet, my lord, and it is cruel of you to tease me about it."

He sighed and toyed with the food on his plate. "My apologies if I have wounded you. The gown is exquisite, fitting for a prize such as yourself. It is the sycophantic ritual it symbolizes that vexes me."

As Lydia met Vincent's gaze, it seemed they shared a deep kinship. She now understood why he avoided London. Both were outcasts, not meant for the pomp and ceremony of High Society. Why could he not see that? Why was he determined to place her in such a role? Why wouldn't he permit her to remain here… with him?

Lydia could not resist a bit of retaliation for his

callous dismissal of her efforts, or of his obliviousness to her feelings. After the meal concluded and they adjourned to the solar, she said, "I understand you are to help me practice proper conduct with my suitors."

"Well, I am rather busy…"

Before he could continue his protest, she warned, "Or in recompense for your earlier mockery, Emma could pin a tablecloth to your back, and you may demonstrate your skill in walking backwards with a train."

"You have me there, Miss Price." Vincent gave her a wink, acknowledging her victory just as he did when she managed a clever move in their chess games. He turned to Miss Hobson. "Who shall I be first? Lord Struttingcock or Viscount Mealymouth?"

Miss Hobson looked down her nose at him and refused to participate in the humor. "We shall start off simply. You may be an earl who wishes an introduction to Miss Price. I shall pretend to be you, her guardian."

Despite the chaperone's attempt to maintain a formal air of instruction with the playacting, it was all Lydia could do to hold in her laughter as she and Vincent competed with each other on who could fabricate the most ridiculous names for her imaginary suitors. For now it was as if they were playing another game.

"You must also know how to respond when a suitor behaves in an ungentlemanly manner. Now, Baron…er…Stuffedshirt, say something improper to Miss Price," Miss Hobson instructed.

Vincent lifted an imaginary quizzing glass and looked down insolently, as if perusing her bosom. "I say, Miss Price, do your garters match your gown?"

Lydia felt herself blush at his heated gaze and

intimate allusion to her undergarments. She nearly answered in the affirmative before Miss Hobson told her to rap his arm with her fan.

"Now turn away and never acknowledge him again." The chaperone had them act out various scenarios until the novelty had long since worn thin.

"Would you care to stroll through the garden, Miss Price?" Vincent asked with exaggerated formality.

Lydia nodded with relief. This farcical play was becoming tedious. She donned her cloak and took his arm. The night air was chilly yet tranquil, redolent with the scent of the newly bloomed spring.

"You look very lovely this evening." Vincent swept her with a glance that warmed her from her toes up. His hair fell about his shoulders, making him look deliciously rakish.

Slowly, his hand crept down to take hers. Shivers broke out on her flesh as his thumb caressed her wrist and the back of her hand. He had such long fingers, she mused.

"I read a poem today that reminded me of you." He gave her another sideways glance, as if confessing something naughty. "Would you like to hear it?"

Her knees quivered beneath her skirts. Perhaps he did feel something for her. *Perhaps he is now going to declare himself!* "Yes, I would."

"Your chaperone is watching us from the parapets. It would be better for me to recite it more privately." With gentle force, he guided her behind a tall hedge.

Lydia's belly fluttered as Deveril took both her hands. His hair gleamed like an angel's wing. Would he tell her he couldn't let her go, that they didn't have to go to London? That instead they could remain here...together?

"*She walks in beauty, like the night,*" he whispered.

> "*Of cloudless climes and starry skies;*
> *And all that's best of dark and bright*
> *Meet in her aspect and her eyes;*
> *Thus mellowed to that tender light*
> *Which heaven to gaudy day denies.*"

Vincent's eyes were like a turbulent sea in a moonlit storm. He gazed at her as though she was something precious. Lydia sighed as his long fingers removed a pin from her hair.

> "*One shade the more, one ray the less,*
> *Had half impaired the nameless grace*
> *Which waves in every raven tress,*"

Her breath caught as he twirled a lock of her hair.

> "*Or softly lightens o'er her face;*
> *Where thoughts serenely sweet express,*
> *How pure, how dear their dwelling-place.*"

His hand crept up to caress her cheek, his intent gaze never wavering.

> "*And on that cheek, and o'er that brow,*
> *So soft, so calm, yet eloquent,*
> *The smiles that win, the tints that glow,*"

His lips curved in a sensual smile as he concluded.

> *"But tell of days in goodness spent,*
> *A mind at peace with all below,*
> *A heart whose love is innocent!"*

For an eternity, they stared as if peering into each other's souls. His fingers slid past her cheek and threaded once more through her hair, sending the remaining pins scattering into the grass.

"Lydia," he whispered.

Then his lips were on hers, warm, silken, teasing. Her limbs melted. Intoxicating heat unfurled low in her body. Lydia reached up to pull him closer, to demand more.

Vincent pulled back before she could grasp him. He took a deep, shuddering breath. "And that is your most important lesson in courtship, Lydia. Never allow a man to get you off alone, especially if he desires to recite poetry, and *particularly* Lord Byron's verses."

A strangled gasp caught in her throat at his duplicity. It had all been part of the game! "You...you..."

He held up a hand. "Now slap me with your fan in retaliation for taking such liberties."

Reeling in outrage, she fumbled in the pockets of her cloak for the ineffectual weapon.

Vincent shrugged, undaunted at her ire. "That is why you should keep your fan at the ready."

Seizing the bundle of cloth-covered sticks, she smacked him soundly on the arm, much harder than Miss Hobson had instructed.

"You are lucky I did not have my gun," she hissed. *How could he?*

To her vexation, he chuckled. "No, a kiss such as that, indiscreet as it was, is hardly a dueling offense." His eyes narrowed, and he stalked closer. Lydia thought of the time he'd told her the story of the wolf. Vincent looked just as predatory as he had that night. "However, if a man kisses you like this…"

With lightning speed, he seized her, pulling her against his body as his lips came down on hers with brutal force. One hand ruthlessly gripped the nape of her neck, while the other grasped her bottom, urging her hips against his. Though it was still part of the game, Lydia was unable to prevent herself from responding. Molten desire flooded her body, flaring brightest within her core. His mouth ravaged hers, his tongue darted in, sliding across hers, coaxing it to tangle with his in a primal dance.

A low moan escaped her throat as she ground her body against him. His hardness pressed, insistent upon her most secret place, making her ache for something only he could give.

With a low growl, he broke away and thrust her from him. His breath came in harsh gasps. "If a man kisses you…like that," he said roughly, "then I shall see him dead."

Panting with need, Lydia met his savage gaze in challenge. "What if I want him to?"

Vincent moved forward. Her lips parted in anticipation. Then he stopped and sighed, running a hand through his hair. "You must save such things for the marriage bed, else you'll be ruined."

"But, Vincent, I want—" He stopped her before she could say, "*you*."

"This must not happen again." His voice was firm, containing an edge of a growl. "I will escort you back to the castle, and then I must go for my walk."

As they walked back, Lydia felt his arm vibrate with tension beneath her hand. Those kisses had affected him as deeply as they had her. She *knew* it! Why would he not admit the fact? Her thighs trembled with unfulfilled desire as her mind raced with the truth of her heart.

Not only did she want Vincent's kisses, she wanted his heart. She did not want or need to go to London to find the man she would love and marry. She'd already found him.

⤫

With a smile, Miss Hobson watched Lydia flee up the stairs. At first, as she'd observed Deveril's stiff stride and turbulent countenance, she'd thought the two had quarreled. Then one glance at Lydia's flushed cheeks, mussed hair, and swollen lips confirmed the earl had finally given in to temptation and stolen a kiss.

She looked back out the window. Her smile deepened at the sight of Deveril stalking off angrily into the night. Miss Hobson would have wagered a guinea that he was cursing himself for his lapse in propriety.

Ah, yes. Things were progressing along quite nicely.

Twelve

VINCENT WALKED AMONG THE VAMPIRES GATHERED within the stone circle. A full smuggler's moon gleamed on the tall gray rocks and moist emerald grass. When all seventy-six were accounted for, he motioned for silence.

"As you all know, I am leaving for London tomorrow. Emrys will be in charge in my absence, and Bronn will act as his second." Giving the younger and more unruly vampires a stern look, he added, "I will also be coming back frequently to check on you."

The blood drinkers under his care bowed deeply. However, Kenan and Daveth, two younglings of about a quarter century, exchanged glances smacking of mischief. Vincent made a mental note to tell Emrys to keep an eye on that pair. The Siddons sisters stood together under Bronn's subtle guard. Vincent was pleased to see that they'd lost much of their wariness. It seemed their time working with Lydia was helping them readjust to social interaction.

"Are there any concerns or grievances before we adjourn?"

A few vampires raised their hands, and Vincent spent the next half hour patiently settling disputes on hunting territories and giving advice on land purchases. When all was at peace, he adjourned the meeting, confident that Emrys and Bronn would take good care of his people.

As the vampires departed the circle to return to their homes, Sally Siddons stepped out from the shadows, her lower lip quivering with uncertainty. "Is all in readiness for our journey as well?"

"Yes, I will be bringing horses shortly after dusk to fetch you, so be sure to feed quickly. And the Lords of Exeter and Bath have kindly offered you and Maria hospitality for your day rest. You should arrive at the town house I leased for you within four nights."

Maria strode forward, visibly trembling in eagerness to set off. "How long shall we be in Town?"

"As long as it takes to see my ward wed, which shouldn't be too long, given her beauty and the magnificent way you've dressed her," he told her sincerely even as he prayed the pair wouldn't cause mischief once they arrived. "Again I must thank you for all your hard work."

"It was an honor as well as a pleasure," Maria said, walking up ahead of her sister. "Miss Price is a delightful young lady and a *fine* painter."

Vincent regarded her with narrowed eyes. "Ah yes, I am well aware of your scheme to throw her in the path of Sir Thomas Lawrence."

Sally shook her head vigorously. "It is not like that, my lord. We do not want him seducing her. We wanted to place him in *your* path so you may tell us how he fares, since we aren't allowed to see for ourselves."

"*And* so she may receive the guidance she desires for her portraits," Maria chimed in. "She is very talented for one of such youth and inexperience and—"

He held up a hand. "I know what your intentions are. And I am not overly worried about the painter toying with her heart. He has to be past fifty by now—"

"Fifty-three," they both interrupted.

"And balding and gout-ridden if your wishes have come true. At any rate, I would not permit her to be alone with the man for a second, and neither will her chaperone."

Maria nodded. "That woman is a dragon if I've ever seen the like."

"So will you take her to see him then?" Sally persisted.

He rubbed his temples. "Since she is so delighted at the prospect of meeting a master painter, I can hardly refuse. What if the man is rich, handsome as ever, and happy with a young, beautiful wife?"

They remained silent a moment before Maria said quietly, "We shall gnash our teeth and pity the wife. He doesn't deserve happiness."

Vincent sighed. That was the best he could expect. "Well, I had better return home and see to Lydia. Remember, if you need anything, do not hesitate to write or send Emrys."

"You care for her very much, don't you?" Sally's large eyes brimmed with sympathy.

"More than is good for me," he answered and left before they could pry further.

By the time he arrived home, it was past midnight,

and the castle was dark and silent. It took every bit of his restraint not to go to Lydia's chamber. Instead, he trudged up to his study and poured a glass of brandy. Tomorrow they would be off to London.

As if by mutual agreement, Vincent and Lydia had avoided all talk of London and suitors for their last days in Cornwall. Instead, they savored their time together, lingering for hours in the game room. Though a measure of their easy friendship remained, it was irrevocably changed after he kissed her.

Vincent could not bring himself to regret those stolen kisses. Lydia had tasted of decadent confections and felt like heaven in his arms. He would cherish the memory until his cursed existence was at last snuffed out.

And he could not suppress a rush of anticipation when Lydia slipped into his study long past the time the household had retired.

"Lydia, what are you doing up at this hour?" he demanded, trying not to notice how delectable her bare toes looked, peeking from beneath her dressing gown.

"I have a present for you, my lord," she said with such cheer he couldn't help smiling.

"A present?" he echoed like a slack-jawed idiot.

She nodded and took his hand. "Come, it is in the library."

As Vincent walked with her, his heart clenched with the bittersweet awareness that it had been centuries since he'd received a gift.

Lydia opened the door with a dramatic flourish, revealing a painting displayed within a circle of lanterns and candles.

"My God," Vincent breathed, stepping forward.

It was a sunrise. Brilliant in its array of colors, the dawn glowed on the branches of the trees, lit up the green grass, and was duplicated within a reflection on the surface of the lake. Unbidden, he reached forward as if he could feel the warmth of the dawn on his skin. How could she possibly know what this meant to him?

"Do you like it?" Lydia asked with aching humility.

"Very much," Vincent spoke past the tightness in his throat. "I feel I could dive into the water, it looks so real." Overcome with piercing emotion, he could not stop himself from pulling her into his arms any more than he could halt the tides.

"Thank you, Lydia." The words were unworthy of her gift, just as he was unworthy to enjoy the warmth of her embrace. "We shall bring it to London with the rest of your paintings."

"We're bringing my paintings?" Her voice was like velvet against his chest.

"Yes, I've had them crated up and loaded onto the baggage cart." He cursed his words the moment he spoke. Awareness of their imminent departure hung like mourning crepe.

"I cannot believe we are going tomorrow," Lydia whispered, peering up at him with wide, bright eyes. "Though I am anxious to see the famed city, part of me longs to stay here."

Every part of me wishes you could stay forever. Vincent held her tighter. "I will treasure your gift forever," he whispered.

Her proximity tempted him to madness. Those silken lips seemed to beckon him closer. Alas, she was not his and never could be.

"Vincent, *please*," she whispered, eyes half-closed and imploring.

One last time. Slowly, giving her ample time to pull away, he brushed his mouth across hers, featherlight, yet rife with longing. The smell of gardenias rose heavy in the air, along with the intoxicating scent of her arousal. Lydia made a small sound against his lips and pulled him closer. He hardened immediately.

It took every vestige of his will to break away before things went further. "You must return to your bed. You have a long journey tomorrow."

She looked up at him like a wounded doe and curtsied shakily. "Yes, my lord."

As she left, Vincent licked his lips, savoring her taste for the last time. "Never again," he whispered.

The words were like a death knell. *Never again.*

❧

Burnrath House, London

"Good God, man," Ian said as he admitted Vincent into his study. "What is so urgent that you had to fly here from Cornwall?"

Vincent gave him a dry stare. "As you well know, I do not fly, I merely…move fast. Where is your wife?"

"She is in her writing room. Do not disturb her." Ian poured him a glass of port. "She *will* bite. She instructed me to assure you that she received a reply in the affirmative from the Lord Chamberlain to her application. Miss Price's presentation to our sovereign will be on Thursday, the sixth, at ten o'clock in the evening, so thankfully we shall all be able to attend and lend our support."

Vincent could not suppress his sigh of relief. "So she has agreed to sponsor Lydia?"

Ian nodded. "Yes, though she remains reluctant."

"I am certain that will change when she meets Lydia." Vincent frowned, recalling another important detail. "What of securing a subscription to Almack's? Miss Hobson informed me such a thing is imperative for a debutante."

Ian studied his glass of port as if it were of paramount importance. "There is a bit of a problem with that matter. Angelica was banned from Almack's only last year. If it were not for our high status and income, her reputation would have been blackened beyond redemption." He laughed. "It was a goal she fervently pursued and nearly achieved, until I unwittingly thwarted her efforts."

"Why *did* you wed her?" Vincent asked without thinking.

Ian chuckled. "It is quite a long story. I originally married her to preserve my reputation. Now I know it is because she is the other half of my heart." He coughed in embarrassment and pointedly changed the subject. "I congratulate you on finding a town house so near to here. Do you think it will be ready in time for Miss Price's arrival?"

"It had better be," Vincent replied. "I've spent more coin than I have in five decades to secure the lease and hire extra servants. Aubert and Cook should arrive with the baggage cart in six days, Lydia and her maid and chaperone are due in seven."

Ian leaned back in his chair, regarding him with half-lidded eyes. "And meanwhile, you will be dashing back and forth across the English countryside to ensure your ward is not set upon by highwaymen during her journey."

Vincent nodded. "I vowed to protect her."

"You cannot protect her during the day," Ian warned. "Soon you must see her safe in the hands of one who can."

Thirteen

"TONIGHT?" LYDIA GROANED. THE EMBOSSED BLACK-and-silver invitation to dine at Burnrath House made her sore muscles protest. "I had greatly hoped to sleep for the next three days. Every part of my being aches so badly that I vow my soul was battered during that journey."

Miss Hobson sniffed. "Such melodrama is unbecoming, as close to the truth as it may be. However, you cannot decline an invitation from a duchess." She rubbed her back, as ill-affected from the trek as Lydia was. "We are not expected for several hours yet. Send a footman with a reply in the affirmative, and we may have a nap."

Lydia's shoulders relaxed at the welcome suggestion. Yet once she was tucked in her luxuriously soft bed, sleep remained elusive. London was an assault on the senses. Her ears rang from the cacophony of noise. Her eyes blurred from the bustling crowds of people, carriages, and stray dogs. And the stench…dear Lord, she did not know if she would ever recover from it. New Orleans had been a busy place as well. However, after months of tranquillity in Cornwall, the English capital was unbearable.

She sighed, knowing she could not lie to herself. The real source of her ill humor was that she missed Vincent. Because of his headaches, he'd been unable to ride with them in the carriage. Instead, he'd traveled ahead on horseback, arriving in time to ensure the town house was outfitted to be a perfect haven for her.

And a haven it was. Flowers and scented candles kept the reek of the city at bay. A walled garden provided a barrier from the noise. Her paintings adorned nearly every room in the house, the sunrise dominating the sitting room, accented by candles infused with lemon verbena. Servants waited to indulge her with the mere ring of a bell.

Vincent was like a guardian angel, transforming her from an unwanted orphan to a pampered princess. Yet Lydia did not want his pampering. She wanted his company, his embrace…his kisses. *And his love.*

If only her painting had been enough to sway him from his decision to marry her to another. At first, she'd thought it was forbidden for a guardian to marry his ward. It would be more bearable if the law kept him from her, for then perhaps she could convince him to take her back to America. Miss Hobson had crushed that hope when Lydia tentatively broached the subject during the carriage ride.

"Unless they are kin, there is no legal impediment against a guardian marrying his ward, though it would raise eyebrows among Society." Miss Hobson had regarded her strangely. "Has Lord Deveril given you reason to believe he would be amenable to such a match?"

Quickly, Lydia had shaken her head, hoping her pain was not obvious. "No, I am merely curious about England's customs."

The suspicious glint failed to dim in the chaperone's eyes, though she had nodded. "Well, his lordship seems to be resigned to remaining a bachelor. It is a bit of a shame, for I believe he is the last of his line." In an offhand tone, she added, "Though that may change this Season when everyone realizes what a catch he is. I daresay many young ladies will be vying to become the next Countess of Deveril. The earl will have to be clever to evade their clutches."

Sick envy had roiled through Lydia at the thought of Vincent with another woman. Only her pride kept her from reacting. Unable to continue the conversation, she'd hidden her face in a novel until they arrived in London.

Now, gazing up at the intricately woven canopy above her bed, Lydia vowed she wouldn't let Vincent's rejection of her affection hurt her any longer. She would not be affected by the other debutantes simpering over him, for she would be too busy with her own suitors.

With that inner promise, sleep enveloped her in its welcome solace, wherein she did not dream of suitors. Instead, her imagination conjured Vincent's lips upon hers, her hands in his hair, the feel of his hardness against her body.

When she awoke, Lydia's mood was improved. Whether from the prospect of meeting a duchess who wrote ghost stories, or because it was nightfall and Vincent was soon to arrive, she could not say. Either way, her heart pounded when she met him downstairs.

Though she did her best not to look at him on the ride to Burnrath House, her few brief glances in Vincent's direction were enough to determine he was in a sullen humor. Was he perhaps nervous? Lydia certainly was, especially once the carriage halted and she caught her first sight of the imposing Elizabethan manor. The monstrosity was nearly the size of Castle Deveril.

A liveried butler greeted them with a low bow. A footman took their hats and cloaks with equal formality before they were escorted to a richly furnished drawing room, decadently illuminated with modern gas lamps that lit the chamber as brightly as day. Lydia couldn't stop staring at Vincent's hair. His gleaming strands shone with molten silver and gold.

"I am so pleased you are here!" A playful voice brought back her attention.

The Duchess of Burnrath was not what Lydia had expected. Besides the lack of a coronet or a regal stiffness like Miss Hobson's, Her Grace was tiny in stature and had an air of mischievousness displayed in her every movement. She looked to be younger than Lydia, yet her exotic black eyes gleamed with astonishing intelligence.

Lydia curtsied low. "Your Grace, I am honored by your invitation."

The duchess returned the curtsy as a black cat wove in and out under her skirts. "It is a pleasure to meet you at last, Miss Price." Turning to Lydia's chaperone, she added, "Miss Hobson, you have trained her well. All the same, I am thankful my mother was unable to afford your expertise."

Miss Hobson inclined her head. "You flatter me, Your Grace, though it seems you have done well without my tutoring."

The duchess laughed merrily and picked up her cat. "This is Loki, the fiercest rat catcher in all of London."

The duke descended the stairs and bowed to the ladies before clapping Vincent on the shoulder. "Deveril, old chap, I am pleased you came. Shall we adjourn to the dining room?"

To Lydia's dismay, she realized that her supposition about aristocratic dining was correct, for the duchess ate as little as Vincent and the duke. It was a shame, for the food was delicious, and it took every vestige of her will to be ladylike and only sample a few morsels of each dish.

Their hosts inquired politely about the journey to London, as well as Lydia's life in America. Lydia observed that they and Vincent frequently exchanged intent gazes and odd frowns. It was as if they were having a conversation without her.

"Tell me, Miss Price." The duchess set down her wineglass and fed her cat a bit of fish. "Are you eager to be presented to the most eligible gentlemen in England?"

I loathe the idea! Lydia longed to shout. *But it is preferable to remaining with a man who does not want me.* Instead, she straightened her spine and fixed the duchess with a placid smile. "Nothing delights me more, Your Grace."

"And what of love?"

Lydia blinked at the unexpected question. *I love Vincent.* "One may always hope. My parents married for love."

"Ah, yes." The duchess smiled at Lydia. "Your father was the scandalous Earl of Morley, who ran off to America with a merchant's daughter. Tell me, did they remain in love?"

Lydia spoke past a sudden lump in her throat. "Until they drew their last breath."

Her Grace gave her a long, considering look, and Lydia feared she had said the wrong thing. Then she replied, "Perhaps my parents should have moved to America."

Burnrath chuckled. "Then you would not have met me."

"That is true." She returned his smile.

His Grace moved on to the next subject. "I gave Miss Price one of your novels."

"Did you enjoy it?" The duchess leaned forward.

"Very much, Your Grace."

Those dark eyes gleamed with warmth. "Please, call me Angelica. I abhor such formality in my home. Tell me, what other authors do you admire?"

The remainder of the meal passed cordially, as Angelica and Lydia discussed literature. They were delighted to realize their tastes were so similar. After the dishes were carried away, Angelica seized Lydia's hand, and they hurried up to the library. Loki scurried after them.

The vast chamber took Lydia's breath away. A cheery fireplace and ornate lamps illuminated the plush burgundy rugs, the inviting overstuffed chairs, and wall-to-wall mahogany shelves holding hundreds of books. Her lips parted in awe. She could spend hours here.

Angelica retrieved a well-worn volume and handed it to her. "You must read this book."

Lydia's pulse quickened at the title: *A Vindication of the Rights of Women* by Mary Wollstonecraft. Just holding the book felt like an act of rebellion. Angelica's eyes met hers, and they exchanged a conspiratorial smile. Lydia knew then that she had made a true friend.

"Do you agree to sponsor Miss Price for the Season, then?" Vincent interrupted the exchange as he regarded them from the doorway.

"Yes, I will. Though I suppose that means I shall have to once more transport myself to the realm of respectability." Angelica looked so dismayed at the prospect that Lydia couldn't hold back her laughter.

"We would like to take you both to the opera tomorrow," the duke said, joining his wife. "It is a way Miss Price can glimpse Society before the Season begins."

"Oh, we should see *The Vampyre, or The Bride of the Isles*!" Angelica exclaimed.

"A vampire opera?" Lydia grinned. "That sounds delightful!"

Vincent, however, glowered at the suggestion of the play. *He must despise gothic tales*, thought Lydia. *Perhaps that comes with living in a real castle.*

❧

"Just what do you think you are about, Angel, loaning her that book?" Ian demanded the moment Vincent left with his charge and the chaperone. "The last thing Vincent needs is for that young lady's head to be filled with seditious ideas."

Angelica's eyes narrowed, flickering with preternatural flame. "You don't believe in female equality?"

Ian raised his gaze to the ceiling, as if to seek divine aid. "You know that I do. I lived through Queen Elizabeth's reign. You also know that a number of Lord Vampires are female. The issue is about Miss Price. She needs to be happily wed and safely out from beneath Vincent's roof before she discovers what he is." He fixed her with an icy stare. "As for that subject, what in God's name would possess you to suggest a vampire opera? Have you gone mad? You may as well bare your fangs at her!"

"And would that be such a terrible thing?" Angelica said softly. "Did you not observe Lydia closely, Ian? She is in love with Lord Deveril."

"What makes you think he would return the sentiment? He hardly acknowledged her presence tonight."

Angelica laughed. "Precisely. He took extra pains with that, as if had he touched her, he would be unable to stop." She shook her head. "It is beyond comprehension why he would throw away an opportunity for happiness."

"The only way he could keep her is to seek permission to make her one of us. I attempted to broach the subject with Deveril during my visit to his castle." He waved off Angelica's hopeful grin. "He is adamantly opposed to the idea."

"Why? You remember how he was at our wedding reception and during my first ball. He was obviously lonely, and Lydia is perfect for him. One would have to be blind not to see it." Angelica reached up to caress her husband's face. "Surely you can persuade him to see reason."

Ian locked his arms around her. "Have patience,

Angel. You forget we have eternity. If Vincent truly loves her, he won't let her go. I'll wager you two hundred pounds he'll submit a request to the Elders to Change Miss Price by the end of the Season. You must not meddle."

Angelica answered as honestly as she could. "I shall endeavor to do so as little as possible."

Fourteen

LYDIA STOOD RAPT IN AWE AT HER FIRST SIGHT OF Somerset House. Illuminated by gas lamps, the "house," a sprawling neoclassical quadrangle, was one of the largest structures she'd ever seen. The Thames lapped against the south wing, and boats actually rowed inside the building under its massive arches.

"Lydia." Vincent's voice brought her back to awareness. "If you want to see the paintings, we had better go inside now or we'll be late to the opera."

She blushed at being caught gaping. "I am sorry, my lord. It is so…" She spread her arms helplessly, at a loss for words. She wished they could have come during the day, but Vincent's headaches prevented it.

"You do not have anything like this in America?" A hint of pride for her home country warmed Miss Hobson's voice.

Lydia shook her head. "The president's home is dainty by comparison."

Both her guardian and her chaperone laughed at the candid remark.

"Is *all* of this home to the Royal Academy?" she

asked, reeling in amazement as they made their way up the large paved drive.

Miss Hobson shook her head. "The Society of Antiquaries, the University of London, and countless public offices hold accommodations here."

Bewigged officials opened the doors for them, and after taking Vincent's card, they led them up a wide, curving staircase to the apartments of the Royal Academy of Arts. When they entered the cavernous receiving room, Lydia immediately wanted to examine the myriad gold-framed paintings adorning the walls. However, there was a man waiting.

"Lord Deveril, I presume?" he inquired mildly.

Vincent nodded. "I apologize for the late hour and thank you for your willingness to give us a tour." He turned to Lydia. "This is Sir Thomas Lawrence, president of the Royal Academy and one of the finest portrait artists to have lived. Sir Thomas, this is my ward, Miss Lydia Price, daughter of the late Earl of Morley, and a skilled painter in her own right." He gestured to Miss Hobson. "This is Miss Sarah Hobson, the most vigilant chaperone in England."

Lydia hid her astonished gasp with her fan as Vincent gave her a wink. She'd known they'd be visiting the Academy, but he hadn't told her they would be meeting Sir Thomas. She quickly curtsied, trying not to ogle the painter she idolized.

He was fairly tall, though much shorter than Vincent. Deep blue eyes, noble Roman features, and rich golden hair fringing his balding head proved that he had once been a handsome man. Was he truly a despoiler of innocents, as the Sidwell sisters had claimed?

"Miss Price, you have your father's unique eyes. He sat for me once, you know." His lips curved in a warm smile. "I am sorry for your loss."

"Thank you." Overwhelmed that he knew who she was, Lydia's curtsy was shaky. "It is an honor to make your acquaintance. I have the portrait you painted of my father. May I see more of your work?"

"Of course." He extended his arm. "Shall we begin the tour?"

Lydia took his arm and allowed him to lead her to the paintings. He pointed out works by Sir Joshua Reynolds, Thomas Gainsborough, and Benjamin West.

She stopped in front of West's roundel, *The Graces Unveiling Nature*. "The texture of their hair is amazing. It appears he used many different-sized brushes."

"You have an astute eye for detail," Lawrence said, eyeing her more intently as he proceeded to show her his own paintings.

His skill with light and shadow was extraordinary. Lydia was also impressed with the romantic, almost melancholy quality of his portraits. She studied each, trying to identify a unifying technique to explain the effect, but could not. A portrait of a young woman caught her eye. There was something familiar about her dark, wavy tresses and pensive gray eyes.

"I've seen her before," she whispered aloud.

Vincent shook his head, expression unreadable.

"Impossible." Sir Thomas's voice turned suddenly melancholy. "That is Sally Siddons, daughter of the renowned actress, Sarah Siddons, who was like a mother to me." He gestured to a portrait of Sarah Siddons, an actress so famous even Lydia had heard of her, before once more regarding the painting of the daughter. "Sally, who was my dearest love, died before you could have been born." Moisture rimmed his blue eyes, and a look of pure agony sliced across his features before he cleared his throat. "Would you like to see the classrooms now?"

"Oh, very much!" she exclaimed, feeling terrible for upsetting him. He must have loved that woman dearly...unless she was one of the "innocents" that Maria had said he'd despoiled.

The unpleasantness was quickly forgotten as the painter showed them the classrooms. "We take on around thirty students a year. First they learn to imitate the old masters, and then they learn to develop their own original techniques."

Lydia's gaze devoured the sight of easels, canvases, paints, and brushes. The acrid odors of turpentine and linseed oil filled her with longing. "It has long been my dream to study here."

Sir Thomas chuckled. "Such enthusiasm. Unfortunately, only males are permitted to attend the Academy."

The offhand statement was like an unexpected slap...as it always was when her gender barred her from something desirable. Every time Lydia thought she was accustomed to such irrational restrictions, a new one would rear its head. This one stung more than others. Why should her sex prevent her from becoming a better painter?

Her fists clenched at her sides. She wished she could rage at his unfairness, like Angelica. "But two of the founders of the Academy were women!" she burst out. Lydia shocked herself at arguing with her hero, yet she could not hold back. "Mary Moser *and* Angelica Kauffman!"

The painter blinked. "I see you are knowledgeable in the history of our beloved establishment. In that case, you *must* know that though both were exceptional artists in their own right, neither studied at the school."

"Perhaps we could discuss arranging some private lessons. Would you at least come dine with us Thursday evening so you may assess Lydia's work?" Vincent asked suddenly. Lydia longed to throw her arms around him and kiss him all over.

Sir Thomas's gaze grew speculative, doubtless at the prospect of dining with a member of the peerage rather than at viewing Lydia's amateur work. "Very well."

Turning back to Lydia, Sir Thomas's smile turned falsely indulgent. Her heart sank.

"Do you paint with watercolors, Miss Price?"

She lifted her chin and tried not to sound impertinent. "Oils."

His grin broadened while his eyes at last gleamed with honest interest. "Female oil painters are rare. I would indeed like to see your work."

"Oh, it is nothing compared to yours," she replied, suddenly shy. What were her paintings compared to those of a master?

Vincent cleared his throat. "It is time we were off. We have another engagement. I look forward to speaking with you again, Sir Thomas."

As they made their way back to the town house, Lydia's heart swelled with gratitude. Boldly, she placed her hand on Vincent's. "Thank you, my lord."

He hesitated a moment before patting her hand. "Do not thank me yet. He may refuse to teach you."

"Your kindness in asking him is enough." With painful reluctance, she withdrew her hand before her touch lingered into impropriety.

❧

Vincent smiled as his valet helped him dress for the opera. Lydia's delight in the visit to the Royal Academy had been a palpable thing, a sojourn back to the hopes of youth. The opportunity to look in on the painter for the Siddons sisters merely gilded the evening.

He hadn't intended on offering to hire Sir Thomas. Lydia had been so crestfallen at hearing that females were barred from the Academy that he'd been overtaken by the urge to bring back her smile. Besides, he told himself, ladies of the *ton* were expected to take lessons in art or music. No harm would be done as long as the old lecher behaved himself.

Just as Ian and Angelica arrived to take them to the theater, Lydia descended in a white satin opera gown that did little to conceal her opulent curves. His fists clenched at his sides. Hell, *he* had better behave himself.

Vincent held back a groan of arousal as he slid into the Burnrath coach next to Lydia. The heat of her proximity was sweet torture. If only Miss Hobson could have come along to dull the mood. With the duke and duchess serving as chaperones for the opera, there was no need.

He frowned once more as they arrived at the

opera house. *A vampire play?* Was Her Grace insane? Ian's countenance was rigid with annoyance while the men exchanged pained looks as they helped the women from the carriage. What if Lydia grew suspicious of them?

Stares and whispers interrupted Vincent's thoughts, bringing his awareness back to their surroundings. The people of London were receiving their first glimpse of Lydia. Several males gazed at her like love-struck swains, and it was all he could do not to pull her into his arms and stake his claim. He gritted his teeth. The more suitors she had, the better. His muscles tensed with the need to tear the fops to shreds. Lydia's hand squeezed his bicep as he led her down the walk, and he resisted the urge to bare his fangs in triumph.

Once they were settled in the duke's box and the curtains lifted, Vincent's earlier worries returned. Thankfully, it soon became clear that he had no cause for concern. The production was the silliest thing he'd witnessed in his lifetime, full of painful melodrama, ludicrous magic ceremonies, and an overly sinister corpse-like actor who bore no resemblance to a vampire at all. At least the singing was good.

Worry quickly turned to amusement, though it was nothing compared to Angelica's response. The duchess had both hands clapped over her mouth as she struggled to contain gales of laughter. Ian gazed heavenward as if praying for divine assistance in removing him from this silliness. Lydia smiled at the performance and frowned in puzzlement at the others' reactions.

Vincent tapped Ian's shoulder in warning. If the

r youth seemed further magnified as she trembled
ore the King. Unlike Lydia, her gown was more
-fashioned and had hoops. That proved to be
fortunate, for she stumbled backward when she was
missed. A servant caught her before she fell, and the
ng dozed on, oblivious. The poor girl quavered as
e was chastised by her grandmother…

My grandmother! Lydia gasped at her first sight
f the Dowager Countess of Morley. Her father's
nother, whom he had defied, and who had exiled
im. Gazing upon a countenance more severe than
hose adorning cathedral walls, Lydia could no longer
oe shocked at such treatment.

Her attention shifted to the man who was dabbing
Georgiana's tears away with a handkerchief. With
the same pale hair and eyes, he had to be the girl's
father…which meant the man was her uncle. This
was her father's younger brother. Lydia could see
little resemblance.

Where her father had been tall and dark, her uncle
vas short and fair. Her father's features had been broad
nd strong. This man's face was thin, and he had
most no chin to speak of. Her father had been bold
red wine. This man had the appeal of lukewarm tea.
t he'd inherited her father's title. The world made
sense.

Vincent touched her arm, pulling her from her
ghts and into physical awareness. "It is time to
urn to the drawing room." His breath on her ear
remors through her being.

dia grasped him, savoring his nearness.
tunately, the duchess drew her away the moment

ducal vampires did not contain themselves, they would
elicit Lydia's suspicion faster than the folderol on stage.

His gaze wandered from the stage to the cheap
seats below the boxes. Two bonneted heads were
averted from the stage, looking up at one of the boxes.
Studying them more closely, Vincent recognized the
profiles of Sally and Maria Siddons. Though they were
thoroughly disguised with wigs and face paint, unease
gnawed at his gut at their solemn expressions, out of
place with the farce on the stage.

He followed the direction of the vampires' tremulous gazes to the private box of Sarah Siddons. Though
age had taken its toll on their mother's once-beautiful
face, her noble stature and vivacity remained. Sarah
observed the play, oblivious to the presence of her
daughters. Her lip curled in sublime scorn for the
atrocious performance before her. Vincent could well
imagine how painful a sight it was for one of the greatest actresses ever to have walked the boards.

Heaving a sigh that should have been felt through
the rafters, Sarah Siddons stood and departed her box
in a disgusted huff.

Sally and Maria immediately rose to follow. Then
their pleading gazes met Vincent's.

Feeling like the cruelest of tyrants, he firmly shook
his head. Tears poured down their cheeks as they
obeyed and sat back down.

Fifteen

"MISS LYDIA PRICE, DAUGHTER OF THE SEVENTH EARL of Morley!" the Lord Chamberlain announced.

Lydia's vision blurred, and dizziness threatened to topple her. Then her gaze locked on Angelica's, and she seemed to gain strength. *You can do this*. It was as if she could hear the duchess's voice in her mind, encouraging her to place one foot in front of the other.

Ignoring the hushed whispers of the surrounding crowd, Lydia made her way to the throne with demure grace. It helped to pretend she was walking to Miss Hobson with the tablecloth pinned to her back. Even so, she nearly faltered when she caught her first glimpse of King George IV.

His Majesty was a formidable sight indeed, a corpulent mass of flesh dripping in jewels. Thankfully, her concentration on her curtsy allowed her to recover from her shock, and she was able to kiss the pudgy royal hand with rehearsed dignity. The monarch's heavy lids barely lifted, and she could smell the stench of sweat and strong spirits emanating from him. Lydia struggled not to stare like a half-wit. King George did

not at all resemble his magnificent portrayings she'd seen. Was this common for rulers nations? Perhaps the etchings of President were also misrepresentations.

The King muttered something unintelligible grasped for a proper response. English mona been known to imprison—or behead—tho invoked their displeasure.

"I am honored, Your Highness," she rep demurely as possible.

George's eyes widened, and he blinked at startled awareness. A stone of terror dropped in L belly. She had said the wrong thing!

Then he smiled. "Your accent is delightful, Price…" He shook his head and wiped a film of sw from his brow. "Miss Price, ah yes, I remember y father. Brilliant chap! And a lucky bastard for hav the courage to marry the one he chose."

Blinking once more, he gave her the formal n approval, and thankfully she was able to neatly her train from a nearby servant and walk bac from the throne room without missing a ste the corner of her eye she caught Vincent's approval before she was flanked by Angelic Hobson. His regard warmed her from h until the Chamberlain announced, "Mis Price, daughter of the eighth Earl of Mo

The breath fled Lydia's body in a ru Eyes wide, she watched the young girl to the throne. Though she had to be Georgiana looked to be about sixteen ing cheeks, doll-like blonde curls, a they'd reached an elegant woman with bright red curls and a stern countenance.

"Miss Price, this is my mother, Lady Margaret," Angelica said with unusual formality.

Lydia curtsied.

"Miss Price." Lady Margaret nodded. "I am honored to meet my daughter's first protégée. Your gown is exquisite, and your manners are better than I've seen in ages." She darted a pointed glance at Angelica. "I look forward to your debut ball at Burnrath House tonight."

"Mother helped me with the preparations," Angelica supplied.

"Her Grace required the aid," Margaret said with narrowed eyes, "as she was once more engrossed in her hobby and neglecting her *duties*."

Angelica flinched at the words. Obviously the mother and daughter had a disagreement about something more significant than her ball.

"I see Princess Lieven," Angelica said stiffly. "I must speak to her about Miss Price's voucher to Almack's. You've met Miss Hobson before, yes?"

Before Lady Margaret could reply, Angelica took Lydia's hand and pulled her away. "Now all have noted that you have Lady Margaret's favor."

Lydia glanced back, seeing that Miss Hobson and Angelica's mother were speaking as if they were the best of friends. It was apparent that Angelica and Lady Margaret had conflicting personalities. Lydia sensed there were heavy implications in her mother's reference to "duties."

As if reading her mind, Angelica raised her fan to

whisper, "Mother thinks because I have not produced an heir, that I am refusing to bed my husband." An impish giggle escaped her lips, and she inclined her head toward the duke. "Who in their right mind would refuse *that*?"

Lydia nodded in appreciation of Ian's dark, handsome features before her gaze strayed from the duke to Vincent, and she imagined *him* in her bed. Her thighs trembled as she studied the strong line of his jaw and the sculpted curves of his lips, lips that had claimed her own in reckless abandon only weeks ago. "Who indeed?"

The duchess followed her gaze and laughed. "I've seen you giving Lord Deveril calf-eyes of late. You must abandon such a habit, else people will assume your relationship is improper... Bloody hell, I sound just like my mother."

Oh, how Lydia longed for an improper relationship with Vincent. She wanted more stolen kisses, more embraces, and other forbidden things. Hiding such feelings would require every bit of her rigid training. Her face burned at being caught. "Please, Your Grace, do not—"

"Your secret is safe with me." Angelica winked before turning away to exclaim, "Princess Lieven! How wonderful it is to see you!"

An astonishingly beautiful woman glided forward to kiss the duchess's cheek. "It is a joy to see you as well, Your Grace." Her accent was heady and exotic, like spiced rum.

Angelica wasted no time. "I would like to discuss a voucher to Almack's."

The princess shook her head. "Your Grace, as

much as I would like to have you back within our hallowed halls, I cannot. Once a voucher is revoked, it cannot be reinstated."

With a trilling laugh, the duchess shook her head. "I am not referring to *my* voucher. You remember I am sponsoring Miss Lydia Price."

Warm brown eyes shifted to consider Lydia, who curtsied obediently. "Ah, yes, the daughter of the late Earl of Morley. I am not certain…"

"She has Miss Hobson as a chaperone," Angelica offered. "It would be difficult for Miss Price to attempt to follow in my footsteps under her vigilance."

The princess smirked. "Yes, I suppose so. I shall see what may be done."

Lydia's eyes widened at the realization that she was looking at a real princess. Life was taking on a surreal quality.

Things became even stranger when her cousin approached her, pale and trembling.

"It is a joy to meet you, Cousin," Georgiana murmured. "Your dress is very pretty."

Lydia could detect no hostility in the girl's tone, so she bobbed a polite curtsy. "Thank you. Yours is lovely as well." A pang of sympathy struck her at the sight of the hoops straining beneath the skirts of her elaborate gown.

Georgiana didn't seem to hear. She darted a timid glance at their grandmother and scurried away as fast as she could in her cumbersome court dress.

"What a whey-faced coward," Angelica whispered behind her fan.

"I think she was rather brave to risk our

grandmother's wrath," Lydia defended, oddly vexed at the insult to her cousin, who'd been nonexistent only moments ago.

Angelica's brows rose as she peered over her shoulder. "It seems she is not the only brave one." She turned away to fetch a glass of champagne from a passing footman as Georgiana's father approached.

Lydia regarded him mutely as he bowed over her hand. This man was her father's younger brother. Her own *uncle*! He was the one who should have taken care of her after her father died. When he did not, she had supposed he was as cruel as her grandmother. Now, as she studied his limpid eyes and hunched shoulders, she knew he was merely weak.

"It is an honor to meet you at last, Lydia," the new Earl of Morley stammered. "You look so much like my brother." He swallowed as if fighting tears. "I missed him terribly when he left. Tell me, was he happy in America?"

Lydia swallowed her own tears at the memory of her father. "Very happy."

"Did he speak of me?" His eyes turned pleading.

Without thinking, she lied. "Oh yes, my lord. Very often." In truth, her father had almost never spoken of his family, and when Lydia had finally discovered they had cast him out, she could not blame him.

"Is Lord Deveril treating you well?" he asked suddenly.

A thousand accusations threatened to burst forth. For all he knew, Vincent could have been the frightening madman he'd been rumored to be, rather than a guardian angel. Instead, she nodded. "Very well, thank you."

He must have seen the anger at his betrayal in her eyes, for his expression swam with guilt. "Lydia, I truly wish I could have taken you in, but Mother—"

"I understand, Uncle." The words came out colder than she intended, and the earl flinched as if she had slapped him.

"I must go now," he said in a strange tone, as if he were afraid.

She followed his gaze and saw Lady Morley's fierce glare. Doubtless he wasn't supposed to speak to her. In muted rebellion, he patted her hand before fleeing back to his matriarch.

Lydia sighed. She wanted to hate him and her sweet, frail cousin, but she couldn't. Pity was the only emotion she could muster on their behalf. Pity, and a complete lack of respect for their weakness. It was no wonder that her father had not seemed to miss them.

"Are you all right, Lydia?" Vincent's welcome voice sounded behind her like a soothing balm. She longed to lean back against his chest.

Though he hadn't wanted her, Vincent had made her feel more welcome than her family had.

To her embarrassment, tears threatened once more. "May we go home now?"

Like a whisper, his hand stroked her back, hidden from view. A covert offering of comfort. Selfish wretch that she was, Lydia wanted more.

※

Vincent watched Lydia descend the spiral staircase to the ballroom. In her pale blue gown of shimmering silk, she was like a wildflower, a symbol of fragile perfection. Her eyes sparkled like jewels…and they were just as cold. Other than that, no sign remained of the emotional turmoil she'd faced at her presentation. Vincent cursed himself for not anticipating Lydia's inevitable encounter with those who'd cast her aside. He should have prepared her better.

Pride filled him at her courage in facing her traitorous relations. And now she was facing the majority of the *ton* with quiet dignity.

He watched her smile at the guests, engaging in cheerful conversation as if nothing was amiss. Dozens of besotted males lined up to fill her dance card as more gathered near, like bees to a rose…or a gardenia. His fangs ached.

All was going as planned. So why did he feel like striding to the dance floor, yanking Lydia from the arms of her suitor, and snapping the fop's neck?

"Lord Deveril, how wonderful it is to see you again!" Another matron interrupted his murderous thoughts.

It was all Vincent could do not to mouth her next words, the same words he'd heard with annoying frequency since Lydia's presentation. "I would like to introduce you to my daughter, as you did not have an opportunity last Season."

Before he could protest, another simpering girl was thrust before him. Vincent struggled to convey polite disinterest and gently disengage her. His irritation and the scent and sound of so much prey made the blood roar in his ears. As if sensing his predatory nature, the girl stammered an excuse and scurried away, to her mother's chagrin.

"I see the *ton* presumes you're on the market as well," Ian noted behind him with a chuckle. "You shall have a *delightful* time at Almack's next Wednesday."

Vincent turned and bared his fangs at the duke. "This is not a matter for amusement."

"You are correct," Ian replied as his gaze narrowed to a point over Vincent's shoulder. "I see my second in command is contemplating your ward. This could be a hazard."

Vincent whipped around with wide eyes. The sight of Lydia in the same room with Rafael Villar made his heart race in panic. He was uncertain of Ian's judgment in choosing Rafe as his successor. Vincent had never met a more foul-tempered vampire. All of London's vampires were terrified of the Spaniard. And there was Lydia, mere yards away from him.

A low growl built in his throat as he strode across the ballroom.

୭ତ

Lydia sighed in relief as she leaned against a pillar, resting her sore feet. Her slippers pinched like the devil, and her face ached from forcing smiles at her inane suitors' compliments. She longed to escape to the library and curl up with a novel. Even more, she longed to take Vincent's hand and run back to Cornwall. Alas, Miss Hobson would bring the roof down on her head if she left this party held in her honor.

To her dismay, a group of pastel-draped debutantes invaded her solitude. Lydia fought the urge to yawn as they chattered on about Lord So-and-So and Baron Whatnot.

"Who is that ugly man by the pillar?" a young blonde asked.

Her friend giggled, and Lydia only just overheard her reply. "That is *Don* Rafael Villar, a hidalgo from Spain and an infamous pugilist."

"A pugilist?" the other repeated quizzically. "How can that be? Look at his arm!"

Lydia turned to peer over her fan at this latest topic of gossip. The man was not ugly, though she could understand why sheltered young girls would think so. His skin was an intriguing shade of cinnamon; his hair fell past his shoulders, an inky black that rivaled the duke's, and his eyes were the color of Vincent's brandy. If that wasn't enough to set him apart from the pale, gilded crowd surrounding him, the left side of his face bore rippled scars, as if he'd been burned.

At last she saw what was amiss with his arm. It hung limp and awkward, damaged from the same burns. It was a wonder he could box with such a disadvantage, albeit believable when one observed his muscled form, thinly disguised under his simple, unadorned attire.

No, this man was not ugly; he was striking with his savagely chiseled features and intent, amber eyes. She would love to render him in charcoals.

The debutante's voice intruded on her speculation. "He is looking right at us!"

"Let us make haste to the retiring room before he attempts to speak to us."

Lydia fought back a gasp, for the man was not looking at them. He was looking at *her*. His amber eyes pierced hers, and his mouth twisted in a fearsome scowl. So she did what she felt was right under the circumstances. She lifted her chin, flicked open her fan, and approached him.

"*Don* Villar." She took care to sound cheery as she curtsied. "I am honored that you attended my coming out."

His scowl deepened. "I believe you are not supposed to speak to me unless we are formally introduced." His voice was gravelly, yet rich with his Spanish accent.

Lydia refused to step back and gave him a wry smile. "*Would* anyone introduce us?"

He blinked as if startled by her humor. "Probably not."

When he didn't say more, she sighed. "Are you always this taciturn?"

He nodded curtly then flicked his gaze around the room. "*Señorita* Price, you should return to your party before your fragile reputation is ruined."

Lydia frowned. These days her reputation felt more like a burden than an asset. Before she could reply, a firm hand grasped her arm.

"*Don* Villar," Vincent said with a painfully slight incline of his head.

Rafael did not bow at all. "Lord Deveril."

They stared at each other with far more intensity than the sullen looks exchanged by Lydia's suitors when they argued about who would dance with her first.

Vincent behaved as if Rafael had committed a crime in speaking to her. He pulled her away, refusing to acknowledge the Spaniard any more. "Come, you look like you need fresh air," he said tersely.

Lydia refused to tremble as he led her out of the French doors and into the spring night. It took all of her effort to hide her alarm. She'd never seen him this angry.

"I don't want to see you speaking with that man again." His tone was rife with command.

Lydia bristled at his autocratic behavior. "Why ever not?"

Vincent gripped her shoulders and brought his face down close to hers. "I don't want you *near* him, because he is dangerous. Even the greenest chits here know that."

Senses electrified at his nearness, she leaned forward until her mouth was inches from his. "Why is he dangerous?"

A low growl escaped his throat, sending shivers up her spine. "It is not fit for an innocent young lady to know."

"Perhaps I don't want to be innocent," she whispered against his lips. Vincent shivered under her touch, and Lydia felt a moment of triumph before he gently pushed her away.

"We must return to the ballroom before people begin to talk."

Flinching at his stiff tone, she lifted her chin and followed him back to the crushing noise of her party. Immediately, several young men flocked to her side, begging for a dance. It took a few minutes for her polite refusal to be heard over the barrage of music and loud conversation.

"I must thank the fine ladies who have attended this night." She seized upon the excuse, seeing a handsome woman seated at the far end of the room, wearing a mauve half-mourning gown that clashed with her auburn hair. Unable to dance, she must be bored senseless.

The woman smiled when Lydia sat next to her.

Lydia returned the smile. "I am honored that you are here, Lady...Rosslyn." She blushed at her difficulty in remembering everyone's names. At least she had remembered this lady was a countess.

"It is my pleasure, Miss Price," the woman replied. "Are you enjoying your come out?"

"It is lovely, thank you." Honesty compelled her to add, "Though it is overwhelming. I have met so many people, and it is difficult to keep all the names straight."

Lady Rosslyn smiled sympathetically. "I felt the same way when I had my come out. Miss Hobson was my chaperone then. I have full confidence she will help you sort everyone out."

"She *was*?" Lydia asked, feeling an instant kinship with the other woman.

The countess nodded. "I found her intimidating beyond measure at first. Eventually, I learned that she has a warm heart under her frigid exterior." Her blue-green eyes held a momentary twinge of sadness. Had they been close?

Reluctant to pry, Lydia changed the subject. "What do you know of *Don* Villar?"

Lady Rosslyn peered over her fan at the sullen Spaniard. "Only that he is a close friend of the Duke of Burnrath. I've seen him here occasionally when I attend the duchess's literary circles, but he's never been receptive to conversation." A faint blush colored her cheeks.

Lydia concealed a smile. It appeared she wasn't

the only one intrigued by Villar. However, this lady's fascination looked to be of a far more dangerous sort. Risking a glance at her guardian, Lydia shivered as she recalled his touch.

Ignoring her petulant suitors, Lydia spent the rest of the evening talking with Lady Rosslyn. It was much more difficult to pretend indifference to Vincent's burning gaze.

Sixteen

As the hour drew near for Sir Thomas Lawrence's arrival for supper, Vincent hid a smile while he watched Lydia pace the length of the drawing room. If she kept at it much longer, she was liable to wear a path in the carpet.

"What if he does not like my paintings?" she asked for the seventh time.

"Then he has no taste," he repeated, trying not to notice the curve of her rear as she continued her pacing.

"What if he refuses to teach me?"

"Then I will hire someone else. However, I am confident that he will accept my offer."

Vincent was more than confident. He'd made discreet inquiries about the painter before the visit to the Royal Academy. Despite Lawrence's fame and lofty position, he was deeply in debt. The man didn't gamble or overindulge in frippery. His loose pockets were the result of being overgenerous to his friends. It was difficult to fault him for that.

Lydia calmed at his reassurance. Her pacing halted, and she lowered her voice. "What is the story about him and the daughter of Sarah Siddons? Miss Hobson refuses to tell me."

The curiosity in her gold-flecked eyes nearly undid him. However, it was best she not know. "It's not a suitable story for a lady."

She sighed in disappointment. "Well, whatever happened, he certainly seemed to be remorseful about it."

Yes, Lawrence had indeed been stricken with guilt. It radiated throughout his entire being. Sally and Maria should be pleased to hear that…and also that he was balding.

Despite the fact that Ian had charged one of his vampires to guard the sisters, Vincent surreptitiously glanced at every window to ensure they were not here to spy on Lawrence.

As if summoned by the thought, Aubert entered the drawing room, escorting the painter. "Sir Thomas Lawrence," he intoned.

Lawrence bowed and shook his hand. "Good evening, Lord Deveril."

Sir Thomas kissed Lydia's hand, and Vincent concealed a frown. In spite of his bald crown and the wrinkles framing his eyes, the man was still far too handsome.

Supper was an amiable affair as Sir Thomas regaled Lydia with tales of all the famous painters he knew, and Lydia described New Orleans. Her words evoked such a vivid picture that Vincent could feel the humid heat, see the riverboats, and taste the spicy food.

After the meal they adjourned to the yellow salon, where Lydia's paintings were set up on display. Sir Thomas scrutinized each so intently that Vincent had to place a hand on Lydia's shoulder to ease her nervous trembles.

"You have a remarkable sense of color," he said finally. "Subtlety in the right places, and vivid hues where it has the best impact. You mix your palette well, Miss Price. I would be honored to give you a few lessons and perhaps even have a word with my fellow Academicians about admitting you."

She beamed at his praise. "Thank you."

Miss Hobson scowled from her seat in the corner. Her dislike for Lawrence was apparent, though at least she did not wish to murder him. Oblivious, Lydia and Sir Thomas sipped wine and spent the next hour in animated conversation about light, color, and texture.

Vincent's gaze locked on Lydia's glittering golden eyes, the flush of her cheeks, and her lush parted lips. He savored the musical passion of her voice. She was like a beacon warding off the darkness in his soul.

"Would you paint her?" he blurted, realizing he must have a way to look upon Lydia after she was taken from him.

Sir Thomas blinked. "Well, between her lessons, my duties at the Academy, and the upcoming exhibition—"

Vincent silenced him, naming a figure that made the poor chap nearly choke on his wine. Lydia gasped, myriad emotions playing across her beloved face.

"I believe that could be arranged." Lawrence coughed, regaining composure. "Shall tomorrow afternoon be agreeable to begin?"

"That is fine, though I am afraid I shall be out." He gave Miss Hobson a pointed look, which she returned with a firm, subtle nod. She would keep Lydia in sight the entire time.

After Lawrence took his leave, Miss Hobson uttered a few cool platitudes about the painter and his scandalous past before changing the subject to Lydia's suitors. Lydia let out a small, unladylike groan, clearly wanting to talk more of painting and scandal. Vincent had his own reasons for disliking both topics.

"It is time for my walk," he said sharply, unable to bear another moment of speculation as to which man would ultimately enjoy her company.

Lydia met his gaze, an unspoken plea for him to remain flickering in her eyes. He wished he could... for eternity.

As he prowled the London streets to slake his unholy thirst, Vincent wondered if centuries later, he'd be gazing at Lydia's portrait with the same mournful longing that was in Lawrence's eyes when he looked upon his painting of Sally.

❧

Lydia trembled with excitement when Sir Thomas arrived the next afternoon. The painter bowed, ignoring Miss Hobson's hostile gaze. Lydia bit back a chuckle. As if she would be interested in the man in *that* way. He was older than her father.

The yellow salon was transformed into a studio, with her easel and paints set near the large picture window where the light was best. She eyed the blank canvas, fingers itching to obliterate the whiteness with creation.

Sir Thomas surveyed the arrangement with an

approving nod. "Well, Miss Price, what would you like to paint?"

"I'd like to attempt a portrait." She tried not to sound too giddy. "I have drawn plenty, but I've never dared attempt to paint one."

He nodded. "Then it would be best to start from one of those sketches. May I see them?"

Smiling to conceal her nervousness, Lydia fetched her sketchbook and handed it to him.

He flipped through the pages as she stared out the window, focusing on a sparrow in the budding lilac bush. The sun was high in the blue sky, so it would be hours before Vincent could join them downstairs. She cursed his headaches.

"Most of these are of Lord Deveril…" Lawrence broke into her thoughts. His tone was bland with no hint of censure.

Lydia dared to turn back around.

The painter continued, "With such striking features, he is a good choice for a subject. You have an artist's eye, I see." He carefully removed the most recent drawing, one she'd begun the night Vincent first kissed her. "I believe this is the best of the lot. You captured…*something* in his expression. Let us hope it shall carry over to the canvas."

As she carefully traced the preliminary outline on the canvas, Sir Thomas pulled out his own sketchbook and began drawing *her*.

Why had Vincent commissioned a portrait of her? Did he intend it for her to hang in her future husband's drawing room? Was that yet another strange British custom? She held her breath as she outlined his firm, angular jaw. Or did he want the painting for the same reason she wanted one of him? Did he want something to remember her by? Something to gaze at long after she was gone from his life?

Once she finished the outline, Sir Thomas nodded in approval and showed her his own sketch. Lydia stared. In minutes, he had captured the shape of her face and features perfectly. "We may begin your sitting tomorrow afternoon, if that is agreeable with your guardian."

He went through her paints and handed her a few colors. "The largest challenge in portrait painting, in my opinion, is mixing the right flesh color. His lordship is so very pale, so I advise only a drop of red."

As Lydia mixed the paint on the palette, Sir Thomas asked about her presentation and debutante ball, and Lydia began to feel at ease with him.

"I understand you met your grandmother for the first time," he said quietly.

Lydia shook her head, despising the ache in her throat. "*Saw* her is more apt. She refused to acknowledge me."

Lawrence made a sympathetic cluck. "I am sorry to hear that. Although I am frankly surprised that Lady Morley continues to bear such venom over your father's marriage. People should learn to forgive and move beyond old grudges."

Miss Hobson raised a brow and gave him a piercing stare. "Some things cannot be forgiven." From the chaperone's censorious tone, Lydia could tell she wasn't referring to her parents' marriage.

The painter knew it as well, for he flushed. "In matters of love, the heart takes precedence."

"Real love isn't fickle and doesn't cause hurt to the objects of its affections," Miss Hobson countered before returning her attention to her embroidery in cool dismissal. Lydia gaped at the crushing set down.

He opened his mouth to argue, then shook his head and turned to Lydia. "That is all for our lesson today, Miss Price. I have other pressing engagements."

"Of course. Thank you very much," she replied, trying to conceal her puzzlement with the odd exchange between her mentor and her chaperone.

The moment Lawrence departed, Lydia whirled to face Miss Hobson. "What in the world was that about? Was he once a beau of yours?"

Unbelievably, the chaperone laughed, a dry, yet somehow still-merry sound. "Certainly not." Her mirth vanished as quickly as it appeared. "One of my first charges was nearly ruined by him—not because she did anything untoward, but because of his reputation. Fortunately, his attention wandered to another as it has always been wont to do. However, she was so devastated that I feared she would never make a good match."

"Ah, so he has a penchant for chasing skirts." Lydia managed a light laugh, though once more, at the mention of his womanizing habits, disappointment gnawed at her consciousness at the thought of her hero being less than honorable. Vincent, on the other hand, was far *too* honorable. If only he would fling propriety to the wind and...and... A memory of his kiss permeated her senses, evoking an aching void of longing in her heart.

If only...

She shunted the thought away and returned her

attention to the subject of Sir Thomas Lawrence. "Well, he is one of the finest painters in the world, no matter his flaws."

"I certainly cannot deny that." Miss Hobson nodded. "If he were not, I would have protested Lord Deveril's hiring him to tutor you. All the same, I—"

She fell silent as Aubert entered the room. "The dressmakers have arrived."

Lydia bit back a curse, every vestige of her being dreading another tortuous fitting, and wishing to continue working on her painting of Vincent.

"Very good, Aubert. Escort them to the blue salon." Miss Hobson beamed, clearly relieved at the change in subject and delighted at the prospect of seeing new frocks and fripperies. Setting her sampler aside, she approached Lydia. "Let us get you cleaned up. I do hope they've finished your new riding habit."

Lydia sighed and removed her painter's apron before she washed her hands and followed her chaperone out of the studio.

Miss Hobson grimaced at the paint staining Lydia's fingers. "Thank heavens for gloves," she muttered before they entered the blue salon.

The seamstresses rose from the settee, wielding their measuring tapes and pins.

"How wonderful it is to see you, Miss Price." Maria's eyes gleamed warmth as she withdrew a carriage dress needing final adjustments.

Sally nodded. "Are you enjoying London?"

Their genuine interest spurred Lydia's excitement over her last few days. "Very much. Lord Deveril took me to visit the Royal Academy, and you will not believe what has happened."

The sisters leaned forward with avid curiosity. "Do not tease, tell us."

"I had the pleasure of finally meeting Sir Thomas Lawrence!" Her words came out in a rush. "He came to supper last night and, afterward, Vincent"—she flushed at her improper slip of tongue—"ah, I mean, Lord Deveril has hired Lawrence to give me painting lessons!"

The dressmakers stared at her, frozen. Lydia looked down in embarrassment at having spoken of her guardian in such an intimate manner. Doubtless they thought she was callous and too American.

"You met Sir Thomas Lawrence?" Sally breathed at last with no hint of censure.

Relieved, Lydia nodded. "And he is teaching me portraiture. Perhaps I may have a piece finished in time for the Royal Exhibition next month."

"What did you think of him?" Maria asked sharply, appearing not to care as much about the Royal Exhibition.

"He is very kind and an excellent tutor." *Though a mite absentminded and melodramatic*, she added silently.

"Is he married?" Sally inquired softly.

"Not as far as I know." Lydia frowned at the intensity of their gazes. Why were they so interested in the man? Had one of them been among Lawrence's fabled string of conquests? Immediately, she dismissed the idea. Both were much too young.

Yet as she studied Sally and the deeply pensive look in her gray eyes, Lydia suddenly realized why Lawrence's painting of Sally Siddons had seemed so familiar to her. *This* Sally bore an astonishing resemblance to the subject of that portrait. They even shared the same Christian name. If the painting wasn't decades old, she would have thought they were the same person. Perhaps Sally and Maria Sidwell shared a blood relation to the Siddons family.

Siddons…Sidwell. Even the surnames were similar. Perhaps a relation on the wrong side of the sheets?

Miss Hobson cleared her throat. "Let us see if that carriage dress suits Miss Price. And how much work is left on her next ball gown."

Maria blinked as if woken from a dream. "Of course."

The next two hours were spent taking measurements and pinning hems. Lydia struggled to remain still and avoid glancing at the clock, wondering when Vincent would return and if there would be time for a game of chess. She couldn't wait to tell him of her painting lesson.

After the seamstresses departed, Miss Hobson shook her head. "Such an irreverent pair. I cannot fathom what they were about in asking you such questions about that painter." Her fingers caressed the embroidered hem of the new carriage dress. "Though for garments as exquisitely and expediently produced, we may endure them speaking above their station from time to time."

"Artistic appreciation shouldn't be limited only to the upper classes!" Lydia bristled, despite the fact that the sisters had seemed more interested in the artist than his work. "Especially considering that most artists are not of the nobility."

Miss Hobson gave her an impatient glance, clearly not in the mood to debate. "That may well be. Now it is time to get ready for Almack's. I hear the Marquess of Stantonbury will be attending. He is one of the most sought-after bachelors this Season..."

Lydia groaned. The marriage noose grew tighter every day.

Seventeen

VINCENT MADE HIS WAY UP THE WALKWAY TO HIS town house, eager to see Lydia. Between her painting lessons, dress fittings, and attending balls and musicales, he'd hardly had the opportunity to speak with her all week. Was she happy? Had any of her numerous suitors captured her interest yet? Miss Hobson hadn't noticed any sign of a budding *tendre* so far.

As he entered the drawing room and Aubert took his coat, he heard Angelica and Lydia laughing together in the yellow salon. He'd forgotten they were attending the opera tonight. So much for having a moment alone with her.

"My lord." Aubert's eyes were wide with a strange combination of excitement and uneasiness. "Viscount Bevin has just arrived. He wishes to speak with you in private. I, ah, placed him in the library."

Not another one. Dread burrowed in his gut. The first one had been a fortune hunter, easy to turn aside. The second had been old enough to be Lydia's father.

Viscount Bevin... Vincent couldn't place the fellow. He'd been introduced to so many knights, barons, viscounts, and earls that the names and faces were a tiresome blur. Aubert must not care for the man, or else he'd have allowed him to socialize with Lydia and the duchess while he waited.

"Thank you, Aubert. You may bring him to my study."

Ignoring the temptation to peek in on Lydia, he reluctantly trudged upstairs.

Pouring a glass of brandy, he sat at his desk and awaited the inevitable.

The young viscount bowed the moment he was admitted into Vincent's study. "Lord Deveril, I humbly request Miss Price's hand in marriage."

A red haze obscured Vincent's sight, blurring out the scrawny lad in front of him. His fangs throbbed with the need to tear the man's throat and drink down his life.

"My lord?" Viscount Bevin asked in a voice tinged with fear.

The dandy would do well to be afraid. Vincent took a deep breath and fought to keep his feral instincts under control. *This man is doing right by offering for Lydia. It is as I planned.* However, he could not bring himself to accept the offer immediately.

"The Season has just begun, and I would like my ward to enjoy a portion of it before she settles into wedlock." How easily those words came. The rest he had to force out. Swallowing the acrid taste in his mouth, he added, "However, I promise to consider your offer."

Briefly, a petulant frown crossed Bevin's countenance, and Vincent's fists clenched. Then the young lord bowed. "Thank you, my lord. May I call upon Miss Price tomorrow?"

I would rather you call on the devil. Vincent gritted his teeth and nodded.

"Forgive me for saying so, my lord." Bevin peered at him with wide eyes. "You do not look well."

"It is another of my headaches. Now if you will excuse me…" Vincent turned to the window, unable to bear the sight of him a moment longer. "Aubert will see you out."

The moment Bevin departed, Vincent slumped in his chair and buried his face in his hands. He hadn't expected Lydia to receive offers so quickly. More would be forthcoming, and he would have to accept one of them. Soon, she would be out of his life. He gazed at Lydia's painting of the sunrise. His heart clenched. It was probably the last gift he'd receive from her.

"Miss Hobson!" he bellowed, caring not a whit for propriety.

The chaperone arrived quickly. Doubtless, she'd been hovering right outside the door. "Yes, my lord?" she inquired levelly.

Vincent rubbed his temples. Perhaps a headache truly was on the way. "Lydia has received another offer for her hand."

Her eyes widened. "D-did you accept?"

"I told Lord Bevin I would consider it. For now, I wish for Miss Price to enjoy the Season a while longer." He looked back at Lydia's painting, avoiding Miss Hobson's hawklike gaze. "In the meantime, he may court her along with the other dandies who have been flocking here."

The chaperone sighed as if she were relieved. Was she

attached to Lydia as well? "That was wise of you. It gives the opportunity for better offers to come along without rejecting him out of hand. Viscount Bevin is of decent fortune and good character. However, I, for one, would like to see Lydia a countess…or perhaps even a duchess."

Vincent suppressed a growl and fought to press on with his responsibility. "It has occurred to me that I know little about anyone in Society, much less anything pertaining to her potential suitors. Could you perhaps edify me on the prospects?"

"Of course, my lord." Miss Hobson sat primly before his desk. "The biggest catches this Season are the Earl of Makepeace, the Marquess of Threshbury, Viscount Sheffield, and, of course, yourself."

"I am *not* a candidate." Vincent forced the words out.

Miss Hobson chuckled. "You'll have a difficult job convincing the *ton* otherwise."

"Please, do not remind me." Vincent sighed despondently in remembrance of the merciless pestering he'd endured from simpering girls and their avaricious mothers. "Tell me more about Makepeace."

Miss Hobson continued to smile. "He is forty-five, his income is twenty thousand per annum, and he sits a horse well."

"He is too old," Vincent declared. "What of Threshbury?"

The chaperone blinked. "Well, his title is certainly the highest, his income is twenty-three thousand, and he is only thirty-two."

Vincent frowned, though the information should please him. "He sounds like a paragon. Pray tell, does he have any faults?"

"Well, he does possess two mistresses. Such is common among gentlemen. Perhaps he will pension one off after he weds." Miss Hobson lost her cheery tone and avoided his gaze.

"I won't have Lydia wed to a lecher," he snapped. "What do you know of the viscount?"

Miss Hobson lifted her chin and replied with a hint of defiance. "He is twenty-three and fond of art. All accounts say he is a proper gentleman, and his income is more than acceptable at fifteen thousand. He and Miss Price seemed to get on well at her ball and at Almack's."

"He is too young," Vincent retorted. The conversation seemed to be like a snare, closing around him tighter with every word. "I am going to White's for a pint. This damn house reeks of flowers."

An odd smile crossed Miss Hobson's lips. Vincent paid little attention.

❧

Fists clenched in his pockets, Vincent entered White's gentlemen's club and spotted Ian at a table in the far corner, playing cards with Rafael Villar.

Holding back a reluctant sigh, he headed in their direction and paused, hearing his name whispered by a group of men gathered around the betting book. Ian shook his head and beckoned him over. Vincent continued on, wondering why he was a topic to be wagered upon.

The moment the men saw him approach, they scattered with sheepish grins.

"You don't want to see it." Ian strode forward. "It

will only vex you, and there's nothing you can do to stop it."

Ignoring him, Vincent read the latest wagers in White's betting book. "*Bloody* hell."

"I told you so," Ian remarked.

Vincent continued to turn back the pages, appalled at the scrutiny he and Lydia were receiving. The first few were about her presentation. Wagers that she'd trip over the train of her court gown, drop her headdress, et cetera. The next few wagers after her debut were more optimistic. Who would steal a kiss from her, who would get two dances…and finally, who would wed her. There were more bets listed than the offers he'd actually received, which meant even more were forthcoming. He should be pleased.

His stomach wouldn't stop churning.

There were the wagers about him as well. Which Society matron he would bed, which debutante he would court, what sort of evidence of his rumored madness he would display. And, of course, there was a wager that he would wed Miss Georgiana Price.

Vincent sighed, remembering how the silly chit had practically stalked him through Almack's assembly rooms as Lady Morley stared over her fan. Even a half-wit would realize she was forcing the poor girl on him. He had no idea what the dowager hoped to accomplish with this strategy.

"It appears you have become quite the catch," Ian noted drily.

"One would think rumors of my madness would be enough to dissuade them."

The duke chuckled. "Not with your title and wealth."

Vincent snorted and stalked back to their gaming table. Rafe looked up and continued to shuffle the cards with his one good hand. The action should have appeared freakish, but he handled the cards with such deft skill that it was like watching a work of art in motion.

As Ian took the cards, he fixed his piercing silver gaze on Vincent. "I understand that your ward has received more than one offer for her hand."

"Yes."

Rafe's eyes narrowed. "Then why have you not accepted one?"

Vincent suppressed the urge to tell the Spaniard to stay the hell out of his affairs. Yet Rafe would be taking Ian's position as interim Lord of London in less than a year, and had every right to be apprised of Vincent's situation with Lydia. "I want to ensure it is the right one."

Rafe's scowl deepened. "The longer she remains under your roof, the more dangerous it becomes for us all."

Vincent sipped his brandy and forced a bland tone. "I am well aware of that."

"I do not think you are." Rafe leaned forward and growled, "If she is not wed by the time I become Lord of this city, I will ban you from London and report you to the Elders."

Ian slammed down his cards. "That is enough, Rafe. I did not invite the Lord of Cornwall here to be browbeaten. I wanted only to verify the rumors of the offers for his ward's hand. The Season has barely begun. Vincent has plenty of time and good reason for making use of it."

Rafe continued to scowl at Vincent while he nodded. "That does not mean I approve of this dangerous charade."

Ian raised a brow. "You did not approve of my marriage to Angelica either."

Rafael made an impatient sound and lit a cigar. "If you don't get the girl married off soon, you'll have more to worry about than pithy human gossip."

The smoke in the club was suffocating. The walls seem to press in on him. Vincent rose from the table, not giving a damn if he seemed rude. "I need to look in on my people." Though the explanation sounded like an excuse, he was vindicated in that it was true. He wanted to make sure the Siddons sisters were staying away from Sir Thomas Lawrence.

Before they could respond, Vincent left the club, walking as quickly as possible without attracting notice from mortals. The moment he was out of view, he picked up speed. The London streets became a blur. To passing humans, he was a gust of wind.

He reveled in his preternatural speed, and a measure of tension eased from his muscles. Moving like lightning was one aspect of his existence that he truly enjoyed.

If only he could outrun his incessant desire for Lydia. And the gut-rending inevitability of her next marriage proposal. As much as he despised Rafe's insistence on haste, the Spaniard was right. A choice had to be made.

Eighteen

GOD, I MISS HIM SO MUCH! LYDIA'S HEART CLENCHED in despair. Vincent had not come home until after she went to bed the previous night. And this evening he had gone off for his walk before she'd cleaned up from her painting lesson, not even bothering to have supper.

Now, Viscount Sheffield was upstairs meeting with Vincent in his study, and there could be little doubt as to the purpose of his visit. Lydia fought the urge to cling to Angelica's hand as the minutes ticked by on the mantel clock.

"That's the fifth gentleman so far," Miss Hobson commented, her embroidery needle flying through the fabric with a vengeance, displaying her excitement. "Truly, it is becoming cruel of the earl to leave them dangling so."

Angelica darted an intent, unreadable look at the chaperone and opened her mouth to reply. Approaching footsteps halted her. All three women turned their heads to the door.

"You have received five offers now," Vincent

announced the moment he entered the blue salon. "Soon, you will have to settle upon one."

Lydia's heart felt as if it were being torn to pieces. *How can you be so cold about this? Why can't you see that I love you?*

Furious with the pain he caused her, she forced a cheery tone. "Viscount Sheffield is very kind. Perhaps I shall do more to encourage his suit."

Before she could gauge Vincent's reaction, Aubert appeared in the doorway. "My lord, Miss Georgiana Price is here...without a chaperone. She, ah, seems to be quite distraught."

Vincent heaved a sigh. "Show her in."

Miss Hobson raised a brow and whispered behind her fan, "This is Lady Morley's doing, I'd wager on it."

Lydia's gut knotted in panic. Was Georgiana making another move on Vincent? Would he be receptive? After all, many gentlemen seemed to prefer a damsel in distress. For the first time in her life, Lydia cursed her strength and self-sufficiency. Perhaps if she had been a little more delicate, then Vincent would have wanted her.

"My lord," Georgiana declared in a breathy sigh as she entered the room in a flurry of golden curls and frothy pink lace. "I am afraid I have become lost!"

"Yet you managed to find your way here," Angelica remarked drily.

Georgiana threw the duchess a panicked glance before dashing to a visibly baffled Vincent, reaching out a trembling hand to cling to his arm. "My lord, if you could please—" Her voice broke off in a piercing cry as she stumbled against him. "Oh! My ankle!"

Vincent caught her before she could fall.

Lydia choked at the sight of him holding her cousin. She'd thought Georgiana was sweet and frail, without a mercenary bone in her body. But Lydia could do nothing to protest. She had no claim on him, and he wanted her to marry someone else.

Angelica rose from her seat, ebony eyes smoldering. "That is quite enough of your theatrics, Miss Georgiana." She turned to Vincent. "Assist her to the sofa. Miss Hobson, fetch some ice from the icehouse for the young lady's injury. His lordship will show you the way."

Vincent and Angelica stared at each other as if having a silent argument. At last, Vincent nodded and bade Miss Hobson to follow him.

The moment they left the room, Angelica stalked over to the shaking Georgiana. "This display was badly contrived, Georgiana."

"Y-your Grace," Georgiana panted, cheeks flushed. "I don't know what you mean."

"You may dispense with the playacting," the duchess said sternly. "You cannot tell me that you had not heard of the events leading up to my marriage to the Duke of Burnrath only last year. For one thing, you could have displayed a measure of originality in your ploy. For another, the scheme would have been ineffective anyway, as this house is suitably chaperoned."

Georgiana gasped and flushed guiltily. "Your Grace, I was not—"

Angelica silenced her with a firm grasp on her shoulders. For a moment, Lydia feared the duchess would shake her cousin. Then, Angelica favored her with a cool smile. "Yes, Georgiana, I am well aware that the plot was contrived by Lady Morley."

The girl blinked vapidly. "How do you know?"

The duchess leaned forward. "The logic is obvious. The old bat hates Lydia and wants to see her ruined. I assume she believes that if Lord Deveril married you, he'd be under her thumb like you and the rest of your spineless family. If that happened, do you think Lydia's Season would continue?"

Georgiana shook her head, biting her lip.

Angelica's gaze suddenly turned slumberous and hypnotic. "You do not wish to wed Lord Deveril at all, do you?"

Not breaking her wide, fearful stare at the duchess, Georgiana shook her head briskly. "Not at all, Your Grace."

"You will cease your pursuit of Lord Deveril immediately, no matter how hard your grandmother presses you." Her gentle voice maintained a steely thread of command.

Lydia shivered. The small duchess seemed to possess an alien power, perfectly capable of bending others to her will.

"Yes, Your Grace," Georgiana replied in a numb voice.

Angelica smiled suddenly, and the veil of threat dissipated. "I am pleased to hear it."

Vincent and Miss Hobson returned with a dressing for Georgiana's ankle. Angelica set it on the sideboard. "We will not need this. Miss Georgiana is unhurt. It seems Lady Morley put her up to this nonsense as part of a feeble campaign to wring an offer of marriage from you."

Miss Hobson gasped, and Vincent stiffened, eyes wide in outrage.

"I am terribly sorry, my lord," Georgiana murmured weakly.

Vincent stalked closer. "Miss Georgiana, you may inform your grandmother that I am not in the market for a bride at all, not now, and not *ever*."

Lydia's heart bloomed with relief at his adamant declaration, even as she silently vowed to persuade him to change his mind as it applied to her.

"Well, what are we to do with her now?" Vincent asked, running an agitated hand through his hair.

Angelica rose to face him. "Do not worry, my lord. I will see Miss Georgiana home. Lydia may accompany me, since we were just on our way out to another literary circle."

"Perhaps I should attend as well." Miss Hobson's eyes narrowed.

The duchess shook her head, and her eerie gaze turned on the chaperone. "Someone respectable should remain behind in case someone comes to inquire after Miss Georgiana."

Vincent regarded Angelica sharply, as if there were some underlying tension between them. He sighed. "Very well, Your Grace. As it appears you have this situation under control, I shall depart." He favored her with a stiff bow before turning to Lydia.

Taking her hand in his, he brushed his lips across her knuckles, capturing her with his stormy gaze. "Stay out of mischief, Lydia."

She was about to argue, but she bit her tongue. "Yes, my lord."

"Well, that was quite diverting, was it not?" Angelica remarked cheerfully once the three women were settled in the Burnrath coach.

A helpless laugh burst from Lydia's lips, and Georgiana looked at both of them as if she'd never seen them before.

"Don't worry, Georgiana," Angelica soothed. "We bear you no ill will, do we, Lydia?"

Lydia faltered for a moment, seething at the memory of Georgiana in Vincent's arms, and finally nodded.

"It is not that, I fear," the delicate blonde whispered. "It is what my grandmother will do when she learns I've failed."

"I wouldn't worry." Lydia couldn't keep the bitterness from her voice. "You are her favorite grandchild...her *only* grandchild, actually, since she refuses to acknowledge me. She will set you on a more suitable gentleman in no time."

Georgiana blanched. "I am so very sorry, Lydia. I'd forgotten grandmother's cruel treatment of you. It was inconsiderate of me to prattle on so about my petty worries."

It was hard to remain angry with the girl. Lydia sighed and forced a smile. "I forgive you, Georgiana. Truly, I consider myself fortunate not to be under that woman's tyrannical thumb."

A small giggle escaped her cousin. "Oh, you cannot imagine." She stopped suddenly, as the driver announced their arrival at Morley House.

Even in the moonlight, the neoclassical behemoth was a blinding white jewel set upon a bed of meticulously manicured lawn and artfully trimmed topiary.

It seemed just as cold and unwelcoming as Lady Morley herself.

"Would you prefer to remain in the carriage, Lydia?" Angelica asked softly.

Lydia straightened her spine, fighting off the feeling of betrayal at the sight of the home she'd been barred from. "No, I believe it is time the old witch faced her prodigal grandchild."

"I agree," Georgiana stated with astonishing severity. "It would do her good to see us together."

Angelica grinned. "Brilliant! It is settled then."

The three linked arms and walked up the drive. They exchanged glances on the doorstep before Lydia nodded and grasped the bronze knocker.

A tired-looking butler answered the door. "Her ladyship is not receiving callers today," he informed them.

Angelica fixed him with an imperious stare, appearing every inch a duchess. "Please inform Lady Morley that the Duchess of Burnrath has returned Miss Georgiana."

"And who is the other young lady?" the butler inquired.

"This is Lady Morley's other granddaughter," Angelica replied with a note of challenge.

His brows drew together. "I am sorry, Your Grace. I am under strict orders that Miss Price is not to be received. I will escort Miss Georgiana to Lady Morley. Good night."

With an insultingly slight bow, the man escorted Georgiana inside and practically slammed the door in their faces.

Lydia turned to look back at the house. The turbaned

dowager's figure in the window was unmistakable, her eyes narrowed with unadulterated hatred.

"I swear," Angelica hissed through clenched teeth as they headed back to the carriage, "that woman has to be the most horrid person to walk the earth."

"I think she is a coward," Lydia said when they returned to the coach. "She knows she treated my father unfairly, and she can't face me because I'm a constant reminder of that fact."

Angelica smiled sadly. "You're probably correct and definitely wise beyond your years."

"Little good it has done me." Lydia could not conceal the bitterness from her voice.

The duchess eyed her sympathetically. "You poor thing, you've been through so much this week. First, with the marriage noose tightening around your neck, then your cousin's vulgar display with Lord Deveril, and finally being snubbed by your own grandmother."

Lydia raised a brow. "If you're trying to make me feel better, I'm afraid you're doing a poor job of it."

"Would you like to have an adventure?" Angelica whispered with such secretive enthusiasm, impossible to resist.

She blinked. "Of course I would. What do you have in mind?"

The duchess grinned mischievously. "Take down your hair and give me your pins."

Full of curiosity, Lydia complied. Angelica sat next to her on the plush seat and braided her hair, pinning it in a tight crown on her head, and then did the same with her own before the coach stopped at Burnrath House.

Once the footman escorted them into the house, Angelica took her hand, and they raced up the stairs to the duchess's bedchamber. An ornate mahogany wardrobe stood in the corner of the small room. Angelica threw it open and tossed Lydia a hat and various articles of clothing—men's clothing.

"The trousers may be too short. The boots ought to conceal the fact." Her voice echoed from the depths of the wardrobe.

"Where are we going?" Lydia could not hide her excitement as she tried on the hat.

Angelica set her disguise on her escritoire and began unfastening Lydia's gown. "We are going to see parts of the city forbidden to decent ladies such as ourselves."

The trousers were indeed too short, and the boots too large. Angelica stuffed the toes with handkerchiefs, and they were comfortable enough. The hat hid Lydia's hair perfectly, and her bosom was concealed by a thick woolen coat. The duchess allowed her one quick glance in the mirror before they crept outside, using the servant's entrance. She looked like a young man, ready to abandon his mother's apron strings and cavort about town.

"I can't believe you do this!" Lydia said as they walked down the cobblestoned street.

"Even a duchess needs freedom," Angelica replied, waving down a hackney coach. "Besides, it gives me inspiration for my writing. Where would you like to go?"

"I haven't the slightest idea." Lydia shook her head at the duchess's insatiable energy. "Other than I would prefer our destination to be somewhat…reckless, with a hint of danger."

"In this city, that hardly narrows our choices." Angelica grinned. "Cutthroats, thieves, and fallen women are a stone's throw in any direction."

A thought crossed Lydia's mind, and she held back a gasp at her own daring. "Do you recall that pugilist whom your husband sponsors? Rafael Villar?"

Angelica's eyes narrowed. "What about him?"

Lydia took a deep breath and fixed her with a firm gaze. "I would like to see him box."

The duchess was silent for the longest time. The horses' hoofs clattered as the coach rolled down the street. "Well, you are correct on that account. That would be most dangerous."

"So we will not go?" Lydia tried to keep the disappointment from her voice.

"Oh, we shall go," Angelica announced with an impish smile. "Only we must be careful that *Don* Villar does not see us."

Nineteen

IAN SIPPED HIS BRANDY AND FROWNED AS VINCENT narrated the incident with Georgiana. "This is very bad, my friend."

"Your wife handled the matter." Vincent shuffled the cards. "Though I cannot say I approved of her mesmerizing the girl in front of Lydia. At least I am certain Miss Georgiana will not pursue me again."

"But what scheme will Lady Morley attempt next?" Ian raised a brow. "And more important, how many other young ladies will employ less than savory methods in an attempt to trap you into marriage?"

Vincent's hand paused in dealing the cards. His shoulders slumped. "This endeavor is more complex than I'd anticipated."

The duke lowered his voice and leaned forward. "Yes, and it is growing more dangerous every night you remain here. You must see Miss Price married soon. Then you must return to Cornwall immediately afterward. You are drawing far too much attention."

"I know, and I told her the time has come for her

to choose among her suitors." His chest grew painfully tight at the words.

"Well, let us hope the man she chooses desires a brief engagement."

Vincent suppressed a growl. Ian was only speaking the truth.

The club manager approached their table with an envelope. "I beg your pardon, Your Grace, but there is a message for you."

Ian took the note and read it after the man departed. He let out a dry, humorless laugh. "That little imp," he muttered. "It seems Angelica has invited Lydia to share in one of her unladylike pursuits."

"And that would be?" Vincent raised a brow.

The duke sighed. "My wife enjoys gallivanting through less than savory parts of town disguised as a male."

"I can see Lydia taking to such an eccentric practice." Then the rest of Ian's words sank in. His eyes narrowed. "What do you mean, 'less than savory parts of town'? Where are they?"

"I mean that as we speak, they are at Scallywag John's, watching Rafe box."

The noise of the club dimmed to a furious buzz in Vincent's ears. He sucked in a breath and stared at Ian, appalled. "Do you mean to tell me that right now, my ward is in an underground club, surrounded by ruffians, gambling on an illegal prizefight—which the constable could break up at any time?"

Ian nodded. "Not to mention the fact that the crowd often becomes unruly after a particularly diverting match. Fisticuffs are guaranteed every night." He rose from his seat and beckoned a servant to fetch their coats and top hats. "I suppose we ought to go fetch them now, shall we?"

A haze of red encompassed Vincent's sight as he donned his coat. "How can you be so calm about this? Our women are in danger!"

"Nonsense." Ian chuckled. "Angelica is capable of defending herself. Also, Rafe won't let any physical harm come to them. However, I *am* concerned with the possibility of them being thrown into Newgate for breaking numerous laws just by being at that club."

The duke's words faded as Vincent strode out of White's, determined to snatch Lydia out of that hovel so fast her head would spin. He was just about to take off in a burst of preternatural speed when Ian clapped a hand on his shoulder.

"We must take a hackney."

"But—"

Ian waved off Vincent's protest. "For one thing, if a duke and an earl arrive without a coach, people will take notice. For another, you cannot use your speed to remove Lydia from the club without eliciting the same response. And it simply would not do to be seen walking back to our neighborhood with Miss Price slung over your shoulder like a sack of grain."

"Very well." Vincent inclined his head in grudging acknowledgment of Ian's logic.

The duke nodded and flagged down a coach. "And remember, we must treat them as young men. We cannot risk revealing their identities, or they truly will be in danger."

Although Ian's advice was sound, it became all the

more difficult to heed once they entered the bowels of the illegal boxing club. The jostling, shouts, and bellows of the rabid crowd, coupled with the pervasive odors of blood and sweat, fed the fires of Vincent's protective instincts. His gaze darted across the rickety building, searching for Lydia amidst the chaos.

Rage filled him with every step. How dare the duchess bring his ward to this dangerous place? A feral growl trickled out of his clenched teeth, making a man in front of him step away in alarm. If Lydia had so much as a scratch on her beautiful skin, he would—

There she was!

The Mark between them pulsed just as the faint scent of gardenias teased his nostrils. Although her lustrous black hair was hidden beneath a shabby cap, the set of her shoulders and her unique poise beneath her homespun jacket and trousers was unmistakable.

Lust, hot and immediate, rose up at the thought of the curve of her rounded backside. If that shabby jacket was lifted…

Only Ian's warning glance stopped him from hauling her into his arms. Vincent ground his teeth and remained still as Ian tapped his wife's shoulder. "Mr. Winthrop! I had heard you were here, old chap."

Angelica spun around, eyes wide in astonishment—and a measure of guilt at being caught. "Your Grace!" she exclaimed in a surprisingly boyish voice. "I…that is, we…"

"Are not where you are supposed to be?" Ian supplied in a helpful tone.

The duchess's gaze narrowed, and she turned around to glare at Rafe, who lounged near the edge of the ring, his match not yet due to commence. "You scoundrel! You tattled!"

At Angelica's shout, Lydia whipped around with a gasp, her eyes locking on Vincent's.

∾

Vincent kept his eyes on Lydia, freezing her in place with his stormy gaze as he addressed Angelica. "Who is your friend, ah, 'Mr. Winthrop'?" His voice was low, silky, and dangerous as he used the duchess's pen name.

Lydia struggled to find breath for a reply.

"This is my mate, Lyle." Angelica's cheery voice seemed oblivious to Vincent's rage. "I thought the lad could use some diversion to take his mind off a very stressful few weeks."

Lydia opened her mouth to warn Angelica to bite her tongue, before Ian stepped in, laughing. "I believe you and 'Lyle' have something to discuss with us in private."

The duchess grinned at her husband. "I imagine we do."

"Are you going to come quietly, or do I need to haul you out of here by the scruff of your neck like a recalcitrant schoolboy?" Vincent hissed at Lydia.

She looked to the duke and duchess for aid. They seemed amused by the earl's ire.

Lydia's fists clenched at her sides. She didn't want to go quietly to anything. Vincent seemed to sense her reluctance and seized her arm with bruising force, following the duke as he dragged Angelica from the despicable hovel. She glanced back at Rafael Villar, and he favored her with a smirk before his amber gaze flicked to Vincent, and he nodded as if in approval. Angelica had been right; he was a scoundrel! How had he been able to notify Ian and Vincent of their whereabouts?

A sodden bear of a man grabbed her. "Don't be a spoilsport, guv'nor. Let the lad stay."

Vincent's fist slammed into the man's face, dropping him like a stone. Lydia gasped. She had never seen him this angry. He appeared to be fully capable of dispatching everyone else in the club with little effort. *What did that bode for her?* The rest of the crowd parted like the Red Sea, and Lydia, along with Angelica, was pulled out of the building with no further incident.

The waiting coach crouched like a sinister beast in the shadows. Lydia tried to pull away.

"Struggle one more time, and I will throw you over my shoulder and haul you into the carriage myself," Vincent growled. His eyes glowed, looking feral in the moonlight.

She swallowed a protest and climbed inside, shivering at the feel of his hand on her back.

"Well, that was most diverting," Angelica said drily.

"To Burnrath House," the duke declared, ignoring his wife. He turned to Vincent. "As we do not want to risk your servants gossiping about your ward's attire, perhaps it would be wise for you both to spend the night with us."

"What of your servants?"

Ian shook his head. "I will ensure their discretion."

Vincent nodded, and the rest of the ride passed in tense silence.

Once at Burnrath House, he fixed his intent gaze

on Lydia, gripping her waist tightly as he lifted her from the carriage.

He remained silent until they were inside the house, then he leaned down, voice rough with command. "I want the smell of Cheapside washed from your flesh, and for you to be clothed as a woman before we speak again."

Overwhelmed by Vincent's harshness, Lydia shrugged out of her shabby frock coat. Angelica took Lydia's hand and squeezed it comfortingly. "I'll ring for a bath." Heading up the stairs, she called over her shoulder, "Come, Lydia, we must find a clean gown. Your walking dress is unsuitable for the hour, though I'm afraid everything I have will be too short…"

The duke bowed and gave Lydia a strange smile, as if he knew something she didn't. Vincent swept her with a heated stare, making her feel warm from head to toe. She gave him what she hoped was a coquettish smile.

"Meet me in the library when you are finished," he commanded before following the duke out of the room.

Lydia watched Vincent as he stalked away. Then, reaching for nonexistent skirts, she followed Angelica up the stairs and into her bedchamber.

The duchess had already thrown open an enormous mahogany wardrobe, revealing a sumptuous array of gowns. After a few minutes of rummaging, Angelica smiled in satisfaction, pulling out the most alluring gown Lydia had ever seen. "Lord Deveril wants you dressed as a woman. Well, he shall get what he asked for."

Lydia gasped, eyeing the scarlet taffeta creation. The bodice was scandalously low, and jet beads glimmered all over the fabric, making the dress shine like a dark ruby. "It's so…"

"Provocative? Indecent?" Angelica supplied helpfully. "You *want* him, do you not?"

Desire flooded Lydia's body at the question. *Oh yes*, she wanted him. So much that her desire was a constant ache between her thighs. Swallowing, she nodded.

"Then tonight may be your only opportunity. For one thing, you finally have a night without a chaperone. For another, he obviously does not have the temperament of a gentleman right now." Angelica looked around and lowered her voice. "Since your mother is gone, I think it is my duty to explain to you what goes on between men and women in the bedchamber."

Lydia raised a brow at the sudden shift in topic. "Are you referring to sexual intercourse? I am already aware of the mechanics behind that."

Angelica's eyes widened, and her cheeks turned crimson. "Do you mean you're not…"

"A virgin?" Lydia chuckled as she pulled off her woolen cap and yanked the pins from her hair. "Of course I am. My maid explained everything to me when I first became a woman. Then my mother explained it again before I attended my first ball in New Orleans."

"Bloody hell!" Angelica exclaimed. "You cannot fathom how much I envy you. My mother told me nothing."

Lydia gasped. "Do you mean you had no idea?"

Angelica shook her head with a rueful smile. "Not until my wedding night."

"Good God, why is it an English custom to keep women as ignorant as children?"

"I don't think this occurs only in England." Angelica held up the red dress. "Back to the matter at hand. Do you want Lord Deveril in that way?"

"Yes," Lydia stated firmly, though her knees weakened at the thought. "Even if it is only for tonight."

The duchess nodded. "Well, let us hope you will be more successful than that." She raised a finger to her lips as footsteps sounded on the stairs. "I'd better put this dress out of sight for now. Mustn't start any more gossip than necessary."

Yawning servants entered with steaming buckets of hot water, and poured it into a large bronze tub; then they withdrew discreetly at a sign from Angelica.

Angelica chuckled as she poured perfumed bath salts into the water. "Deveril looked as if he wanted to devour you."

"I want him to." Lydia removed her boots and unfastened her trousers, shivering as wicked fantasies flitted through her mind.

The duchess smiled knowingly. "When I'm finished with you, he won't be able to resist."

⤳

Ian frowned as he followed Angelica out of the house for their evening hunt. "Let me clarify this situation. You encouraged Miss Price to seduce Vincent?"

Angelica nodded cheerfully. Her steps were brisk on the cobblestone drive. "I am certain this is the best opportunity she will have. I loaned her my red dress."

From the widening of his eyes, it was apparent he

knew to which dress she was referring. "Good God, woman! Vincent's control is tenuous around Miss Price at best. That dress...he might ravage her!"

"I certainly hope so."

Ian raised a brow. "And did you stop in your scheming for a moment to consider that he has not fed tonight?"

"He won't hurt her." Angelica was confident. "He loves her. And you believe that too, or you would have stopped my 'scheming,' as you like to call it. I much prefer the term 'matchmaking.' That is, after all, part of my job."

Twenty

Vincent paced the Burnrath's library like a caged lion. The sight of Lydia's curves in those trousers, so boldly displayed when she'd removed her coat, had driven him to the brink of madness. He thanked the fates the duchess would be able to put her in a proper gown. The scent of gardenias heralded her approach. In a futile attempt to collect himself, he turned to face the fireplace. The dancing flames seemed to echo his raging desire…and blood thirst.

Damn it. He should have fed while she was bathing.

"I am here, my lord." Her voice was like rough velvet. "I hope my attire is pleasing."

"As long as you are out of those trousers, I do not care what—" He turned around, and the breath left his body.

Lydia had transformed into a dark temptress. Her hair tumbled in a midnight cascade past her shoulders, framing her exquisite face and tempting figure. Angelica had indeed dressed Lydia as a woman. Her selection surely was meant to torment him.

And it succeeded. Made of crimson taffeta beaded

with jet, the gown accentuated Lydia's lush body. The low, square-cut bodice exposed her breasts nearly to her nipples, serving up opulent flesh like a forbidden banquet. The shimmering fabric encased her trim waist and hugged her rounded hips tighter than the trousers had. Also, the gown was too short, revealing shapely ankles encased in sinfully decadent silk stockings. Apparently, the duchess had been unable to provide shoes, for Lydia's delicate toes teased him from beneath the thin material.

"Dear God," he breathed.

She stepped forward, closing the distance between them with seductive, graceful steps. The scent of her arousal was an intoxicating drug, taunting him to lay claim to what should be his. She moved until their bodies touched and she had to tilt her head back to meet his gaze.

"Do I look like a woman, my lord?" Her southern American drawl dripped over his senses like warm honey, filling his loins with hot desire.

Vincent wanted to pull her into his arms, grasp that tight bottom and bring her hips closer to his. Instead, he forced himself to grasp her upper arms, unable to push her away.

"Lydia," he ground out against clenched teeth, his body aching with the effort in holding back from ravaging her. "You do not know what you are doing."

"Yes," she whispered and reached up, her fingers gentle torture against his chest as she began to unbutton his shirt. "I do."

❧

Vincent's chest hypnotized Lydia with every inch that was revealed. Then his hands seized hers, stopping her efforts to undress him.

"Why are you doing this?" His voice was hoarse with desire. She recognized that now, for she heard the same need in her own.

Her reply echoed the same roughness. "I want you, Vincent."

"Lydia…" The word came out a tortured groan.

She could sympathize, for the hot pulsing between her thighs was sweet agony. Before he could refuse her, she took a deep breath and forced herself to confess it again, to lay bare her passion for him.

"*I want you.* Please, if only for this one night." Lydia stared deep into his intense blue eyes, begging him with her gaze as much as her words. "*Please*, before you make me go away." Boldly she arched her hips against him. "I want my first time to be with you, not some strange man whom I do not lo—"

She stumbled back as he released her hands, a cry of pain lodged in her throat at his impending rejection. Then his arm caught her about the waist, pulling her against him, and his other hand plunged into her hair.

"Damn it," he whispered before his lips came down upon hers with brutal force.

Her cry turned into a moan of pleasure as his tongue darted inside her mouth, entwining with hers in sweet rhapsody. He released his grip on her hair, and his hands slid down her body to grasp her hips.

Suddenly, he pulled her up so fast that she had to cling to his shoulders to avoid falling backward. Squeezing her hips tighter, he ground her pelvis against his. Another low moan escaped her as she felt his hardness pressing against her center. Lydia wanted more. She wanted, no, *needed* to feel him without any barriers.

He continued to torment her with his deep, spellbinding kisses, devouring her mouth like a man long starved. "We shouldn't be doing this," he whispered between kisses.

Lydia tangled her hand in his hair, reveling in its silken texture as she writhed against him, savoring the feel of his hardness. Vincent broke the kiss, and with a low growl, he buried his face against her neck, sending electric currents of ecstasy shooting through her as he licked and nibbled her skin. One hand held her securely as the other pulled up her skirt. The feel of his fingers toying with the top of her stocking made her want to scream in excitement.

"Please," she whimpered, reaching for the fastenings on his trousers. "Please, now!"

He stiffened in her arms and set her down. "No."

Her heart plummeted. Before she could protest, he spoke once more. "Not here. I cannot have you naked in the duke's library."

With that, he swept her back up in his arms and carried her from the room. Lydia sighed in delight and rubbed her cheek against his chest, inhaling his masculine scent of forbidden spices. "We shouldn't be doing this," he muttered once more.

He carried her through the dark corridor and to the bedchamber the duchess had assigned to Lydia. Instead of opening the door and carrying her over the threshold like the bride she wished to be, Vincent carefully lowered her to her feet.

"Is this truly what you want, Lydia?" His eyes seemed to glow in the darkness.

In answer, she swept her hand under his shirt, marveling at the feel of his heated bare flesh and pounding heart. "Yes, Vincent. I want it to be you." *And only you*, she added silently.

He towered over her, his gaze intent and predatory. "Say it again. Because if we enter this bedchamber, I do not know if I will be able to restrain myself should you change your mind." His voice was savage with deadly promise.

"*Yes.*" A hint of trepidation coated her whispered reply.

This was really happening. Vincent was going to make love to her. Suddenly, Lydia regretted her worldly attitude with the duchess when the subject was introduced. She'd heard the first time was painful. How painful? Would she disappoint him in her lack of experience? Perhaps she should have asked Angelica a few questions.

Her mind spun as he guided her inside the bedchamber. The sound of him locking the door was loud and final. There was no going back now.

Then his mouth was on hers once more, chasing away every vestige of foreboding with his soul-searing kiss. Only one button remained on his shirt, and Lydia snapped it off in her eagerness to touch him.

As the button clattered on the floor, Vincent broke the kiss and raised a brow. "Impatient, are we?"

Lydia nodded, captivated by the sight of him as he shrugged out of his shirt. His hard, lean muscles brought to mind a feral jungle cat. Tentatively, she reached out to touch the firm, ridged plane of his stomach. He stopped her.

"It is my turn now. Grasp the bedpost."

The rough command in his voice made her knees go weak, and her core became even wetter. With a shuddering breath, she obeyed.

In the mirror, she caught a glimpse of him looming over her like a dark archangel. His eyes glowed tempestuous blue-green, and his hair shone like a silvery nimbus in the lamplight. Then, he moved her hair over her shoulders, obscuring her vision with black sheaves.

Before Lydia could ask what he was doing, his lips caressed the back of her neck, sending shivers down her spine. "I need to see how to remove this gown."

Every touch of his long fingers felt like a naughty caress as he gently unlaced the back of her dress. Slowly, he lowered the garment, kissing every newly exposed inch of her skin.

When the dress fell into a pool at her feet, he sucked in a breath. "You're not wearing a chemise or petticoats. Only this..." His hands swept across the flimsy black corset, sliding down her bare hips, and then to the tops of her black silk stockings.

Lydia felt the heat of his stare on her bare bottom as he fingered her red garters. "Does it please you, my lord?"

"Oh yes," he growled into her neck. "Very much. And now I want to see all of you."

With roughness that stole her breath, he jerked the laces of the corset, freeing her from the encasing material in astonishing speed. Gently, he turned her around to face him.

"Beautiful," he whispered, his gaze deep enough to drown in. "So beautiful."

Vincent sank down on his knees as if in worship, though his intentions were far from reverent. As if asking for permission, his hands hovered inches in front of her breasts. Lydia leaned forward in assent, gasping at the rough sensation of his touch.

His eyes glittered up at her; his tongue darted out to lick his lips.

"I want to taste you...all over." And then his mouth was on her breast, kissing, nibbling, and sucking until Lydia was panting in mindless need. Her hard nipples throbbed.

He lifted her onto the bed, rising up to claim her lips once more. Lydia gasped at his delicious weight on her, the feel of his bare chest against her sensitized breasts. Her hips writhed beneath him, grinding herself against his hardness. It wasn't enough. She reached down to tug at his trousers. Vincent dragged his mouth from hers.

"Not yet." He licked her earlobe. "I said *all* over."

With languorous slowness, his lips trailed down her body, kissing her neck, her breasts, her belly. Lydia sucked in a breath as he progressed downward. *Was he...?* Then he unfastened her garter, sliding down her stocking to kiss her bare leg. She shuddered beneath him as he moved to give the other the same attention. Now she was completely naked.

Again Vincent's hands caressed her bare hips, then suddenly clamped down hard as his tongue plunged into her hot center.

Lydia cried out at the intense sensation and tried

to struggle. Vincent's grip was like steel. She had no choice but to submit to his erotic ministrations, squirming beneath him as his lips and tongue explored her female secrets. Her core pulsed. Electric heat flared through her body, obliterating her senses until she could only moan and plead helplessly for release.

"Vincent, please…" Lydia begged. She wanted him inside her, needed it. She needed to become his, if only for this night.

After what seemed an eternity of his sweet torture, Vincent pulled away to unfasten his trousers. In mute awe, she stared as his erection sprang free. Then, his body covered hers once more. This time, there were no barriers, and she could feel his hot, hard length against her.

His eyes were like the turbulent sea as he whispered against her lips. "You are mine."

The words weren't a question. "Yes."

With a growl of triumph, Vincent plunged inside her in one smooth thrust, swallowing Lydia's surprised gasp with his kiss. A momentary pain ebbed as his arms encircled her.

The world vanished, leaving only the two of them, now one. She could feel him trembling in her arms, keeping his strength in check, allowing her body to accommodate him. She could feel his heart pounding in tandem with hers.

Unbidden, her hips moved, finding a rhythm. Primal instinct took over, and her back arched in pleasure as he moved within her. The pleasure built and built, ascending into heights that would surely drive her to madness.

"Yes, Lydia," Vincent said roughly. "Let it come."

He thrust even deeper, and suddenly her universe exploded into particles of undulating light. With a feral growl, he bit her neck, shuddering in her arms as he reached his own climax. The sharp pain nearly brought her back to reality...then the feel of him pulsing inside her sent her back over the edge.

For the longest time, they lay silent and trembling in each other's arms. Gently, Vincent kissed the place on her throat where he had bitten her, as if in apology. Then he pushed himself up on his elbows and stared at her, tracing her cheek with his finger.

"My God," he whispered. It seemed he was going to say more, then he withdrew from her and rose from the bed to put his clothes back on.

Lydia wanted to beg him to remain with her, but she was too overwhelmed to speak. Mournfully, she watched him cover up his delicious body with his rumpled shirt and trousers.

The click of his boots on the wood floor was like a clock ticking away their final moments together.

"I will send Miss Hobson with the carriage to bring you home tomorrow afternoon." He came back to the bed and gazed at her once more, as if committing the sight of her to memory. His lips claimed hers with finality, rife with passion.

Lydia moaned in protest as he broke away. She failed to sway him.

"You should sleep now."

Her body obeyed his command. Against her will, her lids fell heavily as he walked out of the room. It was over.

Twenty-one

"DEAR GOD, WHAT HAVE I DONE?" VINCENT whispered to the empty London streets.

Not only had he allowed his own ward to seduce him, he had bitten her as well. Ah, but her blood had tasted so sweet, so potent. Once his fangs plunged into her delicate throat, it was all he could do to take only a little. And when their lovemaking finished, every cell of his being cried out to take her again and again. Vincent had to use every vestige of his will to hypnotize Lydia and walk out of that room.

"*Please, if only for this night,*" she had begged.

What a fool he had been to believe that such a thing would be possible. After this night, after having her in his arms, touching her and tasting her, there was no way Vincent could let her go. And absolutely no possibility that he could bear the thought of Lydia giving herself to another man.

A wandering cutpurse crossed Vincent's path. He seized his victim swiftly, feeding as quickly as possible. The blood was impotent and flavorless compared to Lydia's intoxicating nectar.

The feeding cleared his head enough for him to realize that he needed to take some time and seriously consider what to do with Lydia. She was no longer a virgin. He had ruined her.

Could he marry her, keep her for a few years? He frowned. It would only be a matter of time before she realized he didn't age. What then? He would have to leave her and watch over her covertly...and see her slowly grow older and die. And what if she discovered his secret? What if she learned what she'd taken to her bed?

Vincent cursed as further implications occurred to him. The Elders forbade mortals knowing of vampires. If Lydia knew the truth, they'd either order her to be killed or, possibly, Changed.

He closed his eyes and leaned against the wall of a vacant shop. For once, he allowed himself to picture Lydia as a vampire...spending eternity by her side. A selfish part of his being reveled at the prospect. However, Vincent's practical side intervened. Even if he had the permission of the Elders to Change Lydia, he would first have to tell her the truth, confess that he was a monster. And grant her the choice to become one.

And what then? Would she be frightened or overcome with revulsion? Or...what if she agreed, only to go mad shortly after the Change, like the Siddons sisters? Hell, such had very nearly been his fate. In either case, Vincent would lose her just as surely as if he continued with his original plan to marry her off. Only, in this case, she would end up despising him.

Vincent sighed and headed back to his town house.

He could not return to Lydia this night. His capacity to resist her had completely dissipated. His mind raced with thousands of potential outcomes.

Two facts stood out clearly in his mind. The first was that he loved Lydia. The second was that he'd ruined her. There was no other choice but to marry her.

His mind tamped down his heart's rejoicing. There were arrangements to be made.

Back at Vincent's town house, Lydia spent the entire next afternoon thinking. By nightfall, she had come to a decision. If she couldn't have Vincent, she would have no one. It would be better to remain a spinster than to live a lie married to someone else. She couldn't bear the thought of sharing a bed with another man while longing for Vincent. It wouldn't be fair to her husband, either. She rubbed the place on her neck where he had bitten her in their lovemaking, surprised that there was no bruising or redness. There had been a moment when she could have sworn his teeth had penetrated her skin. It was just as well, for she would have disgraced herself and her guardian if evidence of their transgression were visible.

When she heard the front door open and Vincent's footsteps on the stairs, she took a deep breath and gathered her will to confront him. Lydia opened the library door and slowly walked down the hall, mindful of the dull ache between her thighs from Vincent's lovemaking.

Miss Hobson's voice broke through the memory. "Lord Deveril, I need to speak with you."

Lydia ducked around the corner before the chaperone spotted her. Miss Hobson had been suspicious enough when she had brought her home from Burnrath House this morning. If she glimpsed Lydia's flushed face now, she might guess what had transpired last night.

"Very well," Vincent replied, sounding tired and irritated. *Had he slept as little as she had?* "Come to my study."

Miss Hobson's brisk steps sounded behind the earl's as she followed him down the opposite end of the hall. "I must admit, the night at Burnrath House must have done Miss Price some good. She was terribly pale after the, ah, incident with Miss Georgiana last evening, and today her color has improved."

Lydia bit back a laugh and crept closer, curious to hear Vincent's reply. The study door was closed, though she heard him cough in obvious discomfort.

"Ah, well, the duchess has taken her under her wing." A hint of sarcasm laced his tone. "Now what is it you wanted to discuss?"

Lydia quietly pressed her ear to the door, hearing the scrape of a chair and a rustle of petticoats as Miss Hobson sat.

"We have not yet had an opportunity to talk about Miss Georgiana's scandalous visit," the chaperone began in a scolding tone. "I believe Her Grace was correct in her speculation that Lady Morley contrived the whole thing." Her voice lowered. "I also believe the dowager is fully determined to win this competition. We must plan our next move."

Competition? Lydia sucked in a breath. *Surely she could not mean…*

"Yes, I have already considered that," Vincent said with painful indifference. "And I am reconsidering one of the possible suitors you had in mind." The cheery way in which he said the last was like a slap in the face.

Vincent was in a competition with Lady Morley. Lydia and Georgiana were merely game pieces. She'd been nothing but a pawn to him. That was why he was in such a hurry to marry her off to someone else. Lydia had heard enough. Searing pain tore through her heart as the universe collapsed around her.

Last night she had given herself to him, allowed him to use her! Agonized panic washed over her mind as she struggled to breathe. She needed to get out. Her chest tight, and eyes burning, she quietly made her way down the stairs, quickening her pace with every step while the walls seemed to close in on her.

Tears blinded her when she rushed past Aubert, nearly knocking him over as she charged out the front door into the pouring rain, breaking into a run. Her skirts tangled around her legs, tripping her. Lydia tumbled face-first into a mud puddle.

A tortured sob escaped her lips while she wiped the grime from her face and struggled to her feet. Hiking up the cumbersome, sodden fabric, Lydia wished she had kept the trousers Angelica had loaned her. She ran as if she could outrace the pain of her shattered heart.

❧

"My lord, are you saying that you will marry Lydia?" Miss Hobson asked with wide eyes as Vincent poured them each a glass of brandy.

"Good God, woman. One would think this was your goal all along." He shook his head and hid a smile at the chaperone's inappropriate enthusiasm for such a scandalous idea. "I am saying that I will consider it. There would be many difficulties if such a thing were to happen."

"Such as?" Miss Hobson arched her brow.

He leaned back in his chair with a sigh, deciding to be as truthful as possible. "For one thing, we would live out our lives in Cornwall. I cannot abide the city." Also, he could not encroach on another Lord Vampire's territory for much longer *or* leave his own land unsupervised.

"I do not see that as being much of an obstacle," Miss Hobson commented. "Miss Price seemed much happier in the country. I do believe she misses it."

Vincent took a deep drink before voicing one of his larger concerns. "I am also unable to give her children."

The chaperone gasped and turned an alarming shade of crimson. "Oh! I see…" Dismay filled her voice as she looked away.

He ran a hand through his hair as irritation roiled within. There was no way to explain that vampires were sterile, yet capable of lovemaking. Instead, he focused on the matter at hand. "I do not know how Lydia feels about motherhood. Either way, it will be painful for her when Society decides she is barren and mocks her for it."

Raw sympathy filled Miss Hobson's eyes. "Yes, they always blame the woman." She pursed her lips and took a small sip of her brandy. "People are already talking about the Duchess of Burnrath…" Her eyes widened and she obviously wondered if the duke was also impotent.

A knock on the door interrupted the awkward conversation. "My lord—"

"Not now, Aubert," Vincent snapped more harshly than he intended. He could not risk the servants learning that he was considering a match with Lydia. Unless he planned carefully, the gossip could ruin her.

Miss Hobson also saw the urgent need for discretion and dropped her voice to a whisper. "And how do you plan on ascertaining Lydia's opinions on... well, that concern?"

"I do not know." His jaw tightened in frustration. "I do not even know how to properly court her without the *ton* thinking I've been dallying with her all along."

"Yes, that would be a terrible shame, especially since you cannot dally," Miss Hobson mused aloud.

Vincent silenced her with a glare. "I had forgotten brandy makes you loquacious."

She flinched, chastened at his icy tone, and stood. "I apologize, my lord. Perhaps you should see what Aubert wanted, and I'll speak with Lydia and attempt to discern her feelings?"

"Yes, that shall do for now. In the meantime, would you see about having this delivered tomorrow morning?" He handed her an application for a special license.

Vincent knew Lydia's feelings. What he didn't know was whether they would change when she discovered he was a monster. Miss Hobson would be unable to help with that, yet it would be useful to see what she could glean as to other matters.

He rose and crossed the room to open the door for her, pride stinging at the false assumption that he was incapable of pleasuring a woman. *I pleasured Lydia last night*, he reminded himself. *And if fate is kind, I will pleasure her many more times.*

Vincent cursed as he discovered Aubert in the hallway, wringing his liver-spotted hands. "I would have thought you were too well trained to eavesdrop."

The butler held his ground. "It is Miss Price, my lord. She's run off. Nearly knocked me over on her way out the door, she did."

"Run off?" Vincent paused and allowed that information to sink in. Torrential rain pattered against the windows. "You mean on foot?"

"Yes, my lord. I daresay she appeared to be quite upset." Aubert blinked up at him. "I tried to inform you—"

Vincent was already out the front door, opening his Mark with Lydia. Her pain washed over him in agonizing waves, overwhelming him to the point that he was almost unable to sense her location. Guilt clawed at his conscience for how coldly he had left her last night, and his callousness in failing to greet her this evening. She must think the worst of him right now.

At last, he sensed her direction. She was to the southeast, nearing an unsavory district. He saw her slight form in the distance. *How had she gotten this far so quickly?* Vincent tensed his muscles to use his preternatural speed to catch up to her. Then a shadow caught his eye. Damn, there were other mortals about.

He quickened his pace, barely maintaining a normal human speed. Rain blurred his vision. The shadow moved closer to Lydia, and he growled. The hair on the back of his neck stood up as all of his instincts told him the other human was a threat.

Lydia continued wandering, too enveloped in sadness to notice her pursuer, who was rapidly closing in on her.

Vincent roared and darted forward, slipping on the muddy cobblestones. He recovered his footing. The man reached her an instant before he did. Lydia's shoulders tensed, and she turned around, eyes wide. She opened her mouth to scream.

Moonlight glinted on a knife blade just as it slit Lydia's throat.

Twenty-two

IN A BLUR OF SPEED, VINCENT BROKE THE ATTACKER'S neck and caught Lydia before she hit the ground. The scent of her blood was thick enough to drown him.

Vincent didn't hesitate. His mouth closed over the wound, drinking down her life force as it poured from her throat. He closed his eyes in pure bliss at her taste. Guilt panged him for enjoying it so much, yet he did not stop until Lydia's heartbeat slowed to a dull thrum.

Quickly, he bit his tongue and laved the knife wound, healing it with his blood.

"Forgive me, Lydia," he whispered. "I cannot let you go." With that, he lifted his wrist and tore his own flesh with his fangs.

Ignoring the pain, Vincent pressed the gaping wound to Lydia's mouth. At first she was unresponsive, and his chest constricted in agony.

"Drink, dearest one," he begged, pressing his wrist tighter to her lips. "Please, drink. Please live." Lydia trembled in his arms as her mouth latched onto his wound, throat working as she drank the dark magic from his veins. His heart surged in triumph as her hands reached up to grasp his arm. "Yes! That's it!"

He let her drink until white spots obscured his vision. Firmly, but gently, he extracted his wrist from her grip. "That's enough."

She whimpered for more before her eyelids fluttered shut and she went limp once more in his arms.

"Egad, what happened here?" a voice rang out.

Vincent stiffened as a drunkard stepped out of the fog, eyes wide as he took in the scene before him. With a dead man lying on the cobblestones and an unconscious woman in Vincent's arms, he could very well imagine what the man thought.

Vincent seized the man, freezing him with his gaze and willing his mind to be as comatose as Lydia's. With a whispered apology, he plunged his fangs into the man's throat and drank enough blood to recover most of his strength. Then he released his victim, erasing the memory of the experience.

As he lifted Lydia in his arms, he breathed a silent prayer of thanks. If it weren't for the man's blood, he doubted he'd have the strength to carry Lydia to safety. Vincent waited until the drunkard shambled out of sight before taking off in a burst of preternatural speed, grateful for the thickening fog.

At Burnrath House, the butler uttered a cry of horror at the sight of Lydia, comatose and covered in blood and mud. Vincent captured his gaze before the man could flee. "Burke, you will retire for the night. You will not remember this incident."

Hypnotized, Burke nodded like a puppet on strings. "Very good, my lord."

Vincent waited for the butler to walk away before entering the house. In the blink of an eye, the Duke of Burnrath stood before him.

Ian's eyes widened at the sight of Lydia's huddled form in Vincent's arms, then narrowed at the blood covering her dress. His nostrils flared at the scent, and Vincent growled in warning.

Respectfully, Ian stepped back. "What happened to her?"

"A man slit her throat." He shook in fury that he had allowed the bastard to get so close to Lydia...that he'd failed to protect her.

"Slit her throat," Ian repeated blankly, eyes roving over the unconscious woman. His eyes bulged as the implication became clear. "You *Changed* her! Without permission from the Elders? Bloody hell, they're going to—"

"I couldn't just let her die!" Vincent countered, unwilling yet to face the consequences of his actions. "Now, may I bring her inside, or do you want someone to see us and further complicate this situation?"

Ian opened his mouth, closed it, and nodded, eyes wide with worry.

The moment they entered the house, the duchess rushed up to them. "What happened to Lydia?" Angelica froze, and her jaw dropped as she sensed the truth. "You *Changed* her! Good Lord! Why—"

The duke cut her off. "He can explain later. Ready the red suite, and put the servants to sleep. I am going to secure Miss Price her first meal, and God help us all."

Vincent followed Angelica up the stairs, keeping

his mind focused on one thing. Lydia was alive. Her heartbeat pulsed against his chest, thawing his earlier icy terror. Everything else was insignificant in comparison.

"It's going to be all right, my love," he whispered as he laid her on the bed they had shared the previous night.

Lydia's lashes fluttered, and an agonized moan escaped her lips. Her golden eyes met his. "How could you?" she whispered. Her voice was weak and piercing with accusation.

Vincent's heart sank. It was as he had feared. She hated him.

～∽～

How could he use me and cast me aside? Lydia's heart clenched as a fresh spasm of betrayal tore through its depths. Her whole body ached as memories of Vincent's lovemaking flashed in her mind, punctuated with a piercing lash every time his conversation with Miss Hobson echoed in her head.

Another memory oozed into her consciousness, gripping her with nightmarish tentacles. *Walking in the dark London streets, throat tight…eyes burning with unshed tears, a dark shadow leaping from the fog, the burning slash of a knife…*

Her throat tightened with a silent scream, and a fresh spurt of agony contorted her body. Suddenly she realized her pain was a real, physical thing, gnawing at her like a ravenous wolf. Light infused the darkness with awareness as her eyes opened once more.

Vincent and Angelica stood over her, their faces

mirror images of worry. Lydia felt a pillow cradling her head and her hands clawing at the plush bedspread. A quick glance over the gas lamps and ornate furnishings verified that she was back at Burnrath House…in the same bed in which Vincent had made love to her last night. She frowned in confusion as she struggled to remember how she came to be here.

Another burst of pain drilled through her skull. This time, she screamed. Vincent's eyes filled with tender worry, and his fingers gently stroked her hair. "It will be all right, Lydia, I promise."

Momentarily forgetting his callous betrayal, Lydia seized his other hand. "It hurts!"

He squeezed her hand. "I know. The pain will end, I promise."

"It will," Angelica echoed sympathetically, lacing her fingers with Lydia's other hand.

At first, a measure of the pain dissipated as she clung to them, taking in their supportive presence like an elixir. Then, her skull seemed to explode as a fresh spurt of agony burst from her teeth. What had happened to her mouth?

"Almost over." Vincent's voice was steady and soothing, a lifeline amidst the chaos coursing through her body.

Wishing she could curl up in his lap and cry, she squeezed his hand with enough force to shatter his bones. "Vincent, what is happening to me?"

His blue eyes were an ocean of mixed emotions. One of them was pity. "You're *Changing*."

"Changing? What do you—" Lydia broke off as a new ache roared through her stomach. An alien hunger tormented her like the fires of hell. It felt as though she hadn't eaten in days. Her mouth filled with saliva as she craved fulfillment.

Footsteps echoed on the stairs moments before the door opened.

"How is she?" The duke's voice permeated the room, holding a new, yet familiar richness.

Before she could wonder about it, a tantalizing scent teased the air, coupled with a delicious, pulsing rhythm. Lydia licked her lips and made a small sound of longing.

"You are just in time," Vincent said, stroking her wrist with his thumb. "Lydia, close your eyes."

She obeyed, sighing as that exquisite smell came closer, filling her nostrils. Something soft pressed against her mouth, and a delicious liquid dripped onto her tongue. She needed no further prompting.

Instantly, the sweetest nectar filled her mouth, warding off her pain like a magic potion. Lydia released Vincent's and Angelica's hands and seized the soft object. Clinging to the source of divine nourishment, she drank down the substance as life infused her body. Greedily, she sucked on the softness, coaxing more invigorating liquid from its orifices.

"Lydia, that's enough," Vincent's voice prodded firmly.

She groaned in protest and sucked harder.

"No, Lydia!" he commanded. "You must stop now, or you'll never forgive yourself."

Heeding the urgency in his tone, she reluctantly tore her mouth away. With a satisfied sigh, she slowly opened her eyes to see what miracle had soothed her.

She held a woman's arm in her hands. Blood continued to trickle from a deep gash in the wrist. *Blood...* she had been drinking blood. Lydia choked on a horrified gasp, terror magnified when her stomach did not roil in disgust. Instead, it seemed to growl for more.

Slowly, her gaze moved up to the woman's face. The overly rouged cheeks and gaudy lip paint revealed her to be a prostitute. She stood over Lydia like a doll, eyes glazed and unaware. Mutely, she watched as Vincent gently eased the drab from her grasp. He raised a finger to his lips and pierced it with a long, white fang. Blood sprang to the puncture site, and he brushed it across the woman's wound.

Lydia stared in rapt fascination as the gash knitted together and faded to smooth, unblemished skin.

The duke took the woman's shoulders, guiding her away from Vincent as if she were a puppet. "You will remember nothing of this night, Maude." His eyes glowed like moonlight reflecting off a mirror. His fangs glistened as he spoke.

Angelica leaned over Lydia. "How are you feeling?" Her maternal smile was at odds with her sharp fangs.

Lydia's frantic gaze darted across the creatures surrounding her. With dreadful suspicion, she ran her tongue across her teeth, flinching in horror as she felt her own fangs.

Twenty-three

"VAMPIRES," LYDIA WHISPERED, HEART POUNDING with shock. "You all are vampires."

Vincent flinched as if it was an accusation.

"And you are now one as well," the duke cut in, voice reverberating with regret. "He did it to save your life." He eyed her sternly, as if daring her to protest.

She looked back at Vincent and swallowed a gasp at the intensity of his gaze. "I remember now." Her voice came out shaky. "A man attacked me...and cut me with a knife."

He nodded stiffly. "Angelica will explain the rest. I must go feed."

Feed...he needs to drink blood. Her gaze shifted to the dead-eyed harlot. *Just like I did.*

"And I need to see this woman safely home," Ian added, following her stare. "Do not worry, she will be all right and won't remember a thing." He reached into his pocket and pulled out a banknote. "She'll also be a hundred pounds richer."

A measure of guilt eased from her conscience. Vincent approached her, and she drowned in his deep gaze, every cell of her being silently begging for comfort in his embrace. Instead, he regarded her with a pitying look she was growing to despise.

"I'm so sorry, Lydia. If there'd been another way…" He shook his head and placed a chaste kiss on her forehead.

Despite her shock at the situation, warmth infused Lydia's body at his touch. She reached out for him, but he'd already turned away and followed the duke out the door.

Angelica plopped on the bed next to her. The vampire duchess patted her hand. "I do hope you are not too angry with him. He couldn't just let you die."

"Of course…" Lydia's breath halted as the reason for Vincent's behavior came clear. "That's why he did not want to marry me…and why he cannot go out during the day, and likely the explanation for all of his strange behaviors."

Angelica nodded patiently, trailing her finger across the embroidered coverlet. "And what of *my* strange behaviors, or my husband's?"

Lydia's eyes widened, and a bubble of hysterical laughter escaped her lips. "I had wondered why you and His Grace found that vampire play so amusing."

The duchess threw back her head and laughed. "We'll have to see it again now that you are apprised of the joke."

Lydia chuckled lightly, then frowned as reality once more intruded. "I do not understand why Vincent did not tell me."

Loki bounded into the room with a meow and pounced on the bed. He sniffed Lydia warily, turned his tail up, and hopped on Angelica's lap. *Cats know we are different.*

"Well, the prospect of you recoiling in terror would be one's first logical assumption," the duchess said drily, stroking the cat's midnight fur. "There's also the fact that it is against our laws for mortals to know of our kind."

Our kind. Lydia spoke her next revelation aloud. "Now I am no longer a mortal." Insane laughter threatened to escape. She'd spent the London Season surrounded by vampires and had been oblivious. The world spun on its axis. "What does that mean? What am I exactly?"

Angelica took her hand and squeezed it comfortingly. "You are a vampire. Like us, you will never age, and you now possess the strength of ten men. You can also run faster than the eye can see. It is quite diverting." Her eyes glittered with life. "And you may develop new powers, perhaps telepathy…or even flight."

"Can you fly?" Lydia asked in wonder.

"No, but *Ian* can." With a mischievous smile, Angelica pointed at a shoe lying on the carpet near the door. "Watch this."

Slowly, the shoe rose up in the air and floated toward them. The cat purred and watched impassively. Just as the shoe was about to reach the bed, it dropped suddenly, thudding on the carpet at Angelica's feet. The cat's ears twitched as if in disappointment.

"Not very impressive, I know, though it is quite an amusing trick at Lady Pemberly's séances." The duchess chuckled. "Power grows with age."

"What is the price of such power?" Lydia asked bitterly.

Angelica sighed. "Well, I'm certain you're aware that you must drink blood to survive. And you cannot go out in the day. The sun will burn you to cinders if you do."

A pang of despair struck Lydia at those words. No more idyllic days at the lake, with the sun on her back, casting her fishing line into sparkling water. And what about her painting? There would be no more sunrises.

Fighting back sadness, she focused on the matter at hand. "What else can destroy us?"

Angelica smiled in admiration for her courage. "Fire, extreme damage to the heart, and I suppose decapitation would do it. We can also starve to death, though I hear that could take decades, maybe even centuries for the old ones."

"Centuries?" Lydia's stomach tilted queasily.

"That's enough on such dreadful topics." The duchess picked up her cat and shifted off the bed. "Let's get you out of that filthy dress and go downstairs for a glass of wine while we await the gentlemen's return."

Once garbed in a light blue muslin gown, Lydia followed the duchess down the stairs, amazed at how bright everything was. The details of the gleaming wood furnishing, the damask wallpaper, and rich oil paintings stood out in stark relief as if it were daylight. The gas lamps on the main floor, however, were almost painfully bright.

"I know it's overwhelming," Angelica commented as she fetched a decanter from the sideboard. "You'll grow accustomed to your heightened senses, I promise."

Lydia wasn't so certain. The smell of the wine lay thick on her tongue, and her bare feet tingled as they sank into the plush Aubusson carpet. The smooth coolness of the glass was such a novelty that Lydia nearly dropped it. Her hand moved in a blur as she caught the stem between two fingers. Only two drops of crimson liquid flew out in hypnotic arcs to bead on the carpet. Lydia watched, transfixed as they slowly bled into the weave.

"Yet another reason I selected burgundy carpet." The duchess raised her glass in a toast. "To your new life, Lydia."

The clink of the glasses pealed like heavenly bells. And the wine, *good heavens*! Its full-bodied sweetness danced across her tongue, though it was like water compared to the blood she'd drunk earlier. The enormity of her situation pressed upon her like an iron shroud. Lydia sank into a nearby chair and took a deeper drink.

"Be careful, or you will get a dreadful bellyache," the duchess cautioned as Loki wended his way around her skirts.

Lydia blinked up at her. "Why?"

"We cannot digest food or drink very well." Angelica shook her head and took a miniscule sip. "Except for water. For some reason we can drink that by the bucketful."

More mysteries were now solved. "Ah, that is why you all eat like birds. I had thought it was an affectation of the aristocracy."

Angelica's laughter tinkled like chimes. "So that was why you tried to do the same. You made Lord

Deveril worry excessively when your appetite seemed to diminish."

The mention of Vincent made Lydia's breath catch. A thousand questions lodged in her throat. Before they could tumble from her lips, the front door opened, and she could feel his presence like a thundercloud over her heart. As multiple footsteps sounded on the wood floor, she could smell him, an intoxicating scent of stormy Cornish seas. She also smelled the duke's musky cologne…and something else, something exotic and spicy.

The duke entered the drawing room and gave her a respectful bow. Lydia had eyes only for Vincent as he came in behind His Grace. Impossibly, he was even more beautiful, moving in sinuous grace like a stalking panther. The strands of his hair gleamed in a thousand brilliant shades of gold and silver in the gaslight. His eyes glowed like forbidden jewels. And his skin, how could she not have realized before how perfect and luminous it was?

"How are you feeling, Lydia?" His voice rumbled within her being, touching places she'd thought unreachable.

Taking a shaking breath, she reached for his hand, gazing up into his fathomless blue eyes. "I am much better." She bit her lip, jumping in surprise as her new fangs grazed the tender flesh. "Thank you for saving my life."

Before Vincent could reply, another voice, heavily accented and full of venom, cut in. "You had better be grateful, *señorita*, for he may very well die for his actions."

Rafael Villar stepped out from behind Vincent's tall form. A bitter sneer puckered the scars on the left side of his face—scars that Lydia now knew came from the sun's deadly rays. The cat flattened his ears and hissed before bounding away. Villar scowled.

Then his words sank in. "What are you saying?" Lydia reeled from the Spaniard's words. Vincent could die because he Changed her?

The Spaniard arched a sardonic brow and shifted his piercing amber gaze to Angelica. "You have not informed her?"

Angelica lifted her chin imperiously. "She has only just been Changed. I assumed you would *all* be gentlemen and give Lydia some time to adjust to her new circumstances."

"There is little time for manners when one of our laws has been broken, Your Grace," Rafael said irritably.

A low growl rumbled in Lydia's throat at his hostility toward those she cared about. She bared her newly formed fangs.

The Spaniard laughed. "You think to challenge me, youngling?"

The duke coughed awkwardly. "We need to have a meeting and discuss this matter at once. I recommend you ladies find a comfortable means of diversion in the meantime."

"Bollocks!" Angelica's voice broke the air. "I shall be included in this meeting whether you like it or not."

"And I as well," Lydia added with a confidence she didn't feel.

"You cannot," three firm male voices echoed in unison.

"Your control is not sufficient to handle the severity of this discussion," the duke said without rancor.

Vincent nodded, expressionless. "I promise I'll inform you of our decision."

"Just as you've *informed* me of everything else?" Lydia's fists clenched at her sides as an unfamiliar fury threatened to overtake her. "I refuse to be subjected to any more secrets."

Angelica placed a gentle hand on her shoulder. "Unfortunately, they are right. Your control is weak, as you are still adjusting to the Change. Things could become unpleasant if you grow upset. That is why I shall attend this discussion. Lord Deveril may keep secrets from you. However, *I* shall not." She ignored the glares and mutters of protest from the men and gave Lydia a reassuring smile. "In the meantime, it would do you good to have some time alone. I recommend a walk through the rear garden. The lilacs are just beginning to bloom."

Lydia sighed in defeat at the duchess's logic. The way she'd growled at Rafe's unfamiliar scent and her primal urge to tear out his throat did indicate that an argumentative environment could cause her to go unhinged.

"Very well, though I insist on being apprised of everything when your meeting is concluded." She imitated a cool British clip and fixed them all with what she hoped was an intimidating stare.

Ian and Vincent bowed respectfully, while Rafael continued to scowl. Lydia made haste toward the French doors, then paused and growled at the intimidating Spaniard once more for good measure.

The cool night air sobered her. Her guardian was a vampire. She had fallen in love with a vampire. She had been kissed by a vampire… A vampire had made love to her. She knew she should feel revulsion, yet all she felt was aching desire for him to take her again.

Twenty-four

VINCENT LOOKED AROUND AT THE OTHER VAMPIRES gathered in Ian's study, attempting to gauge their emotions. These three were his only hope of ensuring Lydia's safety.

Angelica's eyes were filled with sympathetic worry. Vincent was confident he had an ally in her. However, Ian's brow was furrowed in disapproval. Would their longtime alliance and newly formed friendship be enough? Rafe's expression was openly hostile; Vincent hadn't expected any quarter there.

Rafe slammed his fist on the desk hard enough to make an ink blotter leap in the air. "You reckless fool. Do you realize what you've done? The Elders will have your heart on a platter for this!"

"Oh, Rafe, I had no idea you cared," Vincent replied sarcastically.

The Spaniard growled and leaned forward with deadly menace.

Ian held up a hand. "There is no sense in arguing. What is done is done." His voice held more than a hint of compassionate understanding as he cleared his throat and turned to Vincent. "You must file a report with the Elders immediately."

Vincent nodded, though his gut churned with dread at the prospect. "I am well aware of that, Your Grace."

Ian ran a hand through his hair and continued with a weary sigh. "There will most likely be an inquest, perhaps even a trial. I assure you that I will testify on your behalf."

"As will I," Angelica added fervently, placing her hand on his.

A strange yet pleasant warmth crept up Vincent's spine at their support. This was what friendship felt like. He had long since forgotten.

Rafe continued to glare as he leaned back in his chair and lit a cigar. "There will be no bias in my testimony. *I* will tell only the truth."

The duke raised a brow. "You will have to hear the truth before you can recite it." Turning to Vincent, he nodded. "Go on. Lord Deveril, explain what happened."

Narrowing his eyes against Rafe's cigar smoke, Vincent sighed and once again told his tale. "Lydia was upset and stormed out of the house. Just as I caught up to her, a thief slit her throat, so I had to Change her or she would have died. I couldn't let that happen."

"What became of the thief?" the Spaniard interrupted.

Vincent growled. Deadly fury sliced through him at the thought of the bastard who had nearly murdered Lydia. "I killed him." *Though I was too late to protect her.*

"You killed one mortal and Changed another on a public street?" Rafe laughed humorlessly. "The Elders will be delighted to hear that."

"I broke the blackguard's neck," Vincent countered.

"There is no evidence of a preternatural death. He's hardly the first cutthroat to turn up dead on the streets of London."

Ian nodded and fetched a quill and parchment. "You must include all of that in your report. We shall also keep up with the newspapers, and if there is no mention of anything out of the ordinary, we can hope the Elders will be satisfied in that regard."

"He broke the law," Rafe added stubbornly.

The duke ignored him. "Now we must figure out what to do with Miss Price. She needs to adjust to her new form, gain control of her abilities, and of course learn to hunt."

"Then there will be Society to contend with," Angelica put in. "There are flocks of suitors to deter. We must do so carefully, lest the gossip mill begin churning."

Vincent's stomach twisted further at that thought. All of his work to give Lydia a successful Season was now in shambles…and all of his hope to have her as his willing wife was likely dissolved to dust. He avoided the duchess's sympathetic gaze and dipped the quill in the inkwell, determined to get the loath-some chore of his report—or rather, confession—over with.

"There is one thing you could do to mitigate this problem," Ian said speculatively. "You could marry Miss Price. I am well aware that you are fond of her."

A spear of longing pierced his heart. "You're most likely correct. We have no choice but to announce an engagement." Not looking up from his parchment, Vincent uttered the bitter truth. "Though my fond-ness for Lydia doesn't matter. She hates me now."

Angelica let out a choking gasp. "Oh, Vincent, you can't possibly know that—"

He cut off her hopeful speculation. "Either way, it doesn't matter. As Rafe so practically reminded us, I may very well be executed soon."

Rafe blew out a cloud of smoke. "What do you plan to do with your unsanctioned youngling in the meantime?"

Vincent sighed. "For such an unconventional engagement to retain a shred of propriety, she cannot return home with me to my town house." *And Lydia will not take kindly to being under the same roof as the one who ruined her life.* He forced his mind back to practical matters and immediately regretted it as another thought came to him. "Oh hell, what am I going to do with Miss Hobson? And the damned painter?"

"Bloody hell," Ian ground out. Rising from his seat, he fetched a bottle of brandy from the sideboard and poured four glasses. "Damned if this doesn't call for a drink."

"Sack the chaperone," Rafe said blandly as he accepted his glass.

"He can't do that!" Angelica protested. "Miss Hobson is one of the most well-respected chaperones in the country, and you will have to keep her under your employ, or people will speculate the worst. We'll just have to devise a way to lessen her involvement with Lydia."

Vincent took a sip of the blessedly strong liquor. "Speaking of involvement, Your Grace, I humbly request that yours increases."

The duchess peered at him over the rim of her glass. "What do you mean?"

He eyed her severely. "I mean that aside from being Lydia's sponsor in Society, I would like for you to be her guide and mentor in her new life as a vampire."

Angelica's sharp gasp made even Rafe jump. "Do you mean you will not? As her Maker, *you* should be the one in charge of that task."

"What would be the point?" Vincent snapped. "I could be dead in mere weeks. Please, Your Grace, I can better face my fate if I know Lydia is in safe hands."

"The Elders may sentence *her* to death as well," Rafe remarked idly.

"That's enough, Rafe." Ian's eyes glowed deadly silver. "If Miss Price adjusts well to the Change and obeys our laws, there is every reason to believe that the Elders will allow her to live. She is innocent in this, after all."

The duke then turned his full authority on his wife. "Angelica Ashton, as your Lord, I command you to take charge of Lydia Price and instruct her in our ways until Lord Deveril's fate has been determined."

"And after that?" The duchess snatched Rafe's cigar from his grasp and drew deeply.

Rafe scowled and crushed it out when she handed it back.

Ian looked at Vincent while he addressed Angelica. "If he is sentenced to death, I am certain Vincent would prefer for Miss Price to remain in your care—as would I. If he lives, then he should take responsibility for her." Ian turned back to Angelica and Rafe. "I would have a word alone with Lord Deveril," he said formally. They exchanged glances and made themselves scarce.

With an awkwardness Vincent had not seen in him before, the regal duke shifted on his feet and shoved his hands into his pockets. "A little over ten years ago, one of my vampires Changed a mortal without permission. Following protocol, I immediately took him into my custody and reported him to the Elders. They commanded me to execute him…and I obeyed."

Vincent stared at him, horrified. "You've executed one of your own people? I'd thought the rogue who Changed Maria was the only one."

"Yes, I did. It was my duty as Lord, and you should thank God that you have not yet had to face such a loathsome responsibility." Ian ran a hand through his hair. "Let me assure you that the circumstances were far different from yours. From what I gathered from his Maker, Paul had not adapted well to the Change. Barely past his first century, he'd begun to display signs of madness. Then he came upon a woman, fell for her beauty, and Changed her, just like that."

Vincent shook his head at the thought. Madness, indeed. Perhaps not so unlike the Mad Deveril. "What happened to her?"

"Rosetta took well to the Change. She had no love for her Maker, which was no surprise, since she hardly knew him. Often she sought me out, starved for knowledge. In my report to the Elders, I requested that she be allowed to live and swear fealty to me. The request was granted. She became one of my finest vampires"—a strange smile played across the duke's lips—"although not the most obedient."

"And you executed the one who Changed her."

Vincent took a deep breath and plunged on with the next question. "How did you do it?"

Pained regret slashed across the duke's features. "I drank his blood to weaken him. Then I drugged him with laudanum so he would feel little pain." Ian paused, eyes distant in remembrance. His voice shook and resumed. "I drove a stake through his heart, chopped off his head, and burned him in the hottest fire I could build."

⤫

Lydia stood awestruck in the garden, captivated by the beauty of the night. Every detail stood out in exquisite relief, from each tiny blossom on the lilac bushes to every dew-covered blade of grass beneath her bare feet. Her fingers itched to paint this miracle before her. She could imagine mixing just the right shade of blue to render the velvet night sky above…

She stared at the moon, lips parted in rapt wonder. Its silver brilliance turned the garden into a world fit for a John Keats poem.

Inspired, she whispered,

> *"And haply the Queen-Moon is on her throne,*
> *Cluster'd around by all her starry Fays;*
> *But here there is no light,*
> *Save what from heaven is with the breezes blown*
> *Through verdurous glooms and winding mossy ways."*

Quiet footsteps glided on the soft grass, and a heady male scent teased her senses. Vincent's lyrical voice added music to the night.

"I cannot see what flowers are at my feet,
Nor what soft incense hangs upon the boughs.
But, in embalmed darkness, guess each sweet
Wherewith the Seasonable month endows
The grass, the thicket, and the fruit-tree wild;
White hawthorn, and the pastoral eglantine;
Fast fading violets cover'd up in leaves;
And mid-May's eldest child,
The coming musk-rose, full of dewy wine,
The murmurous haunt of flies on summer eves."

He came closer, flooding her awareness with his presence. "'Ode to a Nightingale,' yes?"

She nodded, too overwhelmed by his intoxicating presence to form words. The last time Vincent recited poetry had been the first time he'd kissed her.

Now, instead of claiming her mouth, his lips turned down in a concerned frown. "A melancholy poem. Are you feeling melancholy, Lydia?"

She shook her head. "No, I am only overwhelmed. Please, tell me what you and the others discussed. What is to become of me now?" *What is to become of us?*

"It is against the law to Change a mortal without permission from the Elders." His voice was calm, though every line of his body appeared to vibrate with tension.

Lydia swallowed, longing to touch him, to comfort him. "Who are the Elders?"

Vincent looked up at the moon, yet didn't seem to see it. "They are a council of twelve of the most powerful vampires in our world, who serve as our primary governing system. They make our laws and punish those who violate them."

Her heart froze in her breast as comprehension dawned. "And so you will be punished for Changing me?"

His head dipped in assent, avoiding her gaze. "I could be, if my report does not satisfy them."

"This is what Rafael spoke of." The chill in her heart spread through her body like hoarfrost. "Could you truly be sentenced to death for saving my life?" *Please, look at me!*

Vincent closed his eyes. "Yes. I've already arranged for you to be in the care of the duke and duchess. There is no safer place for you to be than under the protection of the Vampire Lord of London. Angelica will teach you all you need to know."

"You mean you will not teach me?" *Do you loathe the sight of me that much?*

He shook his head, oblivious to her bleeding heart. "I do not think it is best for you. Now I must go and see that your things are packed." He took a deep breath, his features twisted into an agonized mask of what looked like regret. "There is one more thing. In light of current circumstances, we shall have to become engaged, another reason you must reside at Burnrath House."

"*What?*" Her breath came out in a whoosh, chest tightening and stomach sinking with warring joy at the prospect of winning her heart's desire, and dread at his cold tone.

"For one thing, the secrets of our kind must be protected at all costs, so you can no longer carry on with your mortal suitors. An engagement should allay some unpleasant gossip amongst the *ton*, though not all. For another, if we marry, the Elders may be more inclined to show mercy."

A cold weight plummeted in her belly. He didn't want to marry her. She was a necessary obligation forced upon him for the sake of self-preservation. A burden. Guilt twisted through her being. She'd wanted him, but not like this.

Blinking back tears, she nodded stiffly. "I understand."

Vincent cleared his throat, voice rasping. "I know this is difficult for you as well. If things were different…"

Fear and desperation nearly brought her to her knees. Lydia grasped Vincent's arm before he could turn away. "Please, don't leave me!"

For a moment she thought he'd pull back; then his strong arms enfolded her, momentarily shielding her from the horrors of the world. Closing her eyes, she savored his embrace.

"I am so sorry, Lydia, for everything that has happened." His hands moved up to grasp her shoulders, and he forced her to look up at him. "Now, listen to me very carefully. It is of vital importance that you do everything the duke and duchess tell you. Promise me."

The intensity of his gaze and the painful way his fingers dug into her flesh revealed the severity of the matter. There was something he wasn't telling her; she knew it.

"I promise," she whispered shakily.

Vincent bent down until they were face-to-face. His eyes glowed like lightning, and his lips hovered inches from hers. A choking sound escaped him, and in a flash, he was gone.

Because of her, he was facing a death sentence. The weight of her remorse threatened to suffocate her. Lydia sank to her knees. "I've lost him." The words emerged in a broken sob.

❧

A single tear trailed down Vincent's cheek as he walked back to his town house. He couldn't do it. He couldn't tell Lydia that she might be put to death as well. Not when she had every reason to hate him for what he had done to her. Not when every cell of his being longed to fall to his knees and beg for her forgiveness. Not when, even now, he had to fight the urge to pull her into his arms and make love to her where she stood.

"*How could you?*" Her earlier words echoed in his mind.

Straightening his spine, he wiped his face and regained his composure. What was done was done. He had written his confession to the Elders, and Ian had already summoned a runner to dispatch it. All he could do was to await his fate and do his best to ensure Lydia's safety.

Just as expected, lanterns glowed from the windows of his town house, and Miss Hobson awaited him in the drawing room, hands twisting nervously in her lap.

"Where is Miss Price?" she asked sharply.

Vincent took a deep breath and forced a jubilant tone. "Miss Price shall stay at Burnrath House for the remainder of the Season, because it will not be proper to have my fiancée under my roof."

The chaperone's eyes grew wide as saucers. "You proposed already? How wonderful!"

"Indeed," Vincent said stiffly, struggling to hide his misery. "If you would be so kind as to have a notice printed in *The Times*, I would be much obliged."

Lydia had almost been his. Then cruel fate had snatched her from his grasp. Though he had a solid excuse to visit Burnrath House frequently to see her, to make sure she remained safe, it would be torture to pretend that his dreams were coming true.

"Will I be joining Miss Price at Burnrath House?" Miss Hobson pursed her lips as if sensing he wanted to refuse. "Things will appear out of sorts if I do not. And what shall we do about Sir Thomas Lawrence? He delivered her portrait shortly after you both stormed out of the house. Also, she has another lesson with him tomorrow. And we must plan an engagement ball, plan the wedding, have her dress and trousseau made, and—"

Vincent held back a curse. He hadn't considered any of these vexing details. The painter would be easy to handle, but Miss Hobson's presence would cause problems when Lydia's control was so tenuous. "I will decide what to do about Lawrence later. The duchess will be a sufficient chaperone for a few days while you plan the engagement ball and attend to all those other necessities. In the meantime, I'll meet with her suitors and reject their offers."

The chaperone nodded. "An excellent plan, my lord. It will appear much better for Miss Price's reputation if her suitors are deterred first and it becomes known that she is not residing under your roof. Much more honorable, in fact."

Turning away before she could see his pained grimace, Vincent headed for the door. "I must have a few of her things packed. The duchess's gowns will not fit Lydia well."

Miss Hobson halted him. "I almost forgot to offer my felicitations, my lord."

"Thank you." Vincent suppressed a sigh. The woman couldn't possibly know she was rubbing salt in an already throbbing wound.

Her cheery tone was enough to drive him mad. "I had the portrait placed in your study, by the way."

He strode out the door and closed it before she could say more. What were they going to do with Miss Hobson if the Elders summoned him to stand trial? He frowned as he headed up to his study. That would have to wait.

Vincent's breath caught as he beheld Lawrence's portrait of Lydia, already hung behind his desk. The painter had rendered her perfectly. A lump formed in his throat as he gazed upon the gleaming black tresses and sparkling tawny eyes that appeared to reflect the sunlight in the parlor. His eyes traced the line of her jaw, the curve of her lips, the flush of youthful mortality in her unblemished skin. God, he loved her.

What would happen to her if he was executed? He had no doubt that Ian and Angelica would look after her, but for how long would she be comfortable with such an arrangement? Lydia despised city life as much as he did.

He would draw up a will and leave her Castle Deveril. Remembering Lydia's love for the ancient fortress, he felt it only right that it should go to her.

Perhaps it could serve as an apology as well as a declaration of his love for her.

A measure of the crushing weight of despair lifted at the decision. He would meet with a solicitor tomorrow evening, right before he attended to the welcome task of rejecting Lydia's suitors. A slow smile crept to his lips as he left the room to collect Lydia's trunks. Oh, he would enjoy that chore very much indeed.

Twenty-five

LYDIA BIT DOWN ON HER FINGER WITH PRACTICED efficiency, wincing at the pain as she trailed her blood across her victim's wound.

"Very good," Angelica commented behind her. "I can't believe how neatly you made the puncture sites. It took me over a month to do it right. They heal so much more quickly that way. Now wake him up."

Lydia broke her hold on the man's mind. She could hear an audible snap in her skull.

Her victim blinked once and continued speaking as if nothing happened. "If ye take that road and turn left after the Hog's Head, that'll take ye straight to Great Pulteney Street."

"Thank you, sir." Lydia favored the man with a curtsy, struggling with guilt for using a stranger for a meal.

The man tipped his hat and went on his way, displaying no ill effects from losing a pint or two of blood.

Rafael Villar stepped out of the shadows, his ink-black hair shrouding him like a sinister shadow.

Approval gleamed in his amber eyes. "You have mastered the hunt quickly, youngling."

Lydia's jaw dropped. Taking a shaky breath, she gave him a friendly smile. "Thank you, Mr. Villar, you flatter me."

His angular lips curled into a sneer. Immediately, she knew she'd said the wrong thing.

"I never speak to *flatter*," Rafe nearly spat the word. "I speak only the truth."

This seemed to be higher praise. Friendliness seemed to repel him, so Lydia straightened her spine and inclined her head with cool regality.

The gesture seemed to satisfy him, for he nodded in return. "It is time we return."

The moment he turned away, Angelica gave her a wink. "*I think he likes you*," she mouthed so the other vampire could not hear.

Likes me? Lydia fought back an inelegant snort. For the past few nights, the Spaniard had been observing her progress and Angelica's teaching methods, because Ian decided it would be good to have an unbiased witness to provide testimony to the Elders if they decided to put Vincent on trial. Rafael seemed to despise everyone, so perhaps in a way he was unbiased. Either way, his critical gaze on every move she made compelled her to excel at her training, if only to spite him.

As Burnrath House came into view, her heart once more became heavy. The nightly hunts and training did much to distract her from Vincent's impending verdict from the Elders...and his distant manner.

To add salt to the wound, Miss Hobson had arrived only yesterday evening, with Emma in tow, practically glowing with giddy cheer. "Lord Deveril told me of your engagement. I am so pleased that you managed to land the biggest catch of the Season!"

Lydia forced a pained smile as the chaperone prattled on about wedding plans.

It had been agony to feign girlish enthusiasm in the face of the dreadful truth. A wedding was highly unlikely, even if Vincent had wanted to marry her. He could be dead in a matter of weeks. And if the Elders were merciful and allowed him to live, they might not allow her to return to Cornwall with him. She was a London vampire from the moment Vincent put her in Angelica's hands. Rafe had made that clear.

That also meant that once Rafe took over as Lord of London, he would be Lydia's master. Though he had been fair in his observations of her training, she couldn't help quavering in terror at the thought of being under the rule of such an ill-tempered man.

With leaden steps, she followed the Spaniard and the duchess into the house. Only days ago Lydia would have been ecstatic at the prospect of planning her wedding to Vincent. Now she felt only an echoing chord of dread intermingled with guilt at trapping the man she loved.

The butler took their coats and turned to Angelica with a cough. "A Miss Sally and Miss Maria Sidwell are here. They claim to have an appointment for a dress fitting for Miss Price, though I was uninformed of the fact. I placed them in the parlor."

Angelica and Rafe exchanged a pointed look. He scowled, and she shook her head. "Thank you, Burke. Come along, Lydia."

"Deveril will hear of this appointment," Rafe grumbled and stalked up the stairs to Ian's study.

Puzzled, Lydia followed Angelica. What were her dressmakers doing here? She didn't have a dress fitting scheduled until Wednesday.

Once they entered the parlor, everything became clear. The seamstresses grinned at her, revealing their fangs.

"Oh, my God," Lydia gasped. "That is why you only did my fittings at night. Is everyone around me a vampire?"

Maria nodded. "Yes, and when we heard that Lord Deveril Changed you, we had to come right away and see how you are faring."

"We read the engagement announcement in *The Times* as well," Sally added. "We are so happy for you! Deveril is a good Lord Vampire. We'll have to make you a wedding gown worthy of him."

"Thank you." Lydia's stomach churned in despair, more from their felicitations than from anyone else's. They had been with her almost since she arrived in Cornwall and had been the first to learn of her infatuation with Vincent. Which made the fact that he was marrying her against his will all the more agonizing.

Maria seemed to sense her reluctance and changed the subject. "How are you enduring the Change? I imagine with Deveril's blood in your veins you are quite powerful. How long can you keep a mortal under your spell?"

Lydia frowned, suspecting the question was more important than it seemed. "I'm not certain. I've held them only long enough to take sustenance. Angelica, I mean, Her Grace, is much better at that sort of thing.

She used the trick on Miss Hobson and my cousin to brilliant advantage."

The sisters scrutinized her intently before exchanging glances.

"Then we must beg a favor of Her Grace," Maria declared, sinking into a respectful curtsy.

Angelica eyed them curiously. "What would that be?"

"We want to see our mother."

"I see."

Sally approached the duchess, lower lip trembling. "Please, Your Grace, we haven't seen her since your husband sent us away from London, and now that she's retired from the stage, who knows how much time she has left?"

"Did you consider that I could be in trouble with my husband if I agreed?"

"Yes, but from what we understand, you are not averse to trouble."

Angelica regarded them with an impish smile. "Yes, that is true. And I would so much like to meet the renowned Sarah Siddons."

Sarah Siddons...Sally and Maria Siddons... Lydia burst into laughter. There had been something to her suspicions after all. "*Sidwell?* Good heavens, Vincent could have come up with something better. No wonder you were so interested in Sir Thomas Lawrence."

Angelica chuckled. "So you've deduced who they really are."

"Yes, and this explains the painting of Sally at the Royal Academy." She turned to Sally. "Tell me, what happened between you and Sir Thomas? Vincent said the tale was not fit for a young lady's ears."

Maria nodded. "Deveril was correct on that account. Thomas, the cad, wooed my sister, then took advantage of my naïveté and betrayed her to court me, even going so far as to gain our father's permission for my hand in marriage. Then, the moment I became ill with consumption, he forsook me and tried to regain Sally's affections."

"Bloody hell, that's terrible!" Angelica gasped.

Sally spoke up. "He tormented our poor, dear mother, and harassed her friends in a futile attempt to win my heart, even going so far as to threaten suicide if she did not relent and allow him to see me." Her eyes welled with unshed tears. "He was a complete madman. His insane behavior only worsened Maria's suffering, when all I wanted was to nurse my sister back to health." Her words broke off with a choked, pained sound. "All we ever wanted was to be together. Our mother, Lawrence, and our own poor health seemed determined to keep us apart."

Lydia shook her head. "How could he do such a terrible thing? And with Maria so ill?"

Maria picked up the tale. "Things became even worse. When I was ill, I had time to think, and realized that Lawrence had broken my sister's heart when he abandoned her to court me. Even worse, when he defected to Sally, his behavior fractured our family, damaged our reputations, and caused unbearable torment to our mother." She took a shuddering breath. "When I realized I was dying, I prayed for justice. My prayers were answered when I met a vampire in the garden one night. He'd been watching me and Sally for years. He loved my singing and the songs Sally composed on her pianoforte. When I was dying, he offered me eternal life. I took it, and while feigning death, made Sally promise not to marry Lawrence. It took three years before I was able to find another vampire to Change her."

Sally took Maria's hand. "So we could be together, always. It was the happiest moment of my life when I discovered that my dear sister was not dead."

"Why couldn't *you* Change her?" Lydia asked Maria.

"It takes about a century for a vampire to build the power to do so," Angelica explained. "And another century to recover."

Lydia's chest tightened. "Do you mean that Vincent squandered a hundred years' worth of power to save my life?" *How he must loathe me.*

"I wouldn't say 'squandered,' but yes." Turning back to the sisters, Angelica asked, "Who Changed you, and why were you sent away from London? My husband never told me."

Maria flushed. "We were both Changed by rogues. The Lord of London caught us when we were trying to exact vengeance on Lawrence. He arrested us and executed John. Philip escaped."

"We didn't know it was illegal!" Sally added quickly.

Angelica paled. "I had no idea my husband executed someone."

"He was only doing his duty. You cannot blame him for that," Maria said gently. "Besides, he was merciful enough to allow us to live, and sent us to Cornwall."

"W-will Ian have to execute Vincent for Changing me?" Lydia asked through numb lips.

Angelica shook her head briskly. "No, as Vincent

is a Lord Vampire and not a rogue, that responsibility would fall to the Elders." She placed a reassuring hand on Lydia's shoulder and turned to the Siddons sisters. "Enough of this dreary talk. I will take you to see your mother soon. However, you must promise to stay away from Lawrence. If you approach him, I cannot protect you from the wrath of either my husband or the Lord of Cornwall."

Sally and Maria inclined their heads in agreement. "We promise."

Lydia only half listened as the vampires made plans to visit Sarah Siddons. After hearing Sally's and Maria's stories, the possibility of Vincent being executed for Changing her was more plausible.

"I'm afraid you must depart now," Angelica told the dressmakers abruptly. "Miss Hobson has returned, and Lawrence will be here soon for Lydia's painting lesson. We cannot have your presence raise unnecessary questions."

"May we at least catch a glimpse of him?" Maria implored sweetly, though steel glinted in her gaze.

The duchess looked as if she were about to refuse, but then she nodded. "Very well. However, I shall remain with you the entire time."

Lydia realized Angelica agreed only to ensure the pair would not disobey and seek out the man on their own. "I must mix my paints."

Ian had transformed an upstairs chamber into a painting studio for her, with four large gas lamps to brighten the room. Lydia had her palette prepared and Miss Hobson settled into her chair in the corner just as Lawrence arrived.

Lydia regarded the man whom she had once worshipped. How could he have treated so many ladies so poorly? She knew she should despise him, yet he was still the finest painter she'd ever known, and she couldn't stop respecting his work.

Vincent had convinced Lawrence to resume her lessons during the evenings, which Rafe declared was a good exercise in control. He had been correct. The first two nights, her fangs chafed her gums as she resisted the urge to bite the poor man.

Now that she knew of his abominable treatment of the Siddons sisters, the urge returned, stronger than before.

As if somehow sensing the danger he was in, Lawrence was solicitous and praising of her progress. "I cannot believe how quickly your skills have improved," he told her as he peered at her nearly finished portrait of Vincent. "Truly, you do not need to study at the Academy, for you have already surpassed most of the students."

His sugary tone slew her patience. What false flattery had he used on Sally and Maria?

"I am not going to be admitted, am I?" Not that she could anymore, with the necessity of her nocturnal schedule.

He blinked, startled at her bluntness. "It grieves my soul to tell you that I spoke with the officials, and they declined your worthy petition to join our school." Patting her hand, he gave her an indulgent smile. "It is all for the best, as you will be far too occupied with your upcoming nuptials."

"Lord Deveril would allow me to go to school if that is what I desire." Lydia suddenly realized the truth of her words. Vincent had denied her nothing, except his heart.

Oblivious to her revelation, Lawrence nodded placidly. "Then he is a good man. In that sentiment, I can offer you a compromise. Though you cannot join the Academy, you may be able to have some of your paintings featured in the Royal Exhibition."

The breath whooshed from her body. The Royal Exhibition? Surely she hadn't heard him correctly. "I beg your pardon?"

Lawrence grinned. "I said that I could have your work featured in the Royal Exhibition."

"I would be honored!" This was nearly better than joining the Academy, for only a select few students garnered this opportunity.

"There is, however, one condition."

Of course there was. She concealed her disappointment. "And what would that be?"

"Due to the time I've spent on your portrait and your lessons, I'm afraid I've fallen behind on a few of my own commissions for my patrons, as well as for the Exhibition. As president of the Academy, it simply would not do for me to have nothing to show for this sacred event."

Lydia couldn't hide her suspicion. "What does that have to do with me?"

Lawrence gave her a sheepish look. "From time to time I allow my students to apply the finishing touches on my works. Given your astounding skill and speed, perhaps you could finish, say…five of my paintings?"

"Three." Her spite at his treatment of the Siddons sisters and her denial of studying at the Academy compelled her to be merciless.

"A shrewd bargain. Very well, three. I shall bring what I have tomorrow evening."

After he left, Lydia slumped in a chair, dazed. Laughter bubbled from her lips.

Miss Hobson raised a brow. "Are you quite all right, Miss Price?"

"He doesn't even finish his own paintings!" The shock and scorn for yet another transgression her hero had committed warred with elation at the prospect of taking part in creating another Lawrence portrait.

The chaperone smirked. "Yes, well he is a very busy man. Still, that seems less than honest to me."

"At least I will be able to participate in the Royal Exhibition." Joy at grasping one of her deepest dreams surpassed her disillusionment with her idol.

Lydia couldn't wait to tell Vincent about it. Her chest ached as she thought of the easy camaraderie they had known in Cornwall. Although he visited the house every night without fail to assess her progress, emotionally, he seemed farther away than ever.

Twenty-six

VINCENT FOLDED HIS ARMS TIGHTLY AGAINST HIS EVE-
ning coat as he walked to Burnrath House, chilled
despite the warm spring evening. The envelope
containing the missive from the Elders felt like a lead
weight in his pocket. What crime had he committed
to have the fates cause everything to go so terribly
wrong? He'd had Lydia's affection; he'd been certain
of it. Perhaps she would have become a vampire will-
ingly, pleased to spend an eternity at his side.

Eternity. The concept had been his downfall. After
centuries of existence, Vincent had been confident
that he had sufficient time to court Lydia and offer her
his heart and immortality. Not for a moment had he
considered that she did not have the same luxury, that
death could snatch her from his arms at a whim.

Due to his foolish arrogance, her mortality, as well
as his, had crashed down upon them both in one
sound blow. The irony was thick enough to choke
on. Lydia now had the possibility of centuries, while
he likely had mere weeks to live.

Burke greeted him with a bow and took his hat and

coat. "His Grace is expecting you in the study, my lord, along with Mr. Adair."

Vincent felt a small measure of comfort that his summons had been responded to so quickly. "Thank you, Burke."

Ian awaited him in the study, along with Rafe and Emrys. Vincent's second regarded him sympathetically.

"Emrys, thank you for arriving on such short notice." Vincent clapped his second in command on the shoulder. "How fare the blood drinkers of Cornwall?"

His second bowed. "They are all safe and in good health, my lord." He frowned. "Though all of us are dismayed to hear of your predicament."

Vincent straightened his spine. "I did what I felt was necessary."

"I would not expect otherwise, my lord." Emrys nodded in understanding tinged with regret. "Which is why I came as soon as I could. A representative from the Elders has written me. She will be coming to Cornwall in a few weeks to question us on your character and leadership."

Ian snorted behind them. "Well, that is certainly thorough of them."

Emrys inclined his head respectfully toward the Lord of London before turning back to Vincent. "I wanted to assure you that your people stand behind you, and if there is a trial, I am willing to follow you to Amsterdam myself to testify on your behalf."

Rafe chuckled and lit a cigar. "So no insurrections are being planned in Cornwall, then?"

Emrys glared at the Spaniard. "We are loyal to our Lord."

As the seconds continued to stare each other down, Vincent shook his head. Why did the Spaniard insist on being so damn difficult? He turned back to his second. "I need you to remain in Cornwall and watch over my people until this ordeal is over."

Emrys nodded. Rafe smoked his cigar in silence.

Vincent took a deep breath, fixing his second with an intent gaze before asking the dreaded but necessary question. "Emrys, if I am put to death, are you willing to take my place as Lord of Cornwall?"

Ever formal, Emrys dropped to one knee as if accepting a knighthood. "I am, and I vow to strive to look after our people as well as you have."

"I shall express my recommendation to the Elders when they make their decision." Vincent paused at the sound of footsteps and hushed feminine voices approaching.

The scent of gardenias teased his senses when the study door opened to reveal Lydia and Angelica. Both were dressed in male attire, and Vincent sucked in a breath at the agonizing temptation of the sight of Lydia's curved hips and long legs. What mischief had they been up to?

"What is going on here?" the duchess asked, practically quivering with curiosity.

Ian regarded his wife solemnly. "We are meeting with Vincent's second in command, Emrys Adair."

Emrys bowed once more. "Your Grace." He then turned his attention to Lydia, his eyes filled with admiration.

"Lord Deveril's unsanctioned fledgling, Miss Lydia Price," Rafe supplied, blowing out a cloud of smoke.

"Miss Price." Emrys took Lydia's hand and brushed his lips across her knuckles as Vincent fought the urge to kill him. "It is an honor."

Rafe blew a smoke ring and looked on Vincent's ire with amusement.

"We were just finishing." Ian eyed Angelica sternly. "We will join you ladies shortly."

Rafe and Vincent tensed and exchanged glances. Ian's wife did not respond well to commands.

Angelica inclined her head in assent, though the glint in her dark eyes radiated impatience and curiosity. "Very well, we shall see you in the drawing room anon. Come, Lydia."

When the females left, Emrys turned wide eyes to Vincent. "Good heavens, she is exquisite! Once the Elders set eyes upon your fledgling, surely they will understand and show mercy."

Rafe snorted. "If comeliness were justification for violating the law, the world would be overrun with vampires." He added, "On a more practical note, Miss Price has adapted to her new life with astonishing speed and courage. This could prove beneficial to Lord Deveril's case."

Vincent searched the Spaniard's face for a hint of sarcasm and found none. It seemed Lydia had earned Rafe's respect...and perhaps Vincent had as well.

Ian cleared his throat. "Shall we adjourn this meeting?"

Rafe and Vincent nodded.

"I should be getting back to Cornwall." Emrys squared his shoulders and gave Vincent a sympathetic gaze. "I will pray that all goes well for you, my lord."

Vincent closed his eyes. "If God even listens to the prayers of monsters."

～

With identical expressions of solemn dread on their faces, Ian and Vincent joined Lydia and Angelica in the drawing room.

"I received a letter from the Elders," Vincent announced without preamble. His voice was empty and as soulless as a death knell.

"What did they say?" Lydia's knees quaked. How she longed to seek solace in his arms.

He closed his eyes, but not before she glimpsed an answering flicker of fear in his gaze. "I am to be investigated. One of the Elders will arrive on the third of May to question me and observe you."

"But, that's so soon!" she protested. *Less than a month before the man I love could be dead*. It wasn't fair.

Vincent continued as if he did not hear her. "I am to prepare my testimony and gather any witnesses willing to testify in my defense."

"That would be everyone in this room." Ian's brows drew together in sympathy. "I am afraid your reclusive ways have not done you good in this case."

Rafael fixed Lydia with an intent stare. "They will also evaluate you, youngling. So you had best impress them with your adaptation to our ways, or else—"

Vincent slammed his fist on the mahogany table. The sound echoed like a gunshot. "We will discuss that later. It is time for us to prepare for the Wentworth ball."

"A ball?" Lydia choked out. "How can we consider

going to a party at a time like this?" All she wanted to do was take Vincent's hand and flee.

Angelica spoke at last. "We cannot handle problems with Society, in addition to this situation. If you don't appear before them triumphant and acknowledge the felicitations for your engagement, people will speculate the worst. And if scandal is attached to your name, the Elders will learn of it, and that will not bode well for Vincent's case."

"Damn it," Lydia muttered. If she hadn't before had a reason to loathe being a debutante, she now possessed them in abundance.

The duchess screwed her face into a mock expression of pious disapproval. "A lady does not use such language," she said in an eerie imitation of Miss Hobson.

"Double *damn it*!"

Soft laughter echoed around her, lessening the pall hanging over the room. Lydia swore Rafe even cracked a smile.

"Speaking of Miss Hobson, you had better wake her up, along with Emma," Angelica told her husband before taking Lydia's hand to lead her up to the bedchamber.

Lydia glanced over her shoulder at Vincent. He had turned away once more. Rafe's amber gaze glittered enigmatically, and she jerked her face away.

Miss Hobson met them in the hallway, failing to stifle a yawn. "For heaven's sake, the odd hours of this house are enough to do me in. Either that, or it is the confounded lack of windows on this floor."

Angelica ignored the jibe. "We must dress for the Wentworth ball. It is guaranteed to be a crush." She gave the chaperone a wry grin. "It was at one of Jane's balls last year where I met my husband, you know."

"Ah yes, we had best get Miss Price looking her very best," Miss Hobson replied briskly. "Come, Lydia."

Lydia followed the chaperone to her room, where Emma waited with a beaded lavender satin ball gown that the Siddons sisters had recently finished.

The maid favored her with a saucy grin. "The Devil Earl will be pleased to see you in this creation."

Lydia looked down before Emma could see her pain. If only a pretty ensemble was enough to win his love. As the maid helped her dress, Lydia remembered the scarlet gown she'd worn to seduce Vincent. She was tempted to try the scheme once more. Her body ached for his touch, and her heart wanted more.

An hour later, she met the others downstairs. Angelica was resplendent in a low-cut gown of sapphire watered silk. A diamond necklace sparkled at her throat. Ian appeared every inch the duke in his black evening clothes…yet Vincent held her full attention.

His midnight-blue jacket and breeches brought out the color of his turbulent eyes, and the silver embroidered waistcoat complemented the gleaming strands of his hair. His cravat was meticulously knotted, and his hair was impeccably pulled back in a queue, highlighting his sharp cheekbones. Despite the fine picture, Lydia preferred him bare-throated, with his long hair free and rakish, the way she had sketched him so often in Cornwall. From the agitated tapping of his polished Hessians, Vincent appeared to resent the confining attire as well.

Mouth dry with desire, Lydia longed to free him

from his elegant clothes. When he assisted her into
the Burnrath carriage, she had to bite back a moan of
lust at his touch. In the close quarters of the coach, his
masculine scent was enough to drive her mad.

The glittering splendor of the Wentworth ball, and
the warm, pulsing crowd of attendees were an assault
on Lydia's senses. Taking a deep breath, she forced her
heightened perception to dim to a tolerable level. The
scent of blood, countless founts of fresh prey, tanta-
lized her nostrils. Saliva nearly filled her mouth, and
she said a silent prayer of relief that she had fed. Still,
her predatory instincts forced her muscles to tense
and stiffen in the receiving line. Angelica greeted the
hostess with kisses on both cheeks, showing no sign of
wanting to bite the woman. Lydia vowed to behave
with the same control.

"Miss Price, how lovely it is to see you this evening." The Duchess of Wentworth greeted her with
a dazzling smile. "I wanted to felicitate you sooner
on your engagement, but I heard you'd been ill. I am
pleased to see you're now blooming with health."

Lydia curtsied and returned the smile. "Thank
you, Your Grace. It was only a slight cold. It happens
every spring."

As she made her way to the ballroom, a few other
people inquired about her illness and engagement.
Some gave her skeptical looks, as if they didn't
believe her explanation. Lydia shook her head.
Likely some assumed that Vincent had compromised
her. Her lips twisted in ill humor. In truth, *she* had
compromised *him*.

Playing the dutiful debutante proved more difficult

than she'd anticipated, especially since she had to constantly fight the urge to sink her fangs into the men's throats and drain their life force drop by drop. Once she finished placating the last affronted suitor, Lydia quit the floor.

The hairs on the back of her neck stood on end. She turned to see her grandmother approaching her.

The old woman's lips pulled back in a rictus of a smile. "My dear child, I am pleased that your common blood did not prevail, and you have made a match that brings honor to our family."

Lydia froze in shock. First she was an embarrassment; now she brought the family *honor*?

Lady Morley continued merrily. "It is as if it were destined. Lord Deveril's ancestor was betrothed to ours before he had a terrible accident, you know."

"Hmm," was all she could manage.

"Please, come to tea tomorrow afternoon." Her grandmother reached out to pat her shoulder.

Lydia stepped away. "No thank you, Grandmother," she said coolly and turned her back on the dowager, giving her the cut direct.

Immediately, whispers erupted all around her. Some people looked shocked; many nodded in approval. Angelica beamed at her from across the ballroom.

From the refreshment table, she observed the glittering throng. Sparkling jewels and the rainbow of rich fabrics made her think of plumage on birds of paradise. She longed to get away from it all. Her heart ached with desperation to be back in Cornwall in the peaceful solitude of Vincent's castle, to abandon London Society and all of its oppressive trappings.

The beloved scent of sea breezes and masculine spices pulled her from her reverie as the musicians struck up a waltz.

"Will you dance with me, Lydia?" Vincent's soft voice resonated low in her body.

His hand was warm and strong in hers as he led her to the dance floor.

For a while, she merely savored the feel of being in his arms as they moved silently to the music. She looked up at him, increasingly frustrated with his unreadable countenance. If only she could tell what he was thinking! Her breath caught as she remembered that some vampires could read minds.

Looking deep into his eyes, she concentrated.

It won't work, Lydia. His voice spoke in her mind, tinged with amusement. *No vampire worth their salt will succumb to an invasion.*

He laughed aloud at her astonished gasp. Regaining composure, she concentrated on him once more. *We can communicate this way?*

Yes, it is quite useful at times.

Lydia chuckled, feeling deliciously wicked with their secret conversation. *Half the* ton *would give their eyeteeth for an ability such as this.*

She was about to ask him about the Siddons sisters, but then he continued. *How are you handling the evening? Is the hunger becoming unbearable?*

He sounded so concerned that she couldn't bear the idea of increasing his worry. *It was a bit overwhelming at first, but I have gained control of it.* Forcing a smile, she whispered an attempt at humor. "I've been to many parties, and never before was tempted to bite the hostess."

Vincent did not laugh. Instead, his hand tightened on her waist, voice laden with remorse. "I am sorry, Lydia."

His pity stung like nettles. She didn't want his sympathy; she wanted his love. *It wasn't your fault*, she protested silently. *If I had not left your home in a foolish pique…or at least if I'd had my pistol, you wouldn't be facing a death sentence, and I would be engaged to whomever you selected to take me off your hands.*

A fresh spurt of agony burst in her chest at the thought of his previous fervent attempts to get rid of her.

The music stopped, and he bowed before leading her off the floor. His brows drew together in a stern frown before his voice once more penetrated her mind, rife with demand.

What exactly was it that upset you so much you ran out into the night unarmed and unescorted?

"It isn't important." There was no way in hell she was going to subject herself to the humiliation of confessing how his rejection had crushed her heart. Instead, she led him back to the dance floor as the musicians began another tune, and changed the subject. "Sir Thomas Lawrence is allowing me to display my work in the Royal Exhibition."

For the first time since she was Changed, Vincent's eyes brightened with genuine happiness. "That's wonderful! I cannot think of anyone more deserving of the honor. You are a magnificent painter."

"Thank you," she whispered, throat tight at his praise. He truly meant it, yet he could never fathom what that meant to her. "Though Lawrence is doing this only because he wants me to finish some of his paintings for the Exhibition."

He laughed so hard and suddenly that they missed their dance steps and made everyone stare. "He doesn't finish his own work?"

She grinned up at him. "Not anymore. As president of the Royal Academy of Arts, he is too prestigious."

They laughed together and continued dancing out of time with the others. For a moment, all their troubles fell away just as when they were back in Cornwall. Her heart cried for what could have been.

"What did the old termagant want from you?"

"Hmmm?" she murmured, captivated by the metallic gleam of his hair.

"I saw you speaking with Lady Morley."

She recovered her composure and gave him a wry smile. "Oh, yes. My grandmother informed me that our engagement has brought honor to the family, and she invited me for afternoon tea. I gave her the cut direct, as they say here."

"She didn't!" He grinned and held her tighter for a moment. "You did well to give her a dram of her own tonic."

Too soon the dance ended. Vincent's carefree smile faded as he released her. Unable to bear dancing with another man, Lydia fled to Angelica's side.

The duchess seemed to sense her depression. Immediately, she pulled her aside. "Would you like to leave the ball early and meet Sarah Siddons this evening?"

Twenty-seven

VINCENT'S FISTS CLENCHED AT HIS SIDES AS HE WATCHED Lydia leave the dance floor. Every ounce of his being demanded he go after her and pull her back into his arms. He strode to the refreshment table to fetch her a glass of punch. He would ask if she wanted to leave early and play a game of chess…and perhaps talk.

Lady Morley intercepted him by the punch bowl. Her mouth twisted in a querulous frown. He knew she must be stinging from Lydia's rejection of her offer to reconcile.

"You must be very pleased with yourself, Deveril."

"Yes, I am," he said agreeably. *Or I would be if I'd been able to propose to Lydia like a normal human man.*

Her features contorted with hatred—hatred she clearly wanted to project on him because she didn't want to admit it was for herself. "You were so determined to succeed in your hopeless plan to prove me wrong and secure a better match for her, that you took her yourself when no one else would have her." She attempted a scornful laugh, and instead, a feeble cackle emerged. "You may make Lydia a countess, but thanks to my efforts with the Marquess of Stantonbury, my Georgiana shall be a marchioness."

"This is not a competition to me." Though God help him, it had been at the start. "And I'm sorry to correct you, madam. She received five proposals. I turned them down because I want her for myself. She is a joy to know. Pity you didn't give her a chance to realize it." Vincent discovered that he truly *did* pity her.

She flinched as if he had slapped her. Her lips disappeared in a thin white line, and she turned her back and slunk away, a crumpled paper tiger.

Vincent sighed and returned to the task at hand, filling a glass of punch for Lydia. Thanks to him, she could no longer drink the whole thing. Again, the memory of the night he Changed her nearly crippled him—the stunned betrayal in her eyes, the hurt in her voice when she'd said, "*How could you?*"

Yet, from the way she sought out his company, and the heat in her gaze when she looked at him, it seemed she didn't despise him after all. Though he didn't deserve her forgiveness, his heart warmed.

For the first time, Vincent allowed himself to hope that the Elders would be merciful. On the heels of that thought, a deeper hope emerged. Perhaps, given time, Lydia could learn to forgive him, and maybe even love him. If he did manage to escape a death sentence, he could have an eternity to convince her.

Taking care not to spill the punch, he weaved through the crowd, searching for his heart's desire. His eyes scanned the throng for her black hair and lavender gown. He'd last seen her with the Duchess of Burnrath. What had Angelica been wearing?

He didn't see either woman in the ballroom, or in the banquet area. A quick glance out the French doors told him they weren't out in the garden, either. Unease trickled down his spine, magnifying to pure worry when he found Ian wandering through the masses, searching for his wife. Ian appeared more amused than perturbed. "You're missing yours as well, I see." The two Lord Vampires repaired to an alcove with a full view of the ballroom—and with identical frowns on their faces.

"Where could they have gone? Do you suppose Lydia lost control of her hunger?" Vincent asked.

With a light laugh, the Lord of London shook his head. "I doubt it. More likely my wife is up to some mischief and took Miss Price along with her. Let us ask the hostess if she knows what became of them."

The Duchess of Wentworth peered at them strangely. "Miss Price was tired, so Her Grace took her home. I thought she had informed you, Your Grace."

Ian feigned shame. "Oh yes, I do recall her telling me something, but I was so engrossed in my conversation with Deveril about our card game that I'm afraid I did not hear her."

"Well, we had best leave now," Vincent told Ian, hiding his mounting anxiety.

"Indeed," the duchess chided. "Please inform me of Miss Price's health and well-being."

They took their coats and hats from the butler and strode outside.

The Burnrath carriage remained in the drive, vigilantly guarded by Felton, the driver.

"They must have left on foot," Vincent observed.

Ian nodded. "Yes, this definitely smacks of mischief. Though, as they didn't take the coach and have not had time to don disguises, it can't be more than a trifle."

"Do you have any guesses?"

"Knowing my Angel? Not in the slightest."

Vincent gritted his teeth in impatience at Ian's lack of concern. "Have there been any unusual visitors to the house recently?"

"Aside from a few members of Angelica's literary circle, no." The duke's brow furrowed. "Although, the Siddons girls paid a call without an appointment the other night. I think they hoped to encounter Sir Thomas Lawrence, but Angelica saw them out after allowing them just a peek at the man. My wife was never fond of following rules."

"What *else* did she allow them?" A sudden suspicion came over Vincent. Lydia must know that her dressmakers were vampires. She likely now knew who they really were and what had happened between them and Sir Thomas Lawrence. "Although Angelica may have obeyed your edict about the painter, she and Lydia may have decided to be remiss in another regard." Vincent headed to the carriage. "I think I know where they went."

Ian nodded. "Good, would mind fetching them alone? I need to feed and meet with Rafe and Clayton, my third in command. They don't get along, but Rafe has agreed to make the man his second when he takes over."

"You're not concerned about your wife?"

"Oh, I'll deal with her later. Be sure to send her to my study to explain herself." The duke uttered a helpless laugh. "I've learned that my Angel is capable of taking care of herself for the most part, and that if I try to stop her mischief, things become woefully muddled. You may want to keep that in mind when it comes to your Lydia."

"Under current circumstances, I can't afford any trouble. And Lydia has been a vampire only for little more than a week. She could easily be in danger." Vincent shook his head in disbelief as he stepped up into the carriage. "To Marylebone," he clipped out to the driver.

Felton gave the duke a quizzical look, then snapped the reins when Ian nodded and walked away as if to return to the ball.

Minutes later, the carriage rolled to a halt in front of a modest but lovely house on Upper Baker Street. Lydia was there; he could sense it. So were three other vampires. He bared his fangs.

Though the neighborhood was better kept and wealthier than many districts in London, the thought of Lydia venturing out alone at night instantly transported Vincent back to the night in Cheapside when Lydia had run straight into a cutthroat's path.

His possessive instincts roiled at the thought. Yes, she may be a vampire now and was accompanied by another, but she was far from impervious to the dangers that lurked in the shadows.

Only last year a vampire hunter had stalked this city. Rogues were always a concern as well. Humans weren't their only victims.

Suppressing a growl, Vincent walked up the rutted drive and knocked on the door with more force than he had intended.

The door opened and an elderly butler blinked up at him owlishly. "Good heavens, that was loud enough to wake the dead! Whatever do you want at this ungodly hour?"

"I apologize. I am Vincent Tremayne, Earl of Deveril. I am looking for Miss Lydia Price."

"She and the Duchess of Burnrath are visiting Mrs. Siddons, along with two other young ladies in the sitting room." The butler hid a yawn. "I will show you the way."

Vincent nodded and glanced at a pair of maids in sleeping caps peering at him from the top of the stairs. They blushed and ducked out of sight.

Had Lydia and her accomplices disrupted the entire household?

When they reached the sitting room, Vincent bowed quickly, then peered over the butler's shoulder to meet the guilty gazes of Sarah Siddons's guests.

The old actress blinked. "Another visitor? I daresay this dream has taken another strange turn. Do come and take a seat. I was just telling Her Grace and Miss Price about my role as Lady Macbeth." She waved the butler away and he departed gratefully.

At least it seemed they'd remembered to mesmerize Sarah. Else she would be likely be having hysterics at seeing her daughters alive.

Slightly mollified that the woman believed this was a dream, Vincent followed the aging actress into the house. Sally and Maria cringed back from him, making him feel like a brute. A girl of about thirteen, who bore a striking resemblance to Maria, clung to their hands.

Angelica met his gaze with a defiant glint in hers, while Lydia's cheeks flared crimson.

Unaware of the tension between him and the four female vampires, Sarah Siddons turned to her eldest daughter. "Play that song again, dear Sally. Your music was always a balm to my soul."

The young girl released Sally's hand. "Yes, Cousin, please do!" She then led Maria to the sofa, and they sat next to Sarah.

Sally gave Vincent a cautious look as she approached the pianoforte. When he made no move to stop her, she sat on the bench and placed her fingers lightly upon the ivory keys.

An exquisite melody trilled from the instrument, somehow lilting and sorrowful at once. Vincent watched in astonishment. He knew she'd been an accomplished musician in her mortal years, but as far as he knew, she hadn't played since she was Changed. It seemed she hadn't lost the talent.

Maria took her mother's hand and watched her sister, an expression of unadulterated joy lighting up her features like a ray of sunshine. This visit had done more to heal their tortured souls than anything he'd been able to do for them.

Though it didn't change the fact that they had disobeyed him. Torn between compassion and duty, he waited for Sally to finish her song before turning to Sarah Siddons and the young girl, willing them to sleep.

When Sarah's eyes drifted closed and the girl's head fell to Maria's shoulder, he regarded the Siddons sisters sternly. "I told you this was forbidden."

Lydia spoke up before they could reply. "But it isn't

fair! This is their mother! Besides, I didn't know you had forbidden them to see her."

"Yes, but they did." He turned to Angelica. "And so did you."

Angelica regarded him mutinously. "You're not my Lord. And Lydia is right. It isn't fair to keep them from their mother."

"I may not be your Lord, but it was *yours* who originally made this decree." He rubbed the bridge of his nose, trying to decide what to do. "How many people are in this house?"

Maria answered. "Aside from the butler, the servants are asleep, and mother and our cousin Fanny are here. Her Grace and Lydia have used their power to convince them it is a dream."

"We had to make certain they were all right!" Sally added. "And it is a good thing we have."

"Why do you say that?"

Maria eyed him coldly. "Lawrence has been coming 'round, trying to wheedle his way back into our mother's good graces. We think he may have an interest in our dear Fanny."

"The man is obsessed!" Sally's knuckles whitened as she twisted her hands in her lap.

Lydia approached Vincent, golden eyes large and pleading. "Please, Vincent. Don't be angry with them. They want only to protect their family. Wouldn't you do the same?"

Her argument and winsome voice undid him. "Damn it."

Angelica raised a brow. "Does that mean we are no longer in trouble?"

"I didn't say that," he said irritably and turned to the sisters. "However, if it's all right with Ian and Her Grace agrees, she may bring you here to see their mother, providing you are discreet and make sure she remembers nothing."

The Siddons sisters bowed. "Thank you, my lord!"

Turning back to Lydia, he frowned. "You are not to accompany them anymore."

"But—"

"No arguments, or I'll rescind my decision. Now let's see you and the duchess home. Sally and Maria?"

"Yes, my lord?"

"Say your good-byes and go home before they wake. And stay the hell away from Lawrence."

The sisters nodded reluctantly and kissed their mother and cousin before embracing Angelica and Lydia. "Thank you so much for helping us."

Once Sally and Maria left the house and disappeared into the night, Vincent helped Angelica and Lydia into the carriage. As the horses began to pull the conveyance home, he looked at the duchess and shook his head.

"Why do you insist on involving Lydia in every madcap scheme that crosses your mind?"

Angelica grinned, undaunted at his ire. "I see it as my duty as her sponsor, and now her mentor. A woman ought to have a bit of adventure."

"Instead of being locked away like a bauble in a curio cabinet," Lydia added.

Unbidden, the memory of the night he and Ian had caught them at Scallywag John's came to his mind...along with Lydia's subsequent seduction. He turned to look out the window before they could read his expression.

When they arrived at Burnrath House, and after the butler took their coats, Vincent addressed the deviant duchess. "The Lord of London wants a word with you in his study."

"I imagine he does." Her cheery tone remained, though momentary apprehension flickered in her gaze before she lifted her skirts and bravely marched up the stairs to face her husband.

Now he stood alone with Lydia in the foyer.

She suddenly giggled. "Sidwell? Surely you could have come up with a better alias for my vampire seamstresses."

"This is not a laughing matter."

Her mirth lessened a degree. "Why didn't you tell me about them and Lawrence?"

"I didn't have the opportunity before they took it upon themselves to inform you." He couldn't hide the irritation from his voice. He was sick to death of the matter. The pair of vindictive lady vampires should have stayed in Cornwall and he should have found other means of securing Lydia's wardrobe. And why did Lawrence have to be Lydia's hero and teacher? Why couldn't it have been someone less scandalous and meddlesome, such as Reynolds or Gainsborough?

"I do not understand why you are so vexed." She crossed her arms.

He grasped her shoulders. "I am not vexed. I am concerned. You don't understand what a dangerous thing you and Angelica have done. It is forbidden for mortals to know what we are. And if the Elders get wind of what Sally and Maria are up to, we could be in far deeper trouble than we already are."

"But Angelica and I were careful to convince their mother it was a dream."

"That doesn't work all the time. A few humans are immune to our power. And even for those who are susceptible, the effect can diminish. If Sarah Siddons sees Sally and Maria too often, she very well could descend into madness from the fractured memories."

Lydia paled. "My God, I had no idea."

"That's precisely my point." Vincent's fingers tightened on her flesh, longing to pull her into a protective embrace. "You're a youngling, and so is Angelica, for that matter. Neither of you are in a position to make decisions that interfere with a Lord Vampire's decree."

She pouted. "We're not children."

"Compared to vampires older and more powerful, you are." To prove his point, he slid his hands down her arms, holding her immobile. Lowering his head, he grazed his fangs across her neck and whispered, "I could drink you down where you stand." However, that wasn't what he wanted to do with her.

The heat of her body, coupled with her intoxicating scent, was a bouquet of temptation. Before he succumbed and gave in to his desire, he released her—a little more abruptly than he intended.

"If I catch you meddling with the Siddons sisters again, you will be forbidden from participating in the Royal Exhibition."

She flinched as if he had struck her. "I-I understand."

Vincent thrust his hands in his pockets and turned

away to avoid hauling her into his arms and kissing away her hurt.

As he left the house and walked through the dark, foggy streets, he reminded himself that he had to be firm to keep her out of trouble. *Then why do I feel like a villain?*

Twenty-eight

LYDIA SWIRLED THE MIXTURE OF COLORS ON HER PAL-ette, considering how her heightened senses had improved her work. Already she'd finished two paint-ings for Sir Thomas Lawrence: one a landscape that really did need only finishing touches, the other a por-trait of the Duke of Wentworth that not only needed a backdrop, but the man's entire waistcoat painted.

The last was to be the Countess of Blessington, and all he'd provided were sketches and a rudimen-tary outline on canvas. She practically had to paint the whole thing. Thank heavens the woman was a member of Angelica's literary circle.

Angelica had been thrilled when Lydia told her she would be painting Lady Blessington. "An extraordi-nary woman! She wrote *Conversations with Lord Byron*. I can talk with her for hours. You'll meet her soon at my next literary circle."

Lydia looked forward to it, but now she wanted to focus more on the subject for *her* painting for the Exhibition.

The portrait of Vincent seemed to be alive on the

canvas, on the verge of walking out and taking her into his arms. She gazed into his stormy eyes, chest tight as she dabbed her brush in a pot of linseed oil. If only she could paint a new world and walk into it. A world where Vincent was safe and loved her, and they could be happy together.

For now, all she could do was to continue creating illusions and pretending her heart wasn't breaking. Vincent hadn't spoken to her since the night he caught her and Angelica helping the Siddons sisters. Shame crawled through her like an ugly worm. She hadn't known they were putting him at risk. If only she could apologize and take it back.

Angelica entered the studio, pulling her attention from the painting. "Lydia?"

"Yes?" She fought back a growl at the unwelcome intrusion of reality.

The duchess didn't reply at first. Instead, she stared at the canvas, transfixed. "Your talent is amazing."

Lydia warmed at the compliment. "Thank you." She wished she were alone, but she did not want to offend her friend. She forced a congenial smile. "Ah, was there something you wanted?"

"I had noticed that you seem to be melancholy of late, so I have arranged a diverting evening to take your mind off of..." Angelica shrugged helplessly. "Well, you know."

Neither dared to speak of Vincent's upcoming investigation, as if their silence would keep the dreaded event and its impending verdict at bay.

A pang of guilt niggled in Lydia's belly for her resentful thoughts about her time at Burnrath House.

Indeed, she was grateful for Angelica's kindness and unfailing aid with everything, from her seduction of Vincent to her adjustment to her new nocturnal existence. If she had not had such a friend to confide in, she would long since have perished from despair.

Giving Angelica a warm smile, she asked with genuine enthusiasm, "What is this diversion?" The duchess was always good for an adventure.

Angelica grinned. "My literary circle will be presenting a phantasmagoria."

The alien word piqued Lydia's curiosity. "What is that?"

Angelica clasped her hands together like a young girl receiving her first pony. "It is so wonderful I cannot describe it. You shall see. First"—she looked down at the carpet, suddenly appearing nervous—"is everything all right between you and Lord Deveril?"

Lydia bit her lip, reluctant to divulge her heartbreak and humiliation.

"Although you are now practically immortal, you do *not* have eternity to confide in me." The duchess put her hands on her hips and fixed her with a merciless gaze.

A shuddering sigh escaped Lydia's lips before everything poured out in a torrent, like draining poison from a wound. "He can hardly look at me anymore, because he feels guilty for Changing me. He shouldn't! If I had not lost my temper and wandered out on the dangerous streets alone, Vincent would not be facing a death sentence." Her throat tightened. "He should hate me."

Another voice, richly accented, intruded. "He could

never hate you." Rafael Villar stepped into the room, shrinking the space with his powerful presence. "He is far too occupied with hating himself."

Deafening silence greeted his announcement.

Lydia recovered from her shock, eyes widening as his words became clear. "What do you mean?"

"Some of our kind feel that we are monsters. Deveril is one of those," Rafe explained with a shrug. "Like you, he was also Changed without being given a choice, which does not help matters."

Lydia gasped as the implication dawned. "Does he think *I'm* a monster, then?"

"Don't be ridiculous." The Spaniard's scornful tone made the truth of his words apparent.

Angelica nodded emphatically. "If he did, he would not be working so hard to save your life." Her cat leaped up into her arms.

"Save my life?" Confusion filled Lydia at the declaration. "I was under the impression that Vincent was the only one facing a death sentence."

Rafe scoffed. "He wanted to protect you from that knowledge as well."

"It is *highly* unlikely that the Elders will have you executed, especially when you've adapted so well to our ways." Angelica's warm gaze was reassuring as she stroked Loki's fur. "Such a sentence is usually applied only to the ones who go mad from the change."

Lydia's mind raced, cataloging Vincent's behavior with Rafe's explanation. A memory teased her mind of the night he'd told her the story of the girl and the wolf.

"*She* should *get away*," he had said. She'd thought he'd been referring to the girl and the wolf, and perhaps he was…only he thought of *Lydia* as the girl and of *himself* as the wolf. Longing, deep and piercing, thrummed through her being. If only he were here right now. Then she'd pull him into her arms and assure him that he was wrong.

"So he is afraid that *I* now think that I am a monster and resent him for Changing me?" she ventured. Vincent was no monster. He was her guardian angel, her protector.

Rafe nodded, and his voice pulsed with sarcasm. "Your powers of deduction are astounding."

Lydia bristled, fighting the urge to pummel him. "There is no need to be rude."

Undaunted, the Spaniard raised a brow. "Do you see how emotions can overrun your logic? Think *very* carefully about that before the inquest."

Angelica chuckled. "Let us see how well that advice aids you when *you* fall in love."

Rafe's scars puckered as he sneered at the duchess. "I am quite certain my circumstances keep me safe from falling victim to such a malady." To illustrate his point, he shrugged his shoulder, allowing his bad arm to rise an inch, only to fall limp and useless at his side.

There was no regret in his words, only hard practicality. Lydia's heart ached for the Spaniard. She remembered the night of her come-out ball, and how the other debutantes laughed at him and whispered that he was ugly. With his preternatural senses, he must have heard them.

"Lady Rosslyn was quite intrigued with you," she said, hoping to comfort him.

His amber gaze narrowed as a multitude of emotions

played across his scarred face. "Morbid curiosity is *not* admiration. That woman is nothing more than a nuisance. I think her widowhood has driven her mad."

"Cassandra is not mad!" Angelica huffed. "She is the most brilliant woman I have ever met. She wants to be a doctor. Isn't that delightful?"

Lydia nodded as Rafe scowled. "A woman doctor? Impossible. The wench will make herself a laughing-stock if she isn't careful."

The duchess slapped him on the arm with her fan. "Don't be so cynical. And she's coming here tonight, so you had better behave yourself."

For a moment his eyes gleamed with what looked like excitement. Then he shook his head and turned to Lydia, changing the subject. "I am not here to talk about eccentric widows. Time grows short. What made you so upset that you ran out of the safety of Deveril's house and put yourself in the path of a cutthroat?"

Lydia's cheeks burned. To confess her petty and insipid behavior that night to this cold, powerful vampire was unthinkable. Why couldn't they continue discussing Lady Rosslyn?

"Yes," Angelica prodded. "What happened that night?"

Rafe leaned on the door frame as if to block her escape. "As the duchess so wisely declared, you do not have eternity to confide in her. This information could be useful in Lord Deveril's investigation."

"It was so foolish of me," she began in a low voice, turning away to clean her brushes and palette. "I had gone to Vincent's study to announce my intentions never to marry—"

her! She fought to keep her voice level and ——re. "There has been a misunderstanding, and I —opeful it will be solved."

—liss Hobson nodded. "That is good to hear. Now —us get you dressed for Her Grace's literary salon. —e guests are due to arrive within the hour, and you —nnot be in such company with paint on your hem."

Mind racing from her interrogation by Rafe and the —chess and its following revelations, Lydia numbly —llowed her chaperone. Even after the door had —losed behind them, her heightened hearing caught —afe's next words to the duchess.

"So Deveril *did* intend to wed her in the first place. That *is* interesting."

Alternating waves of joy and despair washed over her —s she washed her hands and changed her gown. Vincent —ad wanted her after all. Yet because of her foolishness, —he man she loved could be dead in a fortnight, thus —estroying any chance of them being together.

"*He hates himself,*" Rafe had said.

Tears welled up in her eyes at the thought. She —ouldn't let Vincent die thinking he was a loathsome —onster. There had to be something she could do.

⁂

—ngelica's smile lit up the music room as she intro-—uced Lydia to the literary circle. Lydia recognized —few of the women right away. The Duchess of —'entworth kissed her on both cheeks. Angelica then —troduced her to the Countess of Blessington, the —bject of the painting Lawrence had commissioned —r to finish. As Lydia sought a closer observation of

"Why not?" Rafe interrupted sharply. "It was your duty, and you seemed resigned to it."

Her cheeks flamed further when Angelica explained, "Vincent had *taken* her the night before." She turned back to Lydia. "And so you knew you could not bear to be with anyone else," she whispered with aching sympathy.

Lydia nodded, eyes burning with unshed tears.

A string of Spanish curses echoed in the room. "Foolish man," he growled. "What the devil was he thinking?"

"It was my fault entirely." Lydia pulled off her painter's smock. "*I* seduced *him.*"

"I helped," Angelica added, scratching Loki behind his ears, ignoring Rafe's mutterings of disapproval. "What happened then? Did you quarrel?"

Lydia shook her head. "He was speaking with Miss Hobson. Apparently, he'd been in a competition with Lady Morley on which of her grandchildren would secure the better match." Her voice broke. "I was just a game piece to him."

"Surely that must have changed after the other night," Angelica said softly.

"No. In fact he was telling Miss Hobson that he had reconsidered one of the possible suitors Miss Hobson had suggested." Her fists clenched at her sides. "He sounded damn happy about it!"

To her astonishment, Rafe burst out laughing. "Perhaps you should fetch the chaperone, Your Grace. I am certain she can cast some light on this matter."

A strange smile curved Angelica's lips as she met the Spaniard's gaze. "Yes, I think I shall." With that, she deposited Loki in Lydia's arms and left her alone with Rafe.

Rafe lit a cigar and leaned back against the wall, seeming to be lost in his own thoughts. Lydia sighed and settled into the duchess's chintz seat and stroked Loki. The soft rumble of the feline's purr helped in calming her ragged nerves.

Weary of the awkward silence, she dared to ask, "Do you think the Elders will allow Vincent to live?"

He blew out a cloud of smoke. "To be truthful, I do not know. Vampires rarely violate the cardinal laws. The only one I know of to have committed Vincent's crime was quickly sentenced to death without a trial. Ian carried out the punishment himself." Almost as an afterthought, he added, "The youngling was allowed to live, though."

Lydia shuddered at the image of the regal Duke of Burnrath killing someone in cold blood. Yet she made note to ask him about the incident and glean further details. "Does it bode well that Vincent will receive an inquiry?"

The Spaniard shook his head. "No, that is the usual protocol for a Lord."

Before he could say more, Angelica returned with Miss Hobson in tow. The chaperone gave Lydia a quelling stare of disapproval for being alone with a man as she turned to the Spaniard.

"You wanted to speak with me, Mr. Villar?" She looked down her nose at Rafe in indignation.

Doing little to mask his amusement, Rafe inclined his head mockingly. "I would like to know exactly *which* of your recommended suitors Lord Deveril had

decided to accept for Miss Price's [...] before he changed his mind."

Miss Hobson stiffened and tu[...] Angelica. "I cannot perceive why thi[...] concern of *his*, Your Grace."

"Please, Miss Hobson." Angelica's v[...] with authority. "This is important."

The chaperone sighed and favored [...] a scowl that rivaled his own. "The earl [...] decided that the winning contender for M[...] hand was Lord Deveril himself."

Angelica shared a conspiratorial smirk with [...] am not at all surprised."

The floor seemed to sink under Lydia's f[...] her heart turned over in her rib cage. "What ab[...] competition with my grandmother?"

"You had been eavesdropping for that part,[...] Miss Hobson wagged a scolding finger. "So *tha[...]* you left in a huff. You might as well have st[...] hear the rest of the conversation." Her gaze na[...] "I cannot help but observe that things do no[...] to be going as smoothly as I had planned. You[...] even decided upon a date yet."

"*You* planned?" Angelica's laughter deep[...] was under the impression that the match was [...]

Miss Hobson contemplated the duchess fo[...] gest time before her normally solemn features [...] a wide smile. "Well, Your Grace, it seems [...] have made an alliance sooner." She turne[...] Lydia, and the stern frown returned. "Woul[...] to explain yourself, Miss Price?"

Lydia could have danced with joy. *He* [...]

Lady Blessington's eye color, Lady Rosslyn favored her with a welcoming smile.

"I am pleased to see you again, Miss Price. I have heard much of your skill with a paintbrush. I do hope you will be willing to show me your work at the earliest opportunity."

"You flatter me, my lady." Lydia warmed at the praise. Rafe was mad. Lady Rosslyn was *not* a nuisance, and Lydia hoped she *would* become a doctor. They sipped their wine and chatted excitedly in anticipation of the phantasmagoria.

Angelica clinked her wineglass for attention. "Ladies, it is time. Let us adjourn to the music room."

Lydia followed the group and jumped when someone cried out, "What in the name of heaven is that thing?"

Expecting something horrifying, she was almost disappointed to see the odd object. Concave glass segments, vaguely resembling bowls, were mounted on a shaft upon a small, narrow table. Every section was progressively smaller, making the whole look like a rounded icicle. The smallest end was fastened to a wheel.

"It is a *hydrodaktulopsychicharmonica*," Lady Rosslyn stated smoothly.

Of course, thought Lydia wryly. *Common knowledge.*

Angelica chuckled and explained. "What Cassandra means to say is that it is a glass harmonica. A charming instrument, invented in America." She grinned at Lydia. "By your own Benjamin Franklin, I believe. It shall play an important part in tonight's performance."

Lady Rosslyn nodded in agreement. "Precisely.

Now if you will all be seated, we may commence."
She gestured to a group of chairs that were neatly
arranged facing a black curtain, which hung wall to
wall at the east end of the room, obscuring the fireplace from view.

Lydia glimpsed the shoes of two footmen behind
the curtain, and her curiosity rose.

All lights in the room were then extinguished.
An ominous red glow from the fireplace beneath the
curtain was the only source of illumination. The footmen behind the curtain rattled a sheet of tin to sound
like thunder. Blue light flickered to imitate lightning,
eliciting gasps from the audience.

An eerie melody, high-pitched as birdsong, filled
the air. All turned their heads toward the source. In
the darkness, Angelica's form was barely visible as her
fingers played across the glass harmonica.

Lydia caught a movement in the corner of her
eye. She turned slightly to see Rafe leaning on the
door frame hidden in the shadows. The vampire was
watching Lady Rosslyn intently. She turned away
before he could see her grin. *And he called Cassandra
a nuisance.*

Angelica's voice rang out above the music, recap-
turing Lydia's attention. "An unnatural storm raged
during the night that Death came to claim the true
love of Mary Scofield."

The artificial thunder roared once more, and an
image of a cloaked skeleton grinning at a maiden
appeared. Lady Pemberly shrieked. Lydia squinted
at the image. It was a painting... She could see the
brushstrokes... How had it appeared in this manner?

A murmur of appreciation escaped her lips as she figured it out.

While they'd been distracted by the glass harmonica, a transparent screen had been lowered halfway between the ladies and the black curtain, further adding to its illusion of invisibility. It was upon this surface that the images were being produced by... Lydia turned around once more. The Countess of Rosslyn was operating a strange boxed lantern, which somehow had the ability to magnify and project tiny images painted on squares of glass. As Cassandra moved the lantern up and down, the pictures moved on the screen.

"How very clever," Lydia whispered in awe.

The music grew more ominous as Angelica continued her story. "Mary refused to allow her beloved to die. Instead of humbly stepping aside, she spit in the Reaper's cavernous eye socket. Captivated by her courage, Death offered her a challenge: if she could defeat seven demons, he would spare her lover's life."

Horrid images were displayed as the duchess described Mary's battles with the demons. Many of the ladies cried out as the countess moved the box forward, giving the impression that the monsters were coming to maul the audience. Their eyes and mouths miraculously moved. Lydia saw that Lady Rosslyn was shifting sliders of some sort to achieve the effect.

Droplets of warm liquid struck Lydia, along with the other spectators. The substance would have been evocative of blood if she had been unable to smell that it was water. More footmen had crept behind them to aid in the performance. From the terrified shrieks of the others, the warm water was achieving the desired result. After a while, something thin and damp graced the back of her neck. Lydia glanced over her shoulder to see Emma grinning as she wielded a stick with several wet strings tied on its end. She also noticed Rafe smiling.

Genius! She fought the urge to applaud.

As the duchess narrated, the heroine defeating each demon, the grotesque figures grew smaller in size, as if being carried away into the depths of the hell in which they'd been created. A burst of light signaled each victory, emphasized by ethereal notes on the glass harmonica.

"After the Gorgon was dispatched, Mary dropped her sword into the flames. 'I have fulfilled your challenge and defeated all of the demons,' she declared as Death appeared once more before her. 'Now release me so I may return to my beloved.'"

Angelica paused dramatically and played a long note of anticipation.

"The Reaper laughed. His mirth was the sound of windy tombs and rattling bones. 'I promised only to spare your lover's life, never to release you. For I shall have you as my bride.' From the pocket of his unholy robes, he withdrew a ring carved from human bone. 'Now hold out your hand, dear Mary, and be mine forever.'"

The music once more took on a melody of dread.

"Mary held out her hand, though not in obedience. In the blink of an eye, she snatched the Reaper's scythe and chopped off his head."

With startling speed, the countess manipulated the

slides to make the action seem frighteningly realistic. As a burst of blood exploded from the severed skull, the lurking footmen sprinkled more water over the spectators.

There were more shrieks and nervous giggles, and Lady Pemberly swooned, although no one seemed overly concerned at this development. Angelica played a happy tune. "Mary was transported back to her love, who awaited her with open arms. Since she'd defeated Death himself, they lived happily together for all eternity."

The room filled with light as the servants lit the gas lamps, revealing the screen before them, along with the countess and her miraculous device behind them. Rafe chuckled lightly and disappeared from the room before anyone else noticed.

Lydia stood and applauded with gusto. The others slowly joined her, blinking and dazed.

"Amazing," Lady Blessington breathed. "How did you do it?"

Lady Rosslyn held up her strange box. "This is called a magic lantern." She frowned. "Though it is hardly magic. Anyone with a rudimentary understanding of light and its scientific applications can perceive how the device operates."

Lady Pemberly roused from her faint. "So it was not real? I swear, I could have reached out and touched those monsters!"

"I want to make one!" Lydia declared, overcome with eagerness at the potential for artistic creation. "I wager I could paint even more horrifying creatures."

Angelica grinned. "I wager you could as well." She turned to the countess. "What do you think,

Cassandra? Shall we create another display of horror and mayhem?"

Lady Rosslyn beamed. "I would be delighted."

The ladies of the literary circle all eagerly chatted about the phantasmagoria for another hour before they departed. Most appeared awed and excited on their way out, except for Lady Pemberly, who looked to be rather traumatized. Lydia listened to Lady Blessington's tales of Lord Byron as she memorized the countess's features for her painting.

Cassandra donned her cloak and kissed Angelica on both cheeks before taking Lydia's hands. "I will see about acquiring some blank slides for you to paint as soon as possible. Meanwhile, you and Her Grace should devise another worthy tale."

Miss Hobson yawned as soon as everyone was absent. "I daresay I've had enough excitement for the next year. I shall retire." Turning to Angelica, she fixed her with an imperious stare. "I trust you'll ensure that Miss Price stays out of trouble for what is left of the evening?"

The vampire's lips twitched as she managed a solemn reply. "I always do." After the chaperone left the room, her mischievous grin returned. "Well, Miss Price, if you do not hunt soon, I daresay you might indeed cause trouble."

Once out in the cool night air, under the silvery moonlight, Angelica grinned at Lydia. "I knew Vincent wanted you. I only wish he hadn't resisted you for so long. One would think he'd be able to discern your feelings once he'd Marked you."

"Marked?" Lydia's curiosity rose yet higher. "What do you mean, he Marked me? And when did he do so?"

Angelica lifted her gaze to the heavens and sighed. "I shall let Lord Deveril explain all of that to you, I think. Really, I shouldn't have to do all of his work for him."

Guilt immediately washed over Lydia. "Oh, Your Grace, I'm sorry. I have been such a trial to you, I am sure."

"Not at all!" Angelica said firmly. "It has been quite an enjoyable experience…though I would prefer my tutelage not to be for such dire reasons. Ooh, I see some drunken sods up ahead. Care to race?"

Later, as she worked on the portrait of Lady Blessington, Lydia closed her eyes and allowed the story Angelica had written for the phantasmagoria to replay in her mind. The heroine had defeated seven demons and Death himself to save the man she loved. Could Lydia do the same?

Twenty-nine

AFTER HIS FIRST HUNT, VINCENT WENT STRAIGHT TO Burnrath House, aching to see Lydia again. He savored every moment with her, knowing each time in her presence could be the last.

Ian waited for him outside the gates, fists thrust in his trouser pockets and a pensive frown marring his autocratic features.

"Is there anything amiss?" Vincent kept his tone level while a thousand worries assaulted him. Had Lydia run off again? Had someone hurt her? Or worst of all, had she decided to go out into the sun and end her existence?

Ian shook his head. "I know you want to see Lydia, and she is eager to speak to you as well, but there is something we must first discuss. I explained to you how I was required to execute a vampire who Changed a human without permission. I have thus far refrained from discussing the gory details with Lydia."

Vincent nodded warily.

"Well, Rafe told Lydia what I had done, and she confronted me about the matter."

"Rafe told her such a thing? How could he be so cruel?" Vincent growled, outraged. "She is frightened enough as it is."

Ian shook his head. "I do not think he was trying to be cruel. He likely thought he was giving her a better understanding of the matter."

Vincent gnashed his teeth. *How very helpful of him.* "What did she ask, and more importantly, what did you tell her of the incident?"

"First, I assured her that the circumstances between that upstart and your actions were completely different."

"Did you tell Lydia how you carried out the sentence?"

"Good *God*, no!" Ian's voice was adamant. "It is not my intention to incite bad dreams. I told her only that I tried to make the vampire's death as quick and merciful as possible. It is difficult for creatures such as we, who are so resistant to being killed."

With a measure of relief, he asked, "Why do you suppose Lydia asked you about this?"

"She doesn't want you to die, that much is obvious"—Ian shrugged—"and furthermore, she feels responsible for this whole situation."

"That's ridiculous." Vincent frowned. "If I had given in to my instincts and confessed the truth of what I am to her sooner, I would be holding an approved petition to Change her, rather than a notification of an inquest that could result in my death. Or if I had—"

Ian clapped his hand on Vincent's shoulder, halting the recriminations. "What's done is done, and we must face it. There's no time to dwell on the past. Lydia has some questions to ask you as well, so you had best go to her." With that cryptic statement, the duke took to the air in flight, beginning his own hunt.

She doesn't want me to die. The thought lightened Vincent's footsteps as he approached the house. *What does she want to tell me?* In the tiniest of whispers, his heart dared to voice its hope: *Could she possibly love me, despite what I've done to her?*

Lydia awaited him in the library. The scent of gardenias teased his senses, along with a new, tantalizing scent that made her even more irresistible. The firelight reflected from her silken hair, bringing out the gold in her eyes. Her cheeks pinkened delightfully as he entered the room.

"Good evening, my lord." Was it his imagination, or did she appear happy to see him?

To resist striding across the room and pulling her into his arms, Vincent forced himself to sit beside her in one of the overstuffed chairs. "I understand you have something to ask me?"

Lydia nodded. Her pink tongue darted out to lick her lush lips. "Angelica told me you Marked me when I was a mortal. What exactly does that mean?"

"It means I created a bond between us that is sensed by all other vampires, conveying that you were my property, and to harm you was to incur my wrath." He could not keep a note of possessiveness from his tone. "It also helped me be able to discern your location at all times."

Lydia shivered, whether from disgust or desire, he could not tell. "When did you Mark me, and how was it done?"

"Soon after you arrived. I waited until you were

asleep and fed you a drop of my blood, and then recited the ritual words, which you are not yet allowed to learn."

"Why not?" She frowned.

Laughing at her pique, he explained. "The Elders decree that a vampire cannot perform a Mark until he or she has passed their first century, which is also the age one gains the power to Change a mortal. A vampire must be powerful enough to enforce their Mark."

"Would a vampire Mark someone he disliked?" she asked tentatively.

Vincent nodded, hiding a smile at her worried expression. "Yes, though that is usually done only when a human needs to be watched to see if they are a threat to vampires. I assure you that such was not the case with you. I was fulfilling my responsibility as your guardian to the best of my ability. Rogue vampires had been chased off my lands, and I'd wanted to protect you." He closed his eyes in self-recrimination. "Though I failed to protect you from your own kind."

Lydia placed her hand on his. "I am alive. I hardly count that as a failure. You saved my life, Vincent, and for that I am eternally grateful."

An invisible weight lifted from his shoulders. She understood why he'd had to Change her. He didn't deserve such forgiveness. "Lydia, there's something else you should know."

"Yes?"

He took a deep breath. "That night you were snooping through my castle, looking for secret passageways, I caught you opening the door to my hidden lair."

Her brow creased. "I didn't find anything... I—" Her eyes widened as comprehension dawned. "You mesmerized me, just like we do when we hunt! Did you..."

"No, I didn't take your blood, not then, but I wanted to... I should not have even thought about it..."

"You wanted to and did not—not then..." she mused aloud, rising from her chair. She slowly walked toward him, hips swaying with sensuous grace.

Guilt choked him. "I'm sorry. I—"

Lydia sat on his lap and laid her head on his shoulder. "Did you bite me the night we made love?" she whispered against his neck.

Lust, hot and immediate, pulsed through his being. "Yes."

She shifted on his lap, making his hardness throb. "I wish you hadn't banished the memory. I would have asked you to do it again. Every night."

Her words were too good to be true. "You're not angry?"

"Of course not." She ran a hand through his hair. "Now I have more questions."

With her on his lap, Vincent didn't know if he'd have the mental faculties to answer. "Yes?"

"Do I still belong to you now that I am Changed?" Her lower lip trembled, enticing him to madness.

Another frisson of desire ran through him at her words. If only she could truly belong to him. "In light of the current situation, it is complicated. If I had Changed you legally, then as my youngling, you would be my responsibility until your powers matured." Vincent closed his eyes, despising the invasion of cold truth into their warm solitude. "However, since I violated the law, your care will be decided by the Elders after my verdict has been delivered. I've worked to ensure you will be placed under Ian's authority in the event of my death. The ultimate decision lies with the Elders."

"And if you live?" Her hopeful tone proved the truth of Ian's words.

He dared to speak his ultimate wish. "Then you will likely be relinquished to me."

"They had better let you live." Her voice turned savage. "For you to be punished for something that was my fault is an injustice that defies comprehension!"

A growl built in his throat at her misplaced guilt. "Lydia, it was *not* your fault. If I had—"

"The duke and duchess will be taking us to Vauxhall Gardens tonight. Angelica says the place is a veritable banquet for our kind." She looked into his eyes. "So I have a favor to beg of you."

Mouth dry with desire, his voice came out in a rasp. "And what favor would that be?"

"Be my teacher tonight?" she murmured against his lips. He had to clench his fists at his sides to keep from kissing her. "The duchess has done a fine job, but I would much prefer to learn from you."

"I would be pleased to instruct you tonight, Lydia." Vincent licked his fangs. Oh, but there were other things in which he wanted to instruct her. Things that would be so much more pleasurable.

Thirty

VAUXHALL GARDENS WAS A WONDER TO BEHOLD. Groves of trees adorned with lanterns glowing like captive stars created the illusion of a fairyland. Hedge mazes invited lovers' trysts, while music from the distant concert hall seduced with enchanting melodies. Brilliant fireworks added to the magic, while pavilions of vendors, jugglers, and artists' exhibitions courted any possible fancy. Lydia could not conceal her fascination.

While the duke paid their admission, Angelica leaned over to whisper excitedly, "A vampire could gorge herself every night here without anyone being the wiser."

All of Lydia's predatory instincts rose to a fiery peak as she eyed the multitude of revelers. Unable to restrain the hunger, she licked her fangs in anticipation. A thread of her former humanity whispered a protest, but it was as insubstantial as smoke. She knew she should be ashamed of such thoughts, but she could not manage to do so. For the first time since her parents' deaths, she experienced a sense of belonging.

"Would you care to show me what you've already learned of the hunt?" Vincent's lips caressed her ear, making delicious shivers run down her spine.

Lydia grinned and headed in the direction of the secluded paths, in search of trysting lovers. Feeling Vincent's powerful presence behind her, she felt a kinship…a sense of *rightness* that had been absent with the duchess, congenial as their hunts had been. The sweet aroma of spring flowers added romance to the moment.

As the lanterns grew sparser, Lydia slowed her pace, moving silently across the soft grass. Her efforts were rewarded as her keen eyesight detected her targets. The two were in such a torrid embrace they would likely fail to notice a herd of elephants approaching.

With a mischievous grin, she glanced over her shoulder. "Should I take the gentleman?"

A low growl rumbled in Vincent's throat. "I think not."

"You don't care for the idea of my mouth on his neck?" she teased, hiding her pleasure at his jealousy. He *did* still want her!

"I can think of better places for your mouth." He sucked in his breath sharply. "I apologize for that. Please, carry on. You take the female, and the male shall be my meal."

Lydia hid a smile at his remark and strode to the mortals. She paused and coughed delicately. "Excuse me, could you direct me to the mummers' pavilion? I have lost my way."

The couple sprang apart like guilty children. Lydia and Vincent were upon them in a flash, entrancing the humans like mythical snake charmers. Their eyes

met briefly with an intensity that sent pure lust pool-
ing between her thighs before she sank her fangs in
the woman's throat. Vincent mirrored her movement
with equal grace on the man.

This time a new spice seemed to be present in her
meal. Perhaps it was the sense of rightness she felt with
Vincent at her side, or maybe it was the woman's pulsing desire for the man she'd been kissing. Desire that
echoed throughout Lydia's body as Vincent's powerful
presence made every nerve ending sing.

Carefully, she removed her fangs and bit her finger,
praying her features didn't display the quick jolt of
pain. With a gentle swipe, she healed the woman's
puncture wounds with her magical blood. Vincent did
the same. They stepped back and released their prey
from the enchantment.

The man blinked, frowning at Lydia in irritation. "I
say, madam, can't you see I am otherwise occupied?"
He observed her flushed cheeks and Vincent's tall form
behind her, and his frown turned to a leer. "I daresay,
rather than watching a silly lot of mummers, you look
like you would do better finding a grove of your own
and receiving a good tupping from yon tall buck."

Lydia feigned a gasp of outrage. "Come, Vincent,
we shall find the pavilion on our own."

The man laughed and returned his attention to his
partner in indiscretion.

"You did that very well," Vincent commented,
wiping his mouth with a handkerchief. "I cannot say
I've used such a method before."

Lydia smiled. "That is because men never seem to
have the sense to ask for directions."

They walked in silence for a while before Vincent stopped suddenly. "Lydia? Do you feel any sort of remorse or revulsion for what we have to do to survive?"

Lydia frowned as Rafael Villar's words came back to her.

Some of our kind feel that we are monsters; Deveril is one of those.

Did Vincent truly believe he was a monster? He'd lived for nearly two centuries. She couldn't imagine someone existing with such profound self-loathing for so long. Her chin lifted. No matter, she was determined to change his mind.

She made sure Vincent heard the conviction of her words. "It doesn't hurt them. We take only a pint or two at most. In fact, they seem to be quite euphoric after we're done with them." Lydia bit her lip. In the case of her most recent meal, "euphoric" was an understatement.

Vincent nodded, though he appeared reluctant to believe her. "So you do not regret my Changing you?"

"I am finding great pleasure in this existence." Lydia willed him to see and hear the truth in her words. "My keener vision has revealed untold beauty in the night. Don't you see it?" With a sweep of her hand, she encompassed the brilliant full moon, the silvery clouds, and the cleverly lit trees surrounding them. "I can smell the perfume of a hundred different flowers. My ears delight to hear a nightingale song, the music of human laughter. I've never before felt so alive."

The wonder in Vincent's gaze sent a thrill through her being. "When did you become so wise? So passionate? I had thought…" He shook his head. "No matter. I do not wish to cast a pall on the evening with my regrets."

Lydia's body filled with heat from his words, and she had to clasp her hands behind her back to avoid throwing herself into his arms. "Excellent. Now that you've observed my hunting methods, what can you teach me? I promise to be an attentive pupil."

He studied her intently. "You seem to be proficient at hunting humans. Do you think you can hunt another vampire?"

"Why would I need to do that?"

Vincent's sensuous lips curved in a smile. "Someday you may need to capture a rogue or an unsanctioned invader to your Lord's territory. Or perhaps you may be called upon to observe a suspected traitor without being detected."

A pang of disappointment struck her at his business-like tone. Still, her eyes widened with fascination at this new knowledge. "Shall I hunt you, then?"

"Yes, but due to my age and power, you would never be able to catch me, so I shall make it easier for you." He grinned rakishly. "Although, not too easy."

"And shall I bite you when I catch you?" Lydia couldn't hold back a suggestive smile. "Angelica told me she feeds from her husband on occasion."

She licked her lips at the thought of sinking her fangs into Vincent's neck and tangling her fingers in his moonstruck hair as his rich, powerful blood caressed her tongue. Eyeing his bare throat with desire, she was grateful Angelica had instructed everyone to dress shabbily to avoid being recognized. Now the scheme had even more delightful merit.

"To do so would be considered an insult, for you would be stealing another's power…except in the case of lovers, where it is considered a gift. In this instance, I suppose you may claim a taste as your prize." His eyes glittered with mischief. "*If* you catch me."

Lovers… Lydia blinked, and Vincent was gone.

"Amazing," she breathed, sniffing the air to detect his scent.

A faint trace led her down the easternmost path. Opening her senses to the night, she dashed after him, determined to claim her prize. Wending through the turns of the mazelike groves and past merry revelers, Lydia tracked Vincent's scent. For a while, the taste of him was thick and savory on her tongue. It quickly faded, became elusive, then vanished entirely.

"*Damn!*" she muttered, turning around in futile circles.

Then a thought came to her, curving her lips in a triumphant smile. *The Mark.* Surely it remained, binding them together. That was why his presence felt so right at her side. She closed her eyes, and her mind summoned his essence within her.

A spark ignited, flaring as brightly as the fireworks illuminating the sky. Like a key fitting into the correct lock, her senses felt Vincent so strongly she could find him with her eyes closed.

In an attempt to fool him, she took a circuitous route, humming softly as she passed the concert hall. He was behind a building that resembled a Chinese temple. Lydia ceased humming as she approached the structure, careful to remain in the shadows. On soundless feet, she darted behind statues and bushes until she was only a few yards from the building. Closing her eyes, she thought hard on her strategy.

Angelica had shown her that she could jump high and far. Lydia knew she'd be unable to vault over the temple. However, she could certainly reach the roof. There would be no way she could do it quietly, so she would have to act fast.

As silently as possible, Lydia hiked up her skirts and yanked off her petticoats, stuffing them behind the bush. She then lifted the lower half of her dress and tied it around her waist, freeing her legs.

One last time, she concentrated on Vincent's essence, pinpointing his exact location behind the temple. Tensing her muscles, Lydia took off like lightning, spirit flying as she bounded onto the roof. The moment her boots touched the tiled surface, she sprang again, soaring back into the air, only to come down in a graceful arc.

She landed upon Vincent's back, making him stumble from the impact. With a low growl, she plunged her fangs into his neck, moaning at his potent taste.

An answering groan reverberated from him, sending tremors of desire coursing through her veins. Reluctantly, Lydia withdrew her bite and released Vincent before she lost control.

"Very good, Lydia." Pride filled his voice as he rubbed his neck. "A younger vampire would have been easy prey for you. If you'd had a weapon, even I may have been overcome."

Lydia bowed, flushed from his praise. "Thank you, my lord."

She waited for him to speak again. When she raised

her gaze, she saw that Vincent was staring in undisguised hunger at her exposed legs.

"I, ah, needed more freedom of movement," she explained, her cheeks burning as his eyes slowly moved higher. No doubt he could see through the thin fabric of her chemise. "I'm certain I look ridiculous…"

"You look…delectable." His voice was silken with hunger, his eyes wolfish as they met hers. "Which brings us to your next lesson: there could be a time when you need to evade another vampire, so now I shall hunt you."

Lydia had to bite back a moan of animalistic lust at the thought of him chasing her. Would he bite her as well? The secret place between her thighs pulsed with need at the thought of his fangs penetrating her flesh.

"All right," she whispered.

Vincent's gaze raked across her body, rife with sinful promise. "As you are a youngling, I shall give you a head start, so run…*now*!"

Gasping with anticipation, Lydia obeyed. Vincent's blood did indeed give her more power, for she ran faster than before. Her feet hardly touched the ground as she darted past the pavilions and toward another section of parkland in which the foliage appeared less structured.

Wilderness, a nearby sign proclaimed. There were no lanterns here, and the gurgling sound of running water would surely further disguise the sound of her movement.

When she reached the man-made forest, she felt Vincent's presence behind her just as strongly as her own pulse. There would be no hiding from him…not that she wanted it any other way. Heart pounding in her throat, Lydia ran in a zigzag pattern through the trees.

The thrill of the chase made her want to scream in excitement. She felt him closing in on her, and the sweet ache in her core deepened. Anytime now, he would catch her and—

A primal roar ripped through the air as strong arms closed around her, snatching her up from the earth with dizzying speed. Before she could catch her breath, Vincent deftly turned her around, pinning her against the rock wall of an artificial cave. She noticed he took care not to slam her into the hard surface.

His eyes glowed molten blue, like lightning over storm-tossed seas. A deep growl escaped his clenched teeth again, turning her legs to jelly as he slowly lowered his head.

"Yes," she panted, reaching up to pull him closer.

Quick as a viper, he struck. Lydia cried out in ecstasy as his fangs pierced her flesh. She recalled the night they'd made love. The memory of his rigid length penetrating her body, coupled with the sensation of his mouth sucking on her neck in deep pulls, nearly took her over the edge.

Mad with need, she clung to him and ground her hips against him. He was too tall for her to reach the part of him she most craved. She whimpered in frustration, then disappointment as he withdrew from her.

Vincent's eyes glowed like unholy flames. "I want you, Lydia. And you want me. I can smell your desire. Shall I give you a lesson in vampire lovemaking?"

A pang of hurt struck her heart when he said *want*

rather than *love*. Need for his touch shunted it away. She'd have him any way she could. Lydia reached for the buttons on his shirt.

Vincent seized her hands. "Not here. I don't want your *lesson* to be interrupted."

With that, he scooped her up in his arms and ran. The world flew past in a blur as he catapulted across London with mind-bending swiftness. She was flying. Lydia supposed that with anyone else, she would be terrified at such an alarming rate of speed. Since it was Vincent, she reveled in the safety of his arms, resting her head on his chest. She reached up, feeling his hair flowing around her fingers in the rushing wind.

In minutes, they were at Burnrath House. Vincent held her with one hand as he retrieved the key from his pocket with the other. The mansion was dark and silent; the very air crackled with anticipation of what was to come.

Thirty-one

VINCENT HELD LYDIA TIGHTLY IN HIS ARMS AS HE TOOK the stairs two at a time in a mad frenzy to claim her. Once he reached Lydia's bedchamber, he lowered her to her feet and immediately tore off her dress.

"It was stained from the Gardens anyway," he muttered, half-insane with the need to see her bare flesh. "I'll buy you another one."

Lydia's brow arched before she reached up and tore his shirt open. Buttons clattered on the floor. She could not fully remove it, for his coat remained in the way.

She cursed with impatience.

Vincent chuckled and shrugged out of the garment, tossing it aside. Her eyes flared molten gold as she gazed at his bare chest. The intoxicating musk of her arousal was thick enough to taste…and taste it, he must.

Overcome with desire to touch her, Vincent plunged a hand into her dark, silken mass of hair, breathing in the scent of gardenias, feminine arousal, and the new dark spice of Lydia's power. Tilting her chin up, he claimed her lips, starved for her kiss. His tongue plunged inside her mouth. He lifted her, cupping her delectable rear, squeezing the lush curves as Lydia wrapped her legs around his waist. Slowly, he kissed, nibbled, and licked her neck and shoulders, slicing the straps of her chemise with his fangs. The fabric slid off in a whisper to the floor.

Now she was naked before him, except for her stockings and garters. His cock grew harder as he gazed upon the perfection of her breasts. He needed to taste those as well. Vincent lifted Lydia higher, reveling in his unnatural strength, until the beautiful, rounded flesh was level with his face. He covered her breasts with light kisses, teasing her nipples with his tongue, making them rigid.

Lydia squirmed and gasped from his ministrations, but he was merciless, feasting upon her until he had his fill. Slowly lowering her so he could hold her with one arm, he unfastened his trousers.

"No, not yet!" she protested. "Put me down, please."

Biting back a groan of frustration, Vincent reluctantly complied.

With a smoldering glance under her lashes, Lydia sank to her knees in front of him. "I want to taste you."

Her pink tongue darted out to lick her lips, and he was almost undone. Impatiently, she yanked down his trousers, freeing his erection.

Gently, she grasped his shaft and touched her tongue to the head. Vincent's eyes drifted closed at the electrifying pleasure. Lydia slowly took him into her mouth and reached up to caress his sensitive flesh.

Vincent tangled a hand in her ebony tresses and groaned in bliss with her sensuous ministrations. If she kept at it much longer, he would explode.

⇛⇝

A thrill of sexual power flooded Lydia as she pleasured Vincent with her mouth. His shaft felt like
iron as she worked it with her hand. She swirled
her tongue around the tip, exploring its fascinating
curves and ridges.

"Enough!" Vincent growled, grasping her shoulders
and pulling her to her feet.

Lydia's core flared with heat in anticipation for him
to be inside her.

"Grasp the bedpost." His voice was rough with
command.

Her nipples stiffened at his dominance as she obeyed
him. Lydia curled her fingers around the round, polished oak, legs quivering as the insides of her thighs
grew damp from her arousal. Again, she looked in the
mirror. The view of Vincent looming naked behind
her, his hard length standing up and pointed at her
exposed body, left no doubt as to his intent.

Gently, he seized her hair and moved it over one
shoulder as he kissed the other. He pressed his bare
chest against her back and ran his hands up her rib cage
to cup her breasts. With torturous languor, he kissed
and nibbled her neck while squeezing her sensitive
flesh and pinching her nipples just enough to bring her
to hypnotic heights of pain and pleasure.

"Spread your legs." His breath was hot against her
earlobe, making her shiver. "And do not let go."

As she planted her feet wide apart, Vincent slid one
hand down to toy with her hot arousal. Then, with his
magical strength, he slowly lifted her until the tip of
his hard length pressed against her wet core.

Lydia whimpered with need and clung to the bedpost.

"Are you ready for my next lesson?" he whispered, stroking her clit with his middle finger.

"Please!" she moaned.

His hard length filled her in one long thrust.

The movement was so sudden and intense that her head nearly slammed into the bedpost. Lydia's muscles flexed as she gripped the oak tighter and bent her elbows. Her thighs clamped down on Vincent's hips, adjusting her balance and drawing him yet deeper inside her.

Like a wicked dance, his cock slid in and out of her slowly as his fingers squeezed and teased her swollen clit and labia. The exquisite, simultaneous motions continued until she bucked and squirmed in his grip.

"I want you to come for me now," he commanded roughly.

As if enslaved to his words, her body became electric as the climax shattered her being. He continued his teasing caresses and long, deep strokes until she was reduced to mindless thrashing.

"Vincent..." she moaned desperately.

As the orgasm faded to a thrumming pulse, he grasped her hips with both hands.

"I like the sound of my name when you're in the throes of pleasure," Vincent murmured in a low, wicked voice. "Now let's see if I can make you scream it this time."

With that, he thrust into her hard and fast, gripping her hips with brutal force. The bedpost creaked in protest. The feel and sound of his flesh slapping against hers brought her back to that bewitching realm where pleasure teased the edges of pain.

Lydia threw her head back and cried out in rapture. Her core began to throb once more as the intensity began to peak.

"Scream my name, Lydia," Vincent growled. "Do it, and I will bring you over the edge."

She needed no further urging. "Vincent!"

The moment the scream tore from her throat, Vincent's fangs plunged into her neck, and his mind locked with hers. Suddenly, it was as if they were one being. Lydia could feel Vincent's pleasure, feel how her body clenched his hardness. She could feel his mind inside her and experience his awareness of her ecstasy.

The sensations layered, intertwined, and combusted into a furious torrent as her climax roared through her body in tandem with his. Black spots obscured her vision, and the miracle went on, blurring her consciousness until he took them both over the edge of paradise.

Lydia's awareness faded in and out as Vincent embraced her, his cock still pulsing within. He clung to her as they recovered their breath, then carefully withdrew and gathered her into his arms. As he carried her to the bed, her mouth worked in an effort to speak.

"My God, I had no idea we could use our strength and powers for...for..." Words failed her in dazed awe. Her fingers threaded through his hair, toying with the silver and gold strands. *I love you*, she mouthed, though he couldn't see.

Vincent's heart pounded against her ear, and she felt him tremble as they sank into the soft mattress. He pulled the blanket over them, not releasing her from his embrace.

"I didn't know either." He kissed her lips and cheeks and rubbed her back in slow, soothing circles. "Until I met you. Then I couldn't stop dreaming of trying it."

He continued to massage Lydia until she fell asleep. Her last waking thought was a prayer: *Please, don't let him die!* Her heart clenched in agony.

❧

Before dawn, Vincent carefully removed himself from Lydia's bed, though all of his being cried out in protest. He could not risk discovery in case one of the servants, or worse, Miss Hobson returned to the house.

After dressing quickly, he lingered at the bedside, gazing upon the beautiful woman who had captivated his mind, stolen his heart, and drugged him with her body.

His arms tingled at the memory of last night's exertions. The realization made his gaze snap back to Lydia's slumbering form. Had he hurt her? He had been quite rough...

As if in answer, Lydia made a small sound of unmistakable bliss, a sated smile curving her lips. Vincent's shoulders relaxed, even as he longed to take her again. The urge surprised him. Until Lydia, he'd seen his lust as a minor inconvenience that needed to be assuaged occasionally. Now, carnal visions haunted him constantly. And this night... He closed his eyes as the erotic memories roared over him. Lydia's passion had been just as fervent.

Her *passion*... Vincent shook his head in wonder. She was just as passionate in bed as she was out of it. Contrary to his biggest fears, her exuberance for life did not die with the Change. Instead, her vigor seemed to have doubled.

Lydia had asked Vincent to teach her last night. But she had taught him more. The joy of the hunt, the beauty of the night, and the pleasure of a moonlit frolic… Vincent cursed himself for wallowing in misery these last two hundred years. *All that wasted time…*

Suddenly, he was too tired to think. His muscles became leaden weights. The sun had risen. All of his preternatural instincts could feel it.

Vincent made his way through the dark corridor to the guest chamber the duchess had arranged for him. He admired the clever, windowless setup of this floor. A vampire was free to roam the entire lair of the house, safe from the daylight. Of course, if there was a fire during the day, they would all perish. Thankfully, such was not likely in this sandstone house, with its slate roofs. And fire would be even less likely in his castle, with its thick stone walls, buffeted by damp winds from the sea.

Perhaps if he lived to return home, he would abandon his dismal prison-like cell in the castle bowels, wall up his few windows, and reclaim his former sumptuous chamber. And perhaps Lydia would join him and share his bed—which reminded him he would have to get one with stronger bedposts.

Thirty-two

LYDIA HEAVED A SIGH TO SEE THAT SHE HADN'T MISSED all of the excitement of the Exhibition. Somerset House was a glowing beacon of festivity. Tables lined the courtyard, heaving with trays of delectable confections, while servants carried trays of wine and cheeses. Musicians played jaunty melodies from a pavilion near the river. People strolled arm in arm, chatting merrily. Lanterns were strung across the grounds, making the place resemble a fantastical paradise.

Angelica grinned. "Oh, this is so exciting! How does it feel to be realizing your dreams?"

"Terrifying." Her knees wobbled as they approached the entrance.

Ian laughed. "I don't think vampires are supposed to be afraid."

"Don't worry. Everything will be fine." Vincent took her hand and gave it a reassuring squeeze.

"I hope so." Panic clawed at her throat. What if her exhibit was abandoned?

Her breath caught at the sight of people gathered around the vast array of paintings and sculptures.

David Wilkie's *Chelsea Pensioners Reading the Gazette of the Battle of Waterloo* had been roped off to protect it from the mob it drew. Sir Thomas Lawrence likely didn't approve. She'd heard Wilkie was a rival and in line to replace Lawrence as painter in standing to the King.

Glancing at the swarm surrounding the painting, Lydia shivered. She didn't think she could tolerate garnering that much attention.

She clung to Vincent's arm, and her eyes scanned the great chamber for her paintings. Hopefully they weren't tucked away into one of the shadowy corners, now cast into dark obscurity since night had fallen.

Her heart skipped a beat when she saw her exhibit, just barely visible, but only because she was so short. At least a dozen people circled her works. Some raised quizzing glasses to peruse the brushstrokes, while others pointed and exclaimed about the colors.

As she stepped closer, she heard Cassandra's voice. "Yes, I recently became acquainted with her through the Duchess of Burnrath. A charming young woman, and a brilliant painter."

The Duchess of Wentworth nodded just before her gaze lit on Vincent and Lydia. "Ah, here is the artist in the flesh, along with her handsome subject! Come, Lydia, meet your new admirers."

On shaky legs, she joined the throng. Smiles and compliments erupted all around, far surpassing her most fervent dreams.

"Such talent for one so young and lovely," an older gentleman said kindly.

"You've rendered a remarkable likeness of Lord

Deveril," Cassandra told her. "If he weren't standing before you, I feel he could walk out of the painting!"

The Duchess of Wentworth gave Lydia a mischievous smile before turning to Vincent. "Tell me, Deveril, is that why you requested her hand in marriage?"

"Among other reasons."

Everyone burst into laughter and offered congratulations.

Lydia turned to smile up at him, but froze in awe when she saw two other paintings on display. Her landscape of Castle Deveril hung beside the sunrise she'd gifted Vincent with before they left Cornwall.

"How did these come to be here? I never showed them to Lawrence."

"I did, when I delivered them to him the night before last. We decided they needed to be shared as well."

Grateful tears welled up in her eyes. For a moment, she wished everyone else would vanish so she could throw herself into his arms and cover him with kisses.

Pushing away such an undignified sentiment, she contented herself with squeezing his hand. "Thank you."

His long fingers caressed her wrist, promising more intimate touches later. He bent down and kissed her cheek. "I am so proud of you," he whispered in her ear.

Cassandra approached her with an apologetic smile. "I'm afraid I need to depart. I have trouble enduring large gatherings for very long."

"I understand. Thank you so much for coming." Lydia embraced her and said low, "Were you able to get the last few things for the phantasmagoria?"

Lady Rosslyn smiled. "All is in readiness on my part. Will you have the slides finished in time?"

"I have four more left."

"Splendid."

Ignoring Vincent's quizzical look, Lydia turned and thanked her admirers. "I must go see my mentor's exhibit."

The crowd milling around Sir Thomas Lawrence's exhibit was far larger than Lydia's, as she expected. She was also unsurprised to notice Sally and Maria Siddons, faces painted and wearing mouse-brown wigs. They huddled in the shadows behind the masses, glaring daggers at the man.

Thank heavens Vincent hasn't seen them. Before he looked in their direction, she pulled him closer to Lawrence's exhibit.

Seven paintings hung displayed in the best lighting in the chamber, and to her surprise, the portrait Lawrence had done of her numbered among them. The three she'd finished seemed to be garnering the most attention. Lydia felt a twinge of pleasure at the sight.

"Yours are better than the others," Vincent said as if reading her mind. The twinge became a rush.

The president of the Royal Academy caught sight of them and beckoned them over. "Miss Price! I had given up all hope of you making an appearance! I was overcome with worry that some terrible malady had befallen you."

Fighting the urge to roll her eyes at his melodrama, she gave him a chiding smile. "I'd told you I would be late."

"Ah well, I am happy you have arrived." For a moment, he looked peevish at her reply before he turned to his admirers. "This is one of my pupils, Miss Lydia Price. I painted her portrait and gave her the knowledge she needed to render hers of Lord Deveril. And now they are to be married. Isn't that the most romantic thing you've ever heard?"

As his audience sighed and cooed, Vincent bent to whisper, "He behaves as if he was our matchmaker."

She muffled her laughter with her fan as Henry Fuseli, one of the Academicians, stepped forward. "Yes, I saw Miss Price's exhibit. Your influence is abundantly clear in her work. Observe our president's portrait of the Countess of Blessington." He gestured at the painting which, all but the outline, Lydia had also painted. "The lines, the shadows, the sublime texture is almost as efficiently utilized in Miss Price's portrait of Lord Deveril." He haphazardly gestured in the direction of Lydia's exhibit. "If she were a man, she would be one of our finest students in the Academy."

Fury boiled up through her entire being. This was one of the men who had barred her from the school because of her sex, and he was such a fool that he couldn't recognize two paintings done by the same artist!

"Oh yes." Another man nodded so vigorously he almost spilled his champagne. Clapping Lawrence on the shoulder, he gushed, "Only an artist as remarkable as you could mold such young and frail talent." He smiled at Lydia before turning back to the paintings. "And you continue to improve! This is your best yet!"

Lawrence basked in the praise. "I had an exquisite subject and a sudden irrefutable instinct to use darker hues in the composition." He went on to deliver an unbelievable lump of folderol about brushstrokes,

smiling like a cat full of cream, not saying a word
about Lydia's contribution.

Lydia's fury became an inferno. Gnashing her fangs,
she drew away from Lawrence and his fawning admirers for their own safety.

"I cannot believe his nerve!" she hissed once they
were out of earshot. "He acts as if he painted it himself!"

Vincent shook his head, eyes rife with sympathy.
"Are you really all that surprised? You had an agreement, after all."

She heaved a bitter sigh. "No, but—"

Ian wended his way through the crowd, his features tight with urgency. He whispered something to
Vincent. Immediately, Vincent's eyes widened, and
his lips compressed into a thin frown.

"I have a matter to attend to. I'll return shortly."
He brushed his lips across the back of her hand and
hurried off with Ian.

Alone and despondent with no one to commiser-
ate with, Lydia rose up on her tiptoes, searching for
familiar company. Angelica was nowhere to be found,
and neither was the Duchess of Wentworth.

Her gaze once more lit on the Siddons sisters. They
would understand her vexation. Lifting her chin, she
approached them, reasoning that someone should
check on them anyway.

Sally greeted her with a bright smile. "Your display
was lovely, Miss Price."

"Better than Lawrence's," Maria added. "Except
for the paintings of his that you finished."

Lydia's ire rose. "He is taking complete credit for
them! Look at him strutting about like a peacock

and spouting flowery descriptions of the techniques *he* used."

Sally gasped in horror. "That blackguard!"

"He completed only a rough outline of Lady Blessington. I all but painted the whole thing." Taking a deep breath, she vented all of her frustration to them as they nodded and offered sympathy.

Once Lydia calmed, she came to a realization. "But this has taught me something. Even though Lawrence was once my hero, his acknowledgment and even his very approval of my work doesn't mean a fig to me anymore. Vincent has supported and encouraged me since I first met him, and that is what's important." Her heart immediately lightened at the truth of her words.

Maria smiled and began to reply. Then her attention abruptly left Lydia, and her eyes narrowed dangerously. "Sally, look!"

They turned to see Lawrence talking with Sarah Siddons and Fanny Kemble. A low growl emerged from Sally's throat. "How *dare* he talk to them!"

Maria bared her fangs for a moment and stalked closer before Lydia could pull her back.

Sarah Siddons, however, seemed fully capable of handling the faithless painter herself. "I've told you before, I do not wish to speak with you any longer. I came only out of respect for our former friendship."

"Ah, but my dearest Sarah, my heart has been desolate without your vivacious company! You've been a second mother to me, and a most treasured friend." Bending down to Fanny, he smiled, sickly sweet and somewhat frightening. "And this little poppet is the

very image of my sweet Maria. Surely you will allow
me to paint her portrait."

"How dare you speak of Maria after—" She broke
off and threw up her hands. "I have nothing further to
say to you, sirrah!"

Turning on her heel, she took her niece's hand and
stalked away. As she stormed out of the Exhibition,
she glanced in Sally and Maria's direction and paled.
Then, shaking her head, she departed.

Lawrence heaved a tragic sigh and bade his admirers
and his fellow academicians farewell.

Sally and Maria exchanged glances and followed him.

"No!" Lydia protested. "Don't do this!"

They ignored her and continued on in pursuit.

Frantically, Lydia searched the chamber for sight of
Vincent, Ian, or Angelica. Still, they were nowhere
to be found. But Sally and Maria had to be stopped
before they got themselves and Vincent in trouble.

She cursed them and Lawrence to the lower circles
of hell for once more creating a catastrophe and
making life difficult for Vincent.

Damn, I suppose I must handle this myself. Lydia took
a deep breath and squared her shoulders before hur-
rying after the vengeful vampires. She prayed Vincent
would catch up with her in time.

Thirty-three

"THE ELDER ARRIVED EARLY?" VINCENT BLINKED AT Ian in horrified disbelief.

"I'm afraid so. Rafe just informed me." Ian rubbed the bridge of his nose. "He came to your town house first and then to mine. Miss Hobson told him you were here. He is on his way."

Vincent sighed. "How very helpful of her." He cursed inwardly as dread curdled his gut. Sooner than expected, he would find out whether he would live or die…and what would become of Lydia. "Which one is it? Please say it isn't the Lord of Rome."

"Almost as bad. The Lord of Edinburgh, which is why he was able to come so soon." Ian's face was grave. "We had better fetch Lydia and prepare our defense."

Just then, Sarah Siddons rushed up to a woman behind them, face pale and eyes wild. "Hand me my smelling salts! I swear I have seen my daughters."

The woman eyed her with pity as she rummaged through her reticule. "Oh, Sarah, please calm yourself. You must have imagined it—it's the anxiety brought on from those dreams you've been having, along with speaking to that horrid man again. Let us bring Fanny home and have a nice cup of tea."

Vincent shook his head. This night was only getting worse. He never should have allowed Sally and Maria to visit their mother. Furthermore, he should have sent them away the moment he saw them tonight, despite their clever disguises.

They strode through the exhibits and past the departing patrons. Thomas Lawrence had left his display, and Lydia was nowhere to be seen. Unease curled in Vincent's belly as he searched for her in every direction.

"Do you see any sign of your wife?" he asked, now scanning the area for Angelica. "Perhaps she is with her?"

Ian shook his head. "She had better not be. I sent her to your town house the moment Rafe delivered his missive."

When he opened his Mark and felt Lydia's presence moving away from the Exhibition, his uneasiness increased, especially when he noticed that Sally and Maria were also gone. *And so was Lawrence.*

And Lydia had been infuriated with the man for stealing the credit for her work. Could she have joined the Siddons sisters on their dangerous quest for vengeance?

Although he hoped she hadn't done something so dangerous, the current evidence did not bode well.

His dread deepened when he caught sight of another vampire standing before David Wilkie's painting. The ancient power reverberating from his being marked him as one of the Elders. *The Lord of Edinburgh.* The urge to flee nagged at the back of Vincent's mind, though he knew the Elder undoubtedly had already seen him and Ian.

As if he'd read his mind, the Lord of Edinburgh turned and met his gaze.

"It's always good to see the skilled work of one of my countrymen," he remarked conversationally, gesturing to the painting he was admiring. His eyes turned cold and assessing. "Lord Deveril, I thought I'd have to run pell-mell all over London to find you."

Vincent bowed his head respectfully. "I apologize, my lord. I wasn't expecting you until the night after tomorrow."

"Yes, well it's best to get this over with, don't you agree?" He looked between Vincent and Ian. "Now where is your unsanctioned youngling? I hope you're not hiding her away from me."

"Of course not, my lord." His mind grappled with possible excuses. "She needed to feed."

The Elder's face was inscrutable. "Well, let us go find her then."

Vincent closed his eyes, trying to breathe past the hammering in his chest. He was utterly and completely doomed.

Rafe waited outside, leaning on a walking stick to disguise his bad arm. From the look of his guard-like pose, it was apparent that the Lord of Edinburgh had charged him to watch the entrance to see if Vincent or Lydia attempted to sneak away.

The Spaniard gave Ian a piercing look before

addressing the Elder. "They didn't try to slip away, my lord. Tell me, how were the paintings?"

While Rafe spoke, Ian whispered, "Do you know where she might have gone?"

"I think she went after Lawrence, along with the Siddons sisters."

His brows drew together, and he began to utter a curse, his mouth clamping shut when the Elder turned back to them. "Shall we be off?"

Vincent nodded reluctantly. "If you don't mind, I shall be able to find her more quickly if we walk. It is easier to feel the Mark that way." The last wasn't a lie. However, he needed to stall the Elder as long as possible.

"You Marked her before you Changed her?" The Lord of Edinburgh eyed him quizzically. "Why?"

"Because I was her guardian and wanted to be sure she was safe from rogues."

"Yes, I'd read in your report that she was your ward. But now I understand that she is your fiancée?"

"I thought it the most expedient measure under the circumstances. After all, she can't receive morning callers, much less marry a mortal man anymore." Vincent didn't mention that he'd already intended on marrying her before that.

"Hmm," the Elder murmured noncommittally. "Well, find her Mark, and let's be on our way."

Closing his eyes, Vincent opened himself to the bond he shared with Lydia. Just as he feared, he sensed her to the east, in the direction where Sir Thomas Lawrence lived.

He shoved his hands in his pockets and tried to feign calmness. "She went this way."

Ian and Rafe exchanged glances and followed along behind them. As they walked, for once Vincent was grateful for the presence of mortals. It gave him an excuse to proceed slowly.

Still, they arrived at Lawrence's flat all too soon. The Lord of Edinburgh eyed the building with suspicion. "It is my impression that it is rude to feed from mortals in their own abodes."

Vincent forced a lighthearted laugh. "I'd completely forgotten. Lydia had plans to have tea with her mentor after the Exhibition."

The Lord of Edinburgh gave him a doubtful look. "Without a chaperone?"

"Of course not." Hopefully it wouldn't be discovered that she was accompanied by two murderous vampires. "I'll fetch her. It'll be only a moment."

Rafe gave the Elder an unreadable look before turning to Vincent. "I'll go with you."

The Elder nodded, and so did Ian, the latter giving Vincent a clear message: he would stall the Elder as long as possible.

Vincent headed up the stairs to Lawrence's apartment, praying Rafe would keep his silence.

Not bothering to knock, he opened the door and cursed at the sight before him. Sir Thomas Lawrence lay back on his bed, a blissful smile on his slumbering face as the Siddons sisters lay on either side of him, their fangs plunged in his neck.

Lydia stood before them. She whirled around, golden eyes wide with surprise and guilt.

"What in the hell do you think you're doing?"

Sally and Maria withdrew from Lawrence and

bit their fingers to heal the man's wounds. Vincent breathed a silent prayer of thanks that the troublesome sod was still alive.

"It is not what it looks like!" Lydia exclaimed.

Rafe stalked forward, eyes narrowed dangerously. "Oh? And what does it look like, other than these two trying to kill that mortal?"

"I was *stopping* them," she snapped. "None of you were around when they went after him, so I did what I felt I had to do."

"Is that why they were draining him while you watched?"

"Well, after all he put them and their family through—not to mention his callous behavior regarding my work—I decided they at least deserved a taste."

To everyone's surprise, Rafe threw back his head and laughed. "All right, I can understand that. However, you three had better explain yourselves and do it quickly. The Lord of Edinburgh is outside, waiting to begin Deveril's inquest."

"He's here *now*?" Lydia's choked gasp echoed through the room.

Sally and Maria left the sleeping painter and scrambled off the bed.

"We are so sorry, my lord," Maria told him. "It is only that he was haranguing our mother at the Exhibition and…" Her voice shook in suppressed horror. "And he was eyeing our niece as if he intended to make her his next conquest."

"She's only *thirteen*!" Sally cried, wringing her hands. "We wanted only to protect her!"

Vincent could understand that, however...
"Your own desire for vengeance had nothing to
do with this?"

Maria gave him a direct look and nodded. "Of
course it did. But Lydia had a long talk with us, and
we've realized something."

"And what is that?"

Sally stepped closer and took her sister's hand.
"We learned that revenge doesn't really matter to us
anymore. All we wanted was to punish him for driving
us apart and then causing so much grief that it would
have killed one or both of us. We wanted to hurt him
for separating us."

"But he didn't separate us." Maria smiled up at
Sally. "We are together, and that matters more than
vengeance."

"I am happy to hear that," Vincent said drily, and
he really was. "However, that doesn't change the fact
that yet again you have disobeyed one of my commands. I have no choice but to punish you both. I
command you to return to Cornwall immediately, and
I will deal with you when I get there." Suddenly he
remembered that he might not be alive to do so. He
cleared his throat. "If I am executed, Emrys will carry
out your punishment."

The Siddons sisters bowed. "Yes, my lord."

They headed for the door, but Rafe stopped them.
"I will have someone keep an eye on the painter to
make certain he leaves your kin alone."

Sally's eyes widened. "Thank you. You cannot
know how much—"

"And if he causes any trouble when I serve as Lord

of this city in Ian's stead, I may be willing to make an arrangement with you as to how to handle him."

Maria did not bother with thanks. Instead, she threw her arms around the scarred Spaniard and kissed him on both cheeks. Rafe flinched and gently, but firmly, disengaged her. "Go now. And please take the rear exit. You still have your writ of passage, yes?"

They nodded and hurried away.

Vincent blinked at Rafe, unable to hide his shock at the surly vampire's uncharacteristic display of compassion and disregard for the rules.

"Family is an important thing where I come from. I continue to watch over mine," he said gruffly and opened the door. "The Elder is likely wondering what kept us."

Lydia cast a last look at the sleeping painter. "Are you going to tell him…about this?"

Rafe shook his head. "I see no need to make it worse for Deveril."

She beamed and embraced him. He sighed and patted her on the shoulder. Golden eyes tentative, she walked to Vincent. "Are you angry with me?"

"No, but I was worried." He kissed her on the top of her head. "I still am."

She squeezed him tight. "And I as well."

They encountered the Lord of Edinburgh at the door. "What the devil took so long?"

Lydia cringed and pressed herself closer to Vincent. Before he could fabricate an excuse, Rafe answered.

"The painter had dishonestly taken credit for her work, so she gave him a well-deserved dressing down." Giving Lydia a stern look, he chided her. "There was no need to tell your lord a pretty lie about having tea. Lord Deveril would have understood. Then again, he might have had it out with the lying churl as well."

Lydia pouted prettily and hung her head. "I am sorry." Her trembling hand squeezed Vincent's harder.

"I do apologize for the delay," Vincent told the Elder. "Shall we return to my town house?"

The Lord of Edinburgh nodded, his censorious gaze remaining on Lydia. Vincent pulled her closer, tucking her slightly behind him, every instinct screaming to protect her.

Ian waited outside, casting them an apologetic look before bowing to the Lord of Edinburgh. "My carriage has arrived."

The Burnrath coach rolled into view, cutting through the thick London fog. Its black wood with silver gilding made the vehicle resemble a funeral hack. Vincent hoped the resemblance wasn't symbolic.

Vibrating with reluctance, he helped Lydia into the carriage and pulled her close to him. Propriety be damned. Lydia gave the Elder a nervous look before burying her head against Vincent's shoulder. Rafe and Ian looked out the windows as though to avoid the sight of the couple who might not see the next moonrise together. Vincent's gaze swept over Lydia's face and hair, drinking in her features for what could be the last time. He could feel her heart pounding in time with the clatter of the carriage wheels. Her fear made him feel even more helpless.

Thirty-four

THE COACH ARRIVED AT VINCENT'S TOWN HOUSE, THE horses' shoes clattering on the cobblestones with sharp finality. Ian and Rafe stepped out, followed by the Lord of Edinburgh. They waited for Vincent and Lydia to alight and followed behind like an honor guard.

Vincent rang for brandy and bade Aubert to retire once everyone was settled in the parlor. Angelica perched nervously on the settee, swirling a glass of wine and stealing tremulous glances at the Lord of Edinburgh. Pouring a glass for the vampire who would be judge, jury, and executioner, Vincent fought back a burst of insane laughter. *Such a civilized atmosphere, when I am on trial for my life.*

After handing everyone their brandy, Vincent sat next to Lydia and took her hand.

The Elder opened his satchel and took a sip of the strong liquor. "Shall we begin?"

Vincent took a drink and nodded. Ian and Rafe did as well, their glasses untouched. Lydia only shivered.

Clearing his throat, the Lord of Edinburgh said, "Vincent Tremayne, Lord of Cornwall, you are charged with the crime of Changing a mortal without sanction from the Elders. Do you admit to committing this crime?"

"I do," Vincent replied.

"Please explain the details of your crime and how it came to occur."

Even though everything was in the report he'd submitted, Vincent related the tale, knowing full well the reason for the request. Edinburgh wanted to trap him in a lie.

Once satisfied that Vincent had not deviated from his explanation, the Elder nodded.

"I shall now examine your character and the aftermath of your crime, before your sentence is decided." The vampire withdrew a sheaf of documents. "I will read the reports and testimonies we've gathered from Cornwall, and then I'll hear from the witnesses."

As the report was read, a strange tremor of warmth engulfed Vincent. His people had nothing but good to say of him.

"The vampires of Cornwall deem their Lord to be just and abiding of our laws. Our investigator has determined that they have not made these statements under duress." Shuffling the papers, the Elder added, "I see you also included a petition to name your second, Emrys Adair, to be ruler of Cornwall in the event of an unmerciful judgment."

Vincent nodded, throat tight.

"Very well, now let's hear from the witnesses. Lord of London?"

Ian gave Vincent a compassionate glance and stood.

"Your Grace, please tell us how you came to be involved in Lord Deveril's crime," Edinburgh commanded.

Ian surveyed the ancient vampire with an equally implacable gaze. "The Lord of Cornwall requested temporarily to reside in my city so that he could find a husband for his ward."

"And what did you think of him becoming involved with a mortal in the first place?" A note of derision laced the vampire's voice.

Ian replied blandly, "He was honoring an alliance."

"A *mortal* alliance," the Elder practically spat at Vincent. "Why did you not refuse?"

Vincent fought the urge to grind his teeth. "As His Grace said, I was honoring an alliance. In my mortal days, Lydia's ancestor fought beside me in battle. We swore an oath of friendship between our families. One of the conditions was to become guardian to the other's descendants if needed. The girl's grandmother would have had Lydia thrown into an insane asylum if I had not taken her under my care." He fixed Edinburgh with a pointed stare. "Just because I am now a vampire does not mean I will abandon my honor. I will not break a vow."

With no rebuttal, the Elder turned back to Ian. "Once Lord Deveril and his charge arrived in your city, did he try to find a husband for her?"

Ian nodded. "Yes, he did, and he received five offers."

"Why did he not accept one?"

The Lord of London paused a moment, measuring his words. "I believe he decided he wanted her for himself."

"So you believe his Changing her was deliberate?"

"No, that's not what I am saying!" Ian retorted. "I only mean it is my belief that, had Lydia not suffered the unfortunate accident, he would have filed a petition to Change her."

"Is this true?" he asked Vincent.

"Yes." He heard Lydia gasp, and he squeezed her hand in reassurance. Rafael Villar was then called to testify.

Rafe concurred with Ian's theory that Vincent had wanted Lydia for himself, and added, "However, I believe he was a fool to deliberate so long about it."

"And why do you believe he asked her to wed him?"

"Perhaps he is in love with her?" Rafe's tone held a tinge of sarcasm. "I do know he had intended to do so before she was attacked."

The ancient's eyes narrowed. "How do you know this?"

"Her chaperone, Miss Hobson, informed me. I would have brought her to confirm my statement, but as she is a mortal, I decided that would not be wise." He shrugged. "Of course, Deveril may have become engaged to Miss Price to avoid any more attention from the human aristocracy."

He turned to Vincent. "Which is true?"

"Both," Vincent answered levelly. "I also wanted to ensure that in the event of my death, Lydia would have wealth, land, and a widow's freedom to make her own way in life without scrutiny, thus reducing the risk of mortals discovering what she is."

Edinburgh considered this and appeared satisfied. "Now I'll assess the youngling. I understand that Angelica Ashton, consort to the Lord of London, was appointed the youngling's mentor, and Rafael Villar accompanied her to observe her training. Is this correct?"

Vincent and the others nodded solemnly, and Angelica stepped forward with a bow.

"Your Grace, describe your training of Lydia Price. How is she adapting to our ways?"

Angelica faced the Elder fearlessly as she narrated Lydia's progress in hunting and all the things she had told her about a vampire's strengths and weaknesses. "All around, I feel Lydia's adaption to the Change has been exemplary," she concluded.

"Has there been any sign of madness?" Edinburgh asked sharply.

"Not at all."

Rafe was called on once more. He confirmed Angelica's testimony, although to Vincent's ire, he did not neglect to describe Lydia's awkwardness and mistakes during her first few hunts.

When asked again if Lydia displayed any indication of madness, the Spaniard shook his head. "Not at all. I also add that I am impressed with Lydia's strength and capabilities, and I believe she shall be a fine addition to our kind." Rafe turned away before Vincent could give him a nod of gratitude.

The Elder's gaze locked on Lydia. "Under such satisfactory testimony, I acknowledge you, Lydia Price. Have you anything to say on Deveril's behalf?"

Lydia nodded emphatically. "Please, my lord, don't kill him. All of this is my fault. If anyone is to be punished, it should be me."

Shock waves reverberated through Vincent's body

at the pronouncement. He sucked in endless gusts of air until white spots obscured his vision.

He couldn't believe it.

He had not heard correctly.

One look at the duke's pale face answered his dreaded question. The possibility of living without her was a sentence worse than death. And the torture they would put her through...

As the realization hit him, he released the breath he was holding in an earsplitting shout. "No!" Vincent grasped her shoulder and pulled her against him. "She doesn't know what she's saying."

"Silence!" the Elder snapped and once more faced Lydia. "Why do you feel Lord Deveril's actions are your fault, youngling?"

Lydia lifted her chin and faced the ancient vampire, refusing to tremble as she made her statement. "Because I'm the one who put myself in the position of mortal danger by storming out of the safety of his home and into the path of a cutthroat. If it weren't for his obligation to protect me, he never would have broken your laws."

"I see." The vampire stroked his chin. "Well, killing you would certainly teach Lord Deveril a lesson..."

"Please," Vincent whispered to her in heartbreaking agony. "Do not do this!"

"However, it would be quite a waste, and I cannot ignore the fact that Deveril is still the one who violated the law, so he is the one responsible, regardless of your touching and reasonable defense." Edinburgh's lips compressed in a grim line. "And execution is the traditional penalty for Changing a mortal without our approval."

Lydia clung to Vincent and moaned brokenly, "No, *please!*"

"Yet in this case I find myself reluctant to dispense with a Lord Vampire who has been so obedient and peaceful in the past. Never before have we been called upon to settle any conflicts with you." The Elder paused, watching as everyone held their breath, blatantly enjoying the agonizing tension. "There may be an alternative."

"What?" *Anything.*

"As you well know, governing such a large people across the expanse of the world can be quite costly." Edinburgh smiled tightly. "Therefore, if you pay a fine of say, one hundred thousand pounds, we would feel satisfied leaving you alive."

Ian gasped and sputtered. "*One hundred thousand* pounds?"

"Shut it!" Vincent snapped, not giving a damn that he was speaking to the Lord of London. He met the Elder's gaze. "I agree to the fine." He'd give up his castle and his land if the Elder asked. Though at this sum, he'd have to mortgage them anyway.

"I'll require a down payment of ten thousand, as collateral for your honor."

"Of course." Vincent reached inside his greatcoat for his bank drafts. *I'll bet the other ninety thousand that this will go straight into your pocket.*

The ancient vampire grinned and withdrew a document from his satchel. He dipped the quill and handed it to Vincent. "If you sign here, I can be on my way. And be certain to have the funds deposited at our bank by the end of the month, or else we will have to kill you."

Once the contract was signed, the Elder took another sip of brandy and rose to depart.

"My lord?" Lydia approached the Lord of Edinburgh. "I have one more question."

The ancient paused at the door. "Yes, youngling?"

"Am I a vampire of London or Cornwall?"

He gave her an impatient glare. "As you were Changed in the Lord of London's territory, he could legally lay claim to you, though that is his choice." He strode out the door before she could say more.

"I release you to the Lord of Cornwall," Ian told her. "I have enough mischievous younglings in my territory."

Lydia released her breath in an audible sigh. Angelica leaped up from her seat and spun in a joyful circle. The men remained frozen in disbelief at the miraculous reprieve.

"You're not going to be killed, thank God!" Lydia cried.

When he was at last able to breathe again, Vincent uttered a dry laugh. "I am alive because of a need for government funding. Good Lord." He shook his head. "I have the utmost sympathy for those who do not have that option."

"As do I," Rafe added quietly.

"One hundred thousand pounds?" Ian repeated dazedly. "Do you have that much?"

"Most of it. However, I will still have to mortgage my castle and ask for loans." Vincent sighed and met Lydia's gaze. "I'll be a pauper for quite some time, I'm afraid."

"I don't care!" she said firmly. "You will be alive."

Warmth suffused his heart at her declaration.

Ian stroked his chin. "I can give you a loan. I won't even charge interest."

Vincent held out his hand. "Ian, Angelica, Rafael, you have my eternal gratitude for all you've done for me and Lydia. I am in your debt."

Angelica beamed and gave him a firm handshake. "I am happy that your harrowing experience has a happy conclusion. It has definitely provided inspiration for my writing."

The duchess then gave Lydia a hug. "You were so very brave. I am happy to have you as a friend."

Ian shook Vincent's hand. "You have always been among my strongest allies. It would have been devastating to lose you."

The duke then bowed to Lydia. "My wife is right. You are the most courageous youngling that I have ever beheld. A most fitting bride for the Lord of Cornwall."

Rafe scowled before shaking Vincent's hand. "It was nothing."

Lydia chuckled at his gruffness. The Spaniard met her gaze, and his narrow lips curved in a slight but genuine smile as he shook her hand.

"Well"—Angelica set aside her brandy glass—"that was quite exciting. But now I'd like to go home and finish Vincent's surprise for tomorrow evening." She curled her fingers around Ian's arm. "Shall we be off?"

Lydia shook her head. "I need to feed, and I would like for Vincent to walk me home, if it's all right."

"You're not supposed to be alone with him without a chaperone," Rafe reminded her, though there was a teasing glint in his amber eyes.

Angelica put her hands on her hips and glared at

the Spaniard. "Oh, Rafe, they deserve to be alone after all they've been through." She turned to Lydia. "Though do try to be home soon, or Miss Hobson will be livid."

Although he longed to take Lydia upstairs into his bedchamber, Vincent reluctantly took her hand and led her outside to hunt. They found their prey and fed quickly, getting it done so they could then savor their time together.

Vincent watched Lydia as she walked beside him, amazed at how well she had taken to her new existence. She embraced the night, at harmony with the shadows, and she hunted at his side as if she'd always been there with him. *She belongs with me*, his heart pulsed with conviction.

"Tell me of this surprise you have planned."

A hint of uneasiness flashed in her eyes before she regained her teasing tone. "I am sorry, my lord. You will have to wait." She squeezed his hand. "May we *run* now?"

Together, they took off in a flash, the spring breeze whipping across their cheeks with the scent of newly bloomed flowers. Vincent felt her joy of the run echo his own. *She belongs with me*, his soul repeated.

When they arrived at Burnrath House, he couldn't stop from hauling her into his arms and kissing her good night. Her lips tasted like honeysuckle.

"Stay with me tonight?" she whispered against his mouth.

His hardness ached with temptation. "I cannot. As we are not yet wed, people will talk." He cursed them all to the lowest circles of hell.

She nodded and bit her lip, looking suddenly vulnerable. "Do you still want me?"

Vincent couldn't hold back his laughter. "More than a drunkard wants wine, Lydia. Now I must go before someone sees us." Pulling her into his arms for a last embrace, he inhaled the scent of her hair. "Until tomorrow."

Before he lost his resolve and carried her off to ravage her, he escorted her back to the house and left, reminding himself that he had a surprise of his own planned.

Thirty-five

THE NEXT EVENING, LYDIA AWOKE QUIVERING WITH anticipation. Tonight she would present her own phantasmagoria.

"How do you think he'll react?" she asked Angelica worriedly when they met downstairs.

The duchess remained silent and considering for the longest time. Finally, she replied, "He may very well walk out of the room after the part where—"

Lydia cut her short, fighting back worry. "Could your husband make him stay?"

"I could ask him to try," Angelica replied dubiously.

It was likely the best she could hope for. "And if Vincent remains, what do you suppose he'll think?"

At last, the duchess smiled. "If he stays until the end, I feel it is likely you'll achieve your desired outcome from this endeavor."

Quickly, she and Angelica sought out their first meal and returned to Burnrath House for the preparations. Lady Rosslyn arrived soon afterward with her magic lantern.

When Vincent strode into the drawing room, Lydia

had to clasp her hands behind her back to resist running into his arms. As Ian and Rafe took him off to occupy him with a game of chess, part of her wondered if he'd ever hold her again after this.

An hour later, Lydia paced anxiously through the music room. Everything was in readiness. Chairs for Vincent, Ian, Rafe, and Miss Hobson were arranged before the black curtain. The screen was poised halfway between, prepared to be lowered the moment the audience was distracted. Lady Rosslyn took her place in the shadows with her magic lantern and Lydia's carefully painted slides. Angelica stood by her glass harmonica, resplendent in one of the black velvet cloaks she'd ordered for the occasion and insisted they all wear.

Yes, everything was in readiness, except for Lydia. A thousand questions and doubts raced through her already-taxed mind. In mere minutes, Vincent would hear the story and see the paintings she'd painstakingly worked on. Would he charge out of the room in outrage, as Angelica had predicted? Her heart clenched in terror at the very real possibility.

Or what if Vincent remained and was repulsed by her story? What if it made him further regret the ever-increasing burden she'd been since she came into his life? Crippling guilt threatened to drown her. If it weren't for her, Vincent wouldn't have faced a death sentence and become beggared.

Despite her remorse, Lydia could not bring herself to regret meeting him. Every smile he'd bestowed on her, every time she'd made him laugh, every kiss he'd stolen, every moment in his arms, all were memories she would cherish for the remainder of her existence. And she could never regret his Changing her into a vampire, giving her powers and experiences she'd never thought possible.

Her chin lifted. She would not be a burden to Vincent any longer. She would undo all the trouble she'd caused him. And she would do everything in her power to teach him to find joy in his existence.

∽

Vincent and Ian looked up from their chess game as Rafe entered the room. "It is time for Her Grace and Miss Price's presentation. It shall be held in the music room."

"Splendid." Ian rose from his seat. "I was growing quite weary of being trounced."

As they followed Rafe down the stairs, Vincent grew increasingly maddened with curiosity. Ian seemed to share his sentiment.

"Come now, Rafe," the duke prodded. "You've held your tongue for the entire time. What is this presentation that Miss Price and my wife have been cooking up?"

The Spaniard sighed. "It's only another phantas-magoria."

"A *what*?" Vincent blinked at the strange word.

Ian laughed. "Ah, brilliant! I can imagine Miss Price was delighted to participate in creating such a production. Why didn't you say so before?"

Rafe scowled, seeming to be in a fouler mood than usual. "Because I only recently learned what the blasted things are called."

"What are they?" Vincent demanded, irritated with his ignorance.

The duke clapped him on the shoulder. "They are the most astounding art form ever to be invented. Words cannot describe it. You, my friend, are in for a treat."

Ian opened the music-room door, gesturing for Rafe and Vincent to precede him. The duchess awaited them, dramatically garbed in a black cloak. Lydia and Lady Rosslyn stood behind her in matching costumes, solemn expressions on their faces.

"If you gentlemen would please be seated." Angelica gestured to a group of chairs placed in front the fireplace, which had been blocked off by a thick black curtain.

Vincent, Ian, and a reluctant Rafe joined her. Suddenly, the lights went out and an ethereal melody trilled. Vincent glanced over his shoulder to see the duchess playing an odd instrument that resembled a crystal caterpillar spitted over a desk. The cylindrical object spun slowly on a shaft through a wheel, which Angelica operated with her foot.

Lydia's rich voice rose above the music. "Once upon a time, there lived a young woman who loved to paint. Her parents nurtured her gift."

Ian nudged him, and he turned back to the curtain, though he would have preferred to keep his eyes on Lydia.

Vincent gaped as an image of a black-haired woman smiling up at a happy couple appeared to float before his eyes. He recognized it as one of Lydia's paintings. Before he could wonder how it had manifested, the image seemed to retreat into a dark tunnel until it disappeared. He blinked, realizing that a transparent screen had been lowered in front of the curtain.

Lydia continued the tale: "Then, tragedy fell. Her mother and father both perished from the fever."

Melancholic music played on the instrument as the next vision appeared of the young woman weeping as two coffins were loaded into a funeral hack. Vincent gasped as the realization struck. This story was about Lydia.

As if confirming the thought, Lydia continued. "She was sent on a long journey across the ocean to live with her relatives."

The next picture showed the woman on the deck of a ship, her black skirts blowing in the wind as she faced a terrifying gale.

"Once she arrived in the strange new land, she discovered that her family did not want her. Instead, they had decreed that she was to live with a monster in a haunted castle." Lydia's voice wavered then, and she glanced at Vincent with a wide, unreadable gaze.

The music became eerie as a new image came into focus. The "monster" loomed over Lydia's form, and though he was mostly cast in shadow, Vincent could recognize his own eyes as they reflected the lightning in the background over his castle.

Agonizing pain pierced Vincent's heart at Lydia's description of him as a monster, both in words and in her skilled artistic rendering. He attempted to rise, to charge out of the room and this house, never to return. Ian clamped a hand on his shoulder and forced him back to his seat.

Vincent tensed as Lydia took a shaky breath and continued the tale. "The monster did not want her either, so he did his best to be frightening. But the woman was not afraid."

Angelica played a playful tune on her strange instrument as the next picture was revealed. Vincent recognized the west hill with its great oak, where Lydia had liked to paint. This time, she had depicted him from the back, posing in a caricature of some sort of sinister beast, arms raised and hands reaching out like claws. Lydia's likeness, however, was undaunted. A wide smile shone on her face, and she appeared to be on the verge of joyful applause.

Lydia pressed on. "So the monster thought hard on how to get rid of her. He consulted a witch as well as two other monsters. It was decided that she should be taken to the great city, where many young women were sent to find homes."

A mournful note played as the picture depicted a dour Miss Hobson and a gleeful Vincent, holding up ball gowns and pointing their fingers in command. Vincent heard the real Miss Hobson sniff, offended at being called a witch. His brows drew together in confusion. Where was Lydia going with this?

"The woman did not want to go to the city. She loved the haunted castle and, unbeknownst to herself, had begun to love the monster as well. Since she knew he did not want her, she obeyed him."

The music grew yet more tragic as a heartbroken Lydia was revealed, reaching out to a seemingly indifferent Vincent.

No, I loved you from the start! Vincent opened his

mouth to shout. Then the next part of the story choked off his words.

"She met her family in the great city. She learned that her grandmother was the *true* monster, and the rest of her family bowed down to her as slaves. The monster she'd been sent to live with was indeed no monster at all. He was an angel. And the witch was in truth a saint."

Miss Hobson nodded in satisfaction as a haunting melody played. The next picture revealed a grotesque caricature of Lady Morley wielding a whip and Vincent holding Lydia in his arms, shielding her with gossamer wings.

"The woman longed to prove her love to her guardian angel." Lydia's voice was filled with passion. "She pondered long and hard on the matter. Nothing would truly be worthy, yet perhaps if she showed him what was in her heart when she thought of him, he would feel it too."

And then the sun rose over a verdant meadow. From delicate pink to brightest gold, it filled the chamber with the glory of the dawn. Lydia gave him a sunrise so realistically portrayed that Vincent could feel its warmth upon his face and smell the wildflowers blooming in the field. Her sun did not burn him.

The warm breeze stirred his hair, and Vincent realized that this detail was indeed real. Reluctantly pulling his gaze from Lydia's miraculous creation, he noticed a pair of footmen wafting fans over steaming pots of perfumed water while Angelica used her odd instrument to duplicate birdsong.

Hot liquid trailed down his cheeks. It was not a

trick of the production. It was Vincent's own tears of joy.

His heart cried out in protest as the sunrise faded, taking with it the trilling birdsong. The gas lamps were once again lit, and the curtains parted. Ian, Vincent, and Miss Hobson stood and applauded.

Miss Hobson interrupted with a frown. "How does the tale end?"

Vincent stared intently at Lydia as he abandoned his seat and slowly approached her. "The guardian angel wept with joy at the woman's creation, for she showed what had been in *his* heart all along." Taking Lydia's hand, he gently pulled her toward him. "As for the rest of the tale, we shall see."

He couldn't bear waiting any longer. Reverently, he kissed Lydia's knuckles. "There's something I need to do. I shall return soon."

Vincent met the duke's eyes. "Do not let her go anywhere."

Ian grinned wryly. "You may count on it, though don't be too long, for Angelica and Lady Rosslyn shall likely want to toast the production's success."

⁕

Two hours later, the drawing room had dissolved into an uncomfortable silence as everyone awaited Vincent's return. The only ones seemingly complacent with the delay were Ian, Rafe, and Lady Rosslyn, the latter of whom was settled placidly near the fireplace, reading a copy of Mary Shelley's *Frankenstein*.

"I say, whatever can be keeping Lord Deveril?" Miss Hobson's voice was full of annoyance as she wrapped one hand around her cup of untouched tea and waved off Rafe's cigar smoke with the other. "I would hardly call this a quick errand."

Lydia and Angelica exchanged nervous glances. At first she'd assumed that Vincent had needed to feed, but Miss Hobson was right. It shouldn't have taken this long if he meant to return soon. Panic crawled up her spine anew. Maybe he truly had been revolted by her story and had been too polite to say so in front of everyone. Her hands twisted restlessly in her lap.

Just as her nerves were on the verge of collapse, the door knocker sounded, and she heard the butler say calmly, "Welcome back, my lord."

Moments later, Vincent's tall form filled the doorway. Joy surged in Lydia's being at his return. Another man followed behind him, appearing flustered and exhausted. Without bothering to introduce the stranger, Vincent crossed the room to Lydia.

Taking her hands in his, he sank down to kneel before her. "I know we already are engaged, but I never went about it properly. Lydia Price, would you do me the great honor of becoming my wife?"

Gasps permeated the room as Vincent reached into his pocket with his other hand and pulled out a small jewel case. He flicked the box open to reveal a golden ring filigreed with Celtic knots and adorned with a large diamond surrounded by a rainbow of other jewels.

Lydia's heart lodged in her throat even as unmitigated happiness warmed her body.

"When?" The word escaped aloud before she was aware.

"Now." From another pocket in his waistcoat, Vincent withdrew a small sheaf of papers. "I have with me a marriage contract and a special license. I've also managed to procure a parson at this late hour."

Everyone's gazes flew to the stranger, whose identity was now revealed. The parson yawned as if in emphasis of the inconvenience. All eyes shifted to Lydia, awaiting her reply.

Her knees quaked beneath her gown, threatening to give out and topple her.

"Please, Lydia," he said achingly. "I cannot bear another night of you not being mine."

"Yes." The word escaped her lips past the joy swelling within.

As if afraid she'd change her mind, Vincent quickly slipped the elaborate ring on her third finger and rose to his feet, retaining his grip on her hand. "You've made me the happiest of men," he replied. "Now let's have done with these signatures, so Parson Matheson may perform his duty and return to his home."

Lydia followed him in a daze to the table as Angelica, grinning in encouragement, handed her a freshly dipped quill. Tears brimming in her eyes, Lydia signed the contract. The marriage license blurred in front of her as she signed that as well.

The documents were then signed by all the witnesses, and the parson cleared his throat. "Where shall we have the ceremony?"

"Right here," Vincent commanded. "Right now."

Miss Hobson and Lady Rosslyn gasped. Rafe and Ian raised their brows.

"Wait!" Angelica protested. "Let us at least procure

some flowers." Before anyone could reply, she grabbed Lady Rosslyn's hand, and they headed off to the rear garden.

Parson Matheson blinked sleepily. "And who shall give the bride away? I understand that she is an orphan and the groom is her guardian, so he cannot very well give her away to himself, for that would be"—he floundered—"quite odd…"

"I will," Ian announced, giving Lydia a warm smile.

"I daresay," Miss Hobson finally said, "this is all *highly* irregular. Are you certain you cannot wait to do this properly? We haven't even held the engagement ball, and we should have the banns read, have Miss Price outfitted for a gown and trousseau, invite guests…" She spread her arms helplessly.

"No." Vincent's handsome face was implacable.

Lydia hastened to reassure her chaperone. "All the guests I would have wanted are already here." The truth of her statement warmed her all over.

"But people will talk!" the chaperone protested.

Ian shrugged. "They already *are* talking."

Lady Rosslyn and Angelica returned with a bouquet of lilacs, gardenias, and red roses. As the flowers were placed in Lydia's hand, the parson cleared his throat and opened his prayer book, beginning the ceremony.

After Ian stepped forward and placed her hand in Vincent's, Lydia ceased to hear the parson's words. Instead, she stared up into the turbulent blue eyes of the Lord Vampire of Cornwall and allowed her happiness to carry her soul.

As if in a trance, she repeated her vows. And then it was finished. Parson Matheson pronounced them man and wife, signed the license, and departed without having a glass of champagne.

The celebration was small yet cozy. Everyone repeated their felicitations, and although Miss Hobson could not refrain from a few complaints about the rushed ceremony, the lack of preparation, and even the absence of traditional orange blossoms, her satisfaction was evident to all. Though the means were unconventional, in the end, her charge had secured one of the most brilliant matches of the Season.

Lady Rosslyn finished her champagne and stood. "I am afraid I must be going now. I have my own project to finish." She turned to Vincent and Lydia with a bright smile. "Congratulations to you both. I was honored to witness such a romantic surprise."

Rafe snorted. "Yes, *surprise* would be a very apt word indeed."

The countess glared at the Spaniard, cheeks blazing crimson as her jade eyes sparked. "I don't think you could do any better." With that, she spun on her heel and marched away.

Instead of scowling, Rafe continued to watch Lady Rosslyn's retreating form with a strange, almost hungry expression on his face. Lydia hoped he wasn't planning to bite her. Then Vincent swooped her up in his arms and carried her upstairs, and all other thoughts disappeared.

Thirty-six

THE MOMENT THEY ENTERED THE BEDCHAMBER, Vincent leaned down to kiss Lydia. The pensive look in her golden eyes stopped him short. Carefully, he set her down, reluctantly removing his hands from her.

"What is the matter?" *Oh God, please don't let her already regret marrying me.*

"Vincent?" Lydia's voice was surprisingly timid. "You didn't marry me just to save me from the scrutiny of mortals, did you?"

He laughed, overcome with relief. "Did you not read the date on the special license? I applied for it the night after we first made love—" He held up a hand at her suspicious gaze. "I didn't procure the license out of guilt. I did it because I couldn't bear another day or night without you in my arms. Anyhow, I didn't receive the blasted thing until a fortnight ago. They take time to acquire, you know."

Her lush lips pouted. "Then why did you not tell me sooner?"

He closed his eyes at the painful memory. "I thought you hated me for Changing you."

"No! I thought you were upset with me for causing you so much trouble." She took a shaky breath. "I love you, Vincent. I think I have from the start. Do you...love me?"

He sighed and raised his gaze heavenward. Surely she knew the obvious. "Look at your ring, Lydia."

As she looked down at the bauble, he listed the stones. "Diamond, emerald, amethyst, ruby, emerald, sapphire, topaz... Now what are the first letters of the jewels?"

She studied the ring further then looked up at him with wide eyes brimming with tears. "Dearest! It spells *dearest*."

Warmth filled his heart at the passion in her voice. "Yes, Lydia, *dearest*. I love you. My life was bleak and miserable until you came to me and taught me the meaning of happiness. I thought it would never work for us, because I was afraid the Change would destroy your passion for life."

Lydia laughed. "I have found more enjoyment in this life than I could ever imagine. And as for passion, I have discovered it in boundless amounts, for *you* are my passion, Vincent."

"*Me?*" Joy suffused him as he took in her words.

"Yes. Now I am your bride, so claim this passion before I perish from longing." She reached up, and her fingers caressed his hair in a gesture as delicate as a whisper.

Vincent smiled. Her words were as melodramatic as a gothic novel, yet somehow fitting. Especially with her large golden eyes and lush lips parted in desire for his kiss. "Well, we cannot have that, Lady Deveril."

Her new title was sweet on his tongue, though not as delectable as her mouth when he bent down to claim it. He savored her taste, pulling her closer, marveling at how right she felt in his arms, as if he were at last complete.

Lydia rose up on tiptoe, tangling her hands in his hair as she kissed him back hungrily. Her tongue darted between his fangs, an eager moan building in her throat. Vincent bit back a groan. If she kept this up, it would be mere seconds before he ravaged her.

Gently, Vincent withdrew. "Not so fast. Now that you are truly mine at last, I want to savor you."

Slowly, he sank to his knees and unfastened her gown, kissing her shoulders once they were bared. When the gown pooled at her feet, he breathed a silent thanks that she wore no stays. However, he did not continue undressing her. Instead, he caressed her lithe form through her chemise, delighting at the sight of her tight nipples puckering beneath the thin fabric. He toyed with her garters before he ran his hands down her legs, enjoying her heat through the silk stockings.

With gentle care, he lifted her leg and kissed his way from the top of her thigh down to her trim ankle before he removed her satin slipper. As he moved to her other leg, Lydia's breathing came in quick, sharp pants. Vincent smiled. He had only just begun.

Rising to his feet, he meticulously removed her hair pins, caressing each ebony lock as it was freed. When her silken tresses tumbled down her back, he plunged his hands into the thick mass, breathing in her scent before he took her mouth in another languorous kiss.

Still stroking her hair, he broke the kiss to trail others across her cheek, down her jawline and up her neck just under her delicate ears.

"I love you," he whispered again.

Lydia quivered beneath his lips. Vincent was merciless in his ministrations. Inch by inch, he slid down her chemise, kissing and licking every bit of flesh he uncovered. Once she was naked before him, he removed his own shirt, taking untold pleasure in the way she looked at him.

"Now lie on the bed…on your stomach," he commanded.

Though she blinked at him questioningly, Lydia obeyed. Vincent removed his boots and trousers before he knelt on the bed beside her. He lifted her hair and draped it to the side, exposing her smooth back. Carefully he moved to straddle her hips, hissing in sharp lust as his hardness pressed against her luscious buttocks. That would have to wait.

Sliding his hands up her soft flesh, he massaged her shoulders and neck. Lydia moaned in bliss, and her hips squirmed beneath him, compounding the sweet torture. Vincent then moved to massage her back in slow, tantalizing motions, trailing his fingers across her rib cage to brush across the sides of her breasts.

"So beautiful," he whispered.

Gradually, he moved lower. A small whimper escaped her lips as he caressed her backside, growing louder as his fingers slid lower to trail across her inner thighs.

Again she wiggled helplessly under him. He could feel the heat radiating from her wet center and taste the potent scent of her arousal. Yet he refrained from touching that sweet treasure. Instead, he progressed lower to reverently stroke her legs and shapely calves.

Up and down, he massaged and caressed every exposed inch of Lydia's flesh, except for the source of her desire. When she was limp and trembling, Vincent bent down to repeat the attentions with his lips, taking care to linger on her inner thighs, just a breath from her core.

When he'd kissed every silken place in reach, he bade her to turn over. "Now I must attend to the rest of you."

Lydia gasped and cried out as his mouth covered every inch of her breasts. She giggled when he reached her smooth belly and squealed when he kissed the tender place above her hip.

"Vincent, please," she panted. "Take me now."

Unable to bear the intoxicating torment any longer, Vincent needed no further encouragement. Gripping his shaft, he knelt between her thighs and flicked the tip of his erection across her throbbing clit. Lydia moaned and bucked her hips. He slid his hardness lower, swirling it around her entrance in slow, teasing circles. She squirmed beneath him, gyrating in a frenzy to guide him deeper.

Drawing out the moment, Vincent slid inside her tight, wet sheath with impossible slowness, biting back a growl of triumph with each inch of his entry. Once he'd penetrated his bride fully, he remained still, luxuriating in the feel of their joining, and resumed kissing her silken lips, just as he'd done when he'd taken her virginity.

Lydia trembled with the effort not to move. Her body clenched tighter around his cock, and he gave up the fight, rocking his hips with hers in an intoxicating rhythm. Needing her closeness more than anything in the world, he pulled her into his arms, feeling her heart pounding against his.

She cried out against his lips as her core tightened and pulsed around him. Vincent deepened his thrusts, triumph roaring through him as he rode the wave of her climax and his own began. Something primal within roared. *She is truly mine at last.*

For a second, their eyes met in savage hunger before, in tandem, they struck. Vincent plunged his fangs into Lydia's neck, and she claimed his throat with equal savagery. As he drank down her sweet nectar, his orgasm increased, feeding hers until he was nearly blinded in the conflagration. After an eternity of mind-bending ecstasy, Vincent collapsed on top of her.

"So," Lydia gasped, heart hammering against his chest. "That is what you mean by savoring. May I do the same with you next?"

He licked his lips in anticipation. "Of course, but be warned. I'm not finished enjoying you. In fact, I intend to continue doing so every moment I'm with you, and when we are back in Cornwall…"

"Cornwall," she breathed. "I cannot wait to be home again." Her next words filled him with warmth. "Though I love Cornwall, you are my home."

Epilogue

Christmas 1822

LYDIA EMBRACED THE SIDDONS SISTERS AS THEY TOOK their leave. Sally and Maria kissed her cheeks and thanked her once more for the paintings of Vauxhall Gardens…as well as the humorous caricature of a balding Thomas Lawrence.

"Thank you for the lovely gowns…and the decadent undergarments," she whispered.

She could not wait to surprise Vincent later with the naughty crimson underclothes.

She watched them climb into their sleigh, noticing that they looked much happier and more confident than when she'd first met them. The comforting time spent with their mother…and firsthand witness of Lawrence's eternal guilt and loneliness, had been a balm to their tortured souls. Now they seemed to revel in their work as seamstresses, outfitting the vampires of Cornwall as well as a few wealthy mortals.

With a satisfied sigh, she went back inside where Vincent waited with one last present.

Lydia opened the package and squealed with joy. "A magic lantern!"

"It is more a gift for myself." Her husband grinned, fangs gleaming in the firelight of the Yule log. "I want you to make me more stories and more sunrises."

"Only if we can first enjoy our new bed. I want to test the strength of those iron bedposts." Lydia stopped and put a finger to her lips. "Hush. Listen…" Her preternatural hearing detected the chime of sleigh bells approaching.

Vincent raised a brow. "It seems we have visitors."

Moments later, Aubert announced the arrival of the Duke and Duchess of Burnrath.

The duchess shook snow from her ermine-trimmed cloak before pulling Lydia into an embrace. "Happy Christmas!"

"Happy Christmas to you as well. What a wonderful surprise it is to see you!"

Angelica grinned. "We have just departed for our fifty-year sojourn. I am eager to travel the world, but we wanted to see how you two were getting on."

Before she could answer, Lydia heard Ian comment to Vincent, "She just said her final good-byes to her family. I thought she could use some cheering up."

"We are excessively happy," she told the duchess. "How are you, really?"

Angelica managed a brave smile. "As I have had over a year to prepare, I feel I am handling it rather well. It pains me that I won't have the opportunity to see them again, but I am comforted by the fact that my mother and Papa will be too occupied with their new fortune to mourn me overmuch."

Lydia's heart went out to her friend. She knew what it was like to lose family. For once she was grateful that she had no ties to her remaining kin.

In effort to maintain the light mood, she ventured, "What is the talk in London?"

"Georgiana and the marquess are already expecting a child. Lady Morley defected to her dower house after the wedding and has not been seen since." Angelica lit a cheroot and gave her a wry grin. "People are saying she may have gone mad."

Vincent laughed. "That certainly calls for a celebratory drink. Now tell me, has there been much talk about us?"

The duke looked up from his inspection of the Christmas tree. "There was a whirlwind of gossip when you first departed, but it has since died down. Now the subject on everyone's tongues is our departure and, of course, Rafe. Since I leased him Burnrath House, he's been pestered by countless curious mortals. Furthermore, the Elders forbade him from boxing for the duration of his lordship, and he is chafing under the restriction." He turned to Vincent. "I would appreciate it if you would visit London and look in on him sometime after I am gone."

"I'd be glad to." Vincent smiled. "Perhaps he can take his frustration out on the chessboard. Did he like Lydia's painting?"

"He did. In fact, he hung it up in his study."

Lydia warmed at the honor.

"Rafe isn't the only subject of talk." Angelica leaned forward, dark eyes serious. "Lady Rosslyn caused a bit of a scandal when she applied to medical school." She sighed bitterly. "She was turned away flat...and only because she's a woman."

Lydia's heart clenched in anger and sympathy. "That is completely unfair! Cassandra is the most intelligent person I've ever met. She would have made a fine doctor."

"She assured me that she hasn't given up," Angelica said with a hopeful smile. "Thus far she's retreated to her dower house, doubtless working on a plan."

Ian nodded. "It would not surprise me if the countess found a way around such obstacles. The world is changing."

Vincent nodded solemnly. "But I feel it will be changing faster than even we can imagine."

"It doesn't matter." Lydia rested her head on her husband's shoulder. "As long as we are together, we can face anything."

❧

Rafael Villar stood in the dark drawing room at Burnrath House, watching the snowfall blanketing the lawn. Warm light glowed from the windows of the neighboring houses where families were dining together and enjoying their exchanged gifts.

Far away in Spain, his mortal family was doing the same. Alejandro, his uncle and Maker, should send him a letter soon, letting him know if the presents he'd sent arrived on time. The thought of presents made him think of the ones he'd received, the first in centuries. Vincent's youngling had sent him a magnificent painting of a stormy sea, along with a jesting note saying that it reminded her of his temperament.

Anthony, his third in command, had gifted him with a tin of Turkish cigars. He'd also received a beautifully illustrated copy of *Don Quixote* from Lady Rosslyn. Rafe stroked the cover and scowled.

After Ian and Angelica departed, Rafe had enjoyed his new peace at Burnrath House. No more irrepressible duchesses, no more chaperones looking down their noses at him, no more snobbish, mocking whispers and stares from the *ton*, and best of all, no more inconvenient and dangerous involvements with mortals.

Unfortunately, Lady Rosslyn seemed determined to disrupt that peace. He'd received several dinner invitations, and she'd even attempted to call upon him twice. Angelica's friend had harbored a pointed interest in him since their first encounter at Burnrath House. When she noticed his scars, she did not regard them with disgust or pity like everyone else. She only studied them with curiosity, an unspoken question in her eyes...eyes as bright blue-green as the Mediterranean Sea.

Rafe had rebuffed all of her attempts to further their acquaintance, ignoring her subtle inquiries as to his refusals. He could not tell her that he was the most powerful being in the city. He could not tell her that the longer she remained in his vicinity, the more he wanted to yank out all of the pins restraining her auburn hair, to send the coppery mass tumbling over her perfect shoulders before plunging his fangs in her throat and tasting the very essence of her life.

The front door opened, and a blast of winter air cooled his heated fantasy.

"You missed a jolly good party, my lord." Anthony shook snow from his tousled brown hair. "The champagne flowed, and Madam Florence's girls were in a most generous spirit."

One glimpse of my face would quickly banish their generosity. Rafe frowned and lit a cigar. "Did you look in on the East End before your revels, as I asked?"

His third sobered. "Yes, my lord. There is talk of humans roaming through the cemetery at night, though that seems to have stopped a few weeks ago. I told them to inform you straightaway if they see another one."

"Do you think they were hunters?" Rafe fought back a growl. His burn scars seemed to flare with fresh pain.

Anthony shrugged. "I am not certain. If they were, I'd think they would have made a move by now."

Rafe shook his head and took a deep draw on his cigar. Between a pertinacious countess and the possibility of vampire hunters skulking in his cemeteries, his reign was not commencing as peacefully as he'd intended.

Author's Note

The phantasmagoria was the precursor to modern horror films. Created in the late eighteenth century, the projected images of ghosts were used to fool people during séances. Even after the ruse was revealed, many people found the images so convincing that a 1798 production by Étienne-Gaspard Robert at the Pavillon de l'Echiquier in Paris was halted by police due to accusations that the magician was trying to bring Louis XVI back from the grave. These productions remained popular in Europe and America until the invention of motion pictures. Naturally, with Angelica's taste for the macabre and Lydia's skill in painting, these vampires embraced this invention. However, Lydia's first love will always be traditional painting.

The son of an innkeeper, Sir Thomas Lawrence rose to incredible heights with his gift for painting. He was supporting his family with his portraits at the age of ten. By the time he was eighteen, his work gained the attention of Princess Charlotte, thus granting him esteem—and commissions from the most important people in the country. In 1820, he became president of The Royal Academy of Arts.

Despite his income from his work, Lawrence was frequently in debt due to overwhelming generosity toward his friends. He was also foolish in his love life, first being engaged to Sally Siddons, eldest daughter of the famous tragic actress, Sarah Siddons. Lawrence abruptly shifted his attentions to Sally's younger sister, Maria. He threatened suicide if their mother would not seek Mr. Siddons's approval of an engagement. Then, when Maria was stricken with consumption, he went back to Sally.

Before Maria died (or became a vampire) in 1798, she made Sally promise never to marry Lawrence. Sally kept her promise and followed her sister to the grave (or became a vampire) in 1803. Grief stricken, Mrs. Siddons and her family broke all contact with Lawrence until around 1829, when he was commissioned to draw a portrait of her niece, Fanny Kemble, who was reputed to resemble Maria Siddons. It was his last portrait. Lawrence died abruptly in 1830, reputedly from "ossification of the heart" and blood loss.

Perhaps the Siddons sisters had their revenge after all.

Acknowledgments

I owe my thanks to a lot of people, without whom this book wouldn't have happened.

To Kent Butler: Even though I barely knew you at the time, your awesome hair inspired my muse and gave me a template for my hero. Thanks for being cool about it when I confessed.

To my editors, Deb Werksman and Susie Benton, for pushing me to make the book the best it could be, and for the many fun brainstorming sessions on weaving Thomas Lawrence and the Siddons sisters into the story.

To my awesome publicist, Beth Sochacki, for her hard work in making my first book a success.

To my son, Micah, for drawing an incredible map of the Cornish coast and situating Vincent's castle.

To Shelley Martin, Bonnie Paulson, Michel King, Millie McClain, Rissa Watkins, Dot Dittman, and Tana Essary for their priceless aid in critiquing the book.

To Edward and Candice Francis for an incredible author photo shoot in the cemetery.

To Dean Chamberlain for giving me a phenomenal

release party for the first book and already helping me plan the next.

To all my friends at Gus's Cigar Pub for all of your support and encouragement.

To all the people who saved my butt during times of crisis by providing aid and succor: Danae, Dot, Jade and Arlan, Dad and Kathy, Theresa, Grace, Asa, Aunt Wendy, Dean, Kent, Bill K., Bill F., and Bill S.

And finally, to all my friends and family. You know who you are.

Don't miss the next of Brooklyn Ann's Regency Scandals with Bite:

Bite at First Sight

Scarred, embittered vampire Rafael Villar catches aspiring physician Cassandra Burton alone in a graveyard at night, and you'll never guess what strange bargain they strike…

COMING SOON FROM
SOURCEBOOKS CASABLANCA

Bite Me, Your Grace
by Brooklyn Ann

London's Lord Vampire has problems

Dr. John Polidori's tale "The Vampyre" burst upon the Regency scene along with Mary Shelley's Frankenstein after that notorious weekend spent writing ghost stories with Lord Byron.

A vampire craze broke out instantly in the haut ton.

Now Ian Ashton, the Lord Vampire of London, has to attend tedious balls, linger in front of mirrors, and eat lots of garlic in an attempt to quell the gossip.

If that weren't annoying enough, his neighbor Angelica Winthrop has literary aspirations of her own and is sneaking into his house at night just to see what she can find.]

Hungry, tired, and fed up, Ian is in no mood to humor his beautiful intruder…

What readers are saying:

"It was romantic and quirky and a lot of fun. The author writes with such heart. I can't wait for her next one!"

"I loved this book! Absolutely amazing!"

For more Brooklyn Ann, visit:

www.sourcebooks.com

Forged by Desire
by Bec McMaster

Look for the fourth book in Bec McMaster's highly acclaimed London Steampunk series, coming in late 2014
The captain of the Nighthawk guard has a deadly mission: capture a steel-jawed monster who's been preying on women. Capt. Garrett Reed hates to put his partner Perry in jeopardy, but she's the best bait he has. Little does he realize, he's the one about to be caught in his own trap…

Perry has been half in love with Garrett for years, but this is not exactly the best time to fall in love—especially when their investigation leads them directly into the clutches of the madman she thought she'd escaped…

My Lady Quicksilver
by Bec McMaster

———— ⁓ ————

I will come for you...

He will find her no matter what. As a blueblooded captain of the Nighthawk Guard, his senses are keener than most. Some think he's indestructible. But once he finds the elusive Mercury, what will he do with her?

It's his duty to turn her in—she's a notorious spy and traitor. But after one stolen moment, he can't forget the feel of her in his arms, the taste of her, or the sharp sting of betrayal as she slipped off into the night. Little does Mercury know, no one hunts better than the Nighthawk. And his greatest revenge will be to leave her begging for his touch...

———— ⁓ ————

"McMaster continues to demonstrate a flair for wildly imaginative, richly textured world building. Set in an alternate version of London ruled by vampires...the perfect choice for readers who like their historical romances sexy, action-packed, and just a tad different."—*Booklist*

"One of my top books of 2013... just amazing."—*Royal Reviews*

For more Bec McMaster, visit:

www.sourcebooks.com

Lessons After Dark

by Isabel Cooper

Author of *No Proper Lady*, a *Publishers Weekly* and
Library Journal Best Book of the Year

A woman with an unspeakable past

Olivia Brightmore didn't know what to expect when she
took a position to teach at Englefield School, an academy for
"gifted" children. But it wasn't having to rescue a young girl
who'd levitated to the ceiling. Or battling a dark mystery in
the surrounding woods. And nothing could have prepared
her for Dr. Gareth St. John.

A man of exceptional talent

He knew all about her history and scrutinized her every move
because of it. But there was more than suspicion lurking in
those luscious green eyes. Olivia could feel the heat in each
haughty look. She could sense the desire in every touch, a
spark that had nothing to do with the magic of his healing
abilities. Even with all the strange occurrences at the school,
the most unsettling of all is the attraction pulling her and
Gareth together with a force that cannot be denied.

For more Isabel Cooper, visit:

www.sourcebooks.com

No Proper Lady
by Isabel Cooper

It's *Terminator* meets *My Fair Lady* in this fascinating debut of black magic and brilliant ball gowns, martial arts, and mysticism.

England, 1888. No one has any idea that in a few hundred years, demons will destroy it all. Joan plans to take out the dark magician responsible—before he summons the demons in the first place. But as a rough-around-the-edges assassin from the future, she'll have to learn how to fit into polite Victorian society first.

Simon Grenville has his own reasons for wanting to destroy Alex Reynell. The man used to be his best friend—until he almost killed Simon's sister. The beautiful half-naked stranger Simon meets in the woods may be the perfect instrument for his revenge. It will just take a little time to teach her the necessary etiquette and assemble a proper wardrobe. But as each day passes, Simon is less sure he wants Joan anywhere near Reynell. Because no spell in the world will save his future if she isn't in it.

"A genre-bending, fast-paced whirl with fantastic characters, a deftly drawn plot, and sizzling attraction."
—RT Book Reviews *Top Pick of the Month, 4.5 Stars*

For more Isabel Cooper, visit:

www.sourcebooks.com